The
Triple

Mary Hardcastle

Published January 15, 2016
Fallen Bros. Press
29403 N Enrose Ave.
Rancho Palos Verdes CA 90275

ISBN: 978-0692594131

Cover and interior design: © Guillermo Bosch, 2015

For my mother

Contents   Page

Prologue

She could sense everything from the trapeze platform at the peak of the Big Top. She felt the prairie wind buffeting the tent, the heat rising from the matinee crowd, and the soothing interlude the band leader chose. She felt the sharp gaze of her father as he sat on the catcher's trapeze, rocking impatiently.

When his loud "Hup!" signaled for her to begin, she dusted her palms on the rosin bag and unhooked the trapeze bar. She sailed the bar out alone for a practice flight and watched her father meet its arc then deftly slide down to swing by his knees. Her trapeze returned and as she rose to the balls of her feet to grab it, she caught the strong, earthy scent of air being sucked from the ground.

Suddenly a gust of wind jerked her trapeze off course and caused it to flop and dangle out of reach. She heard a roar like a wildcat and then a fierce Oklahoma gale swept under the canvas sidewalls and instantly filled the tent with choking, brown dust. She strained to see her father, but a cry from the audience made her turn instead and watch the back end of the Big Top rip from the giant center pole and begin to tear apart.

The crowd panicked, scrambling from their seats and pushing toward the exits, their screams drowned by howling wind and whipping canvas. She grabbed the rope ladder and half climbed, half slid downward, her palms and thighs burning on the hemp. Just as her toes touched sawdust, the line to a bale ring snapped and she looked up as two hundred pounds of rigging, block and tackle came hurtling down towards her.

Chapter One: Landing

"Chicago! Union Station!" the bus driver bellowed at the rearview mirror. Sepia started abruptly out of sleep and banged her head on the back of the metal seat as the bus pulled into a cavernous brick terminal and came to a stop.

Bruno dug his elbow into her side.

"Get moving," he grumbled.

She watched her father's dark, brooding face as he swung up into the aisle, tugged a duffel bag off the overhead rack and headed for the exit. Sepia slid from the seat and straightened the cloth belt on her faded yellow dress. She pushed a strand of auburn hair from her eyes, grabbed her own tote bag from the rack and joined the other passengers as they disembarked.

Maybe she should have felt uneasy arriving in the city out of work. It was the summer of 1932 and most people in the same fix were plenty nervous. Sepia and her father, however, weren't most people, and this wasn't the first time they'd lost their job when a show went bust due to what people were starting to call a "great depression."

It was midseason and the chance of joining another circus was slim. Still, it was nothing to get stirred up about.

For most of her seventeen years, Sepia had been on the move, never knowing where she would wake up and never viewing much beyond what she saw, heard or smelled from the circus lot. She recognized a town, not by its name, but by its claim to fame: "the Soybean Empire," "the Hog Mecca," "the Rubber King." Now they stood in the center of "the Gangster Capital" of the world.

Fog muffled the sounds of the city as Sepia hitched her bag on her shoulder and trailed down the street after her father. She stayed silent behind him, knowing better than to ask where they were going. Every so often he muttered more to himself than to her that it wasn't much farther, but he'd been saying that for the last ten blocks. She caught a whiff of fresh baked bread wafting through the haze and the sweet, doughy smell made her stomach growl, reminding her that she hadn't eaten since yesterday. She paused to slide a finger in her right slipper and pull it back on her heel. Her ballet flats were not made for pavement and she stood for a moment, flexing her toes and watching Bruno walk on without waiting.

Always as a child, she had struggled to keep up with him, terrified of being left behind. As she grew older, she lost her fear, but habit made her follow five steps behind since he clearly preferred to walk ahead of her. She remained still now and watched her father disappear into the haze. She let the fog surround her like a woolly cocoon and imagined herself rooted there until a new person formed, a person strong enough to act on her own. She would emerge from her cloud-like shell, transformed, powerful, and ready to strike off in a new direction.

She caught up to Bruno as he reached Michigan Avenue. "Hold it," he ordered as he held out an arm to bar her way.

Sepia heard the faint rumble of a motor and out of the dense fog rolled a black, 1931 Ford Phaeton touring car with its top down and four men in dark suits seated inside. The three passengers gripped "Tommy" sub-machine guns with the butts wedged in their laps and the barrels pointed skyward. As the car passed by, one of the men threw Sepia a cold, dead-eyed stare then the car disappeared into the haze again like a brief apparition. Bruno answered her unasked question.

"Cops or gangsters," he muttered. Unimpressed, he led her across the intersection into Grant Park where the tall elms were shrouded in mist.

Sepia tried to shake the image of the gunman's face glaring at her and pushed away the thought that it was a bad omen. She focused instead on keeping her footing in the foggy path until her toe struck something hard and she nearly tripped on the shiny steel of a train rail. She and Bruno picked their way over the rails and across three more tracks that vanished in both directions.

A foghorn bleated in the distance and Sepia breathed in an odor both fresh and fecund, the smell of Lake Michigan drifting through sodden air. Beyond the tracks, a field of tall, damp grass washed her bare legs and dragged her to a stop. She let the heavy bag slip from her shoulder, and just when she dared ask Bruno to wait, she heard it, an echoing crack of metal against wood, a sound that brought her to immediate attention. She grabbed up her bag again and hurried toward Bruno as another man's booming voice cut through the mist.

"Get that line straighter! Go ahead on number five! Louie, get Rosie and tell her there's a patch job on the short side!"

Sepia watched the curtain of fog suddenly lift and burn

away as a rising sun burst on an open field. She felt a pang of excitement and hope as she stood transfixed watching a flurry of activity unfold before her. Strong-armed men tossed ropes and rigging from horse-drawn wagons. Young boys and girls hauled metal buckets, slopping water as they hurried across the grass. Trainers tugged at the harnesses of camels, zebras, and giraffes that yawned and ambled toward piles of hay already spread on the ground. And behind it all, a mighty canvas tent made a final heave upward, shed its dust and gleamed in the sunlight. A white banner fluttered across the tent entrance with bold letters that proclaimed: "THE OLYMPIC CIRCUS".

A loud metal clang broke Sepia's trance. Nearby, a group of roustabouts wielding heavy iron mallets circled a wooden tent stake. One after the other their swinging mauls struck the wood in such a wave of rapid succession that it was like one loud, resonating crack, the sound that had drawn Sepia from the fog, a sound as familiar as her heartbeat. Her father grabbed her arm.

"Come on," he grunted, as he jerked her toward the man calling out orders.

Chapter Two: Billy

Usually the Boss Canvas Man supervised raising the Big Top, but Billy Thompson, owner and manager of the Olympic Circus, liked to command the crew himself. Billy was like the king pole that held up the center of the tent—solid, sturdy, his stout figure planted squarely on the trampled grass. He stood before the Big Top, waving his arms and shouting orders.

"Quarter poles are in! Take her out!" he yelled.

Immediately the singsong chant of callers began as they ordered their crews to pull, tighten, and stake the guy lines around the outside of the tent.

"Take it!" a caller shouted as his band of men wearing worn overalls and heavy gloves took hold of a guy rope.

"Shake it!" he called next as the gang hauled on the rope, pulling it taut.

"Make it!" he ordered and they cinched the line around a stake and knotted it.

"Break it!" his call went on and the crew let go.

"Go along," came the last command and the men moved on to the next rope.

Billy turned away for a moment as he pushed back his

worn fedora and wiped sweat off his brow. He felt the satisfaction of a morning gone well except for a few minor mishaps; a broken train axle, a lion with a toothache, and a drunken roustabout booted off the lot. He tried to quell the knot in his stomach that reminded him the bank loan was due. Six days in Chicago could put them in the black and give them some breathing room. He let himself gather hope from the blue sky above. He was about to turn back to his crew when he caught sight of a couple walking toward him.

A middle-aged man led the way, unshaven and disheveled with his shoes covered in mud. Behind him trudged a young woman wearing a tattered yellow dress, threadbare slippers and a film of dirt.

Billy knew he was about to be suckered for a handout. These were hard luck times and he was barely keeping the Olympic afloat. Still, he found it next to impossible to turn away the panhandlers that passed through his circus grounds. They always left with a full stomach and sometimes a day's work. The pair heading toward him now, however, had a different look about them. They weren't town suckers and they looked too athletic for bums.

"We're looking for Billy Thompson," the man said.

"Yeah, what can I do for you?" Billy answered, surprising the couple.

The man set his bag down and offered his hand. "Bruno Stefani of the Flying Stefanis," he announced.

Billy shook Bruno's hand. "With the Griffin Brothers?" he asked.

"Yes," Bruno answered, encouraged that Billy knew of them. "They folded a week ago."

"We heard they couldn't make payroll in Cincinnati. Too

bad," Billy said, shaking his head. "It's tough all over."

"We're great flyers," Bruno told him.

"Where's the rest of your act?" Billy asked.

"You're looking at it. Me and my daughter, Sepia."

Sepia smiled shyly and offered her hand. Billy shook it firmly, but didn't return the smile.

"Just you and the girl?" Billy asked.

"Sepia is the best woman ever on the trapeze!" Bruno claimed.

Billy cracked a smile at the boast. "What can you do, kid?" he asked her.

Bruno interrupted. "She can do anything! Wait 'til you see!"

Billy knew Bruno's talk was part of the game. Still, he ignored Bruno and eyed Sepia again.

"Anything fancy?" he asked her.

"I can do a two-and-half," she answered, glancing at Bruno for support.

"In performance?" Billy ventured.

Bruno cut in. "Every time! That's nothing. She's almost got a triple!" he announced.

"A triple! No woman has ever done the triple," Billy said. He was getting annoyed at Bruno's bragging, yet he understood the need behind it. He adjusted his hat and inspected the couple before him. Despite their bedraggled appearance, they made a good-looking pair. Beneath the layer of dirt, Billy saw the delicate features of Sepia's oval face, and the dark, handsome angles of Bruno's. And a flying two-and-a-half was nothing to snub his nose at.

"Tell you what," Billy said. "Go over to the cookhouse and get somethin' to eat. Stay the night. Watch the show. I'll try you out in the morning."

He spotted Louie, his stage manager, crossing the grounds. "Louie! Give these folks breakfast and a bunk!"

Louis Jones didn't break stride when he heard his boss call. If Billy was the king pole of the Olympic, Louie was the guy wire that kept it in place. Tall and lean in his 40's, he spoke little, and because he was a black man in a white circus world, he walked with the pride of hard won respect. He glanced at the Stefanis and raised his eyebrows, but he motioned for them to follow him.

Bruno shook Billy's hand again. "Thanks, Thompson. You won't be sorry!" He and Sepia picked up their bags and caught up with Louie.

"Cookhouse first," Louie announced in a clipped voice as he led them around to the "backyard", the part of the circus lot roped off from town people.

Billy watched them go. Something about the young woman, maybe the sadness in her smile, tugged at his gut even as he chided himself, "Can't say 'No,' can ya? You need another act like a hole in the head!"

Chapter Three: The Olympic

As they followed Louie toward the cookhouse, Sepia couldn't help feeling hopeful. The Menagerie Top was huge, so were the cookhouse and dressing room tents. The Olympic was not the biggest show on earth, but one of the best, and it traveled by train. She would give her eyeteeth to be in a railroad circus. It was definitely a step up from the truck shows she'd been with all her life. There was a keen sense of order here even during the seeming chaos of the set-up. The Olympic was a thirty-rail-car show and had to be a smooth running outfit or it would never last a season. As Sepia scanned the lot, it was hard not to dream of joining on.

Bruno's bragging about their act made her nervous though. She had never seen him so jumpy...or desperate. Losing their last job had shaken him up more than she thought. She wondered if Billy Thompson had seen it, too. Billy was gruff and direct, but there was a kindness in his eyes he couldn't hide. Still, she began to doubt whether they'd get their tryout in the morning. She could already imagine Louie making some excuse to send them on their way. Bruno would find a way to make it her fault and a way to make her pay for it. Despite being almost faint with hunger, Sepia dreaded having to go to the cookhouse now and eat with him. She was exhausted and just wanted to get a bunk and sleep. Instead, she continued to scan the lot, looking for the one thing that would keep her hope alive.

It was then that she noticed the bright red wagon ahead. Large, gold letters flamboyantly scrolled on the side read: ANASTASIA ARTEL, QUEEN OF THE CIRCUS. At that moment, the door of the wagon swung open and Anastasia Artel stepped out wearing a full length, turquoise silk robe. She spotted Billy across the grounds.

"Billy!" she shouted as she continued down her trailer steps and walked briskly toward him.

Sepia had only heard of Anastasia, but all that she had heard made her stop in her tracks and gaze in awe.

Anastasia was the most famous female flyer in the circus, as well known for her violent temper as her explosive performance. Surprisingly small, barely five feet, she carried herself in a way that made her seem much taller. Her trademark hair, golden and curly, trailed to her waist, and what could have been mistaken for padded shoulders were really broad muscles bulging beneath her thin robe. The same build on any other woman would have looked unattractive, but on Anastasia Artel it somehow fit her dynamic presence. What compelled Sepia to watch her though was Anastasia's confident air. Her easy swagger, even when she looked angry, as she did now, made her seem born to be Queen of the Circus.

Anastasia could have clinched top billing in one of the larger circuses, yet she had remained loyal to Billy. Needless to say, she was the biggest act in the Olympic. She was also Sepia's idol. Unable to move from her spot, Sepia stayed within earshot as Anastasia reached Billy and planted herself in front of him.

"I need Rosie to fit my new costume," Anastasia announced.

"There's a rip in the tent. She's fixin' it," Billy told her.

"If she's not at my trailer by noon, I'm not going on tonight!" Anastasia threatened.

"Calm down. You always get riled when we hit this town," Billy answered, trying to keep his voice low.

Anastasia raised hers instead. "I've got a right to be worked up. I almost broke my neck last night!"

As Anastasia's voice grew louder, Sepia heard the hint of a foreign accent, though she couldn't place its origin. "You get me a new rigger or you'll be looking for a new act. Need I remind you my contract is almost up?"

"You're in luck. I hired a new rigger in Milwaukee," Billy said, ignoring her last remark. He glanced over her shoulder. "And here's Rosie with your costume now."

Sepia watched as Rosie Lopez, a heavyset woman in her late thirties, approached with a costume slung over her arm. With her straight black hair and pointed features, Rosie resembled a plump raven. Her eyes darted to Billy with a knowing look.

"Got your costume ready, Miss Artel. Let's go to your wagon and try it on."

"It's about time," Anastasia sputtered. She whirled around and strode back toward her wagon.

"I don't know why I put up with her," Billy growled.

"Because she's worth it," Rosie grinned then she turned and scuttled after Anastasia.

Sepia watched Anastasia disappear into her wagon. To see a woman so brash, so assertive was impressive. She ignored Anastasia's rudeness. After all, she was a star. She had money, control, and power. Sepia had none of those. Bruno had always run her life, had always decided what was best for her. He had long ago drowned any effort on Sepia's part to think for herself. To be like Anastasia, strong and sure, that's what she wanted!

"Sepia!" Bruno shouted as he waited impatiently and motioned for her to come. She took a last glance at Anastasia's trailer then headed toward her father.

The cookhouse tent was emptying out when they walked in. Sepia's mouth began to water the moment she set foot inside and smelled the aroma of breakfast. They sat down at one of the long, cloth covered tables, enough to seat all three hundred members of the Olympic at once. With Griffin's Circus she'd had nothing but porridge and mutton stew for weeks. Now she gazed at the plate set before her, a breakfast she could barely remember; eggs, slabs of bacon, flapjacks, buttered bread, and milk. Neither she nor Bruno bothered to remove their coats. She ate nonstop until she'd swallowed the last bit of egg scraped from her plate with a crust of bread. When she finally looked up, she noticed a circus handbill lying on the table next to her. She picked up the advertisement and began reading.

Bruno finished eating, belched and patted his stomach, then saw the paper in Sepia's hand.

"Give me that," he demanded and she handed it over to him.

"Thompson's picked up quite a few names since Anastasia Artel's been with him," he mumbled as he read. He looked at Sepia. "Now's our big chance. I'm gonna' make you famous and me rich!"

"Why did you say I almost have the triple?" she asked.

Bruno made a motion to shush her and leaned his head closer across the table so no one could hear. "Did you see the look on Thompson's face?" he sneered. "Dollar signs, kid, dollar signs. Besides, you are gonna be the first to do a triple! I've already been thinkin' about it."

"But I can't..."

"Don't say you never thought about it?" he challenged.

"Every flyer thinks about it, but..."

"All right then!" he interrupted, letting his voice rise. "First we need to show Thompson what you got, so you gotta' do good tomorrow." He swung off his seat and got up. "Come on," he ordered. Sepia stood up and followed Bruno out of the tent. He gazed around the circus grounds still buzzing with activity.

"I'm gonna walk around, check things out," he said. "Wait here." He shuffled off, leaving her at the entrance to the cookhouse.

Sepia wanted to walk, too. Her stomach was ready to burst. Unsure when they'd eat so well again, she had stuffed herself and now she needed to move. She watched Bruno disappear behind some wagons, knowing where he was headed. Some roustabout was sure to have a flask of Prohibition whiskey hidden under his coat. Her father would spend the few dollars in his poke for it, too. She didn't care. When Bruno drank, he did it with purpose until he passed out. She knew it wasn't right, but she often helped him get liquor. To her, liquor wasn't bad. It was good. Bruno was only mean when he was sober. Booze sent him to a place where he couldn't hurt her. She knew it could destroy their act, but it saved her life.

She began walking in circles, expanding her range until she arrived at the "backdoor", the performers' entrance to the Big Top. With Bruno nowhere in sight, she ducked inside.

Roustabouts were quickly filling the stands with wooden folding seats, the snap-thud rhythm echoing through the cavernous tent. Sawdust had just been spread and its chaff clouded the air. The low, red, wooden curbs for the three rings were already in place and a thin, platinum-haired woman in tight slacks and sweater was putting her dog act through its paces. An apricot poodle climbed a ladder and at the woman's command, slid down a ramp and raced back to its platform.

A weathered man in a black cowboy hat, dark suit and tie sat perched on the curb examining a fox terrier's paw. He had a proper name, but nobody knew him by anything other than "Doc," and he moved as easily among humans as animals, patching broken bones, extracting teeth, and delivering babies.

"How does it look, Doc?" the thin woman called.

"She's only torn the pad a bit. We'll fix her up just fine," he answered as he carefully picked the dog up in his arms and carried her out of the tent.

As Sepia absently watched the dog act practice, she replayed her conversation with Bruno at breakfast. He was really excited, excited or crazy. The latter was more likely.

She knew of other women who had tried the flying triple back somersault, but none had succeeded. There were only a few men who had done it and there were far more men flyers than women. If women were trained to fly, they often served as decoration or as a warm-up act for the male star. In that respect, Sepia was lucky. She and Bruno had performed with other flyers when she was younger, but now they were a duo. He was her catcher and she was the flyer.

Bruno figured they'd make more money that way, but it was a harder act to sell. If either of them got injured even for a short time, they were out of work. Attempting the triple was assuming a great risk. It was no coincidence that it bore the nickname "leap of death". Many flyers had broken their necks trying it.

Her eyes instinctively darted upward to the ropes and cable at the peak of the Big Top, then an unwelcome memory flooded her.

She was eight-years-old. It was nighttime and she was standing at the performer's entrance with Bruno and Angelina, her mother. Her parents were arguing, but the band music was so loud she only saw their mouths moving. Suddenly, her father's hand flew out and slapped her mother across the face. A drop of red hit the sawdust at her feet then she looked up and saw her mother's bloodied lip and the blank look in her eyes. Angelina seemed in a trance, unable to move until a drum roll sounded and the announcer called their act, then she wiped her mouth and faced the performers entrance.

She watched her parents enter center ring and begin climbing their respective ladders. She didn't notice her mother trembling as she ascended the high ladder. She only saw the same beautiful woman, shiny, auburn hair, dark brown eyes and deep red lips. In her dazzling, sequined costume that sparkled in the lights, she was no longer Sepia's mother, but the most amazing creature in the world.

Angelina reached the platform and dusted her palms with resin. She waited until Bruno was ready on the catch bar, then she grabbed the trapeze and flew out into the air. Letting go of the bar, she twisted three hundred and sixty degrees in the air and was caught in her husband's hands. Sepia watched as the trapeze returned, Angelina grabbed it, swung back up to her platform, and struck a pose. The crowd cheered, but Angelina was not smiling. She was like a statue, frozen, unfeeling. Bruno shouted a signal, but Angelina kept looking at the crowd, seeming not to hear. Finally she turned back to the trapeze, grabbed it and flew out again. She swung out and back then soared to the top of the tent. She spun her body into a perfect one and a half somersault, but instead of opening out and reaching for the catcher, her body stayed curled in a ball and went hurtling downward.

Sepia watched as if in slow motion, as her mother fell through the air and broke through the spreader ropes of the safety net. Then time resumed and her body landed in the sawdust completely still while screams rose from the horrified crowd...

Sepia's hands now unconsciously flew up to cover her ears, then she quickly dropped them back down, afraid someone had seen. She was caught off guard by the memory, one she had worked hard to forget. She drove the thoughts from her head as she strode out of the Big Top. She wanted to get away and headed toward the backyard rope, the border between circus and the outside world.

She stared off in the distance across a field to the Chicago skyline. If she lived out there, would her life be different? Townspeople thought the circus was glamorous and exciting. People ran away to join it, to be free. Sepia felt anything but free. Fear of the unknown kept her from leaving, but that fear only slightly outweighed her dread that she would never be free. She turned away from the outside world feeling trapped and hollow inside. Just then, she noticed a man and woman standing nearby on either side of the backyard rope. The woman was in her thirties, definitely a towner in her polka dot dress and high heels. The man looked circus, with strong muscular arms and a trim body. Sepia guessed he was close to her own age, probably in his early twenties, handsome, with longish, sandy hair. He and the woman seemed oblivious to the world. He whispered something in the woman's ear and she laughed. Sepia started walking away, but couldn't help looking back. There was something about the man's expression that she recognized. Even as his tongue flicked the woman's earlobe invitingly, he seemed detached, mechanical. As Sepia observed him, something happened to her. She slowed to a standstill as the oddest sensation swept over her.

The town woman tried to keep the young man close, but he grinned, pulled away and sauntered off.

Sepia stood fixed by the wild rush that still filled her. She'd been drawn to men before, but never with this sudden flush of feeling. She had no name for it and no idea why this man had caused it.

She was glad he hadn't noticed her. She felt embarrassed, unkempt and unattractive, feelings she'd never had, not because she was vain, but because she'd trained herself not to care. She tried to remind herself that she wasn't interested in being attractive, except to the audience. She didn't want people to watch her for her looks anyway. She wanted them to watch her because she was a great flyer. The only thing in the world that really mattered to her was the trapeze. It was her means of escape, the way to gain power and freedom. Besides, she didn't see beauty as a plus. Her mother had been beautiful.

Sepia returned to the cookhouse and when her father rejoined her, they followed Louie over to the Olympic's train cars resting on the tracks they had crossed in the fog that morning. Bruno was given a space in one of the men's cars where he grabbed a top berth in a tier of three bunks high. Sepia was put with the unmarried women in the "convent car". Billy prided himself on running a clean show, which meant no grifting, no drinking and no improper fraternizing on the lot. Any workman caught talking to a performer was "red lighted," thrown out of the show.

The other women performers were on the circus lot either practicing or helping in wardrobe, so Sepia had the train car to herself. She wanted to get cleaned up, but was too tired. She found an empty berth and dropped her bag next to it then slipped off her damp shoes, flopped down on the small hard mattress and was asleep almost the moment her cheek touched the thin pillow. For once her sleep was deep and empty, not crowded with haunting dreams.

She was startled awake when a group of women burst into the train car, giggling and laughing. She cracked an eye open. All of the women were young, though most had already been performing for years and had the hard bodies and grown-up air of seasoned showgals. Some were in family acts, others on their own, but like all the performers of the Olympic, they were responsible for at least three different duties in the show; set-up, aerial ballet or other acts, and of course, riding in the opening parade spectacle. By the time the women saw Sepia and cut their laughter short, she had already shut her eyes again and pretended to be still sleeping. The women lowered their voices to a whisper.

"Who is that?" one of them asked.

"Look at her," another said. "She's filthy."

"I think I saw her in the cookhouse this morning," whispered a third. "She was with an older guy who looked just as awful."

"Poor thing," the first voice said. "Come on, let's go eat."

Sepia barely heard the women leave. In pretending to fall asleep, she really had.

She woke again hours later to a shouting voice outside the train, and this time she slowly sat up and swung her feet to the floor. She looked out the window and guessed by the golden light that it was near dusk. A calliope was playing faintly in the distance and she realized that the shouting that woke her was probably the ticket superintendent yelling the one-hour warning that meant the Big Top was now open to the audience. Others must have come and gone from the compartment and they were probably all in the dressing room tent now. Sepia ran her fingers through her hair and pushed it back from her face, then she got up and stepped out of the rail car.

She left the train yard and followed the familiar trail of baggage horse dung that led back to the circus grounds. The backyard was deserted, but it was only the quiet before the storm. Very soon the trumpets would blare and the Grand Entry would begin. She spotted a water tank at the backside of the Menagerie tent and headed for it. Finding an empty bucket near the tank, she set it under the metal spigot and began filling it. Animal smells drifted out from the Menagerie, a familiar combination of hay, musk, and manure that was somehow comforting. Still groggy from her long nap, she stood with a blank stare as the bucket filled, then she shut off the water and knelt down over it. She dunked her head into the cold water and groped in her pocket for a bar of soap wrapped in waxed paper. The harsh sting of the lye soap made her scalp tingle, but it helped to revive her. She rinsed her hair, wrung it out, and flung it onto her back. She dumped the water and sat down on a low stool nearby.

As she combed out the wet tangles with her fingers, Sepia dared to raise her hopes again. If only she got to try out for Billy, she would show him what she could do. He would let them join on. He had to. And with that thought, something shifted inside her. Chicago wasn't just another stop, the Olympic, another potential job. She could not go back to the truck shows. She could not keep following her father. If Billy turned them down, she could not go on as before. She'd rather die. Is this how her mother had felt? She knew these thoughts were unhealthy but she clung to them nonetheless. She wondered if she was destined to follow in her mother's footsteps. She remembered little about her mother, but she'd been told repeatedly that she was like her. Bruno had also said over and over that her mother was a coward. What else but a coward would abandon her husband and child?

As she wove her shoulder length hair into a short braid, Sepia heard the single blast of the bugle horn giving the half hour signal. She should try and find Bruno, but she looked toward the Midway instead.

Chapter Four: Showtime

Townspeople streamed into the Midway leading to the Big Top, their path lined with brightly painted banners of wild animals and daring performers. In her street clothes, Sepia fit right in with the crowd that flowed toward the entrance.

A loud talker had begun his grind. He stood on a platform dressed in a rumpled, checked suit and ushered ticket buyers into the Sideshow pit. His hypnotic spiel was nonstop and colorful.

"This way, folks! You are about to witness the most amazing collection of human oddities in the world! See Chaba, half man, half beast; the lovely Tina, weighing an incredible four hundred pounds, and the fascinating Mintook, a man living and breathing in a solid block of ice!"

For those performers whose disfigurements were real, the Sideshow was one place they were accepted. Here they could at least make a living, be independent, and only get stared at for a few hours a day. Far from ideal, it sure beat civilian life.

Sepia noticed a group of city kids stopped dead in their

tracks, their eyes like saucers as they gazed at the sight before them. A black-haired, sloe-eyed woman stared down at them from a large, colorful banner. Along with a scanty two-piece costume, she wore tattoos covering every inch of her body. An emerald ink dragon snaked from her ankle up her thigh and breathed fire that trailed beneath her briefs. An opened oyster was tattooed on her belly and the tilt of her hip revealed a pearl inset on her navel. A slit in the canvas backdrop promised the live version behind as the talker's grind lured the crowd on to the next attraction.

"See the wondrous four legged man, the only man alive who can do the Charleston and the Rumba at the same time!"

The Sideshow was a chance to be hoodwinked by things fantastical and overlook any evidence that the acts were faked. Viewers could recapture the sense of wonder they felt as children when both Santa Claus and monsters were real.

It felt strange for Sepia to be part of the crowd. Like most circus people, she didn't associate with towners, but she often wondered what they were like. There was a time when she had tried to be one of them...

They were living in winter quarters. Bruno wanted time to himself and made Sepia go to school. She had tried very hard to sit in her seat and listen to the teacher, but she kept glancing out the window at the open sky. When the bell rang for recess, she ran outside with the other children. The girls started a game of hopscotch, but she headed for the monkey bars and began climbing. She heard the boys laughing at her, then suddenly felt the breeze on her back and realized her dress had flown up and her underpants were showing. She pulled herself upright, but everyone was pointing at her and yelling, "monkey girl!" She ran back to winter quarters and hid in the Menagerie tent, swearing never to go back to school. She hugged a trick pony's neck and his furry, winter coat grew wet with her tears...

Sepia continued down the Midway, watching couples walking arm and arm, children dashing from one sight to the next and herds of roving teenagers laughing and flirting. Their life was so foreign to her and yet, walking along with them made her realize for the first time what drew people to the circus. It wasn't only the chance to view exotic animals and daredevil performances that brought them here. Standing in the Midway, she saw how their drab clothes were contrasted by colorful scenery and dazzling costumes. She saw how it transformed them, how it made them want to believe in magic. For a few hours, they could escape the woes of the Depression by entering the dream world of the Big Top.

She joined the line entering the Menagerie tent where show animals were viewed before the performance. The crowd ogled the herds of languid camels, dusty zebras, even a hippopotamus in her own steel tank of water. Both children and parents peered wide-eyed and wary through the thick, barred cages of the big cats. Few circus goers questioned the practice of holding wild animals captive and making them perform. Billy didn't tolerate obvious mistreatment, but neither did he pass up the chance to exploit the audience's desire to see animals execute thrilling acts.

The elephants, called "bulls" though usually all female, were lined up at the end of the tent. Several rocked anxiously to and fro and all them used their agile trunks to search for any goobers dropped in the sawdust. Their size always drew crowds. Sepia noticed one bull that knew how to play the audience. She kept raising her trunk, curling and uncurling it and lifting a front leg in a rhythmic stomp. She let out a sudden, loud trumpet call. The crowd backed away, then gradually came closer again as they decided she was merely showing off. Peanuts showered the sawdust at her feet.

As Sepia grinned at the elephant's stunt, an arm reached through the tent flap, grabbed her and jerked her out of the tent.

"What are you doing?" Bruno demanded, still gripping her arm in the darkness outside.

Sepia smelled the stench of whiskey on his breath and saw his red-rimmed eyes.

"I wanted to watch the show," she said, and then quickly added, "I wanted to see the other acts, see how good they are." "Yeah, okay, that's good," he muttered, loosening his grip. "You come back right after."

She nodded, and then Bruno abruptly turned and weaved off into the darkness, not quite drunk enough to pass out.

Rosie approached, struggling to balance an armload of plumed headpieces. She noticed Sepia in the backyard.

"Can you give me a hand, kid? I'm runnin' behind," she said out of breath.

"Here," Sepia answered and held out her arms.

Rosie dumped her load. "Go on ahead. The girls are waiting in the Pad Room, on the right." She pointed then hurried off in another direction.

Sepia carried the costume pieces carefully around the Big Top until she found the right tent. The Pad Room not only held the men's and women's dressing rooms partitioned on either side, but it housed the padded-back performing horses tethered in the center. As she neared the entrance, one of the headpieces slipped out of her bundle and fell to the ground. She balanced her load and started to lean over when a heavy boot crushed the headpiece into the dirt. A body stopped abruptly beside her.

Sepia looked up to see a man wearing the dark costume and loose-fitting black hood of an Executioner. Startled at first, she quickly realized he was part of an act. The man stood completely still though, staring at her with such intensity that she looked away nervously. She picked the headpiece up from the ground, dusted it off on her dress, and moved on. She glanced back, but the man was still standing there frozen as if she had scared him rather than the other way around. There was something about his eyes that both frightened her and seemed familiar. She turned and hurried away.

When Sepia entered the women's dressing tent, a group of showgals spotted and immediately surrounded her. They grabbed the headpieces from her arms and swiftly pinned them on. Only one woman thanked her, Charlene, the oldest in the group. Her short-cropped red hair and crooked teeth matched her cocky manner and raw charm. Out of circus habit, Sepia picked up a discarded dress and fitted it on a hanger as Charlene chatted with a friend and finished getting dressed.

"Finally we're in a burg for more than one night," Charlene said.

Her friend nodded. "You said it, honey. I can't wait to go out and have some fun for a change."

"'Member the name of that club we went to last time?" Charlene asked.

"No, but I remember that guy you was with. What a looker!" her friend said.

"Mmmm. He was nice," Charlene grinned. She pulled up her sequined leotard then glanced over at Sepia. "Hook me up, will ya, honey?" she asked.

Sepia stepped behind Charlene and fastened the back of her costume.

"Just hired on?" she asked.

Sepia started to answer when Louie called from outside the tent.

"Showtime, ladies!"

Charlene thanked Sepia, then muttered to no one special, "Another night, another nickel," as she and the other show-gals quickly headed out of the tent. Sepia followed them to the door flap and looked out.

A line of floats was assembled in the moonlight, deco-rated in an Egyptian motif with golden icons and colorful mosaics. The showgals climbed aboard as Billy stood by.

"Come on!" he shouted. "Let's not keep 'em waiting!"

The most elaborate float was wheeled into position, but sat empty. Billy called out to Louie.

"Go get her, Louie!"

Sepia watched Louie jog over to the large, red wagon and knock on the door.

The door opened and Anastasia stepped out wearing an Egyptian robe and gold sandals. She also wore a black wig with a gilded cobra headpiece.

"We need you, Miss Artel," Louie said.

"You bet you do," she answered with a smile.

She crossed to her float, climbed aboard and sat on a high platform in the center. Billy immediately shouted for the procession to start moving.

Sepia slipped back through the dressing room to the per-formers' entrance and stood gazing out at the audience. The

Big Top was warm with excitement. Children jumped and wriggled in their seats as candy butchers hawked popcorn and lukewarm soda to the packed stands.

The circus band, dressed in bright red uniforms and gold braiding, struck up a jaunty, welcoming tune.

Suddenly, the lights dimmed and the band stopped. Darkness and silence preceded a loud drum roll and crash of symbols as a spotlight hit the Announcer standing in the center ring using only his leather lungs to reach the top of the stands.

"Ladies and gentlemen, children of all ages! We are proud to present to the great city of Chicago, the most spectacular show of exotic animals and death defying feats in the world! And now, enjoy the thrills, the chills, and the magnificent wonders of the great Olympic Circus!"

Behind the Announcer, The equestrian director, wearing red tails, white breeches and black boots blew his whistle to start the show.

The lights came up and the band conductor led a rousing march as the Grand Entry began.

An ornate, gilded circus wagon pulled by six matching black stallions led the parade. The horses pranced a high stepping gait as the crowd picked up their rhythm and clapped their hands. The sides of the wagon were adorned with gold carved figures depicting otherworldly athletes. The wings of Prometheus, the bulging muscles of Hercules, the perfect form of Apollo, the beauty of Aphrodite and the grandness of Zeus. All had their counterparts in the Olympic Circus. It was a bold and alluring comparison, an image the performers loved to aspire to.

Behind the circus wagon came the floats looking like a royal procession from Cairo. Charlene and the other showgals rode a wagon with a golden-winged phoenix spanning the front and a pair of mosaic sphinxes covering each side. Between each float, performers rode horses, camels and elephants draped in vibrant appliquéd fabric. The parade was a glittery, gaudy, fast moving spectacle, meant to dazzle the crowd. If there were any doubters in the audience, the Grand Entry would convince them that they had entered another world.

Finally a float approached that was even grander than the rest. Painted wooden clouds surrounded the golden platform where Anastasia lay on her side like Cleopatra on her royal dais. The crowd cheered wildly when they saw her and she waved graciously to her fans. It was a true love affair, the only kind she really wanted. She bathed in their attention and it was her obvious pleasure at being adored that made the crowd want to love her even more.

Sepia stood transfixed watching Anastasia's power over the audience. Where did she get such confidence? How did she pull everyone's eyes to her and hold them in her spell? The desire to have such power infused Sepia. First she and Bruno must get hired on, and then she would learn Anastasia's secret. Anastasia was the answer to her prayers. Her fate would be life not death. Anastasia, not Angelina would be her inspiration. She was suddenly filled with relief and joy, and she stayed fixed on the exit long after Anastasia's float had disappeared from view.

The equestrian director signaled the end of the Grand Entry and blew the whistle for the first acts. The show was timed to the second and performers scrambled to keep moving.

"And now, in ring one, Wanda and her Wooly Acrobatic Wonders!" bellowed the Announcer. "And in ring three,

JoJo and Roscoe Gomez and their Clowning Canines!"

The same dog act Sepia had seen practicing earlier that day exploded into ring one and began its quick paced and comical act. In ring three, a Kodiak bear climbed onto a bicycle and peddled human-like around the ring.

Unlike the audience who had the pleasant dilemma of which ring to observe, Sepia could take in all the familiar acts like ice cream flavors licked together on a cone and still let her mind wander to tomorrow. Her father was right to have waited to catch the Olympic in Chicago where it would stay for a week rather than the usual one night stand. Billy could afford the time to watch them. She would have to get Bruno up early in the morning so he could lose any hangover from tonight. They hadn't practiced for a week, but if they got their rigging in place early, they would have time to prepare. Hopefully, Billy wouldn't want to see them until late morning or early afternoon. She would have hours to practice, to work the kinks out.

The first acts ended and a clown routine began in center ring. The sheer absurdity of their costumes already had the crowd roaring as they performed to a fast march of giggling flutes and laughing trombones. One clown was dressed as a Poor Man with exaggerated tatters and holes in revealing places. Another clown wore the three-piece, pin-striped suit of a Banker with enlarged fake money hanging from his waistcoat pocket. He was joined by his henchman, an Executioner who wielded an oversized fake axe.

Sepia recognized the Executioner's dark hood and smiled to herself for having been frightened before.

The three clowns played out a story painfully appropriate to the times.

The Banker grabbed the Poor Man. "I want your money!"

he shouted.

"I don't have any!" the Poor Man answered.

"Then I'll take your house!" the Banker announced.

"I don't have a house," the Poor Man responded.

"Then I'll take your car!"

"I don't have a car!"

"Then I'll take your...!" the Banker waved his arms to mean whatever.

"I don't have a...!" the Poor Man also waved his arms.

"What do you have?" the Banker demanded.

"All I have are the clothes on my back!" the Poor Man admitted.

"I'll take those!" the Banker shouted.

The Poor Man stripped off his raggedy garb and stood in his long underwear, shivering. The Banker held up the clothes.

"This is no good! Off with his head!"

The Executioner grabbed the Poor Man, blindfolded him, and laid his head on the block.

"Any last words?" the Banker asked.

"HELP!" the Poor Man screamed.

The Executioner raised his over sized axe as the drum rolled.

"Wait!" the Poor Man shouted.

"What is it?" the Banker asked.

"I just remembered! I have a bag!" the Poor Man said.

"A bag of money?" the Banker asked.

"Nooo," the Poor Man answered mysteriously.

"A bag of jewels?" the Banker asked.

"Nooo," the Poor Man answered.

"A bag of what?!" the Banker demanded.

"See for yourself," the Poor Man said.

The Poor Man pointed toward the edge of the ring where the spotlight hit a large bag. The Banker rubbed his hands greedily and headed for the bundle. The Poor Man pulled off his blindfold and snickered as the Banker carefully loosened the bag…and out jumped a clown in a Gorilla suit. The Gorilla chased the Banker, while the Poor Man grabbed the axe and chased the Executioner. The crowd "hurrahed!" as the chase continued around the arena and out the exit.

Again, the announcer belted out an introduction. "And now, ladies and gentlemen, we are proud to present the Queen of Circus, and the world's greatest aerialist, the star attraction of the Olympic Circus, Miss Anastasia Artel!"

The audience responded with wild cheers and applause as Anastasia made her spectacular entrance. Draped in gold, she walked into center ring and struck a pose. She undid the clasp at her neck, pulled off her cloak, and threw it to her attendant then held the audience spellbound as she began a slow ascent of a long rope suspended from the peak of the Big Top.

Sepia stopped watching Anastasia for a moment to glance at her attendant. He was the same young man she'd seen with the woman from town earlier that day. Even more attractive in his costume, a royal blue leotard with matching tights and a gold waistband, she noticed that he drew the attention of every woman in the audience. Not only were his features striking, there was a roguish air about him as if being Anastasia's attendant was a folly. If she'd thought about it a bit more, Sepia would have noticed his resemblance to the woman in the spotlight above him; the same roman nose, the same brilliant blue eyes. As before, he caused Sepia's pulse to quicken and her cheeks to flush, but also like before, she forced her thoughts away from him. She focused her gaze back up to Anastasia instead.

The spotlight followed Anastasia's stunning figure pulling herself up the eighty feet of rope by repeatedly turning her body parallel to the web, grabbing higher and rolling over. When she reached the top, she took hold of the roman rings, dual rings hanging parallel, of which she had complete mastery, and the crowd became mesmerized by her graceful acrobatics.

Sepia was impressed with how effortlessly Anastasia assumed and then held each position. She performed without a safety net, which added to the thrill of watching her and to the notion that she was, perhaps, immortal.

Charlene and some of the other showgals walked up to the opening and stood nearby. They, too, stared up at Anastasia.

"She's got the crowd in the palm of her hand," one of them remarked.

Charlene scowled. "I knew her when she barely made vaudeville in this town."

"That's hard to believe," the woman commented.

"She started out in a flying return act," Charlene said. "Now she's got what she wanted," she added.

"What do you mean?" the woman asked.

"She's a single act, the star attraction, top billing," Charlene answered.

"She's a star all right," another showgal commented.

"I prefer the son myself," Charlene said with a grin as she stared out at the attendant. Some of the other women nodded and giggled in agreement.

Sepia looked out at the attendant again and the resemblance between mother and son was now obvious. She wasn't only looking at his face, however, but his body, too, an athlete's body. He couldn't just be Anastasia's attendant, she decided, and wondered what act he performed in. She found it harder now to tear her eyes away from his face and his firm and muscled physique. Even his mother could not keep Sepia's attention until she commanded it with the amazing feat she performed next.

Anastasia ended her poses on the rings and thunderous applause greeted her descent. She bowed gloriously then grabbed another rope and was flown aloft to the top of the tent by her son pulling the line through a pulley. The Big Top became still and even the candy butchers were silent as Anastasia began her closing act. She slipped her wrist into a loop attached by a swivel to a hanging rope. She then began a series of full circle turns with her entire body. A drum roll and crash of cymbals signaled each turn and the audience joined the announcer in the count.

Sepia's lips also moved with the count and some of the showgals joined in as the number rose to fifty. As Anastasia's shoulder jerked back and forth, Sepia wondered at the stress it must cause on her body. Others were curious, too.

"I watch her every night and I still don't see how she does it," a newer showgal said.

"Dislocates her shoulder then snaps it back on every turn," Charlene informed her with a grimace.

Now Anastasia's hair loosened from its pins and swung free as she continued her spirals through the air. The count rose to one hundred twenty-five. Finally Anastasia ended on an incredible one hundred fifty revolutions and descended the rope amid a tornado of applause. Sepia was transfixed along with the audience who followed until the last glimpse before Anastasia disappeared from sight.

As Anastasia passed by Sepia, there was a loud commotion outside. Sepia followed unnoticed as Anastasia exited the backdoor and was immediately flocked by newspaper reporters. Flashlights strobe lighted her face as she walked to her wagon. Sepia stayed in the background and watched the reporters battling to question the star.

"What did you think of the crowd tonight, Miss Artel?" one reporter shouted.

"Wonderful! The people of Chicago are magnificent!" she answered graciously.

"What's it like being the biggest star in circus?" another reporter asked.

Anastasia turned toward him coyly. "I finally got my own train car."

The reporters chuckled. A third newsman called out.

"Have you ever thought about doing pictures, Miss Artel?"

"Pictures?" Anastasia asked, playing dumb, then she winked at the reporter. "Oh, you mean moving pictures. Listen, I'm happy right where I am. Circus is still the best entertainment around!" Anastasia reached her wagon and started climbing the steps.

"There's a rumor you'll retire soon. Any truth to that?" a fourth reporter shouted from the back of the crowd.

Anastasia was caught off guard a moment, then she stepped up to her door and spun around. "Whatever gave you that idea, honey?" She posed her body. "Do I look like I'm ready to retire, boys?"

The reporters heartily agreed no.

"You just put in your papers that Anastasia Artel is number one in the number one circus in the world!" She blew them a kiss. "Goodnight, boys!" she called and entered her wagon.

The reporters quickly dispersed and Sepia stood in the shadows staring at Anastasia's door. If she was going to do it, she'd better do it now, she told herself. Another second and she'd lose her nerve.

"Who is it?" Anastasia called from within, responding to Sepia's light knock on her door.

"M...Miss Artel?"

The door opened briskly and Anastasia eyed Sepia coolly. Sepia stood a half a head above Anastasia, but she felt very much smaller.

"Yes?" Anastasia demanded.

"I'm not lot lice," Sepia said quickly, letting Anastasia know she was not a pesky town fan.

"You're with the show?" Anastasia questioned, but waved Sepia in before she could answer. She went immediately to her dressing table where she'd apparently been sitting before.

"Did you hear that damn reporter! Retire, ha! What nerve!" she shouted to her reflection in the mirror. Her fingers unconsciously traced the lines around her mouth as if erasing any signs of age. "Who the hell started that rumor anyway?!"

Sepia didn't attempt to answer. She had been trying to look at Anastasia as she talked, but she couldn't help glancing wide-eyed around the wagon. It was nothing less than elegant. In the corner sat a green velvet covered chaise lounge with rose chintz throw pillows. Beside her stood an Art Deco floor lamp made of thick brass in the shape of a cobra coiled at the base and rising up to hold a fluted, amber globe bulb in its mouth. Anastasia's traveling trunk was also Deco, with walnut veneers running at angles across the front to create a large diamond in the center. The black, lacquered dressing table had thin ivory inlays of oriental design and the Turkish rug under her feet felt like silk. The room was wonderfully extravagant and Sepia thought it was heaven.

Anastasia picked up her hairbrush and pulled it through her long curls as she continued a dialogue with her mirror image. "Maybe it wasn't really me they were talking about. Maybe they meant my act, that it was getting old."

Again, Sepia kept still.

"Yes, that's it!" Anastasia exclaimed with relief. "And they're right! I've let my act get stale. Well, I'll show them! I'll come up with something so daring it'll knock their socks off!" she announced, punctuating the air with her hairbrush. She spun around on her seat.

"Hey, you know, I should thank that reporter! I've been feeling that something was missing and now I know what it is. I need a new challenge!" she cried as she slammed her brush down on the table for emphasis.

Sepia jumped and Anastasia seemed to notice her for the first time.

"What did you want anyway, kid?"

"I, uh, just wanted to say that I thought you were great tonight," Sepia answered.

Anastasia stared at her from head to toe, taking in the ragged coat, thin slippers and dark circles beneath her eyes. "Thanks, kid," Anastasia said. "You said you're with the show?"

"Not yet. My father and I are looking for a job," she replied.

"Well, maybe I can help you. Billy is always looking for new hands," Anastasia offered, but it was obvious her mind was already on other things, principally a grand new trick for her act. She got up and so did Sepia.

"Thanks, but I just wanted to tell you that I admired your performance. Good-night," Sepia blurted, then quickly turned and fled.

Back outside in the darkness, her cheeks burned with embarrassment. She could have talked more! Anastasia offered to help her! Why did she run off like an idiot! She didn't even tell her who she was, that the job she was looking for wasn't to serve food in the cookhouse, or clean out the train toilets. She was a performer. How could she ever dream of becoming a star if she couldn't even talk to people?

She wanted to run away, to get out of her street clothes. She wanted to leave the ground, to be up on the trapeze, to fly! She walked instead, back to the Big Top just as the announcer was introducing the final act.

"And now, ladies and gentlemen, to my right, at the far end of the Big Top..."

The spotlight shone on a red, white and blue striped cannon. "An incredibly daring athlete will be shot from this authentic cannon to the opposite end of the tent! This is a truly death defying feat, ladies and gentlemen, and a spectacular conclusion to our great Olympic Show! And now, the one and only, Carl Reichek, the Human Cannonball!"

A trim, dark-haired man stood at the front of the cannon, waving to the crowd. He wore a gold lame jumpsuit and a playful smile as if he were a child about to climb into a toy wagon, not the barrel of a cannon.

As a drum rolled, Reichek turned and slid into the chamber. An attendant lit the fuse and instantly an explosive BOOM filled the Big Top. A body shot through the air.

Sepia wished it could be her shooting out of the cannon. If only she could sail across the tent and leave her old self behind. When she landed in the safety net, she would jump to her feet and start all over again with a new life and a new destiny.

Reichek landed in the safety net, sprang to his feet and saluted the cheering crowd, his body rushing with excitement and relief. The band struck up a rousing march as all of the performing acts hurried past Sepia to join the final parade. Ten elephants lumbered around the dusty arena track, then stopped and in one joint effort, lifted their great front legs onto each other's backs in a continuous line. They curled their trunks in a unified gesture of grandness and farewell.

"This concludes our show tonight, folks," the announcer shouted. "We hope each and every one of you enjoyed our performance. Bring your family, bring your friends, and come again to the Great Olympic Circus!" He trotted out of the ring and followed the elephants to the exit. The "blow off" or departure of the audience began immediately.

Sepia leaned her cheek against a tent pole watching the crowd walk away, back to their homes and their normal lives. That would never be me, she thought, and in her heart, she knew that wasn't really what she wanted anyway. She wanted something that had nothing to do with regular people or a civilian life. Her life was never going to be normal. She just wanted it to be hers.

She watched a young woman step down from the stands with her boyfriend's hand at the small of her back, guiding her protectively through the crowd. Sepia wondered what it would be like to have someone be nice to her, to care for her, to touch her in a way that didn't make her flinch.

The image of Anastasia's son flashed through her mind and she shook it away. She turned her thoughts to the tryout tomorrow. It was a real way to change her life. When she joined out with the Olympic, things would be different. It would be a whole new start.

As she walked back to the train, she noticed Charlene with several other showgals in street clothes. One of them finished a joke and the group collapsed in a fit of laughter. Sepia smiled enviously at their freedom and friendship. She watched them sneak off into the shadows beyond the smoky kerosene lamps that lined the path back to the rail yard. She didn't see Anastasia's son join them as they headed for the brighter lights of the city.

Chapter Five: When The Lights Die Down

Cole Artel had been antsy to leave the circus that night even though the city they were headed for made him nervous. Not every city, just this one. Chicago was the last place where he had performed before being relegated to the job of his mother's attendant. It was also the last place where he had seen his father alive. His father had been murdered in a back alley outside a vaudeville theater six years earlier. However, tonight more than ever, Cole was feeling trapped at the Olympic, and the distractions of the city outweighed any discomfort he associated with being there.

They were headed for a speakeasy on Wabash Avenue though neither Charlene nor her friends could remember exactly where it was. They searched the street for a land-mark they could recall until Cole glanced down an alley and noticed a group of kids standing on a porch rail. They were gaping through the ventilator of the cigar store next door. Cole led the women down the alley and knocked on a plain, unlit door. A small slat opened at chest level and two fierce eyes peered out.

"Joe sent us," Cole said using the universal password in an easy speaking voice. The door opened and a burly, pug-nosed man looked them over. His muscle bound arms were drawn in half circles toward his body like a bulldog.

"Evenin'" he barked in a gruff voice, one well suited to warning customers before bouncing them out.

The circus group left the quiet, empty alley and entered a loud, smoky room full of warm bodies and live jazz. Heads turned to stare at the newcomers with their cheap clothes, but attractive bodies.

Cole drew several unabashed young flappers like a magnet, but experience led him to a woman in her mid-thirties with shiny, bobbed hair and a black, spaghetti-strapped dress seated at the bar.

"You alone?" Cole asked leaning his arm on the bar and facing her profile.

"Yeah, what of it?" she responded without looking at him.

"Nothin'. I was just surprised that a good looking dame like you wouldn't be with somebody, that's all," Cole said.

The woman turned to give Cole's come-on the brush when she was caught in the gaze of his incredible eyes, blue like the heat of a flame. She forgot what she was about to say, turned her hips toward him and uncrossed her legs. Cole grinned in recognition and she blushed. She wasn't used to being out of control. She needed another drink to steady herself.

"You want one?" she asked, indicating her empty glass.

"Sure, whatever you're having," he replied as if he was used to having women buy him drinks.

"Sam!" the woman called to the bartender. "Two more."

The place was busy, but the bartender left a customer and immediately came over. "Sure thing, boss," he said as he refilled the woman's glass with whiskey and poured a drink for Cole.

"Boss?" Cole asked.

"Yeah, me and a partner own this joint."

"Does the boss have a name?" Cole asked.

"Lila. What about the cocky young stud?"

"Cole."

"Where you from, Cole?" Lila asked, certain that it wasn't this city.

"The circus, I'm a trapeze artist," Cole replied with confidence, knowing it usually got a favorable response.

Lila's hazel eyes widened. That accounts for his spectacular body and his loud, ill-fitting shirt, she mused. She was already imagining what kind of acrobatics he performed outside the Big Top. "Sounds exciting," she said in a low voice.

"I'm sure you wouldn't be disappointed," Cole replied, reading her thoughts effortlessly.

"I wouldn't, huh?" Lila laughed. "I'm old enough to be your mother."

"But you're not," Cole reminded her.

Lila liked flattery as well as the next person, but she was also cautious. She couldn't quite decide how to handle this circus gigolo with the breathtakingly beautiful eyes.

"Come on. I could use a strong pair of hands," she said finally, then downed her shot of whiskey and headed toward a hallway door.

Charlene rolled her eyes when she saw Cole leave, and he winked back at her with a grin as he followed Lila through the door.

Lila led Cole down the hall and into an office. The room was dark and smelled of perfume and cigars as she switched on a lamp sitting atop a wide, oak desk. A worn, Turkish rug covered the concrete floor and a large, metal safe sat against the wall. She walked over to the opposite wall where a painting hung next to a tall bookcase. The painting, faded and dark, was of a gypsy girl smoking a clay pipe. Lila slid the picture askance, pressed a button concealed behind it and the bookcase popped away from the wall like a door. She walked into the black opening and pulled a string that turned on a bare light bulb. Cole followed her into a room about fourteen feet square and lined with cases of liquor stacked like building blocks.

"Mind lugging a case back to the bar for me?" Lila asked Cole.

"Sure. Now?" he questioned. He stood facing her as she leaned against the wall next to the door.

"Yes," she answered.

He turned to get a case when Lila touched his arm. He swung back and stepped toward her instead. Her arm laced under his left shoulder and his right thigh pressed between her legs. Their lips met, opened and formed a long, urgent kiss. The tenseness slowly left Cole's body. He'd been right to come here.

Afterwards, they straightened their clothes in the hidden room and had a cigarette in Lila's office, both of them relaxed and smiling.

"If you ever want to run away from the circus, I'm here," she teased.

"Don't tempt me," he replied, but Lila guessed that Cole's circus blood made him a rover and that he could never stay in one place long. She was sure, in fact, that she would never see him again.

As Cole returned to the circus grounds that night, the heaviness that had lifted for several hours settled back onto his shoulders. He tried to think of Lila and how good it had felt, but even the effect of good sex didn't last. He had lied to her. He was not a performer, not anymore that is. Once, he and his mother had been a flying trapeze act until she wanted the spotlight for herself. Cole gave it to her as he gave everything to her.

No one quite understood the hold Anastasia had over her son, but it was as tight as a lion tamer grips her whip, even if she never uses it. The only time Cole exerted any influence of his own was outside the circus. He had been a good flyer. Now he was a good lover. He made it a rule to only pursue women from town, mostly to avoid trouble with Billy. He conquered women as he had hoped to conquer the audience, with skill and precision. His act won approval, but it never disguised the fact that he only performed outside the Big Top. He had become a gigolo, well liked, but trapped in a life not his own.

***

Charlene and the others had returned to their berths and were dead to the world when Sepia began moaning in her sleep.

A soft, cotton pillow covered her face. It was warm and light at first, but then she sensed pressure and began to lose air. She struggled to push it off, but it was held down too tightly. She tried to scream, to kick, to get one breath, but everything was going black.

Sepia bolted awake gulping for air and drenched in a cold sweat. It was the same dream she'd had since childhood, since her mother's accident. She always woke feeling not only terrified, but guilty, as if she'd done something wrong and was being punished for it.

A thin moon lit the train car. Sepia took several slow, deep breaths, then she lay back down and stared at the curved metal ceiling of the train compartment. She closed her eyes, but she kept seeing Anastasia performing her famous one-arm plunges. She finally fell back to sleep counting swingovers instead of sheep.

Chapter Six: The Tryout

The next morning Sepia rose quietly, dug in her bag, and retrieved a leotard, towel and sweater. She opened the compartment door and stepped out into the sunshine.

Bathing in the circus meant using an allotted two buckets of water outside the Dressing Top, but before she headed toward the circus grounds to wash up, Sepia went to check on Bruno.

She found the right compartment and luckily a roust-about was coming out the door. She asked him to get her father and after several minutes, Bruno dragged himself outside, pulling his suspenders over his undershirt.

"I'm going over to the lot. Here's some soap," she told him as she handed him a piece of hers. "I'll meet you in the cookhouse."

Bruno looked at her surprised, but by the time he grunted his response, she was already gone.

Sepia sponged herself off quickly in the privacy of the canvassed-off bathing spot, then went to the cookhouse.

Much as she wanted to fill her stomach again, she ate only an egg and a slice of bread for breakfast. Bruno finally joined her, hanging his head over a cup of coffee as she finished eating.

"How was the show?" he asked, bleary eyed.

"Good," she answered. "Anastasia was great."

"Anastasia Artel, Queen of the Circus!" he mocked. "Wait 'til she sees you. You're better than her, you know."

"No, I'm not," she said.

Bruno reached over and grabbed her wrist, squeezing. "You're the best. I made you the best. Nobody took care of you the way I done. You just keep doin' what I tell you and we'll make it big!"

She kept her eyes on his until he let go and went back to drinking his coffee.

"I'll go warm up," she said quietly, already losing the bit of assuredness she'd had earlier.

"Good. I need to find Louie and set our rigging," Bruno answered. They were both assuming the tryout was on. If anyone could bully his way into making it happen, it was her father. She was grateful for that at least.

When Sepia walked into the Big Top, the arena was empty and inviting. She liked having the tent to herself in the morning quiet. She walked right into center ring and began stretching out her muscles using one of the huge, center poles to brace against. She placed her foot high against the wooden beam, then touched her forehead to her knee and took a deep breath. When she brought her head back up, she sensed she wasn't alone anymore. Looking over her shoulder, she noticed a figure silhouetted in the entrance to the Big Top. The figure stepped out of the sunlight and she saw a man staring at her, his face covered with deep, shiny, rope-like scars partially covering one eye. A wave of both sympathy and horror rose inside her, yet it wasn't his disfigurement that sent a chill down her spine. The man glared at her with such malice that she slowly lowered her leg from the center pole. She watched as he walked over to the curb and picked up a prop which she recognized as the oversized axe from the clown act. He looked directly at her and started walking toward her carrying the axe. She froze in utter disbelief that he meant to harm her, but at that moment, she heard voices behind her. She turned and saw Louie and her father.

When Louie saw the man with the axe, he called out to him in a quick, but unalarmed voice. "When you're finished fixing your prop, I've got some harness needs repairing."

His prop. The scar-faced man was the Executioner from the clown act. Sepia also noticed that the axe in his hand had torn away from its handle and needed mending. She turned away, embarrassed and relieved, but wondered why the man had looked at her so threateningly. His expression didn't change much when he talked to Louie, however. Maybe he just doesn't like people, she thought.

When the Executioner exited past Bruno and Louie, Bruno stared rudely at his face.

"Poor bastard," he said. "What happened to him?"

"Don't know," Louie answered. "He don't talk. Does good work though. We hired him on as a prop/rigger man and he doubles in the clown act. He can put your rigging up. Don't charge much either. Billy will be over in two hours."

"We'll be ready," Bruno said.

Exactly two hours later, as Sepia swung back up to the trapeze platform and glanced below, Billy walked in the tent. She watched him pick a chair in the audience and sit down.

"Okay, let's see what you've got!" he called up to them.

Bruno was seated on the catcher's trapeze, rocking gently with an arm looped around the rope for balance. He saluted Billy confidently and began swinging.

Sepia shoved a lock of hair back under its pin and tightened her ponytail. She wiped the sweat from her neck and face with a handkerchief she kept tucked in her leotard. Finally, she dusted her palms on the rosin bag and was ready.

Bruno lowered himself into position and coiled his legs like a snake around the thick padded ropes of his trapeze. Sepia grabbed her trapeze bar and flew out. As Bruno swung up to meet her, she sailed head first over the bar in a plange, body flat out, and they locked wrists in what she hoped looked like a perfect hand catch. Her empty fly bar swung away, then, when it returned, she twisted around, grabbed it and flew back to the platform. She grabbed the guy wire and landed with her feet squarely on the board. Many flyers had someone assist them on the return by sending the bar back out and taking it from them when they returned to the platform, but Sepia had learned to handle the trapeze herself.

The trick she performed was an easy one and Billy sat in the stands expressionless, waiting for more. She was sure he had a mental checklist of tricks that were expected from a competent flyer and she was prepared to do them all.

Again Bruno gave a signal. She flew out, pirouetted in the air and was caught again by the wrists.

Billy adjusted his hat and smiled, but Sepia did not notice. She was concentrating on doing every trick as perfectly as she could. She also did not see Anastasia enter the Big Top in her rehearsal outfit.

Anastasia was heading toward center ring when she

looked up and saw the flyers.

"Who are they?" She asked, spotting Billy in the stands.

"The Stefanis," Billy answered.

"Who?" She asked walking over to him.

Anastasia was interrupted by another signal from the air and she and Billy looked up.

Sepia took hold of the trapeze and flew out, tucked her body into a back somersault and this time Bruno caught her by the feet. When she returned to the platform, she risked a glance down and caught what she thought was the beginning of a smile on Billy's face.

"Not bad," he muttered to Anastasia.

"Have I seen her somewhere before?" Anastasia asked him.

"Beats me," he answered.

"You didn't tell me you were bringing in a new act," Anastasia said.

"Didn't know I had to," Billy replied.

"I've got a right to know what's going on," she stated.

"Like you said, your contract is almost up and you'll get offers I can't compete with. I gotta think of the future," he responded.

"I have no intention of leaving and you know it. I made this circus. I'm the star attraction and always will be!" Anastasia yelled a little too loudly. Again she and Billy were interrupted by Bruno's signal.

This time Sepia lifted off and pumped her trapeze out and back, then high up into the Big Top. Releasing the bar, she spun into a two and a half backward somersault. She opened out just as Bruno met her with a hand catch. She returned to her trapeze and back to the platform, unaware that she had caused Billy to rise from his seat. He left the stands and walked out into center ring.

"That was real nice!" he called upward.

Bruno was back in a sitting position on his catch bar. "What'd I tell you? She is great, uh?"

It was time for a decision and Sepia and Bruno waited nervously for an answer.

"Well, it looks like we have ourselves a new act," Billy announced. "Come down and we'll work out a deal."

Sepia's heart leapt. They were in. She smiled broadly down at Billy then she saw Anastasia. She remembered the night before and her face reddened, but she was too happy to care about her foolish behavior now.

"We'll make you even more famous!" Bruno called to Billy. He looked down at Anastasia. "Miss Artel, we're honored."

"Come down and meet our 'star attraction'", Billy called up as he grinned at Anastasia. She frowned back.

Sepia sailed out on the trapeze, curled her body and dropped neatly into the safety net, landing on her back to avoid injury. She bounced up, walked over to the edge of the net and swung down to join Bruno as he walked over to Billy and Anastasia.

"Anastasia, this is Bruno and Sepia Stefani," Billy said introducing them.

"It's a great pleasure to meet you," Bruno said in a servile voice.

"Thanks," said Anastasia, not fooled by his tone. "Actually I've already met Sepia." She furrowed her brow. "Why didn't you tell me you were a flyer?"

"I'm sorry, Miss Artel," Sepia said. "I was so excited to meet you, I forgot."

"Sepia is a big fan of yours," Bruno added.

"You look pretty good up there," Anastasia said to her.

"She's the best!" Bruno exclaimed abruptly.

"Papa...," Sepia pleaded, embarrassed.

"That's okay. He should be proud of you, right?" Anastasia confirmed.

"Come on," Billy said to Bruno and Sepia. "Let's go to my office and talk."

"I make the deals for us," Bruno said. He turned to Sepia. "You go back to the train and wait for me."

Billy raised his eyebrows at Bruno's order, but he didn't interfere. He nodded to Bruno and they exited the tent, leaving the two women standing alone together. At five foot six, Sepia was not only tall for a woman, but very tall for a flyer. She felt awkward and gangly next to Anastasia's strong, compact beauty.

"It was nice to meet you again, Miss Artel," was all she could think to say, then she turned to go.

"Congratulations," Anastasia answered. "You joined up with a great show."

"I know!" Sepia exclaimed, turning back, but Anastasia had focused her attention on Louie. Just before she left the Big Top, she heard Anastasia's voice belting across the tent.

"Louie! Get that trapeze out of center ring! From now on they'll rehearse in three!"

Outside the Big Top, Sepia tried to feel pleased about her good fortune. Like Anastasia said, the Olympic was a great show. Yet instead of being happy, she felt uneasy. Anastasia had been polite but unmistakably cool towards her. Maybe she was angry about last night. Surely she understood that Sepia hadn't meant to fool her.

She stopped walking and shook her head. She was being so stupid! Whenever something good happened, she had to spoil it. She was getting to fly with the Olympic! She was trouping in the same circus as Anastasia Artel! If Anastasia had not immediately embraced her with friendship, it was only normal. She should be thankful that Anastasia even spoke to her!

Sepia remembered her vow from the night before, that if she got into the Olympic, she would find a way to learn Anastasia's secrets. But how?

It was true that Sepia had performed on the trapeze in front of huge crowds and lived among large groups of performers, but Bruno had kept her isolated from them. She didn't know how to talk to people, much less ask for a favor. She needed to learn, however, if she was ever going to achieve the kind of success she wanted.

If she wasn't good at talking, she was good at listening and watching. She decided to find out as much as she could about Anastasia, what she liked and didn't like. There must be something I could do for her, Sepia thought, some way I can get close to her.

As she crossed the circus grounds with new determination, her stomach grumbled. The combination of a light breakfast and a strenuous workout had left her starving. She hoped the flag was still up on the cookhouse and headed for the tent.

As she passed the Menagerie, she noticed Anastasia's son washing down an elephant. It was the same bull that had shown off for the audience the night before. Cole held a canvas fire hose on the elephant's wrinkly back as she tossed her head in grateful pleasure.

Sepia looked for another route to the cookhouse that wouldn't go right past them and found it through a row of wagons. She caught glimpses of man and elephant through the gaps between each wagon. She also saw Charlene walk over to him.

"Late night?" Charlene asked reprovingly. She was wearing a flimsy floral dress that looked new.

"Playing cards in the pie car," he lied, continuing to wash off the elephant.

"Breaking hearts is more like it," she replied with an admonishing grin.

"Me?" he asked, pretending to be hurt.

"You," she answered. "Anyway, like my new dress?" She whirled around to model herself.

"Sure," he said, but he had spotted his mother crossing the grounds and his eye was now on her.

Charlene followed his gaze and frowned. "How'd you get a mother like her?"

"Just lucky I guess," Cole answered sarcastically.

"That woman only cares about one thing, center ring. Me, on the other hand, I'm crazy about you, honey." She smiled and took his arm. "Come on. I got somethin' to show you."

"I already saw your dress," Cole said, turning back to Charlene with a grin.

"That's right," Charlene cooed. She tugged on his arm, making the fire hose fly in every direction.

Sepia felt a splash of cold water on her cheek and gasped. "You want to get us both red lighted off the show? Besides, you know I don't fool around with circus dames," Cole said, pulling the hose back from Charlene and regaining control. "Couldn't you make an exception, lover boy?" Charlene coaxed.

"Nope," he answered.

"You're a little prick, you know it?" she said with feigned

anger.

"Big prick," he replied, correcting her.

Charlene walked off in a pretend huff as Cole watched, snickering. He turned to the elephant and continued her bath. "You love me, don't you, Timba?"

The elephant responded with a loud trumpet call that made Cole burst out laughing. Sepia's heart jumped from the wonderfully infectious sound of his laugh. She watched the sun dance on his slightly damp hair. Like his mother, he moved his body with confidence and ease, but unlike Anastasia, he seemed more relaxed and free. As Cole led the elephant away, Sepia wondered again what Cole did in the show other than help his mother. She hadn't seen him in any other act.

Chapter Seven: Settling In

After breakfast, Sepia returned to the train car where Bruno was waiting.

"What a deal I made!" he exclaimed. "We're makin' double what we was with Griffen. Mr. Big Shot wanted you real bad, asked all kinds of questions. We're on our way, kid."

"When do we start?" she asked.

"Tomorrow. Get your bag. We're movin' into our own dressing wagon. Oh, and you're gettin' a new costume."

Sepia smiled at that. Having her own dressing wagon was pure luxury, and she'd wanted a new costume for a long time. Hers was badly worn and way too girlish.

"Louie will show you where the wagon is," Bruno said, then he left quickly, off to celebrate.

***

Sepia looked around their dressing room, the back end of a prop wagon. It was small, but with a sheet hung across the middle, she had privacy and her own space for the first time in her life. Bruno was lying on a cot sound asleep. After the tryout that morning and a bottle of hooch, he had passed out, but not before telling her over and over how they would practice for the triple.

He was obsessed now, not only with the triple, but with the notion that it was their ticket to fame. Sepia had her doubts about the triple, but she understood Bruno's desire for fame. Being famous would make him important, and feeling important would give Bruno the closest thing to happiness. With fame came money, and with money he could buy the fancy clothes he'd wanted but never had. He could be somebody, someone that others would notice and most of all envy, not only when he was flying, but on the ground, too.

For her, fame meant power, and power would lend her the confidence she'd never had. She knew that she could perform circus tricks extremely well, but so could Jo Jo's dogs. Simply being a flyer did not give her the kind of self-esteem she wanted. Being a famous flyer would be a different story. She was sure of it.

***

She finished unpacking her things and put them in an old, battered wardrobe trunk Louie had provided. She had so few belongings that it was barely a quarter filled. There was her one dress, a pair of practice slippers, a nightgown and her only valuable possession, a hairbrush made of dark cherry and boar's bristles with ivory flowers inlaid on the back. She picked up the brush and held it to her heart. It felt smooth and heavy in her hand, full of remembrance. Why? Why was her mother invading her thoughts again? She remembered so little of her mother and almost nothing that was happy except...

Every night, after her act, she had climbed up on the chair behind her mother and pulled the pins out of her mother's hair slowly and carefully. She spread Angelina's shiny curls onto her back and began brushing. Her mother closed her eyes and purred like a cat and Sepia knew she was doing something that was dearly loved. She could smell the oil from her mother's hair as her fingers gathered and separated the strands of soft auburn into a loose braid. Neither of them spoke, but she felt closer to her mother then than at any other time. It was the only moment of the day when they were alone, safe and quiet...

No. Even this good memory needed to be pushed away. Better not to risk the pain that comes with remembering, she reminded herself.

Sepia set the brush back in the trunk and closed it. She looked around the bare, empty wagon and decided to imagine it differently. Someday, she told herself, she would have her own train car and dressing wagon with her name scrolled on the side. She had dreamed of exactly how it would look. There would be a carved wood bed with a quilted, silk coverlet, thick drapes at the windows and a plush carpet on the floor. A crystal lamp would sit on her night table, and a long, gilded frame mirror would stand against the wall. She would greet visitors from a velvet chaise lounge and serve them tea from rose painted china. She had seen all this in a stateroom car on a passenger train she had boarded by mistake once. She left before anyone saw her, but not before taking a long look at the luxury within.

As she stared around the empty wagon, Sepia heard familiar laughter outside and the sound of voices. She knelt on the cot and peered out the small window above it.

A trampoline was set up nearby and a troupe of acrobats was practicing. They were the five Terelli Brothers, dark haired and olive skinned, between the ages of about eight and twenty. Cole was there, too, leaning against the trampoline, affectionately deriding two of the brothers bouncing on it. They challenged him to do better and Cole swung up onto the trampoline, eager to show off. The two brothers jumped down and observed as Cole began bouncing.

Sepia watched, too, as he pumped himself higher and higher in the air. His white undershirt allowed his bare, hardened biceps to flex freely. Suspenders held up his black stretch pants, revealing strong muscular thighs beneath the thin, elastic material. He bounced up and flipped over backward, then he bounced again and spun into a front somersault. He dove into a handstand, sprang back and spiraled in the air, then landed squarely on his feet in a dead stop. He gave an exaggerated bow and the Terelli's alternated between jeers and applause.

As if aware of being watched elsewhere, he suddenly looked over and saw Sepia in the window. He flashed her such a friendly smile that she instantly smiled back. He motioned for her to come out, but she blushed, shook her head and pulled away from the opening.

Still kneeling on her cot, she pressed her back against the wall and felt a warmness spread through her body. A strange yearning made her heart beat faster and that same odd sensation rushed through her as if something inside her was unfolding. Every nerve, every fiber of her being was feeling excited and relaxed at the same time. Why this man had touched that place inside her she didn't know. She only knew that she suddenly wanted to be near him.

Instinctively, her arm reached for the hairbrush in the trunk. She pulled out her ponytail and brushed her hair down onto her shoulders. She was still in her leotard, damp with sweat, but the only dress she owned was ugly and out of fashion. She cursed herself for not being more womanly, for not even knowing how to be.

Just then someone knocked on the wagon door causing her to jump. She froze on the cot and looked toward Bruno's half of the tiny room, but he snored away uninterrupted. She stood up and slowly walked to the door, but before she reached it, there was another louder knock. She rushed to the door now and flung it open. Cole stood on the wagon steps, glistening with sweat and beaming the same warm smile that made her shiver. He was taller than she had realized, a head above her. His eyes were the most amazing color, like the sky at twilight.

"Hi, I'm Cole. Are you new around here?"

His question was more than an opening line. He hadn't heard of any new act being hired. It was as if she had appeared out of nowhere. She had smiled at him from the window with such innocence that it touched him, even though he doubted that a girl her age could have lived in the circus world and remained innocent. She was definitely circus though. She had the body of an acrobat, strong and firm, with slender yet muscular legs. She also had the face of an angel with enormous brown eyes and deep rose lips. Cole was immediately stirred by the prospect of having her. She looked him straight in the eye and that furthered the notion that either she was so innocent that she knew nothing of being coy, or that she knew exactly what he wanted and was not shy about wanting it, too. When she spoke, he knew that it was the former, that she was locked on his eyes out of inexperience and fear, and this aroused him even further. He wanted her badly. His rule about not fooling around with circus women went right out the tent flap.

"My father and I...just joined on," Sepia said. "He's asleep," she added, nodding toward the wagon.

Cole raised his fingers to his lips to hush her. He took her hand and led her down the wagon steps. He knew how to handle this one, not to turn his face away from her for a second, to keep smiling and assuring her that he was as kind and gentle as she hoped he was. He had long ago learned not to come on too strongly with a girl like this. He had learned patience and knew it was worth the wait to have a virgin want him, not only in her heart, but in her body. It wasn't easy though. He wanted her right now, this instant.

Sepia's heart was racing and her mind was clouded. She was letting this man lead her away as if he owned her. He must have hypnotized her, she thought, like the gypsy woman in the Sideshow. If only he would take his incredible blue eyes off hers maybe she would come to her senses, but she knew she wasn't being led by her mind. Her body had taken over and she would have followed him anywhere. When he touched her it had been like electric shocks to her skin. His warm hand engulfed hers as he led her along, gently squeezing her palm, sending a wave of chills through her body.

Cole led Sepia to the Menagerie. He ducked under the canvas flap and pulled her into the dim light of the tent. They stood facing each other and Cole said his third sentence to her.

"You are beautiful," he murmured in a husky voice.

Sepia barely heard what he said. It didn't matter what he said. She was still locked in his spell and now she was feeling his fingertips running down the length of her arms.

He lifted her left hand, kissed her palm then brushed his lips along the inside of her arm. She trembled as he reached her shoulder then her neck. Still his eyes kept glancing into hers, keeping his hold on her. His hands slid down her hips and moved to her back. He took hold of her and gently squeezed while he lifted her closer to him. Her mouth parted with amazement at how pliable her body had become. As her lips opened, Cole closed his mouth over hers, carefully, softly, mustering the greatest restraint he had ever applied in his life. She sighed and heard Cole answer with a low growl that sounded like baby tigers threatening to pounce. She hadn't blinked in what seemed like minutes.

Cole saw the glazed look in her eyes. He slipped his tongue into her mouth and watched her eyelids finally close. She moaned again and he pressed his body against hers. He knew she could feel his arousal, could feel him prodding, pushing to reach under her. She responded by climbing him like the ladder to her trapeze, her arms gripping his shoulders tightly. He lifted her into the air and her legs circled his waist. He slowly walked over to a pile of straw in the corner of the tent and knelt down. He leaned her into the hay where the sweet musk of animal scents was left behind. Sepia opened her eyes again and Cole assured her with a steady look. His hands were all over her now, roving lightly. His thumbs brushed along her breasts and her already erect nipples. Sepia arched her back until only the tips of her hair touched the straw behind her. He had been right. She was reacting to his touch with small noises of pleasure. His hand covered her mouth for a brief second to let her know that her cries could be heard.

She relaxed her back and blushed with a desire that astounded her. Her hands left his neck and searched tentatively along his body. They moved from his back to his chest, then stomach. Her fingers slid beneath his undershirt, felt the touch of his smooth skin then pushed up through the soft hair of his chest. He followed her actions, but more slowly, opening her sweater, then laying his bare chest against her leotard. He could feel the hardness of her nipples and he wondered if they were the same dark color of her lips. She looked at him shyly, but did not stop him when he lowered his head down and kissed her breast through the thin material. Her hand moved instinctively downward, reaching for him as surely as if she had done this a thousand times instead of the very first. Her eyes widened as she felt his hardness.

God, she was going to explode from so much feeling. There couldn't be more than this, Sepia thought then Cole slipped his hand between her legs and touched her where the burning had not stopped. She didn't mean to, but her head dove into his shoulder and she bit the tender skin there. She couldn't believe she was doing this, but there was no way she could stop. Then she heard the footsteps nearby. Cole felt her body tense as he, too, heard someone coming.

A man appeared carrying a water bucket and Sepia froze as she realized it was the Executioner. At first, he didn't see Cole and Sepia hidden in the shadows. He set the bucket of water down in front of a horse and started to leave, then he stopped. Cole had his back to the Executioner so that Sepia was blocked from view. The Executioner stared at them for a brief moment then turned and walked away.

Cole kissed Sepia's neck and whispered that it was okay, but it was too late. The spell was broken and she could listen to him now without the fog in her brain. She quickly sat up and kept her eyes away from his. Her body was still reeling from incredible sensation, but her mind was operating separately now. She felt such a mixture of happiness and wonder at what she had experienced that it didn't occur to her that she hadn't been fulfilled or that Cole was not pleased, that is, until she heard him cursing.

"Damn idiot," Cole said. "I heard that he practically lives in the Menagerie." Gone were the soft words, the endearments. He didn't help Sepia up from the straw bed either. Instead, he jerked himself up, hopped to his feet and waited impatiently for her to follow. His experience with women didn't go much beyond lovemaking. He definitely wasn't used to making small talk after being satisfied, much less unsatisfied. He did ask her what her name was.

"Sepia," she answered, feeling like a fool now.

"What do you do?" Cole asked next as they stepped out of the Menagerie tent into the bright sun.

"Trapeze," she answered, blinking in the light. She didn't want to talk. She felt awkward now and wanted to get away.

"Yeah?" Cole asked, truly impressed. "When can I see you again? After the show?"

"I don't know," Sepia replied. "My father is very strict."

"But you are a big girl," Cole told her. He stopped and faced her. "Besides, I have to see you again." He cupped her face in his hands and for a moment she was lost again. To feel that feeling, to be wanted. It was irresistible.

"Not tonight," Sepia told him. "We start performing tomorrow. I have to go to bed early."

"Tomorrow then. Promise me," Cole demanded.

"Okay," she said meekly. It was hard to deny him. When he looked at her, she was flooded with the memory of his touch.

"Tomorrow," Cole repeated, and then he trotted off.

Sepia stood watching Cole go, embarrassed for what she'd let him do, yet wanting him to do it to her all over again. Suddenly she realized that her father was calling her. She stared at him across the grounds as if he were a stranger, then reality set in and she slowly walked toward him.

"The seamstress wants to fit your costume now," he said, eyeing her suspiciously. "Come on." He walked off, expecting her to follow, and she did.

Chapter Eight: The First Night

When Sepia stepped into Rosie's costume wagon, it was like walking into a real house. The one small room was overflowing with knick-knacks and memorabilia. There was a sunken, floral upholstered chair with lace doilies on the arms and back, and a tapestry covered sofa with crocheted pillows of colorful fruit decorating each end. A standing lamp with a fringed silk shade stood beside the sofa, and a dark, carved oak coffee table sat in front of it. Every flat surface was laden with cardboard boxes stuffed with sewing paraphernalia, and a metal rack of colorful costumes filled one wall. It was incredibly cluttered, but Sepia loved the sense of permanence it conveyed, a stark contrast to her own bare space in the prop wagon.

Rosie welcomed Sepia and Bruno with a warm hug, her arms enclosing Sepia like huge protective wings.

Wasting no time, Rosie began taking Sepia's measurements. She walked silently around her, stretching the cloth tape along various sections of her body. Rosie's movements had a soothing effect, but Sepia's thoughts were anything but calm.

Her mind was on Cole and what she had done with him.

She had been a fool to go with him she told herself, and yet if she hadn't, she never would have experienced that incredible sensation. She closed her eyes and immediately felt Cole's hands on her body, holding her, caressing her, giving her the affection she had craved for so long.

A moan escaped her lips that made Rosie glance up and raise her eyebrows. Sepia blushed, then her eyes darted to her father, afraid he would somehow guess what was on her mind, but Bruno was staring at the circus photos covering Rosie's walls.

Sepia stared at the hard angle of her father's profile. She thought of the drunken fits when he used to lash out at her with harsh beatings. That was before she'd learned to fly, before she became a prize commodity. When he realized she was worth something, he had stopped beating her. He resorted instead to drowning his frustrations in increasing quantities of liquor. This man took care of her, tolerated her, but had always made her feel that she was unlovable. His coldness was much worse than his bouts of anger and verbal abuse. If he had shown her even the slightest bit of love, she would have gladly followed him anywhere. To know that she was simply his meal ticket left her starving.

Sepia didn't care if Cole cared about her or not. He made her feel good and if she could experience that feeling again, she would. But her father must never find out. He was a fanatic about keeping men away from Sepia, not to protect her, but to preserve their flying act. He let nothing get in the way of Sepia and the trapeze.

"What colors do you like, Sepia?" Rosie asked, breaking the silence.

Bruno answered first. "She looks kinda pale," he said then he walked over to the rack of costumes and rummaged through them. "Put her in somethin' colorful," he stated, grabbing a bright red costume from the wardrobe. "Like this."

"Sorry, that's Anastasia Artel's. "Nobody can have a costume like hers," Rosie said.

"Yeah? Put Sepia in red, too," he insisted.

"I can't do that. Besides, it wouldn't be right for her," Rosie argued.

"I know what's right for her," Bruno announced firmly.

"Look, let me try some things on her, then you can decide," Rosie said. She walked over to the door and opened it. "Why don't you wait outside?"

Bruno frowned at Rosie, but nodded and left the wagon. Rosie closed the door and turned to Sepia.

"Is he always like that?!" she asked.

Sepia laughed. "Pretty much," she answered.

"I'll show you what I had in mind and you tell me if you like it, okay?" Rosie said.

"Okay," Sepia agreed, knowing she had found an ally and friend.

***

When the spotlight hit the arena opening that night, Sepia walked into the blinding light wearing a white leotard with silver belt and trim, perfectly setting off her olive skin and dark hair.

"Ladies and gentlemen, a new addition to the Olympic Show, in ring three, the spectacular aerial feats of the Flying Stefanis!" the announcer shouted.

Billy watched from the performer's entrance, chewing nervously on a piece of straw. Sepia had looked good in rehearsal, but you never knew how somebody would come off in performance, or if they would end up in the crowd's favor.

Sepia's new costume made her seem more grown up, more womanly. It wasn't just the make up and costume that had transformed her. She seemed more confident, more sure of herself in front of the audience. Funny how some people are, Billy thought. For most folks it would be the other way around, stage fright and all, but Sepia seemed to blossom under the tent lights. He watched Bruno boost her up into the safety net then they crossed to their respective ladders.

The band played a romantic waltz as the spotlight followed Sepia up to her trapeze. She quickly reached the platform, checked her rigging, and dusted her palms with resin while she waited for her father to climb into position. Her hair was pulled into a tight bun at the nape of her neck and the lights showed off her striking profile.

Sepia was feeling calm. Any nervousness she felt before had disappeared once she stepped onto the platform high above the crowd. Rehearsal had gone well that day and she was anxious to perform. Every big top was different and Sepia liked the way this one felt, warm but not stuffy, intimate yet airy.

Bruno was ready on the catch bar and gave Sepia the signal. Sepia took hold of the fly bar, lifted off and flew out into the air. She arched her body into a "bird's nest" with her legs curved behind her and her toes touching the bar, and then she released her grip and sailed into Bruno's grasp. The trapeze returned to them, Sepia grabbed it and flew back to her platform. She struck a pose and listened to the polite applause from the audience.

Billy noted the crowd's reaction and looked up at Sepia

hopefully. He felt someone at his side and was surprised to find Anastasia there. She rarely watched other performers.

Sepia swung out again and this time pirouetted into Bruno's hands. The applause grew louder and Sepia waved to the audience gratefully.

Billy's face brightened. "Thatta girl," he murmured under his breath.

On her next flight out, Sepia somersaulted once to her father's catch. This time when she returned to the platform, the crowd burst into applause accompanied by cheers. Some of the other performers joined Billy and Anastasia at the arena entrance. Cole was among them, awed at the impression Sepia was making. He, too, found it hard to believe that she was the same timid girl he had been with the day before. It made him even more determined to finish what he started with her.

Sepia was having fun. She was loosened up now and even began to play with the audience a little. She pretended that making it back to the platform was a little more precarious with each degree of difficulty she added to her tricks. In actual fact, everything she had done up until then had been a breeze. Her father was doing well, too. His timing was better and his grip was surer. Now she would really show the audience what she could do.

Once more Sepia swung out into the air. This time she soared high up into the Big Top. She let go of the trapeze and spun her body into a two-and-a-half backward somersault. She opened out at the last second and Bruno firmly caught her. The audience gasped in unison. As Sepia swung back up to her platform and sprang into a triumphant pose, the crowd broke into wild cheers.

Billy pulled the piece of straw from his mouth and

began pacing the arena opening. "Damn, listen to that!" he yelled happily over the cheers.

The other performers were still watching Sepia as she continued to bow to the roaring crowd. Only Anastasia walked away from the entrance. A performer blocked her way and she glared at him silently until he moved. She strode out of the tent determined that no one else see what was going on inside her, see the hate beginning to build. This girl who had played so innocent, so humble, had certainly pulled the wool over Billy's eyes! Anastasia despised underhandedness and it made her blood boil when hot shots like Sepia tried to push their way to the top. Not here, not in the Olympic, not if she had anything to say about it. Anastasia returned to her wagon to get ready for her act.

Back in the Big Top, Sepia and Bruno were ending their performance. Sepia gracefully dropped into the safety net, swung down and stood before the crowd. Bruno joined her, excited and smiling. They bowed, clasped hands and raised them triumphantly. Applause followed them to the performers entrance where Billy and the others gathered round to congratulate them.

"That was quite a performance!" Billy shouted over the applause and music.

"Thanks!" Sepia shouted back, smiling.

"I told you! She's the best! She belongs in center ring!" Bruno yelled to Billy.

"Did you mean what you said about the triple? You really think she can do it?" Billy asked.

"You give us center ring and we'll give you the triple!" Bruno answered.

Sepia stared out at the audience, her father's words

ringing in her ears. Even she half believed it tonight. Right now she felt like she could do anything and it was a powerful feeling.

Chapter Nine: Sepia Rising

The Executioner lay on a bed of straw as daylight filtered into the Menagerie tent. Louie stood over him, nudging him with the toe of his boot. The Executioner jolted awake and sprang up.

"Take it easy, fella. I need you in the Big Top," Louie said in his usual quick manner, but with a slight edge. The Executioner made him nervous.

The Executioner got up and stood quietly in the tent, trying to shake the sleep from his head. He had been dreaming about his youth, before the accident, before...

He vividly remembered how he looked as a boy, the light brown hair that curled at his nape, the deep blue eyes, the nose that had changed from it its youthful, flared shape to a more narrow, straight form. He had seen his reflection many times in the still water of his favorite fishing hole. First he would lie belly up on the grassy banks of the pond, half minding the tip of his fishing pole resting in the water, and half studying the shapes the clouds formed in the summer sky. After awhile he would roll onto his stomach and gaze at his reflection floating before him in the calm, dark water. He stared at himself not out of vanity, but out of curiosity about who he was, what he was destined for. He had great notions about his future. He wasn't sure exactly what he would do, but it would be of heroic proportions, of that he was certain.

Joining the circus was a common boyhood fantasy, but it was never his. He never imagined in his wildest dreams that he would end up working as a circus rigger, or even more unbelievable, as a clown. But then, he also never imagined that his face would be distorted and racked with numbing scars, never to feel the wind against his forehead or the sun on his cheeks.

It was at a circus performance that he'd met Angelina. A college buddy had dragged him along one night to see a woman he kept raving about, a woman on the flying trapeze. He had laughed at his friend for falling in love with a trapeze artist, but the moment she walked into center ring, he had stopped laughing. He was stunned by the most beautiful woman he had ever seen and was determined from that instant to meet her. Even before she ended her act and bowed before him, he was hopelessly in love. Had he known what that love would bring however; he would have wished he'd never set eyes on her.

The Executioner glanced around the Menagerie at the various groups of animals huddled together. It made sense that this was where he should feel most comfortable. The times he felt the most at ease were the times when he tried to be like them, with no thoughts and content with the bare necessities—food, bedding, shelter, and work. Whenever he began to think, he began to feel, and the feeling of pain and hurt was so overwhelming that it drove him mad. It was better just to exist, not like a human, but like an animal.

***

Anastasia entered the Big Top with a determined air, anxious to rehearse the new trick she had planned. She had put aside her irritation from the night before, refusing to let this young flyer upset her. After all, last night was just one night. It remained to be seen if Sepia could carry on through the rest of the season.

Anastasia walked toward center ring, going over in her mind the steps to mastering her new trick. She looked up toward the rings, imagining herself performing it, then stopped. Suspended on a "web" or rope above her was the Executioner. He had been with the Olympic a week, but Anastasia was seeing him for the first time. He looked like a grotesque monster clinging to the web. He avoided her stare as he looped another rope through a pulley and sent it downward. Louie stood on the ground below, caught the rope, and then attached it to a leather safety belt called a "mechanic", a device to prevent performers from falling during rehearsal. Anastasia walked over to Louie.

"Who's that?" she asked.

"He's your new rigger," Louie answered.

"Is this Billy's idea of a joke?" Anastasia demanded.

"No, ma'am. He's a damn good rigger." Louie replied.

"He makes me nervous," Anastasia said.

"You ain't the only one," Louie assured her.

"Where's Cole?" she asked.

"Last time I saw him, he was headed for the cookhouse," Louie said.

***

Sepia and Bruno were eating breakfast along with the other performers. After last night, Sepia no longer felt like an outsider. Even if Bruno still kept her from mingling, she was part of the Olympic family now.

Bruno was excited this morning, consumed by the prospect of their future. Last night's performance had only added fuel to his fire.

"We got center ring, kid. Center ring!" He said unbelievingly.

"I know, I know," Sepia responded with a smile, still finding it hard to believe herself.

"Now we get down to business. We're going to get that triple," Bruno stated.

"I don't know," Sepia answered. Her feeling of invincibility had waned since last night.

Bruno ignored her. "The first thing you gotta' do is get more height. We'll raise the starting bar, but you gotta' get off the board sooner. You'll be coming out of that triple so fast you won't have a second to think."

Sepia was distracted by each performer entering the cookhouse, but Cole was not among them. The thought of seeing Cole made her heart race and her stomach constrict at the same time. Sepia knew what might happen if she was alone with him again. She thought that was what she wanted, but now she wasn't so sure. It wasn't a sense of guilt or wrongdoing that stopped her. Her father hadn't instilled in her any strict morals. Instead, he had used scare tactics to make her afraid of men.

His method had worked during her impressionable years,

but the effect had faded. She had seen and heard enough to know that men were not the beasts Bruno made them out to be. Besides, his own abusive behavior made him lose all credibility. What was stopping her being with Cole was a growing doubt from within. Sepia wanted to feel good, but never felt she deserved to. After all, there was something inherently bad about her.

Her father knew she was bad. Since she was a child, he had brought waves of incrimination down upon her for the slightest infraction. He warned her repeatedly that she would end up like her mother, and the only context in which he spoke of Sepia's mother was to demonstrate how bad she was. Angelina had destroyed him, destroyed their marriage, their family. Bruno spoke of her with disgust. Sepia knew she looked like her mother and she knew her father hated her for that. It made him doubly determined that she not act like Angelina as well.

He had done his job well. He had convinced Sepia that she couldn't be trusted, that she lacked good judgment.

He is right, Sepia thought. She had gone so easily with Cole. She had used no judgment at all. If her father was wrong about men, he was right about her. Bruno did know what was best for her. Hadn't he gotten them into the Olympic like he said he would? So what if he only cared about the act? The act meant the most to her, too. As her doubts grew, so did her fear of crossing Bruno. Ironically, Sepia knew that the only way she could break free from her father was to stay with him until she was a success.

Sepia looked at Bruno. "So, what are we waiting for? Let's go get a triple," she said.

Bruno broke into an uncharacteristic smile. "Okay, let's go," he answered.

As Sepia and Bruno walked out of the cookhouse, they met Cole coming in.

"Sepia," Cole said, greeting her with a look that made her face flush instantly.

"Cole," she stammered. She hesitated as her heart thundered in her chest, then she lowered her eyes and continued on with her father.

"Sepia, wait." Cole took her arm.

"What is this?" Bruno growled. "Take your hand off her!" His command carried such authority that Cole withdrew his hand immediately, but he watched angrily as Bruno ushered Sepia away.

"Who was that?" Bruno demanded as they headed for the Big Top.

"Nobody," Sepia answered without a glance backward.

Cole watched them go, telling himself that it was fear of her father that prevented Sepia from talking to him, but he knew it wasn't true. Sepia was refusing him. With anyone else, he would have shrugged off a rejection without a second thought. But for some reason, Sepia shook his confidence and reminded him that his ability to woo women was all that he had. No, she wasn't any different, he told himself. If she didn't want him, he'd find someone soon enough who did. He started into the cookhouse when Louie called him toward the Big Top instead.

***

Cole stood in center ring keeping tension on the rope as Anastasia worked on the roman rings wearing the mechanic.

"Let's try it again," Anastasia called down to Cole. She

raised her body into a cross position, arms straight out at her sides, body vertical. She held for a moment then let herself drop so that she hung from the rings. From there she swooped her legs up, attempting a back somersault in the air by letting go of the rings, hoping to grab them again as she finished the turn. She missed, however, and Cole pulled on the rope, keeping her dangling in the air.

"You okay?" Cole yelled up to his mother.

Anastasia reached over and grabbed the rings. "Yeah, I'm okay! I just slipped."

"You're act is good. Why kill yourself?" Cole asked.

"The act is great! I'm getting bored with it that's all. Give me a little more slack this time," Anastasia ordered.

Anastasia gritted her teeth and tried the trick again. This time she missed badly, causing Cole to strain on the rope to keep her from falling.

"Bring me down!" Anastasia shouted.

Cole kept her dangling. "Let me have my own act," he called up to her.

"Get me down, now!" Anastasia roared.

When Cole lowered her to the ground, she ripped off the harness and tossed it to him.

"Don't ever pull a stunt like that again," she warned.

"I want to do more than this," Cole said, indicating the empty mechanic in his hands.

"You should be glad to help me. What's your problem? I don't give you everything you want?" she demanded.

"I want to fly," he said defiantly.

"And you will, just not yet," Anastasia replied, irritated. She grabbed her towel and threw it around her neck. "I'm through for today," she announced and walked out of the ring.

Cole watched his mother go. It was true that Anastasia gave Cole anything he wanted except for the thing he wanted the most. She had promised him that if he helped her, she would make sure he got his own act, but the years had gone by and he saw that her pledge was hollow and full of deception. She couldn't risk sharing the spotlight, even with her son. He knew he should leave her. He could join another circus, form his own act. It was a thought he'd had hundreds of times and yet the same fear always stopped him from making it happen. He was afraid to confront his mother with something that had remained unspoken between them for too long.

As Anastasia strode back to her wagon, she couldn't decide if she was more annoyed at Cole and his behavior or at herself for failing to do the new trick. What had gotten into Cole anyway, she wondered? He seemed so moody and restless the last few days then it dawned on her that she was anxious, too. She always felt a little jumpy when they played Chicago. She supposed it was natural to feel nervous about a place where they witnessed her husband's and his father's murder. She shouldn't have snapped at Cole back in the tent and she vowed to try and humor him when they were together again.

As Anastasia approached her wagon, Bruno caught up to her, then casually slowed down as he came alongside her.

"You saw my girl last night?" he asked.

"I saw her," Anastasia said.

"She's gonna' be a big star, huh?" Bruno said.

"Stardom has a high price. Are you willing to pay that price?" Anastasia asked coolly.

"I been payin' since she was a kid, workin' with her five and six hours a day. It's time I got some rewards," Bruno told her.

"I see," Anastasia said.

"She's gonna' do a triple," Bruno stated.

"What are you trying to do, break her neck?" Anastasia asked.

"No, I'm going to make her the greatest act in circus," Bruno boasted.

Anastasia reached her wagon and faced Bruno. "You push that girl into a triple and you'll be sorry. She can't do it, especially with you catching her. You're out of your league, buster, so back off!" Anastasia entered her wagon and slammed the door as Bruno yelled after her.

"Did you know Billy gave us center ring? We'll see who backs off!" Bruno challenged, and then he turned and headed back to the Big Top.

***

Billy was sitting at his desk sifting through a pile of bills when Anastasia burst into the wagon.

"What's this I hear about the Stefanis going into center ring?" she demanded.

"You heard right," Billy said calmly.

"Did you go soft in the head?" Anastasia asked incredulously.

"They deserve it. The crowd loved 'em." Billy answered.

"We have a good night with a lively crowd and you give them center ring? Who's next? Wanda and her bears?" Anastasia asked in a shrill voice.

"You saw them. The girl is terrific. She's going after the triple."

"She can't do a triple," Anastasia responded in a low dismissive tone.

"She can if that idiot could catch her," Billy argued.

Anastasia studied Billy's face, then a pain of recognition shot through her.

"You're sweet on this kid," she said.

"What?" Billy yelled.

"That young innocent routine got to you, didn't it?" Anastasia needled.

"You're crazy," Billy said. "I just see what she does up there. The crowd saw it, too. I don't know what you're so fired up about. You're still the top act, Queen of the Circus, remember?"

"You bet I am!" Anastasia stated.

"You're not scared of a little competition, are you?"

"You call that competition?" Anastasia sputtered. "I'll be around when that girl has come and gone! Go ahead, put them in center ring. We'll see how long they last!" Anastasia spun around and stalked out of the wagon, leaving Billy with half a smile on his face.

Billy usually enjoyed watching Anastasia get fired up, but what he had just seen in her stormy eyes wasn't amusing. For the first time since he'd known her, he saw fear there, and he didn't like it. He had always thought Anastasia was made of steel, impenetrable. What did she fear from the Stefani girl, he wondered?

Billy had noticed the tension exhibited that first morning when he introduced them. Anastasia had been leery even then. Could it be that she saw Sepia as a rival? Didn't she realize how far Sepia had to go to compete with her? Billy, of course, didn't see it as competition anyway. If Sepia became a hot act, he would simply have two great stars!

He also knew however, that for Anastasia, it was different. She had to be the biggest, the best. He didn't like to think what would happen to her if she lost her status as Queen of the Circus. Anastasia was bullheaded, self-centered, and generally a pain-in-the-ass, but no one had a greater passion and love for the circus than she did, except maybe himself.

He had always gotten along with her, too, being able to quell her temper and cajole her into staying whenever she threatened to leave. Anastasia had stayed, and over the years she and Billy had developed a genuine, mutual respect. It might have seemed natural that they become lovers, but she was too vain and he was too wary to let sex come between them. He did not want to lose her.

Anastasia had said something else that bothered Billy, even if he didn't want to admit it. He had gone soft over Sepia, but not in the way Anastasia meant, at least he didn't think so. He felt incredibly protective about the girl. She seemed like a frightened bird that was able to fly, but not able to feel safe on the ground. He couldn't deny that she touched him, but he reminded himself that circus was his true love. And yet, he found himself thinking of Sepia, worrying about her, caring about her. Hell, maybe he was a little in love with her.

***

Sepia threw herself into her work, rehearsing for the triple during the day and performing in the afternoon and night. She continued to remain in the crowd's favor, receiving the same wild cheers of approval. Anastasia received her usual accolades as well. After accomplishing her new trick in rehearsal, she added it to her performance with great success.

To Sepia's dismay, however, her attempts to get close to Anastasia had failed. Whenever she approached her, she was met with coolness, and she began to think her efforts were in vain. Sepia mistook competitiveness for dislike because she couldn't imagine herself being competition for Anastasia.

The other performers saw it though. They began noticing Anastasia's growing attempts to impress the audience, often in response to the Stefani's act that preceded her. Cole saw it, too. If Sepia tried a new trick or added a particular flair to her act, Anastasia would add something to her performance as well. She had increased the number of her one arm swingovers every night and had now reached one hundred and seventy-five.

Anastasia's effort was taking its toll, however. During her last performance, as she twisted and turned through her swingovers, the leather strap cut into her wrist, causing blood to seep through. For the first time in her life, Anastasia had to force a smile to cover her pain. She finished her incredible one hundred and seventy-five turns, but as she was lowered to the ground, she strained to keep her composure. She bowed to the cheering crowd while hiding her wrist beneath her cape, and when she returned to her wagon, Anastasia pulled off the drape and saw her wrist, torn and bleeding.

The next morning, Anastasia walked into the Menagerie tent, sought out the Executioner's corner and startled him awake.

"I need your help," Anastasia said, avoiding his eyes.

The Executioner pulled into the shadows as Anastasia stepped closer and held out the looped strap she used in her act.

"Can you fix this?" she asked. "It keeps digging into my wrist. Can you make something better?"

The Executioner reached toward the strap, but took hold of her wrist instead. Anastasia flinched as he turned it over and saw the marks where the strap had cut in. She pulled her hand away.

"Can you do it?" she asked.

The Executioner nodded.

"By tonight?" Anastasia asked and again the Executioner nodded. "Good. I'll come back for it later." She backed away, turned and left the tent.

The Executioner remained in his dark corner turning Anastasia's wrist strap over in his hand. He could pad the strap so that it didn't cut her wrist, but he doubted that it would solve her problem. He, too, had been watching Anastasia's increasing attempts to outdo the Stefani act. He saw how good Sepia was and understood Anastasia's dilemma. He felt sorry for her. He knew what it was like to be pushed aside by a beautiful young woman.

After leaving the Executioner, Anastasia fairly burst out of the Menagerie tent. She was used to seeing disfigurement, but the Executioner totally unnerved her. He evoked images of her past, of ugly things she had tried to forget. Anastasia was not one to dwell on the past. It was quickly forgotten along with any pain or guilt that went with it. Some would envy the ease with which she forgot. Most would be shocked by it. For Anastasia, it was a matter of survival. She always looked toward the future. She did not like being around someone like the Executioner who was clearly plagued by the past.

As Anastasia headed for the cookhouse, she noticed Charlene and Cole outside her wagon. Charlene was sitting on his lap with her arm around his shoulder and whispering in his ear.

Cole knew he shouldn't be flirting so openly with Charlene, but he had been more reckless in many ways lately. Billy had caught him drunk before the show last night and would have fired him if it weren't for Anastasia. Something was eating at him and he didn't want to admit what it was. He glanced across the grounds and saw Sepia rehearsing with her father on the trampoline. He turned back to Charlene and planted a kiss on her neck.

"Slow down, honey. We need more privacy," Charlene giggled.

"Cole!" Anastasia shouted across the grounds.

Charlene and Cole both jumped, but she took her time sliding off Cole's lap.

"Gotta' go, sweetie," she said to Cole. "See ya' around."

Cole nodded at her then frowned as his mother approached. Anastasia passed Charlene on the way.

"Stay away from him," Anastasia said.

"It was harmless fun," Charlene said.

"Isn't he a little young for you? First my husband, now my kid," Anastasia sneered.

"I loved Harry," Charlene answered. "You didn't care nothin' about him."

"Harry was a loser," Anastasia said.

"Ain't you got any feelings at all?" Charlene asked.

"I got you this job, didn't I?" Anastasia retorted.

"Yeah, so you could treat me like dirt ever since," Charlene replied bitterly.

Anastasia smiled. "Ah, but you take it so well," she replied then walked off, leaving Charlene in awe of the cruelty she knew, but which never ceased to amaze her.

Chapter Ten: Pushing To The Limit

Sepia believed that if she threw herself into rehearsing and performing, there wouldn't be time to think about anything else, more precisely, Cole. Bruno obliged, working her nonstop. He was a man possessed, and never tired of drilling Sepia on exercises that would help her achieve the triple somersault. Sometimes they exercised on the trampoline, where over and over Sepia bounced and flipped her body into backward somersaults while Bruno stood by, gesturing and shouting at her. Other times, they worked on the ground, Bruno standing with knees bent, hands cupped, then as Sepia stepped into his palms, he lifted her up and threw her over backward into a somersault. During their breaks, Bruno lectured her endlessly. Sepia listened patiently, but most of what Bruno told her she already knew, so his lectures became endless repetitions of the same idea. During those times, her mind wandered and her thoughts always ended at the same place.

Sepia's efforts to forget Cole had failed. She wasn't entirely sure whether it was really Cole or just the experience she had with him that made such an impression, but she found herself thinking about him constantly, recalling the way he kissed her and held her pressed against his body. She tried to remind herself how she felt afterward, how Cole had acted, but her desire overrode her more sensible thoughts and she could not keep him out of her mind. She hid her thoughts from Bruno as he droned on endlessly. Just now she'd seen Cole with Charlene and it had made her burn with jealousy. Why couldn't she get him out of her mind?

After every warm-up exercise, Sepia and Bruno climbed to the trapeze and attempted the triple. Time and again, Sepia sailed through the air, tucked her body and spun three times only to miss Bruno's catch and go plunging into the safety net. The net saved her life, but in truth, it was far from safe. Consecutive landings burned Sepia's skin raw and jolted her body. A bad fall and she could break her neck. It was reckless to keep practicing when she was exhausted, but Bruno continued to push her.

One afternoon, during a particularly grueling workout, Billy walked into the Big Top and stood at the performer's entrance watching. He saw Sepia return to the platform with sweat pouring down her face and panting to catch her breath. Bruno was sitting on the catch bar shouting at her.

"You're too late off the board! And get those knees up! Get 'em up or I'll tie 'em up! Now give me a triple!" he ordered.

"I don't think so, Papa," Sepia called back, still short of breath.

"Let her take a breather," Billy yelled up to Bruno.

"What's the matter? You want the triple or not?" Bruno shot back to Sepia, ignoring Billy. He lowered himself into position and began swinging.

Sepia steeled herself to try again, then grabbed the bar and flew out. After a trial swing, she sailed out, let go of the trapeze and spun her body into the triple. Again she missed Bruno's grasp and fell to the net. She swung down to the ground and Bruno dropped into the net after her. He swooped down and grabbed her arm that was already sore from a bad rope burn.

"What's the matter with you? You don't do nothin' like I told you!" Bruno shouted at Sepia.

"I tried. Our timing was off, Papa," Sepia answered, wincing in pain.

"Whose fault is that? Mine?" he demanded.

"No," Sepia replied.

"Go on!" Bruno yelled as he smacked the back of her head. "I don't waste my time on you no more!"

Sepia ran to the performer's opening with tears stinging her eyes. She sideswiped Billy on her way out of the tent.

"Whoa," Billy said.

Sepia wiped a tear from her cheek. "Sorry," she blurted as she continued walking.

"Sepia," Billy called after her. She stopped, but didn't turn around. Billy was trying to restrain himself. If he had followed his gut, he would have walked out into the arena and thrown Bruno from the ring for what he just did, but it was an unwritten rule of circus not to butt into family business. "He's pushin' you too hard," was all he said.

"I'm used to it," Sepia answered over her shoulder.

"Have you ever worked with a really good catcher?" Billy asked.

Sepia turned around and faced Billy. "My father is good enough. My timing is off, that's all," she said.

"Your timing is perfect," Billy argued. "It's him that's..."

"We're a family act," Sepia interrupted.

"Okay, okay, it's your business," Billy said. "I just think

you deserve the best."

Sepia managed a smile. "I'm in the best circus, aren't I?"

"You win," Billy said with a frown.

Louie approached Billy with a clipboard in hand. "I need you to sign these purchase orders, boss."

Sepia grabbed the opportunity and slipped away. Billy noticed her leave and shook his head, then began looking over the papers.

When Sepia left the Big Top, she didn't go back to her wagon. She strode away from the circus grounds, picked up speed then broke into a run, stopping only when she reached the railroad tracks. She leaned back against the boxcar of a freight train and stared up at the empty sky as tears streamed down her face.

She had thought she was immune from her father's attacks, but she apparently wasn't. More than being hurt, Sepia was angry that she allowed herself to be treated so badly. Never able to do anything about it, however, her anger inevitably turned to self-pity. She was emotionally and physically exhausted and she just wanted to be taken away. She closed her eyes, wishing she could crawl into the boxcar behind her and ride it to the ends of the earth.

"Sepia," a voice said next to her. She turned and saw Cole standing there. "What's the matter?" he asked her.

"I'm just tired," she answered, but her tearstained cheeks told another story. Cole knew it was wrong what he was about to do, but he let his pent up resentment take over.

"It's okay," Cole said, pulling her to him. He stroked her back. "I can make it better," he lied.

Sepia sensed immediately how Cole meant to console her and she didn't resist. She didn't pretend Cole cared this time as he picked her up and held her like a package waiting to be opened. When his mouth covered hers, she closed her eyes and drifted away, wanting to feel wanted.

Cole glanced behind them at the open boxcar then he lifted Sepia up and set her inside. Hopping up next to her, he picked her up again and carried her into the shadows of the enclosed car. Unlike the time in the Menagerie, he refused to look in her eyes now. He was already aroused and totally indifferent toward her feelings. Cole lay Sepia down on the hard floor and straddled her. Instead of moving slowly as he had the first time, he kissed her hard. She responded eagerly at first, then turned her head away as he fondled her roughly. He felt her body go limp beneath him and he stole a glance at her face. There was such an utterly vacant stare in her eyes...that it made him...stop.

His hand slowly reached out, cupped her chin and gently turned her face toward him. As her eyes focused on his, a tear rolled down her cheek. He caught it in his palm and closed his fingers around it like a precious jewel. His thumb softly traced the line of her eyebrow and the delicate curve of her cheek. He stayed locked in her gaze, unmoving then he slowly climbed off of her. She reached up; however, and gently pulled him back. She took his face in her hands and drew him close. Their lips met softly, but almost instantly gave way to an urgent kiss. A desire that neither of them understood filled them, overwhelmed them and carried them to a place where nothing else existed except their two bodies.

Sepia slipped her leotard off her shoulders and down over her hips until she lay naked beneath Cole. He peeled off his tee shirt and shed his trousers until they were bare skin to bare skin. Sepia opened her legs and Cole guided himself inside her. He thrust himself deep and immediately felt the barrier then the soft rupture as it gave. Sepia flinched under him and cried out, but she pulled him in again. They found a rhythm full of urgency until she became lost in waves of sensation. Cole exploded with relief and collapsed on Sepia, his chin resting on her shoulder as their chests rose and fell in unison.

Sepia was terrified to look at Cole. She still didn't know him at all and yet she wanted to cling to him forever. She realized, too, that just having him physically wasn't enough. At that moment, however, he rolled off her, slowly got up and pulled on his trousers.

"That was great," he said coolly, covering his own terror of wanting more from Sepia than her body.

Sepia only saw his apparent nonchalance. She was devastated, but swore to herself not to show it. Instead, she gave him a look he didn't care for, a look matched by her mocking smile.

"Bastard," she said quietly, losing her smile. "My father was right."

"And you, doll, turn from one hot bitch to one cold one real fast," Cole said cruelly, his face burning.

There was no mistake about the look Sepia gave him then. She was still lying naked, but made no move to cover herself. Nothing mattered to her anymore, least of all her modesty. "Go away," she said tiredly.

"Sure," Cole said. "And don't worry. I won't bother you again." He stood at the opening to the boxcar, but Sepia saw only his silhouette in the light, then he jumped down and was gone.

She slowly got up and mechanically pulled her leotard back on. She was sore, but no more so because of Cole than her strenuous workout. She ached all over and was tempted just to curl up there in the train car and fall asleep, again hoping to be transported away. She had stupidly thought Cole would do that, but she was wrong. She felt more trapped than ever.

As Sepia numbly walked back towards her wagon, Rosie stepped out of her own. She took one look at Sepia and immediately called out to her.

"Sepia? Could you, uh, give me a hand with something?" Rosie asked.

Sepia looked at Rosie with complete resignation. "Sure," she answered and walked over to Rosie's wagon.

When she got Sepia inside, Rosie glanced around quickly and walked over to a bureau.

"I've been wanting to clean behind here for weeks. Could you help me push this away from the wall?"

Sepia stepped over to one side of the bureau and Rosie to the other then they slid it back from the wall.

"There, thanks. You want a cup of tea? I just put some water on," Rosie lied.

"I need to go," Sepia answered dully.

"Why don't you sit on the sofa and put your feet up. I'll make you some tea. You look a little tired," Rosie said matter-of-factly, but in truth thought the girl looked like she'd been through the ringer. She went into her makeshift kitchen concealed by a curtain and started a kettle boiling on a small propane burner.

Sepia sat down on the sofa, then after a moment, pulled off her slippers and did as Rosie suggested. When Rosie returned, Sepia had sunk into the corner of the sofa, her head leaning against the back, her eyes closed.

Rosie stared at her for a moment. She's the spitting image of her mother, Rosie mused. Rosie had known Angelina well. They had been friends working in the same circus back then.

At nineteen, Angelina had already made a name for herself as a daring flyer. She performed with her parents and brother, a family fiercely protective of their beautiful and spirited daughter. They never knew that she had already had many lovers. She had also broken many a heart until a quiet, persistent young man finally won hers. Rosie could remember to this day Angelina's excitement as she described how they met. He wasn't circus. He was totally different than any man she had ever known. He had come backstage and stood quietly waiting behind her usual gathering of admirers, but when he caught her eye, it was as if no one else in the room existed. She broke from the crowd and walked over to him. He took her hand and led her out of the tent without a word. Under the stars, he finally spoke, looking directly in her eyes.

"Maybe you think I'm crazy or maybe a thousand men have said this to you, but I can't imagine my life beyond this point without you."

Angelina laughed. "What is your name?" she asked.

"Patrick. Patrick Dannon."

"I don't think you are crazy and no man has ever said what you said or looked at me the way you do, Patrick Dannon."

"Can I take you somewhere, for dinner, or wherever you want?" Patrick offered.

"Dinner would be nice," Angelina said, laughing again at his eagerness. She liked him instantly.

And so it began. Patrick would come for her after the show, then during the day they would steal away and go for long drives in his car. They knew their time was short, but they made the most of it, trying to forget that her circus would pull up stakes in two days. They talked endlessly and easily about everything. She learned about his provincial, middle class upbringing in St. Louis. He learned about her exotic life in the circus.

Their second night together, they were driving in the country and stopped to take a walk on a tree lined dirt road. Moonlight filtered through the leaves, dappling the road with patches of light. A horse whinnied nearby and Angelina walked over to a fenced pasture to meet the animal seeking company in the darkness. As she stroked the horse's muzzle, Patrick came up behind her. Her hands left the horse and reached behind her, pulling him nearer. The horse made a small snort at being forgotten then trotted off in the moonlight.

Patrick wrapped his arms around her and she moaned softly as she leaned her head back against his chest. His lips caressed the tender skin behind her right ear then moved down her neck and along her shoulder. His fingers glided down the silky folds of her dress, then drew the material up until he felt the smoothness of her thighs and the round softness above. She slowly turned around and his hands slid to her back. They locked in a deep kiss that never broke even as she unzipped his pants, was lifted up against the fence, and joined with him forever.

By her last night in town, there was no question that Angelina's future was linked to Patrick's. They planned to reunite at the next stop on her tour. Each told their family of their decision and as expected, both sets of parents were dead set against the union.

Patrick's parents were shocked to find out that he actually intended to marry this circus girl he told them about. They were an upstanding family from St. Louis and they weren't about to let some woman dupe their son into a marriage that would never last.

Angelina's parents were equally distraught. They had wanted to match their daughter with another circus family and carry on a new generation of trapeze artists. They forbad Angelina from seeing Patrick. The couple made secret plans to elope. He telegraphed her to meet him at the railway station, but his train never arrived. The drunken engineer chose that night to plow his cars into an opposing train. Patrick barely survived the crash. His parents refused to let Angelina see him, blaming her for the tragedy. They tried to convince Angelina that Patrick had changed his mind and wanted nothing to do with her. She didn't believe it.

Angelina waited and waited but when Patrick never came for her, she broke down completely, not only from losing him, but because she discovered that she was carrying his child. The circus moved on and she went with it. Her spirit crushed, Angelina was quietly married off to a catcher, Bruno Stefani, who performed in another show. She started flying again, but never with the same passion. Years later, Rosie received news that Angelina was dead.

When Rosie first saw Sepia, it was like seeing the young Angelina again, and when she heard Sepia's last name, she realized immediately who she was. Rosie wondered how much the girl knew of her past.

The whistle on the kettle blew, interrupting Rosie's thoughts and causing Sepia's eyes to fly open.

"It'll just be a minute," Rosie said, going back into the kitchen.

When she walked out the second time, Sepia was staring straight ahead with tears in her eyes. Rosie set the tea tray down and sat on the sofa next to her.

"Sepia, what is it?"

She leaned over and pulled Sepia into her cavernous arms. "It's all right, honey. You go right ahead," she whispered, gently rocking Sepia as she began to weep.

Normally, Sepia would have damned her feelings and pushed them away. Somehow, in the safety of Rosie's arms, she opened herself to the flood of pain inside. She felt hurt, ashamed, angry, and humiliated over what had happened with Cole. She told herself it didn't matter, but it did. Again, her need for love and closeness had been betrayed by lust for this same man. Cole cared as little for her as she did for him. They had simply used each other.

Sepia saw herself as the woman her father had always described her mother to be, a destructive, self-pitying fool. Bruno had not succeeded in saving Sepia from her fate.

Rosie could only guess what was troubling the girl, but she had heard enough exchanges between Sepia and her father to know where part of her troubles lay. Rosie had heard Bruno accuse Sepia of being like her mother. Rosie saw immediately what Bruno never understood, that Sepia was nothing like her mother and never would be. Where Angelina had been high strung and impulsive, Sepia was calm and patient. Angelina had craved interaction, Sepia liked to observe. Each, however, had a strong spirit that Bruno had successfully broken. The only thing Sepia had left was her desire for accomplishment.

"Try to remember why you love to fly," Rosie said quietly when Sepia's tears had lessened.

She's right, Sepia thought. Flying is all I have to live for. When I fly, I am free. It is my salvation, my escape. Flying will make me famous, and becoming famous will change my life.

Sepia closed her eyes and dreamed of her future. Her body grew heavy and Rosie felt the slowed breath of sleep on her arm. She gently set Sepia back on the sofa and covered her with a shawl.

When Sepia woke hours later, she had no sense of how long she'd been in Rosie's wagon. Rosie was not there. She quietly got up and left.

She could tell by the long shadows that it was nearly dusk. The day already seemed a week in length and she still had to perform that evening. She felt rested though. The deepness of her sleep had restored at least her body. Her mind was a different matter. She'd allowed her feelings to surface where they remained raw and vulnerable.

Sepia remembered what had started it all, her father's anger that morning. Bruno had not struck her in a long time, the mental abuse having been enough to give him the control and satisfaction he needed. Sepia had learned to push away the emotional abuse Bruno showered on her. She had learned to shut down, to force her thoughts else-where. Try as she might though, she couldn't do it now. It was all she could do to make it back to her wagon and get ready for the show.

Chapter Eleven: The Triple

Inside the Menagerie, the Executioner anxiously paced the tent, mimicking the wild cats in their cages. His head was throbbing with pain. Ever since that first morning in the Big Top, he had avoided Sepia. A circus is a hard place to avoid someone completely though. Each time the Executioner came in contact with Sepia, the torture and anger he felt increased. He had been in the Big Top this morning when the Stefanis were practicing. As Bruno shouted at Sepia, as he swung and hit her, the Executioner had stood in the shadows watching. When the father struck her, something inside the Executioner snapped. No matter how hard he tried to stop the memory, it kept coming.

After the accident, his parents told him that Angelina abandoned him when she heard about his injury. He was too weak and in pain to protest. Months later, after a slow recovery and no word from Angelina, depression set in. He tried to convince himself that even if Angelina had come to him, he would have sent her away. He did not want her to love him out of pity. Still, she never came. The wounds on his face eventually healed, but the wound in his heart never did.

Every day since, he had been tortured by her memory. This girl, this Sepia, reminded him so much of Angelina, the same eyes, the same mouth. He hated her.

***

Sepia and Bruno performed their usual act that evening, but it was somehow different. Billy sensed it. Even Sepia's smile was forced. The audience didn't seem to notice, however, and when the Stefanis ended their act, they were greeted with loud cheers and applause. They bowed to the crowd and ran out of the arena. Sepia made it to the arena opening, then abruptly collapsed in pain. Billy helped her to a seat and Bruno began massaging her calf.

"She's fine. It's just a cramp," Bruno said.

Billy studied Sepia's face. "You okay, kid?" he asked.

Sepia grit her teeth and fought back the tears. "Yes," she answered quickly as Bruno continued massaging her leg.

"She was great tonight, uh? They were crazy for her!" Bruno crowed. He stood up. "There. Good as new! Get up, Sepia."

Sepia slowly stood up as Louie ran into the tent. "There's some reporters out back that want to talk to Sepia."

Bruno broke into a huge smile. "You see?" he said. He put his arm around Sepia's waist and ushered her outside where a group of reporters immediately surrounded her. Word of mouth had spread about the new young star. Even under stress, Sepia had proven herself to them tonight.

"How long have you been flying, Miss Stefani?" the first reporter asked.

"Since I was nine," she answered.

"Not many women have done the two and a half. Did it take you long?" another reporter asked.

"Not really. I..."

Bruno broke in. "She got it like that!" Bruno said, snapping his fingers. "She's a natural!"

Anastasia walked toward the group unnoticed and stopped short when she saw Sepia with the reporters.

Bruno continued. "That's nothin', boys. My girl will make history!"

"A triple?" the first reporter guessed.

"The first woman in the world!" Bruno shouted. Bruno caught sight of Anastasia and grinned. Anastasia whirled around and stormed away. A photographer, on his way over to the others bumped into her.

"Sorry, lady. I'm in a hurry," he said. He rushed on, leaving Anastasia stunned. She pulled herself together and strode back to her wagon.

Sepia and Bruno continued answering the reporters' questions. "So tell us a little bit about yourself, Sepia," one of them urged.

Bruno took over the interview, but Sepia didn't mind. She was overwhelmed by the attention and was content to bask in the light of the flashbulbs as photographers snapped her picture. She tried to forget everything else, everything that had happened before. The only thing important now was the future, her future. The photographers captured the excitement in her flushed cheeks and the smile spreading on her lips.

***

Anastasia charged inside her wagon and banged the door shut. She planted herself at the dressing table, picked up her brush and started to run it through her hair, then turned and hurled it like a missile across the room.

"Ow!" a voice called. Cole popped up from the shadows of the chaise lounge cupping the hairbrush in his belly.

"What are you doing here?!" Anastasia asked without apologizing.

"Waiting for your act, what else?" Cole answered.

"Get out," Anastasia said.

"What's eating you?" Cole asked.

"I said get out," Anastasia demanded.

"Okay, okay. I'm goin'," Cole said, however, during the moment it took him to reach the door, Anastasia had begun talking.

"The Stefani girl is going for a triple," Anastasia said.

Cole paused. "So?"

"She's trying to take my place," Anastasia told him.

"Never happen," Cole replied, still facing the door.

"What makes you so sure?" Anastasia asked.

"She doesn't have what it takes," Cole said, turning to look at his mother. "She's a good flyer, but the crowd will never love her the way they love you."

"They might if she does a triple," Anastasia remarked. "I can't let that happen," she added slowly as she looked at Cole.

"What are you saying?" he asked with a nervous laugh.

"I'm saying I want you to stop her," she said.

"Jesus, Mother," he said, turning to go, sure that she was joking.

"You owe me, kid," Anastasia said. "If it wasn't for me, you could have ended up in juvenile hall or worse," she added.

Cole turned and stared at his mother, incredulous. "It was an accident," he replied quietly.

"I knew that, but the cops didn't," Anastasia continued.

"Did you want to risk going to court to prove it?" she asked.

"I thought he was going to kill you," Cole said, instantly replaying the scene in his mind.

"He might have," she said, implying the opposite was also true then she changed her tactic. "Look, I know you didn't mean to do it. You were trying to protect me. We protected each other. That's all I'm asking you to do now."

"Just what exactly are you asking me to do?" Cole asked his mother.

"Stop Sepia from performing a triple. Do it any way you want," Anastasia said coldly.

"This is crazy," Cole said. He turned again and grabbed the door handle.

"Stop Sepia and you can have your own act," Anastasia offered.

Cole halted and stared at the floor as her words sank in. She must be very desperate, he thought. He had never known his mother to be scared, not even that night when his father attacked her.

It had happened here in Chicago six years ago. Cole was fifteen. They had just finished a vaudeville performance and were leaving the theater. As they carried their bags and rigging out the stage door and into the alley, Anastasia informed Cole's father, Harry, that she wanted to be on her own. She told him about the contract she'd made with a circus. Harry was furious, accusing her of using him and casting him aside. He called her heartless and cruel. Anastasia responded by asking Harry for half of their earnings, but he refused to give it to her. Instead, he picked up his suitcase and headed down the alley.

As Cole stood by and watched, Anastasia picked up their trapeze bar and hit Harry across the back of his head. When he fell to the ground stunned, she knelt down and rifled through his pockets until she found her money. As she stood up however, Harry reached out an arm and grabbed her ankle. This time, Anastasia fell. Harry crawled on top of her, grabbed her arm and twisted it behind her back. As he pushed her face into the pavement, Harry demanded that she give back the money or he would break her arm. When Anastasia refused, Harry twisted her arm farther back. She cried out and Cole finally moved from the spot he'd been frozen to, grabbed up the trapeze bar, and as Anastasia had done, he swung it at his father. The bar struck Harry across his temple. Harry slumped to the ground and lay still. He never moved again. Later, when the police arrived, Cole was unable to speak. Anastasia said they had all been attacked by a robber who stole their money. Harry was buried, and she and Cole moved on.

Cole remained in shock for some time after. Anastasia, on the other hand, acted as if nothing had happened. In fact, she had never mentioned that night again, until now. But for Cole, the events of that evening had continually haunted him. The guilt and remorse were overwhelming. He had loved his father. He knew that the things Harry accused Anastasia of were true, but he also adored his mother. She treated him totally different than she did Harry and there was no question that Cole would have gone with her when she left Harry. Lying to the police had sealed a bond between them that could not be broken. It was the reason Cole had continued to stay with his mother and let her dominate him. It was the reason he never took responsibility for his actions. It was easier to do his mother's bidding than to assert himself. Cole loved flying and desperately wanted to be part of an act, but even that he gave up for his mother. Anastasia's offer to give him his own act was not as generous as it seemed. It was bait to get Cole to do what she wanted, knowing full well that she might not have to give the reward.

Cole didn't respond to his mother's offer. He simply opened the door and walked out.

***

Sepia lay awake most of the night despite being totally exhausted. The reporters had changed something for her and her mind would not stop imagining what it meant. The interview had been like a magic tonic. They had wanted to know about her, her! Her scalp prickled at the thought of it. In asking Sepia over and over about the triple, the reporters had made it real. They wanted it. She would give it to them.

***

Billy was in his office drinking his morning coffee when Louie burst in.

"She got it, boss! She got the triple!" he shouted.

Billy smiled, picked up his hat from the desk and followed Louie out of the wagon.

When Billy entered the arena there was already a crowd of performers gazing up in the air. Billy looked up and saw Sepia on the platform, breathing deeply, but with a huge grin on her face. He smiled up at her and cocked an eyebrow.

Sepia stepped up onto the starting bar. She could do it again. She knew it. She took hold of the trapeze and lifted off. Sailing out and back, then out again, Sepia pumped herself high into the peak of the Big Top. She let go, and Billy watched her body spin like a flipped coin three times in the air. She opened out as Bruno swung up and grabbed her wrists.

Billy's mouth fell open and he whispered to himself, "Well, I'll be damned!"

Sepia returned to her trapeze and back up to the platform midst the hoots and hollers of her fellow performers.

Standing in the middle of the group, stark still and the only person not cheering was Cole. Sepia had done it. The next step was to perform the triple before an audience and her father was now yelling his intention to do just that.

"Didn't I tell you she would do it, Billy?!" Bruno shouted downward.

"Yes, you did!" Billy yelled back, grinning broadly. "Yes, you did!"

"Tonight, we do it for the crowd!" Bruno announced.

"Tonight? Whoa! Slow down, Bruno. Wait 'til she's ready," Billy said still smiling, sure that Bruno was kidding.

"We only have two more days in Chicago, right? I want to show them a triple where it counts!" Bruno said, dead serious.

Billy stared up at Sepia, looking as if she could fly without the trapeze. "What do you say, Sepia?" Billy called to her.

"If my father is ready, then I am ready," she called back, her voice trembling with excitement.

"You win!" Billy yelled to them both. "Tonight Chicago sees the first woman in the world complete a triple back somersault!"

Another "hurrah" rose up from the crowd of onlookers, but this time Cole was no longer among them.

Cole saw Anastasia at the edge of the crowd. Nothing needed to be said. He looked at her a moment, then walked out of the tent. He knew what had to be done. The only problem was that he'd stayed awake all night trying to convince himself to do it.

No matter how hard Cole tried to think of Sepia as the same as other women, the moment he saw her, everything had been different. He had let his feelings get involved. He had let himself get angry, frustrated, even humiliated. Why then, did he care what she thought of him? Why did he still want to see her when it was clear she did not want to see him? Why, even now, was he tortured by the memory of her body, her taste, and her smell? She was causing him to lose the only control he had on his life.

Cole knew his mother well, but even he couldn't believe what she had asked him to do. "Stop her from performing the triple," she said, but what did she mean? Keeping Sepia from performing the triple one night wouldn't stop her from doing it the next. Anastasia meant for him to destroy Sepia. Cole realized now how scared Anastasia was. He knew how much of a threat Sepia was to her. What he didn't understand was his mother's intent behind the offer to give him his own act. It was so clearly an attempt at blackmail, and yet, she was also making a sacrifice. The fact that she was asking him to solve her dilemma either showed how much she thought of him or how little. He truly did not know. He was already losing control of his feelings. Now his mother was making him lose his mind.

***

Anastasia was troubled by what she had seen in Cole's face.

He was having a problem with what she'd asked him

to do. She figured it was a matter of conscience. She had no idea of Cole's conflicted feelings over Sepia. She knew nothing about them being together. All she knew was that she could not count on him to help her.

Anastasia entered the Menagerie tent and found the Executioner grooming a horse. The Executioner glanced at Anastasia, but kept working.

"You did a good job on my wrist strap," she said.

The Executioner nodded at her.

"I want you to do something else for me," Anastasia stated.

When the Executioner didn't respond, she went on. "The Stefani girl is going to try her triple tonight. She is out to ruin me. She threatened to take my place, but it's not just me she is after. I heard her talking. She doesn't like you. She wants to have you sent away."

The Executioner stopped brushing the horse and looked at Anastasia.

"She has to be stopped," Anastasia continued. I don't care how you do it, but I want her stopped for both of us. If you do this, I'll make sure you have a home here forever."

The Executioner looked into Anastasia's eyes and she knew not to waver, to hold his gaze and make him trust her. The Executioner slowly nodded his head. Anastasia smiled at him. Now that he had joined her, she was no longer repulsed by him.

He would be the one to do her bidding.

When Anastasia returned to her wagon, Cole was waiting there. The troubled look had not left his face.

"I know what you're going to say. Don't worry, I found somebody else to help me," Anastasia told him.

"Who?" Cole asked astonished.

"It's rather amusing, really. He's the rigger, otherwise known as the 'Executioner' from the clown act," Anastasia said with a smirk.

"What's he going to do?" Cole asked.

"I left that up to him. My guess is that something might happen to Sepia's rigging, a tragic accident," Anastasia said, emotionless.

"You're out of your mind," Cole told her.

"Don't get any ideas, Cole. Just stay out of the way," Anastasia warned him, then she softened her expression. "Look, I've been thinking. The offer to have your own act still goes. When we leave here, we'll start planning it, okay?"

"This is sick," Cole answered before he turned and left.

Chapter Twelve: The Big Night

For the first time in a long while, Sepia was nervous before her performance. Never had so much excitement surrounded her. She tried to tell herself it didn't matter if she did the triple tonight. She would do it some night. She had broken the barrier and that's what mattered. It was no longer a question of "if" she could perform the triple in front of an audience, but "when." And yet, she wanted it tonight. She had experienced a taste of what it could bring her, and she wanted more.

Sepia left her wagon and walked around the circus grounds, hoping it would take her mind off her act. When she passed the Menagerie tent, she stopped and went inside. A line of horses was tethered nearby and she rubbed the velvety muzzle of one of the black parade ponies.

"Sooo, boy. That's a boy," she murmured in a low voice as the horse's ears flicked back and forth to the soothing tone. Next to the blacks was Princess, a pure white Arabian mare that performed tricks with her rider, Sheik Amali. Sepia scratched the short rough hair on Princess's forehead, then laid her head against the horse's smooth neck. Princess stood still as Sepia calmed herself with the warmth from her body. "Think I'll make it tonight, girl?" Sepia asked.

Princess whickered softly in response then raised her head up suddenly. Someone moved in the shadows across the tent and Sepia saw the Executioner step out into the dim light of the overhead lantern.

Other than that first morning in the Big Top when she had been alone with him, Sepia had seen little of the Executioner except for the moment he discovered her with Cole in the Menagerie. Sepia sensed that the Executioner disliked her. She just didn't know why.

The Executioner started to walk toward Sepia, but this time she faced him unafraid. He looked in her eyes, slowed his pace then stopped. His expression suddenly changed. His eyebrows were knit, not with contempt she realized, but with anguish. For the first time, Sepia noticed that he looked at her as if he knew her, then it dawned on her that he was not really looking at her at all. He was looking at a memory. She reminded him of someone. Sepia also realized that whoever the woman was, she was someone he had cared about deeply. He had loved her even though it caused him great pain. She smiled at the Executioner and saw his expression change again. The hatred flooded his eyes once more and Sepia became truly scared. At that moment, however, someone else entered the tent, and Sepia turned to see Rosie.

Rosie looked curiously at Sepia and the Executioner then handed Sepia a small box.

"Anastasia asked me to give this to you," Rosie said.

Sepia opened the box and found a note inside that read: "Good luck, Sepia." It was signed: "Anastasia". She held up a delicate necklace with a small gold charm in the shape of a horseshoe.

"It's beautiful!" Sepia cried.

"How unusual," Rosie commented, surprised at Anastasia's gesture.

A ray of sunlight shining through the tent struck the gold charm and it glinted in the Executioner's eyes. He backed away and walked out of the tent. Rosie watched him go.

"What was he doing in here with you?" Rosie asked.

"I don't know. He looked at me as if he knew me, but I think it's only that I remind him of someone," Sepia said.

"Who?" Rosie wondered.

"Someone he loved," Sepia answered. "Someone he lost. I could see the pain in his eyes."

Rosie stared at Sepia then toward the direction the Executioner took. A sudden look of recognition swept across her face, but she tried to conceal it.

Sepia didn't notice. "I guess I better get ready," she said.

"Yes," Rosie mumbled absently. "I'll see you before you go on."

Sepia left Rosie standing in the Menagerie, seemingly lost in thought.

***

When Sepia had gone, Rosie's face changed to near panic. If what she was thinking was correct, it was truly extraordinary, and if the Executioner was who she thought he was… Rosie tried to remember back to the last time she spoke to Angelina. Angelina had been totally distraught. She had tried again to see Patrick and been refused by his parents, and her own parents were forcing her to leave with them. That was the last Rosie knew of Patrick's whereabouts.

Rosie began to wonder what Patrick must have thought

during that time. Did he know that Angelina had been trying to see him? Did he think she had abandoned him? And, of course, he wouldn't have known anything about Sepia. So, where would a disfigured, lost soul go to fit in? Where is a place that welcomes both misfits and dreamers? He had come to the circus.

Rosie walked out of the Menagerie in search of the Executioner. She found him in the Big Top, but he was up in the air, checking rigging. Rosie had too much to do for tonight's performance to wait. She would have to come back later.

***

High up in the shadows of the Big Top, the Executioner examined Sepia's trapeze rigging. His fingers moved along the ropes as if searching for the right spot, then his hand moved to his belt where a knife rested in its sheath.

"Need any help?" a voice asked.

The Executioner turned quickly, startled to see Cole Artel.

"My mother wanted me to check her rigging again," Cole lied.

The Executioner's thick scars allowed a slight grin.

"I heard Sepia Stefani is going after the triple tonight," Cole said.

The Executioner shrugged his shoulders with seeming indifference.

"I hope she makes it. I hope the crowd doesn't get more than they bargained for," Cole said looking straight at the Executioner.

The Executioner moved over to the ladder and began

climbing down. Cole quickly checked Sepia's rigging, saw that it was secure then followed the Executioner. As he reached the bottom, Louie happened to walk by. Cole caught the look of Louie's surprise then curiosity at seeing Cole descend from the rigging.

**

Sepia was wearing her new necklace as she and Bruno waited at the arena entrance to go on. Billy walked over to them.

"Nervous?" he asked.

"A little," Sepia answered.

"She'll be famous after tonight," Bruno said.

Anastasia walked into the tent and over to Sepia. Billy watched with surprise and pleasure as Anastasia hugged her.

"Good luck, Sepia. Ah, you're wearing the necklace," Anastasia said, smiling.

Sepia kissed Anastasia on the cheek. "Thank you!"

"It's a good luck charm, you know," Anastasia told her.

"I hope so. I'll need it," Sepia replied.

"You'll be great I'm sure. It's a good crowd tonight," Anastasia commented as she stepped up to the arena opening and looked out at the audience. Her eyes moved to center ring, where the roustabouts were hoisting up the safety net under the trapeze, then she glanced up into the darkness at the peak of the tent.

The clowns entertained the crowd with the Poor Man, Banker routine while the roustabouts finished raising the safety net.

Cole stood at the animal entrance keeping an eye on the

clown act. The Banker held up the Poor Man's clothes.

"This is no good! Off with his head!" the Banker yelled.

The Executioner put the Poor Man's head on the block and raised his axe.

"Any last words?" the Banker shouted.

The Poor Man answered, "HELP!"

Anastasia turned and smiled at Sepia.

Sepia smiled back. She was quite overwhelmed by Anastasia's sudden kindness. The gift meant a lot to her. She had almost given up trying to get close to Anastasia. The more she had tried to be friendly, the more stand-offish Anastasia had become. Sepia chalked it up to the natural wariness of someone people were always attempting to approach. Yet, Anastasia had come through on the very day that was most important to Sepia. She had felt calmer ever since she received the necklace and she reached up now and touched it for reassurance.

The clown act was ending as the Poor Man grabbed the axe and chased the Executioner around the arena track and out the exit. Cole was waiting there. He watched the clown disguised as the Executioner pull off his hat, but froze when he saw that there wasn't a scarred face beneath it.

"Damn, this hood is hot," the clown said, tossing it into a costume box. "Anybody know what happened to the other guy?"

Cole shot a glance up into the dim peak of the Big Top, then over to the performer's entrance.

"And now, high above center ring, Bruno Stefani and his daughter, a daring young woman on the flying trapeze, the lovely Sepia!" the announcer shouted to the audience.

Cole dashed out of the animal entrance and ran around the Big Top to the back door.

Sepia and Bruno entered center ring, saluted the crowd and swung up into the safety net. They crossed to their respective ladders.

Cole ran up to the arena opening, past his mother whose mouth tightened to a thin line.

Bruno had reached the catch bar, climbed on and begun swinging. Sepia was already on her platform, dusting her palms with resin.

Sweat poured down Cole's face as he fought the voice inside him. He swung around and was about to call to Billy when Anastasia walked toward him quickly.

"If you say a word, we're finished. You are no longer my son," Anastasia growled in a voice only Cole could hear.

"I can't let you do it," Cole told her.

"Do what?" Anastasia asked him. "Who will believe you? You think that freak will tell anyone? By the way, Louie asked me what you were doing up in the rigging before the show."

Cole looked at his mother, stunned. It was as if she had walked up to him and driven a knife into his chest. All he could hear was a ringing in his ears. It drowned out the melodic waltz playing in the arena. It made him move like a dead man past his mother and out of the Big Top. Anastasia calmly returned to Billy's side to watch the Stefani's act.

As she sent the trapeze bar out for a trial swing, Sepia took a moment to concentrate. She tried to forget the group of reporters below. She must think only about her act. Bruno lowered himself into position and Sepia grabbed the bar and lifted off. The crowd swayed to the tune of "The Daring Young Man on the Flying Trapeze" and smiled as they watched Sepia's obviously female body sail through the air.

Everything felt great. Sepia had lost her nervousness the minute she hit the air. She swung high, pirouetted and landed in her father's grip with dazzling perfection. The crowd burst into applause as Sepia returned to her platform.

Billy broke into a smile. "They're hot tonight! I can feel it!"

Anastasia stood next to him, stone-faced, staring at the crowd. Her eyes moved upward to the peak of the tent, as if she could actually see the supporting ropes of the trapeze becoming frayed.

Outside the Big Top, Cole could hear the crowd cheering. He paced back and forth, torn between his mother's threat and doing what was right.

In center ring, Sepia continued to wow the audience. She performed a single and a double backward somersault, and then the announcer filled his lungs.

"And now, Sepia will attempt a feat never before achieved by a woman! She will execute a triple somersault into the hands of her catcher! This is an extremely difficult feat, ladies and gentlemen, and we ask for your total silence, please!"

There was a loud drum roll then the band fell silent.

This is it, Sepia thought to herself. She thought of all her heartache in the past and cast it aside. She thought of her mother and vowed to change her own destiny.

Bruno dried his palms on his thighs as Sepia climbed to a higher starting bar.

"Go get 'em, kid," Billy mumbled under his breath as he crossed his fingers.

Still outside, Cole stopped pacing, turned and dashed back into the Big Top.

Sepia took the bar and flew out for her trial swing. On

her return, she soared to the top of the tent. It was at the height of her swing that she felt the snap.

Cole ran to the arena opening just as the crowd gasped with horror. A supporting rope broke and one side of the trapeze bar dropped. As Sepia was flung away, Bruno swung up, reached for her and amazingly caught one of her wrists. He held on with all his strength, but the strain was too much. Sepia slipped through his fingers and fell. She landed at the edge of the safety net and tumbled through the guy ropes into the sawdust. The audience screamed as Billy rushed out to her. Sepia lay still on the ground for a moment, but even before Billy reached her, she began to move. Roustabouts quickly surrounded Sepia as the band covered with a gentle melodic tune. Billy knelt at her side.

"Don't move," he said.

Bruno descended from the catch bar and ran over.

"What happened?!" he shouted as he broke through the circle of roustabouts.

"I'm all right. I'm okay," Sepia said with surprising clarity.

Billy ordered her to lie still until help came. Doc ran into the tent carrying his medical bag and knelt down next to Sepia. He asked her to move certain areas of her body, and when he was satisfied that it was safe, Billy and Bruno carefully helped her stand.

Cole had watched everything from the animal's entrance. Sepia seemed miraculously unhurt and she bravely signaled to the crowd that she was okay. They applauded as she walked out of the arena supported under each arm. Cole breathed a sigh of relief, but the tightness in his stomach did not go away.

Anastasia walked out to meet Sepia. "Take her to my wagon," She offered to Billy. "It's closest."

Billy agreed and he and Bruno walked Sepia out of the Big Top toward Anastasia's wagon. Anastasia started to follow them when she noticed a glint of metal in the sawdust at her feet. It was Sepia's necklace.

The announcer called to the audience. "Folks, the little lady is fine. She's going to be okay. What an athlete! What courage! I'm sure we'll see her back again soon performing her amazing aerial acrobatics!"

Anastasia stepped on the necklace and ground it into the sawdust as she left the arena and headed for her wagon.

***

Sepia lay on Anastasia's bed as Doc examined her one more time. Anastasia, Billy and Bruno looked on.

"I'm really okay," Sepia told them.

"Doc?" Billy asked.

"She seems all right. No broken bones. We should keep an eye on her though. She's got quite a bump on her head."

"What happened out there? " Bruno demanded, changing his focus now that he was sure Sepia was okay.

"I don't know, but I'm sure as hell going to find out," Billy assured him.

Louie stepped into the wagon and motioned Billy over, out of earshot of Sepia. Bruno followed.

"Take a look at this," Louie said. He handed Sepia's trapeze bar and rope to Billy.

Billy fingered the jagged piece of supporting rope. "It's been cut," he said angrily.

"Let me see that," Bruno demanded and took the rope from Billy. "Who did this?"

"Louie, find out if anybody saw anything," Billy said,

trying to keep his blood from boiling.

Anastasia broke in. "You'll upset Sepia with all this talk. She needs quiet. You men go on and leave her with me."

"I'll take her back to our wagon," Bruno argued.

"Anastasia's right, Bruno. Let her stay here. C'mon," Billy ordered.

Anastasia ushered the two men to the door and they left the wagon.

When they got outside, Bruno headed angrily back to his wagon, but Louie pulled Billy aside.

"I saw Cole up in the rigging just before the show," he said.

"Cole? What are you saying, that he...?" Billy asked in disbelief.

"I don't know," Louie answered, shaking his head.

Billy looked off in the distance as a dark cloud crossed his face.

"Find Cole and bring him to me."

As Louie took off into the darkness, Rosie ran over and met Billy.

"Is Sepia okay?" she asked, clearly disturbed.

"Seems to be," Billy said with relief, though his thoughts were drawn elsewhere.

"Thank heaven," Rosie said, relieved, then she remembered her mission. "Have you seen that rigger, the clown Executioner?"

"No, why?" Billy asked.

"Nothing," Rosie mumbled, and then she turned and hurried away, more upset than ever by the turn of events. She kept telling herself that the Executioner couldn't have had anything to do with Sepia's accident, but her gut instinct didn't agree.

She should tell Billy about him, but something made her wait. She wanted to speak to the Executioner first.

It was then that Rosie spotted him, his palms pressed against a wagon as if he was trying to push it over. She walked up to him, but he was like a piece of stone, refusing to acknowledge her presence. Rosie began talking.

"I need to speak to you. I need to ask you...are you Patrick Dannon?" she asked.

The Executioner lifted his head up ever so slightly, but it was all Rosie needed to know that she was right.

"I used to be a very good friend of Angelina," she said.

The Executioner whipped his head toward Rosie and she saw the wild, dangerous look in his eyes.

"She waited for you to come for her. She was forbidden to see you. She tried many times. Your parents told her that you didn't want her, but she never believed it. She waited and waited, then finally lost hope. She was so young, so afraid and her parents forced her to go on with them. She also had to think of the child."

The Executioner had not blinked an eye until Rosie's last word, but now he closed his eyes for a moment then stared at her again.

"She was carrying your child when her parents married her off to a catcher named Bruno Stefani. She didn't love him. I heard that she was killed in a flying accident years later, but I didn't believe it. Angelina died of a broken heart."

The Executioner looked away now as if Rosie had merely related the time of day.

"I want to help you in any way I can," Rosie said again. "Sepia is your daughter and I believe that she has not lived a very happy life with Bruno. I believe that she would want to know the truth."

The Executioner refused to look at her.

"Did you hear what I said? Sepia is your daughter."

The Executioner began to shake his head. He motioned Rosie away, first gently, then violently.

Rosie backed off, not knowing what to do, afraid that she had done the wrong thing in telling him. Maybe he was too unstable to even understand. She should tell Billy now. If the Executioner did have anything to do with Sepia's accident, Billy would know how to handle it. She left the Executioner in the same position she found him, standing like stone, staring ahead.

***

When Billy and Bruno left her wagon, Anastasia locked the door behind her. She went back over to Sepia and sat on the edge of the bed.

"What were Billy and my father talking about?" Sepia asked.

"Don't worry about that now," Anastasia said.

Sepia desperately wanted to talk. The numbness had worn off and the defeat of her fall and failure to do the triple had begun to sink in. She needed reassurance that her dreams were not totally destroyed, but a fuzziness filled her head and blurred her vision.

"I shouldn't have tried the triple," Sepia said as her eyelids began to close. Her words became slurred. "I wasn't... ready..."

Anastasia watched, amazed, as Sepia's condition suddenly deteriorated. Sepia put her hand on her forehead.

"What's wrong?" Anastasia asked her.

"I feel...so dizzy. I think when I...when I hit...," Sepia's voice trailed off and she closed her eyes.

"Sepia," Anastasia called. "Sepia," she said louder.

Outside Anastasia's wagon, the Executioner quietly approached the window and peered in. Sepia lay on the bed with her eyes closed, but her chest rose and fell in even rhythm.

The Executioner had heard what the seamstress said. He had heard the words, but he couldn't seem to sort them out. The woman lying on Anastasia's bed was his child? This woman that he tried to hurt was his daughter? No, it couldn't be...

The Executioner watched Anastasia rise from Sepia's bedside and back away. She looked around her wagon, picked up a throw pillow from her couch, then moved back to the bed and stood over Sepia. The Executioner's head began to throb as he watched

Anastasia lower the pillow over Sepia's face and hold it firmly down. His fist clenched and he raised it up to the window to bang against the pane. Someone else however, knocked against the wagon door instead.

Anastasia froze and released her weight on the pillow.

Louie called from outside the wagon. "Miss Artel, you're on!"

Anastasia removed the pillow from Sepia's face. Her hand trembled as she pulled up a strand of hair from her neck and secured it with a pin.

Louie called again. "Miss Artel?"

Anastasia answered, "I'm coming."

She grabbed her cape from a chair, looked back at Sepia and left. She stepped outside the wagon and quickly closed the door behind her.

"How is Sepia?" Louie asked.

"She's asleep. Don't bother her," Anastasia said curtly.

"I can't find Cole," Louie told her.

A look of disgust crossed her face, but Anastasia was not surprised that Cole had disappeared. She would just as soon not see him now anyway.

Louie followed Anastasia toward the Big Top while the Executioner watched from the shadows. When Anastasia had gone, the Executioner quietly slipped inside her wagon. Moments later, he came out carrying Sepia wrapped in a dark blanket. He glanced around and moved off into the night.

The Executioner brought Sepia into the Menagerie tent and laid her in the shadowed corner where he slept. He crouched next to her and stared down at her sleeping face. Sepia looked completely peaceful, like an angel, like his Angelina. She had finally come back to him and he would keep her forever now. He would never ever hurt her again. As he gently brushed a lock of hair from her cheek, he heard someone enter the tent.

The Sheik led Princess into the Menagerie and tethered her for the night. He picked up a brush and ran it over the horse's pure white coat.

"You were perfect tonight! Did you see how they loved you, my clever beauty?" the Sheik praised.

He set the brush down and walked over to get a bucket of water sitting inches from the Executioner. The Executioner pulled into the shadows, remaining crouched, ready to spring. The Sheik picked up the bucket and returned to Princess. She took a deep, long drink.

"Thirsty, uh? You will sleep well tonight my precious, my treasure," the Sheik cooed. He kissed the horse on her forehead and walked out of the tent.

The Executioner heard the Sheik's footsteps disappear then he sank down in the straw next to Sepia. He felt the warmth of her body. If only he could lie there next to her and sleep forever. Just as he started to close his eyes, a figure appeared over him. He looked up and saw Anastasia's son.

Cole had followed Sepia's every move since the accident. He had watched her being taken to his mother's wagon and he had seen Billy and the others leave. He had not, however, seen what Anastasia had attempted to do to Sepia. He had been waiting for Anastasia to leave then he, too, planned to take Sepia from the wagon. The Executioner, however, had gotten to her first.

"Let me have her," Cole said, calm but firm. The Executioner instead rose up over Sepia protectively, taut as a guy rope.

***

There was a rumbling in the sky as Anastasia ended her act and hurried from the Big Top. She crossed back to her wagon, entered it, and stopped short when she saw the empty bed. She burst out the door and ran over to the Stefani wagon.

Bruno sat on the edge of his cot with a bottle in his hand. He took a long swig of whiskey and ran his fingers through his hair. It had to have been Anastasia, he thought, yet even he found it hard to believe she cut Sepia's trapeze or hired someone to. But who else had a reason to hurt Sepia? He shouldn't have left her in Anastasia's wagon. He better go get her...after one more drink. As Bruno lifted the bottle to his lips, someone knocked on his door. He got up, steadied himself and answered it. Anastasia faced him.

"Is Sepia here?" Anastasia demanded.

"What do you mean? She's supposed to be with you," Bruno said, confused.

Anastasia pushed Bruno aside and searched the wagon.

"What are you doin'?" Bruno yelled.

"I came back to my wagon and she was gone," Anastasia replied.

"Gone? Where?" Bruno asked angrily.

Anastasia ignored him and rushed out of the wagon. Bruno stumbled down the wagon steps and shouted after her.

"I'll find her and when I do, I'm keepin' her away from you! There's somethin' going on here and I don't like it!"

Again there was a rumble in the night sky as the wind picked up.

The performers were lined up for the Grand Finale when Anastasia rushed into the tent and anxiously looked around.

She pushed past the floats toward the arena opening, and tried, with no luck, to spot the Executioner. As she turned to leave, Billy grabbed her arm.

"Up you go!" Billy commanded as he assisted Anastasia onto her float where she was forced to wait in the parade finale.

"How's Sepia?" Billy called up to her.

"Sleeping," Anastasia lied, hoping Billy wouldn't learn otherwise until she'd found Sepia. She was trying to keep the panic from rising inside her. Having Sepia disappear had not been part of her plan.

Inside the arena, Reichek was preparing for the final act of the show. The fuse was ignited on the canon and a loud BOOM was heard; however, it was eclipsed by the even louder explosion of a huge thunderclap.

Billy looked toward the sky as the Grand Finale proceeded into the arena.

"Call a 'John Robinson' and get the funny ropes on the quarter poles! Wrap it up and get these people out of here!" he yelled to Louie. "There's a storm comin' fast!"

Just then, a roustabout ran into the tent. "Boss, Menagerie got hit by lightning! There's a fire!" he screamed.

Billy dashed out of the Big Top, but stopped short when he saw flames leaping from the peak of the Menagerie. He ran to the entrance and heard the cries of animals inside. Billy shouted to the roustabouts already scrambling to put out the fire.

"Get the animals out first! Break it down. Get every bucket you can find and start a relay!"

Trainers hurried out of the tent, leading their blindfolded animals. The fire was spreading rapidly aided by the wind. A cloud of smoke billowed out of the tent making it impossible for anyone else to get inside.

"Is everybody out of there?" Billy shouted.

"Yeah, boss," a roustabout coughed as he dashed out of the choking tent.

***

Inside, the tent was full of smoke. The figure of a man stumbled toward the exit, but stopped to cut one last horse free from its tether before heading to the opening. Just then, a burning tent pole collapsed and fell on him, pinning him unconscious and unseen beneath the blazing log.

***

Billy watched from a safe distance as the tent became consumed with flames. Sheik Amali came running over to him.

"Princess! Where is my Princess?!" he screamed. He started toward the tent, but Billy grabbed him.

"You can't go in there!" Billy shouted.

"I must! My Princess is still inside!" the Sheik demanded.

Billy gripped him tightly. "I'm telling you, you're not going in there! It's too late!"

The bucket relay was a pitiful attempt against the raging fire. The fire hose was no better. The Sheik shook his fists at the turbulent sky.

"A curse on Allah!" he shouted.

The heavens responded, bursting forth with a downpour of rain, but it was too late to save the burning tent.

***

The Executioner, wearing his dark hood, stared at the red glow of the fire from across the field. He sat astride Princess holding Sepia still unconscious in his arms. As it began to rain, the Executioner turned Princess around and rode away from the circus.

Chapter Thirteen: Rumors

The grey dawn found the flags still waving at the peak of the Big Top, but nearby, smoke rose from the burnt remains of the Menagerie.

Doc tended the elephants now staked in the open air. He rubbed a salve on Timba's burned legs.

Billy and some of the roustabouts sifted through the wreckage of the fire, uncovering the charred body of a zebra trapped in the blaze. Suddenly, Billy stopped.

"Doc, come here quick!" Billy called.

Doc left Timba and ran over to Billy. They stared at the body lying under the tent pole.

"Who is it, Doc?" Billy asked.

"Can't tell, too badly burned."

"It's the freak rigger," a roustabout piped up.

"How do you know?" Billy asked.

"He slept in Menagerie," the roustabout explained. "Poor bastard couldn't even call for help."

Billy shook his head sadly. "It's a damn shame. Somebody help Doc. We'll take him into town. I'll make sure he gets a proper burial."

As bad as it was losing the menagerie tent and some of

the animals, Billy had felt lucky. He had escaped a fire in the Big Top, a circus owner's worst nightmare. Billy did not, however, feel lucky now. He tried not to view The Executioner's death as an omen. But combined with Sepia's accident and the fire, he had to face the fact that bad luck had come to the Olympic. Superstition was very real in circus.

Billy headed toward his office, but stopped when he heard someone yelling nearby. He walked toward the voice as the shouting escalated.

He found a very drunk Bruno Stefani banging on the door of Anastasia's wagon.

"Come outta there! I know you done somethin' to her. Come out before I kick the door in!" Bruno threatened. His leg was poised to do what he said as Billy ran up and tried to pull him away.

"Hey! What's goin' on here?" Billy demanded.

"Leave me alone! I'll handle this!" Bruno insisted as he pushed Billy off and staggered toward the door again.

This time, Billy grabbed Bruno's arm and locked it behind his back.

"Get away from there, Bruno!" Billy ordered, then he called out toward the wagon, "Anastasia, are you in there?"

Anastasia's voice called back from inside. "Have you got that lunatic under control?"

"It's okay. You can come out," Billy told her.

Anastasia opened her door and cautiously stepped out. Bruno struggled to get free of Billy's grip.

"I want him out of here," Anastasia said. "He tried to kill me!"

"What did you do with Sepia?!" Bruno shouted.

"What is he talking about?" Billy asked Anastasia.

"Sepia's gone, left my wagon last night," Anastasia explained. "I tried to look for her, but Stefani told me to butt out," she added.

"She's lyin'," Bruno growled. "She done somethin' with her. She was jealous of Sepia and she done somethin' to her. I know it."

"Shut up, Bruno," Billy warned.

"See? I told you he was crazy," Anastasia said.

"Crazy and drunk, but the important thing is to find Sepia," Billy said. He forgot the fire, the death, everything else.

"Go back to your wagon, Bruno, and stay put. If you threaten Anastasia again, I'll have you locked up. And stay off the booze or you're off the show!"

"You find my girl, Thompson," Bruno warned, "or I'm callin' the cops!" He gave a last menacing glance at Anastasia, then staggered back to his wagon.

"I want him out of here," Anastasia repeated to Billy when Bruno had left.

"I'll deal with him later," Billy answered. He was scanning the circus grounds, trying to spot Louie. "I need to have Louie start searching the grounds." A knot was forming in his stomach as he turned back to Anastasia. "Have you seen Cole?"

"No, he didn't come back last night," Anastasia said bitterly.

The knot tightened in Billy's gut. "Would Cole have had any reason to hurt Sepia?"

"What are you talking about?" Anastasia asked, irritated.

"Nothing else makes sense. Bruno was harping about you thinking Sepia wanted to take your place. Maybe Cole thought so, too. Maybe he was trying to protect you. Awhile back, Bruno came to me all hot and bothered because he thought Cole was after Sepia.

"That's crazy," Anastasia said, but her face was growing red with anger. Cole with Sepia. Now Anastasia understood why her son hadn't been willing to help her. He had, in fact, betrayed her. "I didn't know anything about this," she said to Billy. Betrayal could work both ways she decided.

"We need to find them," Billy said, looking around for Louie again. "Either we find them or I'll call the cops."

"You would bring the cops into this?" Anastasia asked.

"He tried to hurt Sepia," Billy said.

"I thought we always settled our own business," Anastasia said accusingly.

"This is different," Billy told her. "We pull up stakes tonight, but I'm not leaving 'til Sepia is found." He had spent too much time talking. He left Anastasia and headed toward his office.

Billy forgot his other problems and thought of nothing but Sepia's disappearance. He had never been this concerned about anyone before, but he was beginning to understand that his feelings for Sepia were not the ones Anastasia had accused him of. The protective feeling Sepia had inspired in him was not born of lust or desire. It was something else which at first confused him. Billy had never been a father, so he had not recognized his feelings as paternal. He was certain of them now though because along with a father's love, he was also experiencing a father's terror for the safety of his child.

Anastasia watched Billy go. When she had learned of the Executioner's death in the fire, she had felt coldly relieved. There would be no trace to her plan or deed. The suspicions about Cole and Sepia gnawed at her though.

She couldn't believe that they had run off together. If it was true, however, she was sure it wouldn't last. Like the others before, he'd soon figure out Sepia was not worth it.

News of the death in the fire spread like lightning through the Olympic. News of Sepia and Cole's disappearance traveled fast, too, and along with it came the rumors. No one dared believe Bruno's accusations against Anastasia, partly because of her powerful position, but mostly because it seemed ludicrous that Anastasia would be so afraid of Sepia that she would actually try to hurt her. People were willing to believe the rumors about Cole, however. Even Bruno had stopped pointing the finger at Anastasia and leveled it at her son instead. He spouted his accusations to anyone that would listen and many were beginning to believe him. They knew how close Cole was to his mother and suspected what he might do to protect her.

When Rosie learned about the Executioner's death, she immediately went to Billy and told him the truth about the Executioner's past and that he was Sepia's real father. Billy was taken aback by Rosie's news, but when she began to reveal her suspicions about the Executioner being the one that cut the safety net, Billy stopped her.

"Why would he want to hurt her?" he asked.

"He was all mixed up," Rosie explained. "He thought Sepia was Angelina and he had the wrong idea that she ran out on him.

"Maybe so, but I've got a different idea about who tried to hurt Sepia. Cole Artel is missing. He's the one we're after."

"And you think Sepia is with him?"

"Damned if I know. One way or the other, I want to find her."

The news about Cole made Rosie confused, wondering if

she had been wrong about the Executioner after all. Rosie knew how tightly bound Cole was to his mother and if what everybody was saying was true, it was conceivable that he would try to protect her no matter how unfounded the idea of Sepia as a threat might be. Conceivable but not convincing. Rosie had a hard time believing Cole acted on his own. He was much too irresponsible and cavalier to have committed the deed he was being accused of. Besides, though she didn't particularly care for his sexual escapades, she had always thought he was basically a good kid.

Rosie had never trusted Anastasia, however. As hard as it was to believe she would do such a thing, Rosie knew Anastasia was certainly capable of devising such a plan. If indeed she had gotten Cole to cause Sepia's accident, then Rosie was frightened for Sepia's safety now.

Rosie wasn't the only one who had a hard time believing the rumors about Cole. Where Rosie was only suspicious of Anastasia, Charlene was absolutely sure that if something evil had been done, Anastasia Artel had done it. Charlene would never forget what she had seen Anastasia do before.

Charlene had been a showgirl in vaudeville when she met Harry Artel. She'd never known a more miserable man in her life. At first, she suspected he was acting so sorry just to get her attention, but when Charlene met Anastasia, she understood where Harry's misery came from. It was obvious Anastasia didn't care for him, maybe never had.

Anastasia had already been on quite an odyssey before she met Harry. She grew up on a German potato farm in a family of six girls, headed by a strict Prussian father who expected his daughters to work hard and dutifully until they were married off to neighboring landowners. He was a cold, inflexible man who demanded obedience under the threat of beatings. Anastasia had tested her father more than once and carried the memory of his belt against her bare skin, but she could never resign herself to the life he meant for her. A visiting aunt who lived in Munich had told her about the city, about fine restaurants, museums and the theater. Her aunt's descriptions of vaudeville filled Anastasia's head with dreams and she was determined to see it. She begged to be allowed to visit her aunt, and her father finally consented. That was the last he saw of his spirited daughter. If she never scrubbed another potato in her whole life, it would be too soon. She was sixteen.

Munich was just as her aunt had described, but Anastasia had to take a job in a cannery to support herself. She loved her independence though, and saved every penny to go to that magical place her aunt had described, the vaudeville theater. One night, a trapeze act was performing and Anastasia was spellbound as the three Artel brothers amazed the audience with their daring tricks. It struck such a chord in Anastasia that she made her way backstage as soon as the performance ended. The oldest Artel, Harry, was also the best looking, with wavy brown hair and hound dog eyes that drooped in a sleepy, seductive way. He was first to spot Anastasia in the crowd of fans at the stage door. Her piercing blue eyes held him enraptured and when she offered her body to him that night, he thought himself the luckiest man in the world. They were married the next day.

Anastasia began to learn the trapeze and within a year, was instrumental in breaking up the Artel brothers and forming a husband/wife act instead. Next, she bought one-way tickets on a boat to America. Harry didn't mind. All he wanted was for his wife to be happy and for them to be flying. Anastasia's ambition, however, was far greater than Harry's. Her plans were delayed by pregnancy, but as soon as her son was delivered, she got herself back into shape and back on the trapeze.

Cole spent far more time with his father than his mother, though his mother adored him. At a very young age, Cole began learning acrobatics from Harry. Anastasia decided that Cole should go to boarding school, but Harry wanted the boy with them. They fought bitterly and as their relationship declined, Harry began to look elsewhere for female comfort. Anastasia didn't seem to mind.

By the time Charlene met them, Anastasia had almost removed Harry completely from her life. She was sick of the vaudeville circuit and was biding her time until her lucky break arrived. It came by way of a contract with the Olympic Circus, a contract for her only.

Charlene had listened to Harry's laments over his marriage, but beneath his pain and resentment, she had discovered a sweet, gentle man who was simply lonely and unloved. Harry was grateful for Charlene's attention and they soon ended up in each other's arms. Despite his unhappy marriage, Harry wasn't sure he wanted to leave Anastasia. He was crazy about his son and didn't want to lose him. Anastasia, however, made the decision for them.

Charlene wasn't at the theater the night of the murder, but she was heartsick over Harry's death. She never quite believed the story of the mugging, but she let herself be led by Anastasia's pretense at mourning and her offers to help Charlene. Charlene guessed that Anastasia was only placating her, but she was raw from her own grief over Harry's death and she joined the Olympic to change her surroundings and forget.

It was probably a mistake to stay close to Anastasia, but

Charlene fell in love with the circus and learned to avoid contact with its top performer. She had watched Cole grow more and more dependent on his mother, and she often wondered at the tight hold Anastasia had on him. Cole had the potential to be a powerful man, yet he deferred to his mother completely. His charm and personality won the heart of every woman he met, but his relationships were no more than brief encounters, always to return to Anastasia... until now.

Ever since Cole had disappeared, Charlene had been filled with curiosity as to what made him go. There was only one part of the rumor about Cole she hoped was true, that he and Sepia were together. Charlene liked the girl, and if Sepia had been the one to break Anastasia's grip on Cole, then Charlene wished them well. She would never believe that Cole had harmed Sepia. It had to have been either Anastasia or someone else.

Chapter Fourteen: The Executioner

A morning haze blanketed the woods as Sepia lay asleep under a bramble of honeysuckle. A drop of dew struck her cheek and she opened her eyes to a wall of yellow blossoms. She sat up and breathed in the sweet smell of nectar, then spread some branches and looked out. A dense stand of trees was behind her and a vast rolling meadow in front. She was still in her costume and a morning chill made her shiver as she crawled out of her shelter. She looked up at the grey sky and the dark, ominous clouds in the distance.

"Papa?" she called, but got no answer. She heard no sounds of the circus or of the city. She did hear the gurgle of a stream nearby, the sound of which triggered an incredible thirst. Her mind was in a fog and she was having a hard time recalling the events of the last twenty-four hours. She remembered her fall from the trapeze and Billy and her father helping her to Anastasia's wagon. She remembered Anastasia sitting at her bedside talking to her, but then her memory faded. Where was everyone? How did she get here?

Sepia followed the sound of water to a small brook. She knelt down and dipped her hands into a deep pool and drank several palmfuls. The surface cleared and Sepia stared at her reflection in the dark burn, hoping it might somehow jog her memory. Her likeness was joined, however, by another image behind her. She whirled around and found the Executioner standing over her in his black hood.

"Where...am I?" Sepia asked, edging away.

The Executioner didn't respond.

"Did you bring me here?" Sepia asked him and the Executioner nodded. Sepia slowly stood up. "Are we alone?" she asked tentatively, afraid of the answer.

Again the Executioner nodded. Sepia glanced around and noticed Princess grazing nearby. Seeing the horse calmed her slightly.

"I want to go back," she said.

In response, the Executioner walked over and picked up a length of rope lying on the ground. Sepia looked at the Executioner, then at Princess, gauging her chances. She dashed toward the horse and swung herself onto Princess's back only to be pulled off by a powerful grip.

"Let me go!" Sepia yelled. She fought to get free, but the Executioner covered her mouth and pinned her against his chest. She gradually stopped struggling and he removed his hand from her mouth to gather up Princess's reins.

"They'll come looking for us," Sepia said, breathing fast. "You don't want to get into trouble. Let me go and I won't say a word. I swear it," she promised.

The Executioner slowly released her, but took the horse with him as he walked back to retrieve the rope. Sepia glanced at the surrounding woods. She hesitated for a moment then took off running toward the trees. The Executioner did not move to stop her.

The forest was thick with brush and Sepia crashed

through brambles that scraped her bare arms and legs. The air became suddenly still and the sky turned black as night. Within moments, the woods were blanketed by a downpour. The rain drove through the canopy of trees, soaking her costume and washing the blood from her scratches. The sky lit up and thunder shook the ground, but the brief light showed an outcropping of boulders nearby. Drenched and out of breath, Sepia crawled into a niche between two rocks. Though her body was hidden, there was no cover overhead and she sat huddled in a ball, wiping the rain from her eyes, watching.

She prayed that this was a nightmare from which she would soon awaken, but knew it was not. It was all real; the accident, her failed hope, the Executioner. What she had thought would be her salvation with the Olympic had really been her ruin. Lightning flashed and Sepia looked up. Again the Executioner stood before her as thunder exploded around them. Sepia cared little what he did to her now.

The Executioner pulled her up and led her toward another opening in the rocks, this one a cave. He pushed her inside, but went back out into the driving rain, returning a moment later leading Princess to the entrance. He slid the dark blanket from her back and ducked into the cave then oddly, he held the blanket out to Sepia in what seemed a gesture of kindness. She took it, wrapped it around herself and huddled against the cavern wall. Soaking wet, the Executioner sat against the opposite wall and they faced each other in silence. She waited.

Several hours passed before the rain stopped. Sepia lay asleep on the cave floor. The Executioner was also asleep, still propped against the wall. Princess was grazing peacefully outside the cave entrance when her ears pricked up and she lifted her head.

Sepia woke to the sound of someone moving through the brush. She quietly sat up and looked out of the cave. She could barely make out the figure of a man passing through the trees. The Executioner wakened, too. He also saw the man and the shotgun under the man's arm.

Dressed in a brown vest and cap, the hunter paused and bent to examine some fresh tracks. Sepia was amazed he hadn't spotted Princess's white coat through the brush until she realized that the rocky formation hid the horse from view and the man would have needed to look back over his shoulder to see her. Sepia stared at the hunter. Her mouth was open, ready to call for help, when she turned back and glanced at the Executioner. Their eyes met, and for the first time, Sepia realized that he no longer looked at her with malice. His eyes were full of despair, almost a mirror of her own feelings. She hesitated.

The hunter stood up and started to walk on. Sepia's gaze moved from the Executioner back to the hunter, but she remained silent as she listened to the hunter's footsteps fade in the distance.

"Why did you take me away?" she asked quietly.

The Executioner reached into his pocket and pulled out the length of rope from before. Sepia drew back, but he merely handed it to her.

She examined the rope with recognition now rather than fear. "It's from the trapeze. Did you cut it?" she asked.

The Executioner slowly nodded his head.

"Why?"

The Executioner looked down at his feet and shook his head as if he didn't know.

"You wanted to hurt me," she answered for him.

"Yes," the Executioner said in a harsh, guttural voice.

The sound of his voice startled Sepia more than his answer.

"You can talk!" she exclaimed.

"Anastasia," the Executioner went on in a low, raspy tone. "Anastasia wanted to hurt you, too. She asked me to do it."

Sepia's eyes widened. "Why would Anastasia want to hurt me?"

"She thought you'd take her place. She had to stop you," he told her.

"I don't believe it," Sepia said, staring at the rope again.

"You don't know her," the Executioner replied.

"Why did you take me away?" she asked again, but the Executioner didn't answer. "What happens now?" she asked.

"You'll go back. Anastasia would be crazy to try and hurt you again," The Executioner said. "I won't hurt you either," he added.

Sepia looked out toward the woods.

"Where are we?"

"I'm not sure," said the Executioner, then he stood up. "It stopped raining. We should go."

Sepia rose and shivered from the dampness. The Executioner took the blanket from her. He pulled out a knife and made a slit in the center of the cloth, then he lifted the makeshift poncho over her head and down on her shoulders.

"Thanks," she said softly.

They left the cave and began walking through the woods with the Executioner leading Princess.

"I wonder where they think I am? Will they know you

took me?" Sepia asked.

"I don't know," the Executioner answered.

"I'll tell them you helped me. I won't say anything about the accident," she said.

"You would forgive me for what I did?" he asked.

"Yes," she told him. The answer came easily, though she wasn't sure why. "I'll only tell them you helped me," she added.

"It doesn't matter anyway," the Executioner said. "I'm not going back."

"Why?"

The Executioner didn't answer.

"I'll tell them about Anastasia," Sepia said, surprised by the anger in her voice.

The Executioner stopped and faced her. "Who will believe you? How will you prove it?"

Sepia couldn't answer and they walked on in silence.

The knowledge that Anastasia had tried to harm her was devastating, but along with the feeling of hurt and anger, Sepia recognized that Anastasia did what she did because she truly believed that Sepia could take her place. It amazed Sepia that Anastasia viewed her this way. She took it as sort of a bizarre compliment. Instead of destroying her, Anastasia had given Sepia the recognition she sought. This fact alone was saving Sepia from despair.

As she began to comprehend everything that had happened, there was still something Sepia did not understand. Why had the Executioner changed from wanting to hurt her, to wanting to save her life?

"Where will you go?" she asked him.

"I'll find work with another show," he answered.

"Have you always been in circus?" she asked.

"It's the only place I fit in," he replied.

They came to a small clearing and found an old stone foundation overgrown with vines and surrounded by weeds. Sepia spotted the fuzzy canes of wild raspberries. She plucked some and quickly devoured them, then collected another handful and held them out to the Executioner. He took the berries and ate hungrily then they both began gathering more.

"It feels good to be away from circus, but strange," Sepia said as she stuffed another handful of berries in her mouth. "When I was little and my father used to take me into town, I pretended I was like all the other girls, that I lived in a house, went to school, and wore dresses every day. I wanted to be them."

"And now?" The Executioner asked, swiftly plucking berries.

"I couldn't live anywhere but circus," she replied. "Flying is everything to me. Besides, now when I'm on the outside, I feel like a..." her voice trailed off with embarrassment.

"Freak," he said finishing the sentence for her. "You're hardly a freak. You are...beautiful."

Sepia blushed. "I don't want people to watch me for my looks. I want them to watch me because I'm a great flyer."

"That's why you want the triple," the Executioner said.

"Yes," she answered.

The Executioner looked up at the sky. Night was falling and he saw the glow of lights in the distance. "We're close to the city. We can go back tonight or wait until morning." He saw the look on Sepia's face. "Are you scared of me?"

"No," Sepia half-lied. There was a part of her that was not ready to go back to the circus yet. There was another part of her that was nervous to be alone with this man.

"I'll look for some wood and make a fire," he said.

"I'll help," Sepia offered.

Darkness surrounded Sepia and the Executioner as they sat opposite each other across a small campfire. The firelight danced in their eyes, the dark brown of Sepia's and the deep blue of the Executioner's. Sepia found herself feeling suddenly peaceful. It was as if at last, she had finally been taken away from everything that plagued her. Though she hadn't completely lost her fear of the Executioner, at least she no longer distrusted him. She wished, however, that he would remove his black hood. To her, the mask was more frightening than his scarred face. She decided to ignore her uneasiness however, and take comfort in the ease she felt talking to him.

"I was just thinking how angry my father must be," she smiled. "He would be even more furious knowing I was alone with a man," she said, embarrassed.

"He doesn't let you see men?" the Executioner asked.

"He scares them away. I mean, not that there have been many," she said.

"I bet there have been a lot," the Executioner said.

"I say hello to a man and my father goes crazy," she told him.

"He treats you badly."

"I'm used to it."

"Maybe he only treats you like that because he knows you'll take it."

"When I'm on the trapeze, all the bad things go away. The people who come to see us think we live in a fairy tale," Sepia said.

"There's no such thing," the Executioner replied.

"You rescued me. That was like a fairy tale," she said shyly.

"I'm no knight in shining armor," he answered.

"I was scared of you before," she told him.

"You had reason to be. But the others are, too. I like it that way. They leave me alone," he explained.

"Don't you ever get lonely?" she asked.

Before the Executioner could answer, Princess snorted loudly and startled Sepia. She jumped toward the Executioner and caught him off balance. He fell backward, carrying Sepia with him, but he quickly and gently pushed her off and sat back up.

"It was just the horse," he said gruffly.

"Then why are you scared?" Sepia asked.

"I'm not," he replied.

"You're shaking," she said, touching his arm.

The Executioner withdrew it, then abruptly stood up and threw some more wood on the fire.

"That should last awhile. There's more if you get cold," he told Sepia. He walked to the other side of the fire and lay down with his back to her.

Sepia watched him through the flames. It was odd, but she wanted him to like her. He was the first man who had ever really talked to her and she wanted to be his friend.

She sat for a while, thinking again about the accident and Anastasia and what she should do when she returned to the Olympic. The Executioner was right. She needed to stand up for herself. It sounded so easy. It should be easy. She was a grown woman who could work and earn her own living. She needed to tell her father to stop treating her the way he did. If she didn't make him stop, he would go on doing it forever. She would also have to put the accident behind her. The most important thing now was to decide what she wanted to do next. The triple? It had not only been her father who drove her to try it. She had wanted it, too. It was every flyer's goal. She would go back and make it happen. It seemed so simple, so clear. If only she had the strength to do it.

She looked over at the curved dark back of the Executioner. He believed in her more than she believed in herself. He listened to her and treated her like an adult. She wished they had more time together. Maybe in the morning she could convince him to go back to the Olympic. She finally lay down and pulled the poncho around her.

She was standing on an extremely high trapeze platform with Anastasia who handed her the same small gift box as before.

"Good luck, Sepia," she said. Sepia opened the box. Inside was the gold necklace with the horseshoe charm. Anastasia smiled.

Suddenly, the necklace turned into a deadly viper that lunged and bit her neck. She screamed and dropped the snake.

It landed at her feet and continued to strike at her legs. She backed up as Anastasia began to laugh. She felt her heels touch the edge of the platform. She lost her balance and fell. She dropped a long, long way, hearing Anastasia's echoing laughter until she abruptly hit the ground.

Sepia woke with a cry and found herself in the Executioner's arms, her body drenched in sweat.

"Shhh, it's okay," he said.

"It was Anastasia," she murmured, still pulling herself from the nightmare.

"I know," the Executioner said. He stroked Sepia's hair while she let the dream pass.

"I'm afraid to go back," she told him.

"You've got to stand up to her," the Executioner said.

"It's not just Anastasia. It's my father, too."

"Then be as strong on the ground as you are in the air," he said.

"I wish you were going back with me."

"You can do it alone," he assured her. He continued to smooth her hair with his hand and the hypnotic comfort of his touch calmly put her back to sleep.

***

Sunlight warmed Sepia's face and she woke to find the Executioner gone. She sat up and saw him through the trees, kneeling at the brook. She stood and started walking toward him, then stopped as she realized that he had removed his hood. Not wanting to intrude, she waited in the trees. The Executioner was splashing water on his face, but when he finally raised his head, Sepia sucked in her breath and froze. It was not a scarred, disfigured face she saw. It was Cole's.

Cole heard Sepia gasp and whirled around. He grabbed up the Executioner's hood from the ground and gripped it tightly in his fist.

Sepia stared at him in shock.

"I don't understand," she said.

He strode toward her.

"Forget you saw me," Cole said in his normal voice.

"But, it couldn't have been you," Sepia said in disbelief.

"Take the horse and do like I told you. Go back to the circus," he told her as he walked abruptly past her back to the campsite.

Sepia stood stock still in total amazement, trying to sort out what happened.

It couldn't have been him! It wasn't only that Cole had

disguised himself and lied to her that confused her. There was also the fact that he had kidnapped her to save her life. But far more difficult to believe and what she simply couldn't accept was that the person she had spent the last twenty-four hours with, the man who had talked to her, been kind to her, and genuinely seemed to care about her, was Cole.

Before, Sepia had convinced herself that no matter how attracted she was to him, Cole was totally wrong for her, irresponsible and unfeeling. But now she was utterly perplexed. Cole had revealed a completely different side of himself whether he intended to or not.

She turned and looked back at the campsite. Cole was not there. She quickly glanced around, but he was nowhere in sight. A feeling of panic swept over her. She ran back to where Princess stood grazing near the charred remains of the fire.

"Cole!" she called, but she knew he was gone. He'd left her.

It had been difficult enough to know that the Executioner was not returning to the Olympic, but to realize that it was really Cole she might lose meant something all together different. She remembered how he urged her to go back to the circus and take control of her life. He had wanted it for her even if he wouldn't be with her. No one had ever cared about her that way. His feeling had seemed so strong, so much like what she imagined love would be, and yet, it couldn't be love. If he loved her, why had he left?

Then it slowly dawned on her. It wasn't love Cole felt for her. It was pity. He was like a hunter who pulls an animal from a trap and in a moment of compassion spurs it back to its own kind. He had only saved her in order to stop Anastasia and that was all. He felt guilty that it was his mother who had tried to hurt her, and he saved Sepia's life in order to soothe his conscience. He could not betray his mother so he had left, pure and simple.

Sepia didn't blame him. She even tried to tell herself that it was easier this way, that it didn't matter how she felt about him because now he was gone. But it did matter. She didn't want Cole's pity. She wanted him to know that she was worth more than his clean conscience, and she wanted the chance to find out if what her heart was telling her was true, that she should not let him go.

Sepia untied Princess's reins and hopped on her back. She chose a direction and rode Princess into the woods. She searched for hours, but found no trace of him, and unsure of which direction to take next, she picked up the trail of the brook and began to follow it. It meandered through stands of trees and along edges of crop fields. It began to grow wider until it became a deep creek, then wider still as it curved east. Sepia became tied to the flow of water though she had no idea where it would lead. She rode through a dense stretch of forest, hugging the river's edge, then suddenly broke out of the trees and stood on the bank of Lake Michigan. Waves rolled off the lake like an ocean, and the dark grey water spanned to the horizon. The wind blew at its usual brisk speed, but it hit Sepia like a burst of sorrow, and she sat astride Princess feeling its power.

"Cole!" she cried above the rushing wind.

He had said he wasn't returning to the circus, but Sepia had no idea where else to look. The only other person who might know where he would go was his mother. Sepia rode down the rocky shore until the click of the horse's hooves was muffled by the sandy beaches of the city. Sepia could see the tall buildings off to her right. She heard a train whistle and steered Princess away from the water. She found the railroad tracks and began to follow them.

Chapter Fifteen: The Mask

Where Sepia had gone south and east, back toward the circus, Cole went west, away from it. He broke out of the woods and began to cross an open field, the Executioner's mask still clutched in his hand. The rain and dark sky from the day before had passed, leaving a clear, blue sky overhead.

It would be so easy now, Cole thought. He could go anywhere he wanted, as far away from the Olympic as possible. He could hook up with a new show, join another act or try to form his own. It was as if the whole world had opened up to him and it was an amazing feeling. He should have left a long time ago. He had let his mother hold him hostage with fear, but not anymore. Anastasia had severed the bond between them when she tried to destroy Sepia.

Sepia. He had to forget her. He couldn't go back to the Olympic now or ever. Sepia would be okay. He was sure Anastasia would not dare try to hurt her again. Sepia would perform the triple and become a great star. He had been wrong. The crowd would love her even more than Anastasia. They would love her as he...

Cole stopped in the middle of the field as his thoughts

overtook him. He was flooded with her smell, the taste of her lips, the depth in her eyes. He had learned too much about her. He had learned the shape of her ears and the softness of her hair. He knew the way her fingers swept the air when she talked. And when she sailed through the air on her trapeze, he knew exactly how to catch her.

His heart started pounding and the only way he could stop it was to keep moving. He shoved the Executioner's mask in his pocket and continued toward the city.

It was still morning when Cole knocked on the door to the speakeasy and stood waiting. The pug-nosed bouncer opened the door and stared at Cole with bloodshot eyes.

"Yeah?" he said.

"Is your boss here?" Cole asked.

"Lila?"

"Yeah, Lila," Cole said.

"She ain't here," the bouncer told him.

"Can you tell me where I can find her?" Cole asked.

"Why should I?" the bouncer responded.

"She told me I could come here if I needed a job, that she'd help me."

"Huh," the bouncer snorted. "Come in and wait."

Cole walked into the speakeasy. It was empty and quiet in the dim light that filtered down from a louvered window. A grizzly-chinned man was sweeping up spent matches with the patience of age. A collection of dirty glasses sat on a table and the room stank of used smoke and spilled whiskey.

The bouncer left Cole and went behind the bar. He reached under the counter, pulled out a telephone, and set it on the counter. He dialed a number and after several moments got an answer.

"Mornin', boss," he said apologetically. "...I know, but there's somebody here to see you." He looked up from the phone. "What's your name, kid?" he called to Cole.

"Tell her I'm from the circus," Cole said.

"He's from the circus," the bouncer repeated with a frown.

"Okay, boss," he said and hung up. He grabbed a note pad from under the bar and scribbled down an address. He walked over and handed it to Cole. "Mind your manners, kid," he warned. "Or you'll have me to answer to."

***

Cole stood at the bottom of a flight of stairs leading up to a narrow brownstone building. He checked the address on the slip of paper, then climbed the steps and rang the doorbell. Several minutes passed before Lila answered the door wearing a flowered blue kimono.

"Kinda early, isn't it?" she asked yawning.

"You want me to leave?" Cole asked.

"No," Lila answered and opened the door wider to let him in.

"You want some coffee?" Lila asked when he stepped inside.

"Sure," Cole said, then followed her down a hallway toward the kitchen. He glanced in the room they passed, a warm and comfortable parlor, eclectic in its mixture of antiques and art work, with rich earth tones in the upholstery and large throw pillows on the floor.

Lila led Cole into a light filled kitchen with a large farm table near a window that looked out onto a small garden in back. She poured them both a cup of coffee and sat down by the window. She rested her feet on the chair beside her and Cole sat down on the other side of the table.

Cole didn't seem to notice how the daylight revealed the lines around Lila's eyes hidden before by make up and the low lights of the speakeasy. Her bobbed hair, combed straight before, was in a disarray of soft curls and the sun picked out the silver highlights among them.

"How's the circus?" she asked.

"I quit," Cole told her.

"How come?" she asked curiously.

"Got tired of it. I wanna' do something else for a change," he said.

"What did you have in mind?"

"I don't know. I'm good with my hands," he said.

"Yeah, I know," Lila replied, grinning.

"I thought maybe you could give me a job," Cole said, not smiling at her remark. He was starting to feel panicked, out of control.

Lila saw the tenseness in his jaw. "I could probably find something for you," she said. "You want some breakfast?"

"Sure," he said, only to change the subject, but when she set a plate of eggs and toast in front of him, he practically inhaled it.

"Don't they feed you at the circus?" she asked as she lit a cigarette and leaned against the kitchen counter watching him.

"I left two days ago," he said and his jaw tightened again. "You should have come here sooner," she said softly. She put out her cigarette and walked around to the back of Cole's chair. She smoothed down some strands of his sandy hair then slid her hands gently down his chest. "You look tired. Come on, let's go upstairs."

Cole stood up and followed Lila obediently out of the kitchen and up the stairs. He was dead tired and he didn't want to think anymore. He would have given anything to have his mind cleared of thoughts.

Lila's bedroom was similar in taste to the downstairs, warm and comfortable but decorated almost entirely in soft pastels, including the chain pattern quilt on her bed.

Cole stood as Lila pulled off his t-shirt and unbuttoned his dark cotton trousers. She saw the black hood stuck in his pocket and pulled it out before he could stop her.

"What's this?" she asked as the empty holes of the mask dangled eerily from her hand. "Planning to rob a bank?

"It was part of a circus act," Cole replied, trying to sound nonchalant as he took the hood from her and jammed it back in his pocket.

"Sounds interesting," she murmured as her arms circled his waist and her robe fell open. She pressed against him and he felt the warmth of her body.

He needed her. He needed to forget. His mind was becoming filled with thoughts of the circus, his mother and...

Lila kissed Cole and pulled him into bed. She felt his urgency as they began to make love, but then he gradually slowed and became completely still above her.

"What is it?" she asked.

His arms, braced against the mattress, began to shake. His eyes filled with tears and he looked down at Lila as he spoke in a barely audible whisper. "I'm sorry."

Lila pulled him close. "It's okay. It's okay."

She had known something was wrong in the kitchen, but she figured he was just a mixed up kid trying to figure things out. But these aren't the tears of a kid, Lila thought. This was a man trying to hide his pain, to control his quaking body.

"It's really okay, Cole. Trust me," she said gently. She gripped him tightly as his body became racked with sobs. She stroked his back and continued murmuring soothing words. She was glad he had come to her, be it for sex or solace. She was prepared to give both, especially when she saw how different he was now. He was definitely not the cocky young man that had seduced her less than a week ago. The man lying in her arms had been humbled by some experience, and it made her want to help him. Cole's body gradually relaxed and his breath became slow and even. Lila held him in her arms as they slept into the afternoon.

Chapter Sixteen: The Finishing Touch

Anastasia sat in her train car waiting for the Olympic to finish pulling up stakes. She was definitely feeling more relaxed now than she had in the last two days. The Olympic had put on good shows despite the aftermath of the fire. The Executioner was gone and so was Sepia. Cole was her only remaining concern. The train was leaving in an hour, but she was convinced that he'd return in time. Whether he'd been with Sepia or not, he would come back. He had run off before and always returned. Anastasia recalled with relish her fortune in walking by Billy's wagon earlier that day and overhearing Rosie explain to Billy the relationship between Sepia and the Executioner clown. "He's her real father," Rosie had said. "I'm sure of it." Anastasia couldn't wait to tell Cole. Her thoughts were interrupted when someone knocked on her door.

"Who is it?" she called out.

"Sepia," came the answer back.

Anastasia's head whipped around and she stood up. She slowly went to the door, opened it and found Sepia standing in the dark, exactly as she had first seen her, hair tangled, her clothes disheveled, and with dark smudges under her eyes.

"I need to talk to you," Sepia said.

"Come in," Anastasia replied, glancing around to see if anyone had noticed them. She made no pretense at welcoming Sepia back or being glad that she was okay. She already guessed that Sepia would know it was false sentiment.

"Where's Cole?" Anastasia asked coldly.

"I don't know," Sepia answered.

"You weren't with him?" Anastasia asked.

"Yes, but not anymore. I'm trying to find him. I thought maybe you would know where he is."

"So, he left you," Anastasia said.

"Yes," Sepia said again.

"Then why are you looking for him? He obviously doesn't want to be with you," Anastasia said. She was gaining control, getting a feel for what to do now. Sepia was clearly upset.

"I...need to see him...to talk to him," Sepia said, her eyes filling with tears.

"You're in love with him," Anastasia said.

"Yes."

"Yours isn't the first heart he's broken, or the last. You better start forgetting about him right now. Are you back to stay?"

"I don't know," Sepia answered.

"Billy is not going to be happy to see you, Bruno either. You see, they found out certain things about you."

"What things?" Sepia asked, confused by the shift in the conversation.

"I really shouldn't be the one to tell you," Anastasia admitted, pursing her lips. "Rosie is the one who knew it all.

She should have told you."

"Told me what?"

"Why don't you sit down? I think you should know the truth." Anastasia waited until Sepia took a seat on the couch. "It seems that Bruno is not your real father."

"What?" Sepia asked in disbelief.

"Your mother was with another man before him," Anastasia explained, repeating what she had heard. "They were lovers. They were going to run off together, but the man was in a train accident, an accident that left him with a badly scarred face. Can you guess who that might be? "

"What are saying?" Sepia asked incredulously.

"I'm trying to tell you that freak rigger, the Executioner clown was your real father," Anastasia said.

"You're lying!" Sepia said, her voice full of shock and horror.

"Am I? Your mother left him after his accident. She was already pregnant with you, so she had to find a man who would have her. She probably tricked Bruno into marrying her, even though she didn't love him. Your mother was a cruel person."

"No," Sepia said, overwhelmed by what Anastasia was saying. It couldn't be true! Even as she denied it though, she knew there was something to what Anastasia said. Sepia knew her mother did not love Bruno. She had always known it.

There was also some truth to what Anastasia said about the Executioner. She remembered how he had looked at her as if she reminded him of someone, someone he had loved and lost. But still, it didn't mean that he was her father! He couldn't be her father. He had tried to... No, she told herself. Cole said Anastasia had gotten the Executioner to cut the trapeze.

"You made him hurt me," Sepia said.

"Who told you that? Cole?" Anastasia laughed. "Cole would say anything. We had an argument and he left angry. Cole is totally unreliable. You should know that by now," Anastasia said. She was wrapping Sepia perfectly around her little finger.

Sepia hated to admit that Anastasia was right about Cole. But more devastating now was what Anastasia had said about the Executioner.

"But, if he was my father, why would he want to hurt me?" Sepia asked painfully.

"Maybe he didn't even know who you were. He was mixed up in the head. Anyway, it doesn't matter anymore. He's dead. He was killed in the fire."

"Fire? What fire!?" Sepia asked. She was mixed up herself and beginning to lose touch with reality.

"The night you left, during the storm, the Menagerie was hit by lightning. The Executioner was trapped in the fire." Anastasia watched as everything that she had told Sepia began to sink in.

"Billy is in a mess because of you. He even called the cops to find you. He thinks his luck has gone bad, what with the fire and a man dead. He'd just as soon not see your face around here again. Bruno knows you were with Cole. He doesn't want you back either. Frankly, I think it's best if you leave."

"I...don't know where...to go," Sepia said in a total stupor.

"I could give you some names," Anastasia offered. She walked over to her desk. "You know what your problem is? You tried to make it to the top too fast. If you really want to be a circus star, you've got to pay your dues. You've got to work your way up like I did. I'll give you the name of somebody right here in Chicago. It's where I started."

"Thanks," Sepia murmured absently.

Anastasia had done it. Sepia had gone from thinking Anastasia had plotted to kill her to thinking Anastasia was her only friend. Sepia had also forgotten about Cole. She was so consumed by what Anastasia told her that there was no room for her to think about finding Cole. Anastasia was right. She could not stay at the Olympic. She couldn't face Billy after what she'd done. She could not face her father either. Her father. He wasn't even her father. She would rather die than see Bruno now.

Anastasia picked up a circus handbill and wrote a name on it. She gave it to Sepia saying, "Tell him I sent you." Then she guided Sepia to the door.

"Good luck. I'll try to let you know if things smooth over. Maybe you'll make it back here someday."

She opened the door and Sepia stepped off the train. "Things are never as bad as they seem," Anastasia reminded her, smiling.

Sepia nodded and walked off into the darkness completely dazed. She headed away from the train then stopped and looped back. She found Billy's train car and stepped aboard. Anyone walking by might have seen her through the lit window standing at Billy's desk writing a note, but everyone was still busy breaking down the show. The letter she left on Billy's desk was written in a wobbly hand and read: "Dear Billy, Sorry for the trouble I caused you. I'm leaving for good. Sepia."

She slipped back out of Billy's car and left the circus grounds in the dark of the night, hearing the tinkling strains of the calliope fading in the distance.

Chapter Seventeen: Hit The Road

By ten o'clock the speakeasy was packed. Cole stood behind the bar; washing glasses in a tub of warm soapy water, his thoughts miles away. The Olympic's last show would be over by now and he could almost hear the clacking of the wooden seats being folded flat as the Big Top was dismantled. He pulled a handful of shot glasses out of the washtub, set them on a towel, and began to wipe them dry. He tried to concentrate on the task at hand, but the work was mindless and his thoughts flew back to the circus.

The Olympic was leaving Chicago, taking with it the two women that gripped his heart and twisted it inside him. He knew it was best that he was away from them both, but he also guessed that physical distance would not wipe away their hold on him. He still felt mainly hurt and shock when he thought of his mother. She had made it devastatingly clear how she felt about him and it stung like the lash of an animal trainer's whip. Now, any caring memory he had of her vanished, leaving him only with a dark wound of rejection. If it were possible for Cole to be objective, he might have seen that his mother was scared, so scared that she was willing to destroy the bond between mother and child. But

Cole could not be objective. He saw only that his mother, who he thought had protected him out of love, had only been protecting herself. He was convinced now that when she lied to the police about his father's death, it wasn't to save Cole, but to stop her name from being dragged through the newspapers. All the times he had hoped that he was part of his mother's concern, he had only been secondary in her thoughts. It made him feel worthless. If the woman from whose loins he sprang did not care about him, then he must not be worth caring about.

Besides being hurt, Cole was angry, but only on Sepia's behalf. He refused to recognize his own deeper anger at his mother. It smoldered inside him like a dried leaf near a flaming hearth, waiting to burst into flame.

Still, it was not thoughts about his mother that made him stop wiping the shot glass and grip it tightly instead. While the pain of his mother's rejection seared his heart, thoughts of Sepia burned his very soul and made the knuckles clenching the shot glass whiten.

Cole had never believed someone could touch him the way Sepia had done. Beneath the safety of the Executioner's mask, he had allowed himself to do things he had never done before. He had never talked to a woman like he had with Sepia. It had made him feel vulnerable, but also secure. Where his love for his mother was cluttered by self-doubt and fear, his feelings toward Sepia were amazingly clear. He felt a passion for her that was pure and intense, and it was only when he was not with her that his insecurities emerged. He was scared that his link with Anastasia made him unworthy of Sepia's love. He felt guilty that he hadn't protected her from his mother before the accident. He felt ashamed that it was his mother who had tried to hurt her. His fears had won out against his love, but it left him in constant turmoil, yearning for a different outcome.

"A penny for your thoughts," Lila said.

Cole looked up and saw Lila leaning against the bar watching him. He was still holding the same undried shot glass in his hand.

"Sorry," he said, quickly rubbing the glass dry and picking up another.

"That's not what I meant," Lila said.

The door of the speakeasy opened and a uniformed policeman entered. Cole stiffened, but noticed that Lila remained calm, even smiling as she walked over to the cop.

"Hi, Charlie, what brings you in off the street?"

"Just thought I'd see what kind of riff raff you're catering to lately," he told her. He glanced around the room, his eye resting on Cole a moment then he turned back to Lila. "Who's the kid?"

Lila turned briefly toward Cole who was keeping busy behind the bar.

"Him? I needed more help." She responded.

"Mmm," Charlie grunted, raising his eyebrows at her. "Where's he from?"

"I don't know. Why?" she asked innocently.

"We're supposed to be lookin' for a young stud from the circus, a young woman, too, for that matter," he explained.

"What'd they do? Let the tigers out of the cage?" she joked.

"I ain't sure. We're just supposed to bring them in for questioning."

Lila glanced over at Cole again. "He's not your man."

"Just askin'. You're too trusting, Lila. On the other hand, for somebody living on the edge, you always seem to keep out of trouble."

"You mean this place? You know my customers are mostly good working stiffs. We aren't harming anybody."

"If I thought otherwise, I wouldn't be standing here in uniform shooting the breeze, now would I?"

"That's what I like about you, Charlie. You're reasonable and you're willing to look the other way...for the right price," she added with a smirk.

"It don't pay to break the law...unless the law is unreasonable," he grinned.

"Like I said, you're a reasonable man," Lila said.

"Take care of yourself," Charlie said as he headed for the door.

"You, too," Lila answered as she watched him go. She turned towards the bar in time to see Cole breathe a visible sigh of relief.

Later, when they returned to Lila's house, she began making up a bed on the couch in the living room.

"It's not that I don't want you upstairs, but I think it's better this way," she said. "Can you tell me about her?" Lila asked as she billowed a sheet out over the sofa, then tucked it in around the cushions.

Cole looked at her, surprised.

"I wasn't born yesterday," Lila said. "You've fallen for some gal. Hard."

"She's just a kid. I, uh, helped her when she was in trouble," Cole said.

"And you're still worried about her?" Lila asked, guessing that Cole had done more than just help this young woman.

"I guess," Cole said.

"She's from the circus I take it?" Lila asked as she finished making the bed.

"She's a trapeze artist," he told her.

Already, Lila was impressed. "She must be very talented," Lila replied, smiling. She took a seat on one of the large floor cushions.

"She's incredible," Cole said a little too quickly.

Lila laughed. "You reveal your feelings faster than green grass through a goose. Is she why you left?"

"She's not the only reason I left," he said then looked away.

"Do you want to talk about it?" she asked gently.

Cole looked into Lila's soft, hazel eyes and they worked like a truth serum. He sat on the arm of the sofa and began telling her everything that had happened; about meeting Sepia, her quick rise to prominence and Anastasia's growing jealousy. He told her the truth about the accident and how he had helped Sepia escape from the circus. And when he had recounted the recent past, he did not stop. He began to tell her about his life, and in the very end, about his father's death.

Lila sat quietly listening, fascinated by the enormity of what Cole had been carrying around inside. When he finally finished, she stayed silent for a moment, letting all that he told her settle on them both.

"You left out one thing," she said and watched Cole knit his brow. "You haven't told me the real reason you came here."

"Yes, I did. I needed a job," he said a bit more bluntly than Lila wanted to hear. "And because I like you," he added quickly.

"I'm glad you added the second part," she laughed. "I'd hate to think you were just using me," she added grinning.

"I used to use women," Cole said very serious. "It was the

only thing I was good at."

"You were," she agreed.

"I'm not using you," he said.

"I know you're not, at least not in that way, but I do think you're using me just like I used you," she said. "We're both afraid to go after what we really want."

Cole looked at Lila with surprise. "What do you want?" he asked.

Lila laughed again. "You say that as if you think I've already got everything I could possibly want: a business, a home and great company! Believe it or not, I want more. I want a legit business, a house in the country, and a man that can think as well as act." She saw Cole wince. "That didn't come out like I meant it to," she went on. "I think you're terrific, Cole, but you're like I was at your age. The whole world is just opening up to you. I've already lived my youth and I'm ready to settle down a bit. And quite frankly, I don't want to risk falling for somebody who's in love with someone else," she said. Cole started to object, but Lila continued.

"The way I see it," she said, pulling her knees up and wrapping her arms around them, "You are never going to be able to have Sepia until you sort out this thing with your mother and the only way you're going to do that is to start feeling good about yourself. I might think that I could help you, but from what you've told me, there is something else you need and it isn't washing shot glasses in a speakeasy. My guess is that it involves you on a trapeze in a Big Top," she told him. "Don't get me wrong, I want you to stay here as long as you want, but I think in another week, you'll be ready to climb the walls."

Cole's jaw dropped open at her speech. How could she

know what he was thinking? He suddenly realized that she was one of the first people to see him as he really was. She also seemed to really care about him. It lent him a new confidence, the confidence to know she was also right about what he needed. It was time to go after something that was completely his.

"You are amazing," he said for lack of words to convey his admiration.

"Or completely nuts," Lila said looking up into his beautiful eyes. "On the other hand, I might decide to hold you captive here forever," she told him; almost wishing he'd give her a reason to do so.

Chapter Eighteen: Finding Work

Sepia woke to the cooing of pigeons waddling around her park bench. She was curled in a ball, pressed against the hard wooden slats at the back of the bench. She sat up and stretched the stiffness from her legs. Her stomach ached with hunger and her throat was parched from thirst. She rubbed her face in her hands, stood up and started walking toward the park's exit, passing other sleeping bodies curled on benches. In fact, every bench in Grant Park held a slumbering figure using old newspapers and rags for bedclothes. Around these prone human bodies scrambled what seemed like hundreds of sleek, grey squirrels scampering up and down the large oak trees lining the path.

Sepia left the park, crossed Michigan Avenue and headed into the city streets. It was warm already, and the heaviness of the air foretold the muggy day to come. She passed a cafe and the delicious smells drifting out the door nearly made her faint, but she stopped only to ask someone leaving if they knew the address written on the circus handbill. The man pointed down the street and waved to the left then Sepia thanked him and moved on.

The Depression had settled on the city like a heavy

blanket, and if Sepia looked desperate, she certainly did not look out of place. There were plenty of people walking the streets more destitute than her. At least Sepia held a piece of paper in her hand with the possibility of hope.

Sepia had replayed her conversation with Anastasia over and over in her mind as she made her way from the circus grounds to the city the night before. The things Anastasia told her made Sepia's whole life seem like a bizarre, sordid history filled with people who were monstrous in one way or another; her mother, Bruno, the Executioner.

The revelation about the Executioner was the hardest for Sepia to bear. She didn't think it was possible to believe any less of herself, but this news about her father brought her to a new low. The Executioner was her father and he had tried to kill her. Nothing could be worse than that, not her mother's death or Bruno's brutality, nothing. It made her feel totally worthless, numb.

Where once Sepia believed she could change her life, now she barely cared what happened to it. If she didn't care, why should anyone else? As if to drive home the point, she found herself standing across the street from the address written on the handbill, an old rundown theater, its ticket and advertising windows boarded up. It looked as if it had been closed for years.

"Can I help you, miss?" a voice asked behind her.

Sepia turned and saw a white haired man wearing a work apron standing in the doorway of a corner market.

"I...I'm looking for a Mr. Tyler. Mr. Roscoe Tyler," she said.

"You a relative?" the man asked.

"No," Sepia answered.

"Roscoe Tyler, huh? He's not so easy to find anymore.

He used to run that vaudeville house across the street, but it closed down three years ago. He got into another line of business after that."

"Somebody who used to work for him gave me his name. She thought maybe he could help me. Do you know where I can find him?"

"You might find him over at the barber shop, two blocks over, or at least somebody there could tell you how to find him. If you don't mind me sayin' though, I'd hate to see a nice girl like you get mixed up with his kind."

"Thanks," Sepia said, ignoring his last remark.

"Wait there a second, miss," the man said and disappeared into his store. He returned a moment later and handed her a small paper bag. "This might come in handy," he said.

Sepia thanked the man again and walked off. She opened the bag and found a hard roll, an apple and bottle of soda with the cap half-popped. She devoured the roll immediately and washed it down with the lukewarm soda. She kept the apple in the bag and held it under her poncho.

The barber shop was open and Sepia stepped into the pungent odor of witch hazel and aftershave. A heavyset man with his chin covered in lather filled one of the barber chairs. A thin, mustached man in a barber's shirt was just beginning to scrape away the soap with a straight edge razor when he looked up and saw Sepia.

"Can I help you?" he said.

"I'm looking for Mr. Roscoe Tyler," she said.

"Who sent ya?" the barber asked.

"A woman named Anastasia. Anastasia Artel," Sepia replied.

"You don't say," piped up the man sitting in the chair. He could barely see Sepia from his position, but he raised his head so he could get a better look. "Anastasia's a real big shot now, ain't she? I always knew she was gonna' do something big. That lady has more balls than an elephant," he said chuckling. "Come over here. What's your name?"

"Sepia Stefani," she said.

"Where you from, doll?"

"I'm from the circus, too," she answered.

"You are, huh? So, what did Anastasia send you to me for?"

"You're Mr. Tyler?" Sepia asked.

"Call me Roscoe."

"I need a job," Sepia said.

"I don't book circus acts no more," Roscoe said, smirking.

"Oh," Sepia said quietly.

"That don't mean I can't help ya," Roscoe said. The barber finished, and Roscoe sat up and wiped his chin off with a towel. "Look at that face, Artie. She looks like a fuckin' angel. Take that thing off you're wearin' so I can get a better look at ya."

Sepia pulled off the poncho shyly. Her costume was torn in several places and she tried to cover the holes with her arms. Both Roscoe and the barber gave her the once over, slowing at her long legs. Roscoe noticed one of the rips in her costume.

"You must of left in a hurry, eh? You in some kind of trouble?"

"Sort of," Sepia said.

"You ain't knocked up, are ya?"

"No."

"Okay, here's the deal. I've got certain clients that like to be entertained. You go out with them, eat, drink, have fun. They're happy. I'm happy. I'll pay you fifty a week."

"I don't understand," Sepia said dumbly.

Roscoe looked at Sepia like she was from Mars. "When businessmen come into town, they don't know nobody," he explained slowly as if she were a child. "We try and show 'em a good time, got it?" He snapped his fingers at the barber. "Artie, take her over to Flora's and buy her a dress," he ordered. He pulled a wad of money out of his pocket and handed some bills to the barber then he turned back to Sepia. "I got some clients comin' in tonight. You come along. There'll be some other girls there that can show you what to do. I gotta go." Roscoe suddenly stood up and disappeared through a door into the back room.

Artie looked at Sepia with a frown. "Come on. Let's go." He led her by the elbow toward the door and Sepia went along obediently. She was relieved to have someone tell her what to do. She had only been on her own for two days, but already she didn't want to think for herself anymore. She didn't want to think at all.

That evening Sepia found herself sitting in the back seat of a black touring car with two other women. Roscoe and his driver were in front. Sepia hadn't ridden in many automobiles, so the sharp turns and fast speed kept her off balance. She was scared. The dress she wore was so thin it made her feel naked. It was a flowery chemise and the silk slip beneath glided across her nipples and made them stand up beneath the fabric. Her new pumps with a leather strap pinched her feet and the bargain perfume the women had doused her in was making her feel sick.

The two women were jabbering away about their hair dresser. The one named Loretta was blond with sharp features that her plucked eyebrows and thick eye shadow did nothing to soften. The other woman's name was Ginny.

She had dark hair like Sepia's though shorter and parted on one side with a sweep of loosely permed waves curving along her face. She had round owlish eyes and wore thick makeup to cover her blemished skin. Both women were in their twenties, but their faces had the hardness of years spent in the company of fast crowds and cheap booze. Loretta was expertly fixing her makeup in the mirror of her powder case despite the twists and turns of the car. She covered her lips in cherry red and drew perfect lines of kohl black along each eye lid. The women tried to include Sepia in their conversation, but she had nothing to offer so they finally gave up.

Sepia stared at the passing sights of the city. It was dark and the street lights and store signs streaked by her view, slightly distorted through the scratches in the isinglass window. She couldn't help noting that it must be around show time wherever the Olympic was playing now, St. Louis she remembered Billy saying. Her heart began to thump. She shouldn't be here. She had no idea who these people were or where they were going. The women's incessant chatter rang in her ears and the men in the front seat became huge, dark blobs wafting the smell of cheap cologne and cigar smoke. Sepia wanted to get out of the car. She gripped the door handle in a panic, feeling that if she stayed in the car one more second she would suffocate. Just as she was pulling the handle back, the car slowed to a stop in front of a hotel. Ginny nudged Sepia and she opened the door. Roscoe got out and started up the front steps of the Palmer House Hotel. Sepia stepped out on the sidewalk and took a deep breath of the cool night air. She could run away now and go somewhere else, any place, back to the woods if she had to. She turned away from the hotel, but Loretta hooked her elbow and pulled her toward the steps.

"Come on honey, don't keep Roscoe waitin'," she warned.

The lobby of the Palmer House had a marble floor and a long, drop crystal chandelier suspended from the ceiling. Sepia was briefly distracted from her fear as she stared at the velvet upholstered chairs and the large oil paintings on the walls then two men came walking toward her and her stomach tightened.

Both men were middle-aged. One had a paunch like Roscoe's and a large bulbous nose, and the other man was short and trim with a mean mouth and beady eyes. The larger man got to Sepia first and took her arm, smiling.

"What's your name, honey?" he asked, staring at her breasts.

"Sepia," she answered, blushing.

"My name's Joe," he said, stirred by the flush in her cheeks.

They followed the others toward the dining room. Sepia realized that Loretta must be Roscoe's girlfriend as she leaned on his shoulder comfortably.

They all walked into the Empire Room, an opulent dining hall filled with tables fanned around a shiny, wood parquet dance floor. The maitre d'hotel showed them to a choice spot and they sat at a circular table. At the back of the dance floor, a full live orchestra played the new popular hit "Night and Day". Roscoe and the other two men immediately began talking business and the women discussed their shopping preferences. The hotel strictly obeyed the law, so the group sipped alcohol free cocktails and listened to the music.

Sepia looked around at the other patrons eating dinner,

laughing, and enjoying themselves, all of them dressed in tasteful evening attire. The flapper look was passé as women opted for a more sophisticated style of broad, padded shoulders, slender hips and long, clinging evening gowns. Hair, too, was longer and more loosely waved. Sepia unintentionally fit the fashion with her small bosom, slim waist and shoulder length hair, and she caught the glances of more than one man around the room. In fact, she couldn't help noticing that one of them kept staring at her, though she tried to avoid looking in his direction. He was in his early forties with thick black hair and a hint of silver at his temples. His eyes were dark also, and his chiseled features and fit body were enhanced by an impeccably tailored suit. An attractive, platinum-haired woman with an upturned nose and large, blue eyes accompanied him. She was smoking a cigarette and looked very bored. Even as Sepia tried to listen to the conversation at her table, she could feel the man's gaze on her from across the room.

"Did you bet on the Cub's game today, Joe?" Roscoe asked Sepia's date.

"Sure. Made fifty bucks," he answered. "I'll bet a grand we play the Yankees again for the series."

"Only a sucker would bet against the Babe, Gehrig and Combs," Eddie scoffed. The others nodded in agreement.

Roscoe ordered dinner for them all and though the food was delicious, Sepia ate very little. During the meal, an announcer wearing a black tuxedo brought a microphone to the middle of the dance floor and stood it before him. "Ladies and gentlemen, the Empire Dining room would like to present a lady whose voice will break your heart, Miss Betty Frazer."

The audience clapped as the lights dimmed and a woman

walked into a spotlight. She was dark-skinned, in her thirties, dressed in a white gown with her hair pasted close to her head. As the first black woman invited to perform in the hotel, Betty Frazer intended to make sure people understood what they'd been missing. The moment she opened her mouth, the room became hushed by her powerfully pure notes even as she slid them together in a bluesy melody. It was a new tune called "Stormy Weather", but it immediately grabbed the audience with its sad, haunting theme.

Sepia had never heard a live nightclub singer, and at first she was simply awed to see such talent and hear the music coming from the woman's mouth, but the soul of the song began to sink into Sepia's heart and it touched the pain she had buried there. "Can't go on, everything I had is gone, stormy weather. Since my man and I ain't together, keeps rainin' all the time."

Cole returned to her thoughts full force even as she tried to push them away. She instantly felt the softness of his warm mouth, the musky smell of his chest, and the touch of his large hands. She remembered how he held her gently in his lap that night in the woods. She hadn't even known it was him, but now she would remember forever.

"Don't know why there's no sun up in the sky. Stormy weather"…

Sepia looked down and blinked a teardrop onto her dress, darkening the fabric against her slip. The music was killing her and she could not listen anymore. She abruptly stood, searched for an exit and quickly headed for it. Roscoe snapped his fingers for Loretta and Ginny to follow.

Sepia found herself confused in a hallway until a bellboy pointed to a door and she entered a powder room. She walked into an empty stall, closed the door and sat on the toilet seat. A wave of emotion overwhelmed her and she hugged herself to try and stop it. She took long, slow, deep blowing breaths, rocking herself, but the pain rose in her chest and a loud sob escaped.

It felt foreign and retched then she remembered where she'd heard such a sound before. She'd once seen a mother Chimpanzee have her baby wrenched away and shoved in a cage on a truck. The screams of both mother and baby were the primal cries of hurt and grief, hearts breaking.

The powder room door opened and she heard the clack of high heels. Loretta called her name.

"Are you okay, honey?"

Sepia dug her fingernails in her arms, gripping the pain and forcing it back down inside her. "Yes," Sepia answered in a garbled voice. She heard Loretta whisper something to Ginny.

"We'll wait here for ya, sugar," Ginny called out.

Sepia was trapped and she knew it. She had nowhere to go and no one to help her. She slowly reached over and gathered some sheets of toilet paper, dabbed at her eyes and wiped her nose. She then cleared her throat, stood up and finally emerged from the stall.

Loretta and Ginny were seated at a long mirror fixing their make-up. As they powdered their noses and foreheads, they discussed what couldn't be said at the table.

"What do you think?" Loretta asked.

"Does it matter?" Ginny frowned. "Ah, Eddie's okay. I bet he's cheap though. Are we gonna stick together tonight?" she asked.

"Roscoe wants to head over to the club for awhile then we're goin' back to his place," Loretta answered.

"Good. I want to get Eddie good and drunk," Ginny

announced with a smirk. She looked up and saw Sepia through the mirror standing behind them. "You wanna borrow my compact?"

"No, thanks," Sepia answered.

"Roscoe said you just came to town," Loretta said, trying to be friendly.

"Yes," Sepia replied, searching for something else she could add. "I knew somebody that used to work for him. Anastasia Artel."

"Hmm, never heard of her," Loretta said.

"I have. Ain't she a circus star?" Ginny asked.

"About the biggest there is," Sepia answered.

"Are you from the circus, too?" Ginny asked, interested.

"Yes," Sepia replied, feeling uncomfortable about the way the conversation was going.

"What did you do?" Ginny persisted.

"Trapeze. I was a flyer," Sepia answered quickly.

"Holy cow, that's really somethin'," Ginny said, clearly impressed. "I love the circus! My daddy always took me when I was a kid. One of the only times I saw him sober," she said with a sad laugh. "So, how'd ya end up here if you don't mind my askin'?" Ginny said.

"I don't want to talk about it," Sepia replied.

Ginny and Loretta exchanged glances, but didn't say anything more.

"Joe's a pretty nice guy," Loretta said changing the subject to Sepia's date.

"Yeah, I was with him once. He was okay," Ginny agreed.

The women finished their primping and the three of them returned to the table. Just as they sat down, the dark-haired man from across the room approached the table with his blond companion on his arm.

"Hello, Roscoe, Joe, Eddie," he said "Ladies," he added nodding his head toward each of them and lingering on Sepia, then he touched the platinum-haired woman's arm. "You all know Kay," he said. Everyone said hellos.

"How's business, Tony?" Roscoe asked.

"Could be better, but I can't complain," Tony replied.

"Come on over to the club later," Roscoe said.

"We might do that," Tony replied, again resting his eyes on Sepia before he took Kay's elbow and led her away from the table.

Joe leaned over to Sepia. "That guy's loaded. He owns a whole stockyard."

Sepia nodded her head as she watched him go.

A short car ride brought Sepia and her group to Roscoe's club located in the back of a billiard hall with the entrance from the alley. It was a speakeasy to be sure, but classier than most with art deco furnishings, elegant walnut veneered booths and etched glass sconces. It wasn't that Roscoe had particularly good taste, but he had emptied the vaudeville theater of its furnishings before it closed down and they added a unique flair to the surroundings. Roscoe led them to a corner booth where Sepia sat wedged between Joe and Eddie.

Drinks were immediately brought to the table. Roscoe toasted their health, and Sepia took her very first slug of hard liquor. The straight gin burned her throat and tasted like bitter metal. She coughed and nearly spit it back out. The others watched her and laughed, surprised at her innocence. Sepia took smaller sips after that and quickly understood why people learned to like it. The gin formed a warm fire in her belly that gradually spread to the rest of her body. It wasn't much longer before she even found herself smiling at Joe's attempts to be funny. Most of his jokes centered on the Depression.

"Hey, did you hear the one about the guy who was about to register for a hotel room, and the clerk asks him, 'For sleeping or for jumping?'" He laughed and slapped the table with his hand, then put his arm around Sepia's shoulder and squeezed it. She downed her glass and another round was brought. Various clienteles stopped by Roscoe's table to say hello. A live jazz band was playing in the background and Ginny pulled Eddie up to dance.

When Loretta couldn't get Roscoe on his feet, she persuaded Joe to dance with her. They moved off to join the others in the middle of the room. As Sepia watched the couples dance to a lively tune, the music filled her head and seemed to echo through her brain. Two drinks on an empty stomach were taking effect, and not an unpleasant one. Sepia was grateful to have her senses dulled and she didn't mind the off-kilter way she was seeing things. She wondered how liquor could make people mean like it did Bruno. She could barely make a fist. As she leaned her head back against the booth, someone slid into the seat beside her.

"You're looking quite happy...and beautiful I might add," Tony murmured in her ear. He was by himself and when Sepia glanced around the room, Kay was not visible.

"Glad you made it Tony," Roscoe said. "Freddy!" he called and the waiter went for another round of drinks.

"So who is this lovely lady," Tony said.

"Sepia. Sepia...," Roscoe floundered, forgetting her name.

"Stefani," Sepia answered for him.

"Sepia. What an interesting name," Tony said. "Like the color of your eyes," he noted.

"That's what my... mother used to say," Sepia replied, surprising herself with the memory.

"Would you like to dance, Sepia?" Tony asked.

"I don't know how," she said.

"You don't have to. You just follow me," he told her as he took her hand.

Sepia would have preferred to stay in the booth alone, but she allowed Tony to help her to her feet. She was shocked by how unsteady her legs felt, but Tony put his hand at her waist and deftly guided her to the dance floor. Facing her, he placed her arms on his shoulders then his hands circled her and pulled her close. She hadn't noticed until now that the music had changed to a slow, swinging melody.

"How'd you get mixed up with Roscoe?" Tony asked.

"Everybody keeps asking me that. What's so bad about him anyway?" Sepia asked, her voice sounding a bit slurred.

"Nothing if you're into bootlegging, extortion and gambling," Tony laughed. "I personally have nothing against him," he added with a smile.

"A friend sent me to him. I thought he ran a theater," Sepia explained.

"Are you a performer?" Tony asked.

"I used to be," Sepia said.

"But not a dancer," he teased. "I knew there was something special about you though, something besides those brown eyes," he said as he whirled her around once, then continued his slow rocking lead.

"Joe said you were loaded," Sepia said dizzily.

"He's right," Tony laughed. "Does that impress you?"

"I'd rather be famous," she said.

"Maybe I can help you. I know a lot of people. You wanna' get out of here?" he asked, glancing around.

"What about Roscoe?"

"I'll take care of Roscoe," Tony said. "Come on."

Tony led Sepia out the alley door and down the street to a sleek, new Cord sports car with a hood that resembled a coffin and large pipes curling out of both sides. He opened the passenger door and she got in then he went around and slid into the driver's seat. The car pulled away from the curb with a rumbling exhaust and drove off into the night.

Sepia was feeling incredibly sleepy as Tony smoked a cigarette and weaved the car through the city streets. She wanted to close her eyes, but every time she did, the car made a turn and jolted her awake. Tony finally pulled up in front of the Stevens Hotel, a thirty story brick building on Michigan Avenue, its 18th century French architecture lending it a warm elegance. Tony got out, came around to Sepia and helped her out of the car. A valet took his keys and Tony led Sepia into the lobby where they crossed the marble floor to the elevators.

As they waited, Sepia stared up at clouds painted on the ceiling and faces of cherubs smiling winsomely down at her. The elevator door opened and Sepia leaned into Tony's chest to steady herself as the operator took them up through the building to the top floor. The doors opened and Tony walked Sepia to an entrance that he unlocked with his room key. She stepped into a luxurious penthouse and instantly made her way to the walls of windows that looked out over the city in one direction and at vast dark space in the other.

"Like the view?" Tony said coming up beside her and following her gaze toward the lake.

She nodded and he left her, walking over to a bar where he poured them both another drink. He brought Sepia's back to her as she stood at the window still staring out.

"Here."

"I better not," Sepia said. "I think I drank too much."

"I won't hold it against you," Tony assured her.

Sepia took the glass and drank a sip. "It tastes so much better now than at first," she said drowsily.

"Lots of things are better after you get used to them," Tony said. He took her glass away and set it down on the window sill. He lifted her chin and kissed her lightly on the lips.

Sepia closed her eyes, but the room started spinning, so she opened them again. "What about Kay?" she said.

"She's just a friend," he said then he pulled Sepia into his arms and kissed her again. Tony's mouth was so warm, his arms so enveloping that when he picked her up and carried her into the bedroom, she didn't resist. He laid her down on the bed and pulled the covers from under her. She was so tired and it felt so good to lie down, she told herself. The room was dark, but moonlight filtered through the glass curtains at the window and cast a single ray of light across the room. As if in a dream, Sepia watched Tony pull off his hand-painted silk tie, unbutton his custom made shirt, slip off his Italian leather shoes, and step out of his tailor made trousers until he stood naked next to the bed. Sepia wasn't sure she wanted what was about to happen, but her leaden body could not seem to move. Tony leaned over the bed, climbed on top of Sepia and kissed her again, this time sliding his tongue into her mouth. She tried to push him away, but her arms were like two heavy stones. He lifted her dress over her head in one motion and tossed it on a chair then he crawled back on top of her naked body.

She was so firm and lithe beneath him. His mouth covered

hers and he thrust his tongue in, roving and penetrating, mimicking his next move. That came shortly after, when his knee pushed open her thighs and he shoved himself inside her. Sepia wasn't ready, but it was clear now that Tony didn't care either if she was ready, or if she gained any pleasure from his pursuit.

As his tongue continued to plunge into her mouth, he ground himself into her body, pushing his full weight onto her, crushing her chest. Sepia was totally overwhelmed now, not only with a desire to stop him, but from the sheer physical effort to breathe. Tony never noticed that her throat was gagging and her breath was coming in too quick of gasps. The combination of the alcohol robbing the oxygen from her brain and Tony forcing it from her lungs, made a dark cloud pass before her eyes and she blacked out. Completely absorbed in his own pleasure, Tony didn't notice that Sepia had gone limp beneath him. He finished quickly and rolled off of her in sweaty relief.

When he realized that she had passed out, he figured it was from the liquor and decided not to waken her. He climbed out of bed, stood up and dug his cigarettes out of his coat pocket. He opened his monogrammed case, lit a cigarette with his silver lighter and stood watching Sepia in the moonlight. She looked so young now with her hair spread across the pillow. He needed to have that feeling of youth near him.

Sepia didn't know that she had met Tony at a turning point. He had reached that stage where the rest of his life was laid out before him with no probable struggles and no mystery either. The son of a meat packer, he had inherited a successful business that even the Depression hadn't threatened significantly. Divorced from his wife of twelve years and with no children, he found himself needing to be revitalized, to know that this wasn't all there was. He had begun to go out more and hang around with increasingly shadier characters, Roscoe being one of them. The underworld held an excitement that his legitimate life did not. He began to drink more and stay out later with each venture into the night. So far, his night life hadn't cut into his work, and it made him feel powerful that he could do both. He began to pick up looser women, too. They were more apt to please him in bed and make him feel virile.

When he spotted Sepia with Roscoe's group, she was clearly a diamond in the rough. She wasn't a mob girl, but she wasn't exactly legit either. There was classiness about her, yet also something mysterious. He was surprised and intrigued by her innocence. She was shy and vulnerable, yet charming in an open and honest way, a total contrast to the loose, blowzy women he'd hung around lately.

As he stared down at her lying peacefully on the bed, he sensed that she needed protection, that she was out of her element and still very immature. On the other hand, she had to grow up someday, and there was a certain power derived from showing her the way.

Chapter Nineteen: Tony

Sepia woke the next morning, embarrassed to find herself naked in Tony's bed, and with very little recollection of how she got there. Tony had already showered and shaved and was knotting his tie in front of the dresser mirror. Sepia wanted to get up, but her clothes were lying too far away to reach without leaving the bed, and her head was thumping like a tent stake driver.

"Good morning," Tony said, glancing at her through the mirror as he cinched his tie. "I'm going into the office, but I'll be back around noon. Call room service on the telephone and they'll bring some breakfast." He walked over and sat on the edge of the bed, putting his hand over hers. "I want you to stay here." Before she could respond, he kissed her forehead, then got up and disappeared through the bedroom door.

Sepia sat against the headboard with her knees drawn up to her chest and the sheet held tight against her shoulders. The quiet in the room was unnatural. She had never experienced such silence. No voices, no movement, no noises of any kind could be heard in that high, insulated space of the hotel. It was a deprivation that both fascinated and terrified her. For the first time in her life, she was completely alone. There was nowhere she had to go, nothing she had to do. She was left with nothing but time to think, yet everything that came into her mind was everything she did not want to ponder. Her throat tightened and her fingers gripped the sheet still pulled around her. She must not, must not let the thoughts come, and most of all, she must not listen to her heart.

Sepia slid quickly out of bed and walked into the adjoining bathroom. Her head was still throbbing and her bladder was near bursting. She sat on the toilet and stared around at the gleaming, tiled floor and the shiny white porcelain. The room was still humid from Tony's shower and she saw his damp towels hanging on the rod. She looked over at the knobs marked hot and cold, reached out, and broke the silence with a burst from the shower. Within seconds, the steam was rising from the spraying water and after adding some cold, she stepped in. As she turned her body under the hot flow of water, she felt a million miles from her life before. In the circus, if she wanted to bathe with hot water, she had to have it brought boiling from the cookhouse, and poured into a large metal tub.

It was so odd what had happened, that she should be in this hotel room by herself. It was not at all what she had envisioned as an alternative to her life before. She remembered little about last night, but she knew Tony had had sex with her even before she felt the stickiness between her legs as she rose out of bed. It was not what she wanted, but she was beginning to realize that it was mostly what men wanted. Sepia remembered what Tony said about being able to help her. Anyone who lived like this must have influence. She had no other plan for what to do, and the thought of returning to Roscoe was not at all appealing.

She amazed herself at the thoughts that were running through her mind now: to stay and find out how Tony could help her, to sleep with him again if she had to, to use him. She had never been so calculating before and the two women from last night flashed in her mind. That was how they were, doing whatever was necessary to get what they wanted; money, food, shelter, clothes, jewelry, furs, status. Sepia told herself she would never be like them. She wanted more than that. She would only do what she had to until she figured out something else. She never considered that by then she might already be lost.

As the warm water rushed down her face and along her slender body, Sepia felt it wash away her conscience. As long as she could step into this shower every morning, she could do most anything. It was a cold, unemotional thought. It was also incredibly destructive.

When Tony returned, Sepia was dressed in the only outfit she owned, the dress Roscoe had bought her. She had no other possessions to her name. When Tony realized this, he turned right around and led her out of the hotel and down the block to a woman's dress shop and bought her three new outfits, one for evening and two for daytime. Sepia went along with it all quite naturally, used to being fitted for clothes. It was also exciting and seductive to have salespeople wait on her, then with a signal from Tony, watch them write up a sales ticket. She had little to say in the choices, but since she had no sense of the current styles, it was better that Tony expressed his apparent good taste. He seemed to enjoy it, too. The Pygmalion aspect of giving Sepia a new look gave him obvious satisfaction. He was attracted to her youth, but he wanted her to look womanly, mature enough to pass in a classy crowd.

The tailored styles he chose were perfect on her slim figure and small bust line. The evening gown was a simple but elegant white silk that clung to the subtle curves of her body. The other two dresses were practical but chic, a ubiquitous blue and white plaid with sashed belt and bow collar, and its match in style but in solid red. Sepia loved them. She was not shy at all about modeling for Tony. He could see that she was used to being looked at and that she came alive in front of an audience.

When Sepia accompanied him to a business function wearing the white gown that evening, Tony noticed that her charm and presence appealed to others as well. He was somewhat shocked to see how easily she moved in his circle of friends. She genuinely seemed interested in learning the most mundane aspects of his friends' businesses even from the most blowhard, boring of his peers.

What Tony didn't realize was that Sepia had never had a chance to talk to people about anything other than circus, and she was truly curious about the outside world. Almost everything she was experiencing was new and different, from the food she ate to the expensive scent she wore dabbed behind each ear. She was like a child in a candy shop and she tried everything offered to her; exotic appetizers, drinks, cigarettes. She quickly understood that Tony liked to socialize and that he could move easily from a normal group like the business function to the less legitimate crowd they ended up with later that night.

Tony drank a lot and his resistance to alcohol was high. Sepia knew she could not keep up with him, so she tried to find a drink she could sip slowly. She discovered that a gin fizz could be made to last an hour without being conspicuous. She was more subdued around the rougher crowd, but still listened intently as they talked about sports, business and politics. She learned that Charles Lindbergh's baby had just been found dead two months after being kidnapped and less than five miles from their home. She heard that Al Capone was making an appeal on his tax evasion rap from prison. She found that people were ecstatic that a man named Jack Sharkey beat the German Max Schmeling to bring back a world boxing title. She tried to keep her head clear of alcohol to hear all of these things, but even so, by the time they returned to the hotel, she could barely walk on her own. Tony supported her into the elevator and up to his apartment.

"You'll have to learn to hold your liquor, doll," he said affectionately, quite pleased with how the evening had gone.

"It happened before I knew it, not being able to walk I mean," she replied in a slurred voice.

"You'll get better at it," he said.

Just like the night before, Tony helped Sepia into the bedroom, let her down on the bed, but didn't undress her.

"You can get undressed by yourself tonight," he said.

She nodded, not wanting to admit what was about to happen. She dizzily got to her feet again and went into the bathroom. She closed the door behind her, went to the sink and looked into the mirror. Her eyes were bloodshot from smoke and the late hour. Her cheeks felt heavy and her throat ached from harsh, unfiltered cigarettes. She ran cold water over her wrists and splashed some on her face, and then she took a tumbler from its brass holder and drank a glass full. She was taking her time, hoping that when she returned to the bedroom, Tony would have fallen asleep, but when she finally stripped to her slip and opened the door, Tony was sitting up in bed, bare-chested and smoking a cigarette.

"I thought you had fallen asleep on the john on something," he joked. He patted the bed beside him.

Sepia climbed under the covers and saw that Tony was naked. He reached over, stubbed out his cigarette, turned off the light then immediately rolled on top of her. In a repeat of the night before, Sepia again suffered from too much alcohol and Tony's crushing weight, only this time she didn't pass out. Her lungs drew in just enough air to keep her conscious and she discovered what it felt like to have sex with Tony.

Despite his good looks and trim body, she was not physically attracted to him, but when she tensed up under him, it hurt. She tried to stop her muscles from tightening and found that if she concentrated on relaxing her body, she could almost forget where she was. If Tony had been the least bit sensitive, he probably could have aroused Sepia into wanting him. His lovemaking however, was too short lived and self-serving to give her any pleasure. After it was over, she rolled over and pretended to be asleep.

When Sepia woke the next morning, her head was pounding again. It was Saturday and Tony was still asleep next to her. She carefully slipped out of bed and went into the bathroom. She reached for the shower knob and blanked out the hammering in her ears with the sound of water, then stood under the hot spray for ten minutes without moving.

When she came out of the bathroom, Tony was on the phone ordering breakfast and when it arrived, he took out a bottle of gin from the living room cabinet and poured a shot into each of their glasses of orange juice.

"Hair of the dog," he said, then saw her perplexed look. "It'll help your headache," he explained.

Minutes after she drank her juice, she was grateful for whatever part of a dog had relieved the pounding in her head.

She put on one of her new dresses and stood at the window looking out toward Lake Michigan, barely visible in the mist that covered the city. Tony ate his breakfast from the coffee table in front of the couch as he read a morning paper in his bathrobe.

"Looks like the democrats are going to nominate this Roosevelt. Hell, why not? Guess we can't get into any more of a fix than we're already in."

"Nominate him for what?" Sepia asked turning from the window.

"President," Tony said with surprise. "Where have you been anyway, locked up in a closet?"

"No," she answered defensively.

"Where did you say you used to act or perform?" he asked.

"The circus," she answered quietly.

"No kidding," he said. "I thought you were in vaudeville or something. Circus, huh, so what'd you do?" he asked, more interested now.

"Trapeze," she said.

"Like the flying trapeze?" he asked, incredulous.

"Yes," she said.

"I'll be damned! Did you like it?" he asked.

"Yes," she answered, turning back to the window.

"So, why did you leave?" he finally asked.

"I don't want to talk about it," she said.

"Well, it sure explains that body of yours. I've never seen

muscles like that on a woman, not big I mean, but strong."

Sepia nodded.

Tony got up from the couch and headed back into the bedroom to dress. He called out to her.

"I'm going out to play golf with some buddies 'til late afternoon." He came back with his wallet. "Go out and buy yourself another dress for tonight. We'll go somewhere special." He pulled out a wad of bills and pressed them into her hand then he walked back into the bedroom.

Later, Sepia did leave the hotel and was glad to get out on the street in the fresh air. She had never felt so cooped up before. Despite the cramped living quarters at the circus, she didn't spend much time in them. She was used to being outdoors or under a large tent.

The mist had faded and the sun was out. Sepia began to walk the streets with no particular idea where she was going. She hadn't been in the city during the daytime since the morning she arrived looking for Roscoe. She had been caught up in her own depression then and she hadn't noticed the one that gripped the city. She was aware now of the number of people standing on the sidewalks. She had heard, of course, that the economy was bad, but she had only seen how it affected the circus box office. Now she noticed a man curled asleep in the doorway of a closed bank. She watched a woman rifling through a garbage can for breakfast. She saw a child gripping his mother's hand as they stood in a bread line that snaked around the block. Whole families stood in that line, the children wondering when they'd have a home again, and their parents wondering if a rich governor from New York would understand their troubles and bring them jobs. They had heard Roosevelt's pledge of a "New Deal", but it sounded more like politics than a real promise. All they could hope was that this bread line was as bad as it would get.

Sepia felt ashamed for her new dress and her luxurious life with Tony. Even though it seemed more like years, she and Bruno had walked through this city cold and hungry only two weeks ago. She passed the end of the bread line where a small girl stood clutching the back of her mother's leg. Sepia pulled out one of the bills in the pocket of her dress and stuck it in the little girl's chubby hand.

"Mama, look," the little girl said holding the folded bill up toward her mother. The woman glanced down in a reflex reaction then did a double take as she saw the twenty-dollar bill in her daughter's hand. She looked around, but Sepia had disappeared down the block.

She passed a vacant building and at first didn't notice the advertisements daubed on the deserted front. When she finally looked up, she froze in her tracks and stared into the eyes of Anastasia Artel gazing down at her. It was a lavish and colorful pose, Anastasia swinging on the roman rings, a charismatic smile on her face, surrounded in the background by various other performers of the Olympic. The poster had not faded in the sun and still leaped out boldly at the viewer. Sepia felt like a hammer had struck her chest and she quickly walked away. Tears stung her eyes and she gasped for breath. She walked faster and faster then broke into a run, not stopping until she reached the hotel and the safety of Tony's apartment.

Sepia drew the bottle of gin out of the cabinet and poured a large shot in a glass, then downed it quickly. The liquor burned her throat, but the moment it hit her stomach she felt the sensation of warmth that she knew would quickly rise through her body and dull her mind.

She poured another drink, finished that one and had still another. When Tony returned that afternoon, he found her sprawled across the bed asleep.

"Sepia!" he yelled, shaking her after he noticed the empty gin bottle on the nightstand. He heaved her up to a sitting position and she moaned.

"What the hell are you doing?!" he shouted, more perplexed than angry. She didn't seem the type to become a boozer.

"Come on, get up," he said as he stood her on her feet and walked her to the bathroom. With her eyes still closed, he turned on the shower, pulled off her dress and stood her under the flow of cold water.

"Ow!" she screamed, opening her eyes wide now.

"Stay there," he commanded then he went back into the bedroom and ordered coffee from room service.

Sepia wakened fully under the freezing water, and gradually began to sober up. She stepped out of the shower shivering, and rubbed her skin with a towel to bring back her circulation.

After a cup of coffee and a lecture from Tony about drinking during the day, Sepia put on the white silk gown and waited for Tony to shower off his sweat from the golf course and change into a suit. She rested her head on the arm of the couch as she sat in the living room. She was too groggy to feel much besides stupid for having been found drunk. She thought of her father and the thousands of times she had seen him in a similar condition. If she had abandoned her mother's path of destruction, she now seemed to be following Bruno's. She actually laughed out loud at the idea.

Sepia hadn't thought of Bruno much. He certainly wasn't one of the people who constantly sprang to mind when she couldn't help it. She wondered what he was doing now without her. He was most likely hitting the bottle hard. It made her laugh again. Bruno had no one to push around, no one to yell at...and no one to perform with. Her laughter stopped. Circus was Bruno's whole life. If Billy couldn't find a place for him, Bruno would end up on the street the same as the people she had seen that day. It was bad enough for a civilian to be out of work. It was death to a circus performer like Bruno. Sepia derived no particular pleasure from knowing that she might have destroyed him. It was not how she had wanted to break away. What she had chosen seemed a coward's way and she felt guilty for it. She looked toward the bottle of gin on the nightstand, but it was empty. Luckily Tony took her to a place that night where she forgot everything.

They ate a light dinner first at a small French restaurant. Tony tried to humor Sepia by telling her stories about his younger days in the meat packing business. He described the time he was locked in a meat freezer for two hours and how the piss in his pants had frozen him to the seat by the time someone rescued him. He told her about getting knocked out cold by a swinging cow carcass moving along a cable line. He revealed how he fainted dead away the first time he saw a cow bludgeoned with a mallet for slaughter. Sepia both smiled and cringed at his tales, but it did not stave off what was eating away at her mind—that she had run from everything she wanted.

She should have gone back and faced up to what happened, but every time she thought of the Olympic, she remembered what had driven her away. The memory of the Executioner made her sick with shame. He had wanted to kill her. She tried to remind herself that it was all because of her mother. She wondered how her mother and father had met and if it had really been as Anastasia said, that her mother didn't want him after he was disfigured. How could she have been so cruel?

They left the restaurant and drove to Roscoe's speakeasy. Sepia felt uncomfortable about seeing Roscoe, but apparently Tony had worked things out with him because they greeted each other warmly and Roscoe winked at Sepia good-humouredly.

"He's pretty slick, this guy," Roscoe said nodding toward Tony. "Steals away my new girl right from under my nose. But hey, what are friends for, right?" he added with a friendly snort.

Tony chose a booth at the center of the wall so they were near the action. People came and went from their booth, staying for a drink, swapping jokes, making bets, then moving on to another party. The din of voices and haze of smoke grew with the amount of booze consumed. Sepia had done her share to break the law, neatly finishing three martinis. Tony had been resting his arm on Sepia's shoulder and it grew heavy as his body relaxed into drunkenness.

A thin, pimply-faced man with greasy hair walked over and slid into the booth next to Tony and whispered something in his ear. Tony's eyebrows raised and he nodded his head. A few minutes later, he nudged Sepia and they got up to leave, following the thin man who Sepia learned was named Jimmy.

When they entered the alley, Jimmy led them to his car, a faded blue Chevy with a large dent in the passenger door. Sepia got into the back seat and Tony sat up front with Jimmy. They wound through the streets toward a section of the city Sepia had never been to, Chicago's small but bustling Chinatown.

Tony pulled up in front of what looked like a laundry. The sign above the door was written in Chinese characters and the stacks of brown paper packages and hanging suits in the window advertised the business inside.

An old woman was working through the night, but pretended not to see as Jimmy led Tony and Sepia past her, then down a flight of stairs to a closed door. He made a series of knocks on the door and it opened slightly. A face peered through the crack and after recognizing Jimmy, the door swung open to let them in.

The room they entered appeared as if it ran the length of several stores above. Metal warehouse lamps hung from the ceiling, casting eerie shadows on the large tapestries covering the walls. Sepia was amazed by the crowd of people lounging either on large square cushions arranged on the floor or on ornately carved rosewood bunks stacked three high against the walls. She noted curiously that the clientele were of various nationalities, skin color, and social class unlike the world above where separation was strictly defined. The atmosphere was also strangely subdued as most of the people actually appeared to be asleep. Low tables sat next to each cushion and on each table rested a small oil lamp under whose glass flue a flickering light was haloed by the smoke-filled air.

Sepia realized that the room was not smoky from cigarettes as she'd been accustomed to in the speakeasies. This smoke was bluer and the odor sweeter, like some kind of herb or flower. As a scratched recording of eastern music tinkled in the background, a Chinese man in a dark silk jacket and rounded hat moved slowly about the room carrying what looked like a fat wooden flute in his arms. Sepia guessed that it couldn't be a flute however, because instead of finger holes, there was a small bowl attached to the outside near the end of the tube. She saw that some of the people on the cushions were holding a similar tube as well. She watched a man rise up to his elbows, put one end of the tube to his lips and hold the other end so the bowl met the top of the flame in his oil lamp. Then he proceeded to suck on the end as if it were a tobacco pipe using his fingers to control the draw by opening and closing them over the other end of the tube.

She realized that a pipe was exactly what the device was when smoke curled out of the small bowl after the man stopped filling his lungs with whatever had burned there. He seemed to barely have time to rest the pipe on the table before sleep overcame him and he was forced to lie back on his cushion again.

The Chinese man walked over to Sepia, Tony and Jimmy and motioned for them to follow him. Sepia stared at the long, smooth braid hanging down the Chinaman's back as she trailed behind him to an empty set of cushions in the corner. Sepia gripped Tony's arm in the dim light as she knelt down on her cushion.

"What is this place, Tony?" she whispered.

"An opium den," he told her with a half smile of what seemed both anticipation and fear. He had lost interest in spending late hours drinking in the speakeasies. He was seeking a new thrill.

Before Sepia could ask anything more, the Chinese attendant knelt down and offered the pipe to Jimmy, letting him demonstrate for Tony and Sepia. Jimmy indeed took hold of the tube with an experienced hand and sucked on the tip in short puffs, inhaling the smoke until it filled his lungs. He kept the drug inside his body, letting it filter from his lungs into his bloodstream until he couldn't hold his breath any longer, then he slowly exhaled a wave of used sweet smelling smoke.

Tony was next to take a drag from the pipe. He began to inhale, and then coughed immediately from the different intensity of the opiate smoke. He followed Jimmy's example, taking small draws that made a strange clacking sound through the pipe.

Jimmy had already begun to feel the drug. A dreamy look filled his eyes and he sank back into his cushion. The attendant then handed the pipe to Sepia, but she waved it away. Tony exhaled and motioned for the attendant to give it back to her.

"Try it. Don't worry. It'll be okay," he said.

Even drunk, her brain warned her to be wary of this new experience, but when the attendant kept the pipe held out to her, she finally took it. She held the tip to her lips and took a small breath. It actually felt smoother than cigarettes and she wasn't even sure she'd gotten any of the smoke until a second later when she exhaled a stream of bluish haze. The attendant encouraged her to take several more puffs then he took the pipe, silently got up and moved on.

Sepia looked at Tony and saw that he had joined Jimmy in a transfixed state of apparent bliss, caring little if the whole world collapsed around them. Sepia felt frightened and alone until someone gently touched her. She turned to look, but no one was there and she suddenly forgot that she was by herself.

At first she couldn't tell if the drug was everywhere in her body or just in her brain telling her body it was, but she felt as if every cell of her being was invaded by a sensation that was so utterly peaceful that it brought tears to her eyes. She forgot where she was. She forgot Tony and Jimmy and the place they were in and her life before. She even forgot the ache in her heart for the person her thoughts refused to name anymore. She forgot flying. She was higher now than she'd ever been in a Big Top, higher than the clouds, floating in some kind of deep space that hugged her and kept her safe. She needed no love or closeness, no food or shelter. She was completely content and she never wanted to leave that space. She had some notion that her body was moving, but she had no idea that she was retching her dinner and whatever alcohol was left in her body into a bowl the Chinaman held under her chin. She felt no fears, no insecurities, no worries about the future, nothing but tranquility. It was heaven.

Tony slowly roused from his drugged state and tried to focus his eyes on his wristwatch. It was nearly 5 a.m. He turned to look at Sepia and started. She was lying face up across her cushion with such a distant and vacant look in her eyes that at first he panicked. He quickly leaned over and laid his head on her chest. Her heart was beating and she moaned slightly. Jimmy was wide awake already, finishing his lotus blossom tea and getting anxious to leave.

"Are you ready yet?" he asked Tony.

"I don't think I can walk," Tony answered with wonderment still filtering from his brain.

The Chinaman brought him a small bowl of tea and left one for Sepia. Tony tried to wake her with his voice, then later by shaking her, but it was apparent that opium gripped her tighter than it did others. He tried to force some tea down her throat, but it dribbled out the side of her mouth. The Chinaman brought over a small vial and placed it under her nose. Her head jerked to the side to avoid the strong ammonia scent, but it had an effect. Her eyes fluttered open and she reluctantly joined the real world again.

Tony sat her up and put the cup of tea in her hands. He helped her raise it to her lips and this time she swallowed. Her throat was dry from vomiting and the tea felt soothing. After another few minutes, Tony pulled Sepia to her feet and they joined Jimmy who was already heading for the door. Tony stopped to pay the man at the door then he let them into the hallway. They followed Jimmy up the stairway and through the store just as daylight broke on the streets outside. The prune-skinned old woman was still working in the laundry, but stared through them as if they were ghosts.

Tony spoke little during the ride back to get his car and then to the hotel. His only comment to Sepia was, "You liked it, huh?"

Sepia didn't respond and when they reached the hotel, she headed for the bathroom immediately, intercepting Tony's thoughts for a shower. She stood under the steady stream of water and tried to force herself to accept her surroundings, but the water felt too hot this time, and even after she lowered the temperature, she was stifling. The shower was no longer a refuge as the bathroom walls pressed in on her and she crumpled to the floor and began to cry. She wanted to run back to the opium den and return to that world of painlessness, but she realized stupidly that she didn't even remember where it was. She crawled out of the shower and found the next best thing.

Tony didn't seem to notice when Sepia came out of the bathroom with a towel wrapped round her and walked over to the liquor cabinet. Her hands were trembling as she pulled out a bottle of gin and poured herself a drink. Tony finally looked up from his newspaper and saw her.

"Hair of the dog," she mumbled.

"Okay, as long as you lay off the booze for the rest of the day," he commented. He watched her standing at the window as she downed her glass. She looked beautiful framed against the blue sky with her dark hair dripping down her back. Tony realized that he had wanted her last night but had been too overwhelmed by his first experience with opium. He was ready to make up for lost time now though and he called Sepia over to him.

"Sepia, come here," he said. She turned and walked over. "Sit down," he ordered. Sepia lowered herself onto the couch. They had never made love in the daylight, but Sepia recognized the look in his eye and a shiver ran down her spine. Tony was mostly pleasant to be with, but she needed to be drunk to have sex with him and even then it hurt.

"I want you to do me," he said abruptly and he began to unzip his trousers. The previous times they'd had sex she had been nearly oblivious, but now she was fully aware and definitely being asked to do something against her will. She felt humiliated and the gin that had warmed her stomach a moment ago threatened to come back up. Tony laid his head against the back of the couch, but when he reached over and pulled her toward him, she resisted.

"I can't," she said quietly.

"What's the matter?" he said, irritated. "You're the one who came out here half-naked and paraded yourself in front of me. What do you think I'm made of, stone?" then he changed his tone. "I want you, doll. Please." He stroked the back of her arm as he made his plea, but it only made her stiffen. Again his tone changed back to one of annoyance and growing anger. "Do it or get out, right now," he said.

Sepia wasn't even exactly sure what he had meant by "do me", but fear of leaving him made her lift the towel away from her thighs and start to climb onto him. Tony pushed her away.

"No, with your mouth," he said angrily, but with a slight look of surprise. He realized that she didn't understand what he meant her to do and that roused him even more. She hadn't lost all of her innocence yet. He grabbed a clump of hair at the back of her head and pulled her forward.

The shock of what he was asking made Sepia go rigid. Tony twisted his hand in her hair and showed his teeth under a curled smiling upper lip, and she whimpered in pain. She had never seen him angry, but she knew what anger made people do, and she was startled into submission. She did not want him to hurt her. She had learned the consequence of fighting back and the memory of Bruno's beatings flashed in her mind. It occurred to her now that she had been incredibly lucky that Bruno never sexually abused her, but she guessed that his anger toward her was of a very different nature and sex with her would have been just as revolting to him as it would have been devastating to her.

Sepia slid off the couch to her knees and crawled in front of Tony, tears welling in her eyes as he parted his knees and pulled her into his crotch. He let out a sigh when her lips closed around him, but he did not release his grip on her head. She still wasn't sure what to do, but his hand guided her, pulling her head up and down over him. Sepia suddenly realized what was coming and her eyes widened with resistance, but Tony held her tightly until the very end and she was forced to swallow the slippery, salty fluid. Tony finally pulled her off and let go of her hair. In a daze, Sepia managed to stand up, pour a new glass of gin and walk back into the bathroom.

She closed the door, took a gulp of gin and let it travel around her mouth and bubble in her throat before she spit it into the sink. She took another pull on the glass and swallowed. She looked in the mirror at her tear stained face and puffy cheeks and tried to find the remnants of the woman she had at least known if not especially liked before. She despised the person in the reflection and the amazing thing was that she was likely to become even more hateful. The woman who stared back at her was a coward, a weakling and a liar. She had promised herself she would never become like Loretta and Ginny, but in less than a week, she already fit their description to a tee. She was made for this kind of life. She had the ideal personality; insecure, stupid and scared. She should be lucky she ended up with somebody like Tony. She could have been washing her mouth out from Joe or Eddie or worse.

She could learn to handle it. She could maybe even learn to use it to her advantage. There was one way she was still different from Loretta and Ginny. They were tough. She could learn to be tough, too, to harden her heart and stop letting people hurt her. They could only hurt her if she let them. Someone had said that to her before, but her mind was half delirious trying to overcome what had just happened and she couldn't remember who. She decided to stop being a victim. Whatever she did from here on would be because she decided to do it and there would be no regrets. Regrets were for suckers.

A small voice inside warned Sepia that she had just rationalized her life away, but she chose to ignore it. She was, after all, willing to accept her own deceitfulness now. Lying to herself was necessary for her survival.

From that day on, Sepia began a life of mere existence. She slept most of the day then dressed to accompany Tony at night. She pretended to enjoy his friends and laugh at their jokes. She drank as much as she could handle and still stay on her feet, and she learned to cover the liquor on her breath after drinking during the day. The alcohol was affecting her body and soon her hard muscles began to dissolve into fat. Tony noticed the bulges in her tight fitting dresses and started getting after her.

She tried to remedy the problem by eating less, but it took its toll on her health. Between smoking and drinking, her complexion had gone from a healthy olive to a sickly yellow. Her shiny hair was growing dull and she developed a cough that wouldn't go away. Tony saw that the innocence had finally disappeared from her eyes and been replaced by a dullness. She gave him sex whenever he wanted it, even becoming adept in a mechanical way, and though he still enjoyed the youthfulness of her body, her charm was wearing off. She persuaded him to go back to the opium den as often as possible and they usually saw Jimmy there.

During this time, her nightmares returned about someone trying to suffocate her, but there was one difference. Where before, the person trying to hurt her had been an anonymous, shadowy figure, now Sepia felt as if she knew the person even if she couldn't say who it was. When she woke in a sweating panic, she had to calm herself on her own, embarrassed for disturbing Tony. He was not sympathetic to her late night outbursts. He saw them as simply another annoyance in the growing list of irritations she caused him.

One afternoon while Tony was at work, Jimmy stopped by the penthouse. Sepia was reluctant to let him in, but she shrugged her shoulders and opened the door.

"How are things?" he asked. His eyes darted around the penthouse as if he were casing it out.

"Okay," Sepia answered. "Tony's at work."

"Yeah, I know. That's why I came now," he explained.

Sepia eyed Jimmy suspiciously, but his demeanor, though nervous, did not appear dangerous. She had gotten used to his ferret-like behavior, dodging and darting his body as he moved and talked. He walked in and came right to the point.

"I noticed how much you like opium. If you get hooked on that stuff though, Tony will dump you fast. I got something you could try. It's not the same, but you don't have to go to Chinatown to get it." He reached in his pocket and brought out a small wooden box about two inches square. He opened it, licked his finger and dipped it into what looked like baby powder. His finger came back out and he held it toward Sepia. "Cocaine," he said simply.

Sepia had heard of cocaine by now in passing conversations at the speakeasies. She'd even met people whose business was selling it, but she'd never actually seen it. "So, what do you do with it?" she asked.

"Smoke it, snuff it, sniffing is easiest," he told her.

He put his hand in his pocket again and pulled out what looked like a tiny measuring spoon. He dipped the spoon into the white powder and held it under his nose. "Hold one nostril closed and sniff it up with the other," he instructed then demonstrated. She watched the powder disappear from the spoon into Jimmy's nostril, leaving a few stray specks of white clinging to his nose hairs. He sniffed a few times to draw the powder up into his sinuses then he dipped the spoon back into the powder and held it out to Sepia. She hesitantly followed his example.

"Don't let any air out through your nose or you'll blow it away," he warned her.

She took hold of Jimmy's hand to steady the spoon under her nostril then she sniffed abruptly like Jimmy had done. The foreign powder stung the inside of her nose like sharp cold air, then the lining of her nostril immediately discharged mucus to carry the intrusive powder down her throat where she tasted its bitter flavor. She involuntarily sniffed to try and relieve the rawness in her nose. She couldn't imagine that such a small amount of a substance could have any affect, but as she handed the spoon back to Jimmy and started to ask him if he wanted a drink, a sensation began to spread up through the sides of her face and into her head. Jimmy was right, it wasn't the same as the opiate high, but she could already tell that it had the power to quell the anxious thoughts in her mind. It felt like a wall of glass was rising up around her, separating her from the outside world.

Jimmy had been watching the drug take affect on Sepia and a smirk appeared on his face. He liked Sepia even though he wasn't attracted to women, but he had seen her change from a young, sweet looking dame to a hard, worn-out looking broad. Of course, he'd seen it before, especially this last year when more young women ended up on the streets after they couldn't find the typical waitress, secretary or bank teller jobs. The Depression was bad for everybody, but it was especially tough for young women who'd gotten a taste of liberation in the gay twenties, then had the doors of opportunity bang shut when the stock market crashed.

Sepia moved around the room, picking up a throw pillow and tossing it back on the couch, straightening up the glasses on the bar, and rearranging the angle of a chair. She felt a burst of energy and a feeling of elation. She could already see the advantages of this milder high. It put her in a state, but not a stupor. It also left no telltale odor on her breath. "Is it hard to get?" she asked Jimmy.

"I can get it easy," he assured her. "You give me the dough and I'll make sure you get what you need. Just don't let Tony find out. For some reason, he's got a bum idea about cocaine. Maybe he just doesn't like the cost, you know. He can be a real tight wad about some things, and besides, he doesn't need this stuff like you and me.

Jimmy was right, Sepia thought. Liquor and drugs were purely social for Tony. He sought diversions from his dull job, but he had no need to block out the world the way Sepia did.

"How did you meet Tony?" Sepia asked. She suddenly felt like talking and it was the first time she'd said more than two words to Jimmy since they met.

"Me and Tony go way back, grew up in the same neighborhood. We didn't see each other much once he went into his old man's business, but I ran into him last year at Roscoe's place. I was pretty surprised to see a guy like him hanging around that joint, he's always been so legit. On the other hand, he was always the one goin' off and trying new things, dangerous kind of shit when we was kids. He'd try anything once. I doubt he'll hang around Roscoe's much longer 'specially since Prohibition's gonna end anyway.

"It is?" Sepia asked. She'd heard everybody talking about it, but she didn't believe it. After all, Prohibition had been going on for twelve years.

"I betcha by this time next year, Roscoe will be out of business and lookin' for a new racket. This'll be the stuff to make money on then," Jimmy said, holding up the small box of cocaine before he shoved it back in his pocket.

Sepia figured he was right. It worked for her and probably would for others too. It took such a small amount to achieve the effect she needed. Cocaine would be hers and Jimmy's secret.

Jimmy got up to go, but pressed a tiny package into Sepia's hand before he left. It was a piece of paper, carefully folded to contain a small amount of cocaine powder inside. "I'll collect some dough from you next time." He let himself out the door without saying good-bye, leaving Sepia wondering when that next time would be.

Sepia saw Jimmy the following evening at Roscoe's and when they had a moment alone, she asked him for more cocaine. After that, she began to see him frequently when Tony was at work.

She decided Jimmy wasn't as objectionable as she'd first thought, and he became, in fact, her only friend. He told her funny stories and liked to gossip about the shady crowd he hung out with. Sometimes she and Jimmy would go to the movies or get a bite to eat. As her need for cocaine grew, her appetite for food lessened and she became even thinner than before. Jimmy tried to tell her to go slow, but she required increasing amounts of the drug to get the same effect. Jimmy knew that Tony would guess something if she kept the pace she was going, but he couldn't seem to stop her. He also knew if he limited Sepia's supply of cocaine, she would just find somewhere else to procure it.

It had only been five months since she left the Olympic,

but it would have been hard for Sepia to convince anyone that she had ever been a circus performer, much less an aerialist. Her strong muscular frame had become weak and flaccid. Tony was growing tired of her constant sniffling and irritable moods during the day. He kept asking her what was wrong, but she convinced him that her sniffling was due to a flu she couldn't shake and that her irritable mood was from lack of sleep.

Tony suspected she was lying, but he hadn't guessed what was really happening. He knew she wasn't drinking heavily, but he hadn't suspected drugs. He began to wonder why he kept her around and yet, when they went out at night, she seemed to come alive with seemingly boundless energy. And despite her gaunt appearance, there were times when he'd catch her standing at the window in the half light of dawn and she still looked heart stoppingly beautiful, like an angel waiting to ascend into another world.

One afternoon, however, everything fell apart. Tony came home early and surprised Jimmy and Sepia sitting on the couch with a bag of cocaine lying open on the table.

"What's going on?" he asked angrily.

"Nothing, Tony," Jimmy said as he hastily grabbed up the bag and stuffed it in his pocket. "We was just talkin'."

"What's in the bag, Jimmy," Tony asked threateningly.

Sepia sat frozen on the couch, already terrified of what was about to happen. The cocaine she had just consumed vanished from her brain.

"What is it?!" Tony repeated though he guessed he knew.

"Coke. Cocaine. We was just trying it. A buddy gave me some," Jimmy lied, knowing it was useless.

"Just trying it, huh. Get out, Jimmy."

Jimmy stood up and abruptly walked to the door. He

gave a quick helpless glance at Sepia then disappeared.

Tony turned to Sepia. He walked angrily over to the couch and raised his hand to hit her. She cringed under him and he wavered a moment, then dropped his hand to his side. "Well, I guess that explains how you've been acting," he said bitterly. "And why you look like a worn out whore."

The words might have stung Sepia three months ago, but she was too far-gone to care now.

"It isn't doing any harm," she said feebly. "It helps me."

"I never would have guessed you were such a loser," Tony continued, ignoring her comment. "I used to think you were something special, but I was wrong. You had a pretty good deal here, but if you'd rather shove that garbage up your nose, go right ahead. Don't you think I know about the money you've been stealing from me?"

"Whores get paid, don't they?" Sepia said in an uncharacteristic tone.

Tony glared threateningly at her again, but did not touch her. "I want you out of here before tonight," he said with disgust, then turned and left.

Sepia knew she'd never see Tony again just like she knew that the pain in her heart would never end no matter how much cocaine she used. She stuffed one dress and her comb in a shoulder bag and left an hour later.

She spent that night in a church shelter and ate breakfast at a long table with a room full of homeless. It reminded her of the circus cookhouse, only here everything was drab and spare and the people ate in dispassionate silence.

She tried to find Jimmy, but no one had seen him. She had enough cocaine to last a day, but her mind was beginning to beg for more and she began to sweat with fear. She went to Roscoe in hopes he would take her back in, but he had heard she was hands off from Tony.

By late afternoon, she was desperate. She thought of only one other place to try, a house Tony had pointed out to her once, laughingly saying it was where he'd lost his virginity.

Sepia walked up to the entrance of the wooden Victorian and knocked on the door. A woman answered looking very grandmotherly in a prim, high collared dress and her hair pulled loosely back in a chignon. Only the red rouge and buxom figure matched the image Sepia had had in her mind of a madam. Her name was Sadie, and the flophouse she ran was extremely clean and orderly. She had no room for Sepia, but she led her into the kitchen and gave her a cup of tea. Sadie noticed Sepia's trembling hands and sweaty brow as she drank it.

"Are you sick, honey?" she asked.

"No," Sepia answered then gave a revealing sniffle.

"Drugs?" Sadie asked. "Sorry, honey, even if I had a place for you here, I don't allow that stuff. My advice would be to get yourself off it right now, before it's too late."

Sepia nodded, but knew it was already too late.

The house was absolutely quiet and she guessed that the employees must be upstairs sleeping. Sepia almost wished she had come to Sadie's first before she ever went to Roscoe six months ago. She might not be sitting here with her skin crawling and feeling like she was going to vomit.

Sadie was having a similar thought. If she'd caught this girl sooner, she could have made some good money with her. Despite looking thin and washed out, she had the face of a Madonna. Sadie reached in her dress pocket and sighed. She pressed five dollars into Sepia's palm as she led her to the door.

"You promise to get some help, okay?" she asked.

"Okay," Sepia lied and guiltily stuffed the money in her purse.

Sepia entered the opium den searching for Jimmy. She found him slumped on a cushion asleep and shook him awake.

"Jimmy, it's me, Sepia. I need some cocaine."

Jimmy opened his eyes slowly and looked at her. "Tony told me to stay away from you. He said if I gave you more coke, he'd kill me."

Sepia had never heard Tony threaten anyone with violence, but she saw the scared look on Jimmy's face. She wondered why Tony even cared what she was doing. She wasn't able to consider anything, however, except the quaking urge inside her.

"You've gotta help me, Jimmy," she said desperately.

Jimmy saw the crazed look on Sepia's face and knew she was in bad shape. "Go to 53 Grove Street and ask for Ned. Don't tell him I sent you. He'd kill me."

If Tony's threat had been questionable, Sepia could see that this other warning was real. She considered staying there with Jimmy, but even in her desperate state, she had to think beyond the next two hours. She left Jimmy reaching for the long wooden pipe and sucking needfully on it like a mother's tit.

Chapter Twenty: The Snakecharmer

53 Grove Street was an auto repair shop and when Sepia asked one of the grease-faced mechanics for Ned, she was led into a back office of the brick building. It was a dirty room, smelling of motor oil, cigars and sweat. Ned Davies was seated in a swivel chair with his feet propped up on his desk. His fleshy chest was covered only by a stained undershirt tucked into striped trousers shoved low without a belt. His face was pudgy and pale, but he was not without vanity. The few strands of blond left on one side of his head had been combed over his bald scalp to create a pretense of more hair, but resembled a near empty spool of thread instead. His body was molded to the chair as if it had been years since he performed the work being carried out in the front bays.

Sepia was trying to keep from trembling as Ned looked her up and down and asked what she wanted.

"I want to buy some cocaine," she said in as low and steady a voice as she could muster. She felt like her insides were caving in.

"Oh you do, do you? Who sent ya?" Ned asked.

"A man, I don't know his name," she answered haltingly.

Ned sighed, knowing he should pursue her connection, but tired of having to deal with the distrustfulness of drug users.

An idea dawned on him however, and the scraggly looking woman before him took on a new meaning. She wasn't much good for anything else. She was thin as a rail and looked ready to climb the walls.

"You got any money?" he asked Sepia. He noticed the fabric of her dress was not cheap goods.

"Yes," she said.

"How much?" he asked.

Sepia was unsure how to reply. She had exactly ten dollars to her name including the five dollars Sadie gave her. "Enough," she replied.

Ned smiled. Beneath her unwashed face and sunken eyes, he detected a faint spark of courage. He decided to test it.

"Tell you what. You do somethin' for me and I'll do somethin' for you." He opened his desk drawer and took out a brown paper bag. "I want you to deliver this to somebody. When you get back, I'll give you the white stuff."

"Couldn't I have it now?" she asked a little too like a child begging for a sweet.

"I told you the deal. Take it or leave it," Ned replied coldly.

Sepia couldn't afford to take too long to think. She picked up the bag.

Ned scribbled down an address. "This is the place. Just tell 'em I sent ya."

Sepia took the address and the paper bag and hurried out the door. She had to travel across town to reach the place written on the piece of paper and as she sat wedged between passengers on a crowded bus, she tried to concentrate on something to help her stay in control. She counted the ridges on the rubber floor mat and picked out the letter "T" in the billboards outside. She was mentally connecting liver spots on the woman's hand next to her, when a face jumped out at her instead. It was Mintook, the caveman frozen in the block of ice from the Sideshow. Sepia shook her head and the image disappeared. Seconds later, the tattooed lady undulated her hips in the aisle of the bus. Sepia closed her eyes for a moment and that figment vanished also. The faces kept appearing though, one after another, all the disfigured and dissembling performers from the Sideshow began to parade before her eyes. They were mocking her, their sneering smiles belittling her for trying to outdo them with her fakery, her pretense at being a human being.

Sepia had to use all of the energy she had left to make her tormenters retreat. Her body was covered in sweat and she felt nauseated. She squeezed her eyes shut with such intensity that she was attracting the attention of the passengers around her. Just as a scream was about to escape her lips, the bus driver announced her stop and she fairly jumped up and shot out the door.

Sepia climbed the steps of a pre-World War building made of thick brownstone. She found the apartment number written on the now damp paper clenched in her palm and knocked on the door. It opened only a crack and two snake-like eyes appeared. At first Sepia thought it was another hallucination then the owner of the slitted eyes spoke.

"What do you want?" he asked and Sepia swore that even his tongue flicked reptilian-like.

"I have something from Ned," she said.

The door opened wider and Sepia stepped inside. The

living room looked more like a cheap hotel than someone's apartment. The furniture was shabby and sparse with no knick-knacks or memorabilia of any sort. The only warmth came from the stifling heat outside, a burst of Indian summer to tease those nervous about winter coming.

The snake man had disappeared into an adjacent room, but another man was sitting in an easy chair with his back to her. Smoke trailed from his cigar.

"Come here," a voice ordered in a hoarse tone.

Sepia walked around the chair and faced its occupant. She had expected to see someone around Ned's age. Most of the underworld figures she'd met had been older, at least in their late twenties. The man in the chair, however, looked only slightly older than her. He was small, too, almost elf-like that added to the contrasting figure in her mind and almost made her laugh. The man seemed used to the reaction he inspired, because he immediately threw her a look that told her not to reveal what she was thinking.

"Give me the bag," he said in his raspy voice.

Sepia handed him the brown bag and the young man opened it, glanced inside then wedged it in the seat next to him.

"Do you know what's in it?" he asked curiously.

"No," she said truthfully. It hadn't even occurred to her to look. She had been too busy trying to keep herself in one piece so she could make it back to Ned's. That thought propelled her now. "Can I go now?" she asked.

The fact that she was asking his permission gave him the feeling of authority he liked. He looked Sepia over with his large, grey, elfish eyes.

"No, you may not," he said simply. "Ned owes me a favor. You get to return it for him."

The man then stood up, barely reaching eye level with Sepia and she noticed for the first time the thin moustache above his lip. It looked fake, as if penciled on to make him look older.

"In there", he said motioning toward the adjoining room.

Sepia went rigid, but the man gave her a forceful shove and she started walking in front of him. They moved into the next room, which Sepia quickly realized was a bedroom. The young man thumbed the snake man out then he closed the door and faced her.

"Take off your clothes," he ordered.

Sepia began to shiver and hugged her arms protectively.

"I have to go," she begged.

She heard a clicking sound and looked down to see the glint of metal flash in the man's palm, a switchblade pointed toward her.

"Fraid not, doll. Now, off," he repeated, waving the blade at her clothes.

Sepia slowly began to move, keeping her eyes fixed on the knife as if she were a cobra hypnotized by its command. She removed her dress, her slip, garter, stockings and finally her underwear while the young man watched with a cold, unemotional stare.

"Lie down on the bed," he ordered.

Sepia moved to the bed and lay down on the nubby cotton spread. Terror had quelled the earthquake inside her and she felt amazingly numb. The young man walked over to her.

"Turn over," he commanded.

Sepia rolled over onto her stomach and realized she was crying when she saw a teardrop hit the spread then she felt a prick in her back and froze. The man ran the knife tip between her shoulder blades and down her back to the top of her buttocks with just enough pressure that she had no idea if he was drawing blood or not. The knife lifted from her skin, but a second later, she felt something thrust between her legs. She cried out, then realized not without horror, that it was the man's penis. He pulled her into his body and she lay halfway over the edge of the bed as he humped against her. Even he sensed the frailty of Sepia's body as his hands closed around her hips and he felt her sharp bones just below the skin. She was limp beneath him, but he easily moved her to suit his needs. He pulled out of her once, jerked her down to the floor and continued with her under him, barely on all fours as he gripped her from behind. As he grunted and finished, she collapsed to the floor sobbing while he stood up and zipped his pants.

He reached down and dragged Sepia to her feet, then leaned her against the wall facing him. She was wondering where the knife had gone when he thrust it under her chin. This time she felt a pop where it broke the soft skin on her neck.

"You're all right. You were nice and good. I like that. How did you get mixed up with Ned?"

"I wanted...cocaine," she answered nicely like he said.

The young man started to laugh. "I shoulda known by the way you was shakin'. Hey, I can fix you up. You shoulda told me. You want cocaine? I got cocaine." He withdrew the knife from her neck and walked over to his bureau. He opened a drawer and pulled out a substantial looking bag. Sepia stared wide-eyed as he thrust the knife in and came up with the tip piled high with white powder. He came over and held it under her nose.

Sepia disgusted herself completely by leaning over and

snorting it rapidly from the blade. She wiped her nose and looked away.

"Feel better?" he asked.

Sepia nodded.

"Listen, I want you to stick around here for awhile. I want you with me later. Clean yourself up. We're goin' out. Have all the stuff you want for now," he said, indicating the bag on the dresser. He opened the door and left Sepia leaning against the wall, sinking into a state of disgrace.

Chapter Twenty One: The Restaurant

Lila hadn't heard from Cole until the day she received a postcard with a large elephant on the front and bold letters on the back that read: "Am now a member of the Flying Zambinis!" Under it was scribbled, "See you in the spring. Cole". Lila would have been lying if she'd said her heart didn't feel a slight pang at seeing Cole's words, but mostly she was proud of him. Besides, there was a new man in her life who had attracted her attention with more than just his offer to turn her speakeasy into a restaurant once Prohibition officially ended.

Ending Prohibition was the talk everywhere. Roosevelt had won the election and though the future was shaky, it was pretty certain that the Democrats would end the long ban on booze. Sure enough in late February, 1933, Congress passed the Twenty-first Amendment and Prohibition was dead. The new law was toasted nationwide.

Lila panicked a bit over the end to her livelihood until a man she had seen maybe once or twice in her speakeasy introduced himself and proposed a deal. His name was Jack Riley.

They sat down at a table together and Jack immediately

began to outline his plan. It was a little hard for Lila to concentrate on what he was saying though. She was so charmed by his twinkling eyes and Irish brogue that she had to ask him to repeat his offer. By the time they shook hands over dinner a week later, Lila had fallen hard for her new partner.

Jack's feelings appeared mutual, but Lila swore to herself to keep him at arm's length until they opened their restaurant. She was more than skeptical that the scheme would work and she didn't want a little thing like sex to get in the way.

America was no longer denying its dim future. With one in four wage earners out of work, two thousand banks closed, people mining the garbage dumps for food, and no federal relief, opening a new business seemed risky indeed. Lila was not without hope, however. President Roosevelt had given the best damn inaugural speech she'd ever heard, and his wife, Eleanor, was a First Lady with both brains and heart.

Jack, an eternal optimist as well as a former carpenter, proposed to do much of the work on the restaurant himself. They rented a small warehouse space and combined the furnishings of his old coffee shop with Lila's bar. Whatever else they needed, Jack built. By the time Prohibition ended, they were halfway finished, and by springtime, they were ready to open.

Lila wondered if anyone still had enough money to go to a restaurant, but by buying from local farmers in need of unloading their surpluses, menu prices were kept low and people who could barely afford to eat out, came to Jack and Lila's. They both had loyal patrons from their former businesses, so the restaurant was busy right from the start.

It had taken all of Lila's restraint to keep her relationship with Jack strictly about business. He guessed her reluctance was tied to finishing the restaurant and it added urgency to his work. Sure enough, when they opened the doors to the public, Lila opened her bed to Jack. She had figured sex would be good with him, but when they lay together in the morning light wanting each other yet again, she was surprised at the depth of their passion. She'd been in love before, but never like this.

***

One evening, Lila was at the restaurant filling in for a sick hostess. She had just shown a large party to their table and was heading back to the front when she stopped. Standing at the door was a tall, bronze-skinned, sandy-haired young man wearing a broad smile. He had already gathered stares from the clientele nearby, but it actually took a moment before Lila realized who he was.

"Cole!" she called out as she walked quickly to him and threw her arms around his neck. He gave her a bear hug in return, lifting her completely off the ground. When he set her back down, she stood back and looked him over.

"You look terrific," she said in total honesty. Where he had been extremely attractive before, now he had an inner glow of confidence.

"So do you," Cole replied, equally earnest. Lila had her own sort of glow and when Jack walked over and she smiled at him, Cole saw where her happy look came from.

"I'm hopin' this is a long lost relative, otherwise I'm gettin' very nervous," Jack said to Lila with a grin.

She introduced them and the men shook hands.

"I didn't tink you got those muscles workin' in an accountin' office. Lila's told me all about you, well, almost all maybe," Jack said winking at her.

Lila turned beet red, confirming Jack's suspicions, but he put one arm around her shoulder and his other arm around Cole's and ushered them toward the bar.

"Let's have a drink, shall we?"

As Cole sat down at the bar, he glanced around the restaurant approvingly. It reminded him of Lila—warm, classy, and comfortable. "You really did it, Lila. This place is swell."

"Hey, she had a bit o' help, you know," Jack said.

"He just meant that I'd gotten something I wanted very much," Lila assured Jack. "And what about you?" she asked Cole.

"I'm getting there," he replied, and over a mug of beer, he began to tell Lila and Jack the story of his last nine months.

Things hadn't gone well at first. He'd had no luck joining up with a circus, so he joined the thousands of boxcar bums riding the rails in search of work. While Cole warmed himself at campfires near the tracks, he listened to the stories of these disillusioned travelers. Sometimes they shared a can of beans or a pot of coffee, but mostly they warmed themselves on a bottle of whiskey passed around. Old-time drunks and hobos were mixed with newly laid off auto and steel workers, yet nobody much cared who was what. No matter where they came from, there was an overwhelming feeling of helplessness. If the government didn't think they deserved help, then maybe there was something wrong with them; maybe they caused the fix they were in.

Cole headed west, then south, then north again until he found himself in Detroit, wandering the streets, hungry and anxious. Detroit was a place with so little hope he could feel the depression in the air. He pulled an old copy of Billboard magazine out of his pocket and opened it to a page that gave the schedule of a small circus called Halley. They were supposed to be in Detroit in two days. There was nothing else to do but wait. It was getting dark and Cole decided to head back to the rail yards to find a place to sleep; however, he noticed a young boy sitting on a shop door stoop with his forehead sunk on his knees. Cole reached down and touched the boy's shoulder.

"You okay, kid?"

The boy looked up. His curly brown hair was matted with burs and his cheeks were covered with dirt except where tears had washed them. He straightened his shoulders and swiped his cheeks with a shirt sleeve.

"I promised Ma I wouldn't come back 'til I got some food."

"No luck, huh? Me, neither. You should head on home anyway."

"Got no home," the boy answered.

"Where's your ma?" Cole asked.

"In Hoovertown with the others," the boy said.

"Come on, I'll take you there."

"I can take care of myself," the boy said, thrusting out his chin.

"I know, but I could use some company, do you mind?"

"I guess not," the boy said as he stood up.

"What's your name?" Cole asked as they started walking.

"Ralph," he answered.

It was a moonless night and when they approached what seemed a large vacant lot, it was pitch black. The boy found his way easily though, leading Cole through a seemingly endless maze of shacks. The glow of a campfire appeared ahead, then more fires dotted the darkness until Cole found himself in the midst of a huge encampment of people. It was a typical "Hooverville", the name given to the makeshift housing of the evicted and unemployed, the people President Hoover refused to have on the dole. They honored him with namesakes made from cardboard and tin.

Cole was shocked by the conditions in the camp. He was used to a gypsy lifestyle in the circus, but it was nothing like this. Even in the darkness he could see the filth and squalor. Some people had made shelters out of cardboard, others lived in holes dug in the earth and covered with scrap tin roofs. Ralph stopped at one such shelter and called out toward the dark hole.

"Ma, it's me," he said.

A woman crawled out of the black opening with a sleeping two-year-old clutched in her arm. She was probably at most in her late twenties, but the lines of worry and despair made her look twice her age.

"Any food?" she asked her son hopefully.

"No, mam," he answered, hanging his head miserably.

A mixture of anger and frustration filled the woman's eyes, then they softened in resignation and she touched the boy's head gently.

"Don't worry, son."

"There's no food to be had, mam," Cole said from behind Ralph.

"Who are you?" the woman asked, looking up at him in the dark.

"My name is Cole Artel. I'm looking for work."

"Who isn't," she muttered, too tired to question him

further.

"How long since you've had anything to eat, mam?" Cole asked.

"The Red Cross handed out bread this morning," she answered.

"My pa's gonna' get a job in Pittsburgh, then we'll have plenty to eat," Ralph said, his stomach voicing its hope with a loud grumble.

"That's right, son," his mother said with a half smile. "My husband left us here 'til he gets work," she explained.

A large, burly figure appeared out of nowhere and addressed the woman. "How you doin' this evenin', Helen? And how's my Molly," the figure added, chucking the child under the chin.

"Could be better," Helen answered as she shifted Molly onto her shoulder. "This here is, uh, what'd you say your name was?" she asked Cole.

"Cole Artel," he said offering a hand.

"Danny Jarrett."

When Cole shook the hand offered back, he got a better look at the owner's face, realizing with a start that it was a woman. Danny grinned widely at his surprise. She had large, round cheeks and slanted eyes like a cat. In fact, she reminded Cole exactly of the Cheshire cat in Alice in Wonderland, the only book he'd owned as a child, given to him by a family of actors he met on the vaudeville circuit.

Danny was dressed in men's trousers, Henley shirt and vest, but she wore soft, leather moccasins that made her footsteps light and soundless, allowing her to come and go like her storybook counterpart. The resemblance stopped there, however, for Danny was neither frivolous nor mocking like the famous cat. "I'm head of this camp," she said in a strong, clear voice. "We formed a group to run things, keep the place in order. You passin' through or stayin' awhile?"

"Just passing through," Cole answered.

"You want some coffee?" she asked hospitably.

"Sure."

"I'll stop by in the morning, Helen. The Red Cross truck should be comin' again," Danny said.

"We ain't goin' nowhere," Helen answered. She watched Cole follow Danny toward the glow of a campfire then she and her children crawled back into their foxhole shelter.

When Cole joined the group of people surrounding a campfire, he lost track of Danny who faded into the darkness after putting a tin cup of hot coffee in his hands. Cole noticed that the faces surrounding the fire were divided into white and black.

"We had twenty more evicted come in today," one man announced. "And two people dead from hunger," he added bitterly.

"We've gotta do somethin'," a voice hollered.

"The mayor's got to find us some relief," someone else agreed.

"It ain't the mayor. It's the government that thinks we're all bums and drifters," another said. "They say there are jobs for people willin' to work."

"There's jobs," another man stated. "It's just that any jobs go to white folks. The work that wasn't good enough for them before is all a sudden real desirable. My wife just lost her house cleanin' work to a white woman."

"My wife didn't get no such job," a white man responded.

"I'm sayin' your chances is a lot better than mine," the black man continued. "You think that Apple Shippers Association is going to give apples to us coloreds to sell?"

Some of the white men around the fire tightened their lips into thin lines.

"The man is right," Danny said, appearing suddenly. "It's not hard to see who's worse off. But fightin' among us isn't gonna' get any of us fed. We need to let the government know what's happening, that we aren't just loafers and bums. There are families starvin' here. They don't want to recognize us, so we're going to have to make them see. We tried marchin' to get our jobs back from Ford and we know where that got us."

Even Cole had heard of the march on the Ford auto plant two months ago. When the police ordered them back, the crowd refused, and the police threw tear gas. The marchers responded by hurling rocks, metal and mud. The fire department was called in and sprayed the protesters with a blast of freezing water, but the marchers congregated in a field outside the plant, determined to keep going. That was when the first shots were fired. By the time it ended, twenty five people had been wounded and four killed.

"I'd rather risk gettin' shot at than sit here starvin' to death!" a man shouted.

"Maybe so," Danny said. "But this time we won't march for jobs, we'll march for food. We'll organize a protest and go right to city hall. If we get enough families to join us, they can't ignore women and children that are hungry. They'll have to do somethin'!"

Several voices of support rose from the group.

"We've had it bad so long, we've started thinkin' nothin' good can happen," she continued. "But I'm tellin' you it can. We've just gotta stick together. We've got to organize so all our voices can be heard!"

Another rally of support rang in the darkness.

"You just give the order. Our people'll be ready," a black man told her.

"How do we know the mayor will listen if there's a bunch of colored's there?" a white man blurted out. A tense silence hung over the group.

A black man stood up. "The man has a point. The mayor's not gonna listen to a bunch of shiftless niggers," he said, curling his lip at the white man. "That's why you folk gotta show your white faces right up in front. We'll stay in the back...as usual," he added with a sly grin.

"We're all in agreement then?" Danny asked and saw the nodding of heads around the fire. Her voice dropped to normal. "Okay, spread the word. We'll march day after to-morrow. Ben, you and Abe are on the Red Cross truck in the morning, right? Make sure things go peaceable."

One of the men she singled out nodded his head.

"Good," she said then displayed one of her wide smiles. "I ain't gonna' keep talkin' over my grumblin' belly, so I'll see you in the mornin'," she called as she padded out of the circle. Most of the black men and women got up together to return to their own encampment nearby. The whites began to disperse also though some remained to talk about the new plan. It gave them something real to focus on, to live for. If they couldn't fill their stomachs, they could fill their minds. Danny had provided the spark they used to build a flame of hope.

Cole stayed near the campfire as it died down to glowing embers. A gaunt-faced man began to play the guitar and hum a tune. Several men had already curled up on the ground near the heat and Cole did the same, falling into a restless sleep of dreams he forgot by morning, waking only with a feeling of sadness.

Well before the Red Cross truck arrived, a line of people waited. They were laid off auto workers, busted farmers from the surrounding countryside, migrants from the south, and anyone else who was hungry. When Cole joined the line, he noticed Helen, Molly and Ralph toward the front.

A car pulled up and a man got out. He spotted Danny talking to a young couple that had just entered the camp carrying battered suitcases. He walked over to her.

"I've got bad news. Hoover ordered a freeze on any kind of relief. No more handouts."

"Jezus H. christ," Danny muttered. "You tell them, not me," she said indicating the waiting crowd. The man nodded and started toward the line, but Danny stopped him. "I'll tell 'em. You might not make it out of here alive."

She climbed onto the bumper of the man's car and called out to the crowd.

"Everybody, listen up! There ain't going to be any food today."

Angry shouts were heard from the line as it broke apart and formed around Danny.

"The fact is, there ain't gonna be any more food given out at all." She was drowned out by another wave of fury. "Hold it! HOLD IT! All of you listen to me! Save your voices. It's time to let the mayor know what's happening here. There's no better opportunity than now. I say we march to city hall! Who is going with me?!"

"We are!" came the unanimous cry.

"All right. But keep it orderly! Don't give the cops an excuse to hurt anybody! Let's go!" Danny jumped down from the car and headed for the street. The crowd joined her, nearly two hundred strong.

Cole stood aside. They were not his people. They were towners, outsiders, suckers, and yet he felt guilty watching them go. He had been with them on the road. His belly ached from hunger the same as theirs. He wasn't so different. As the black unemployed joined the back of the march, Cole stepped into the line with them and followed the crowd.

Townspeople watched from the sidewalks and store windows as the hunger marchers passed through the downtown. A sign reading "STOP HUNGER" was quickly painted by a sympathetic bystander and handed to the front of the line. Many unemployed transients stepped off the sidewalks and joined the march.

They got within five blocks of the Hall of Justice when they were stopped by a blockade of uniforms. Danny had figured this would happen since the police headquarters were only a few blocks away. She held up her hand to stop the march then she called out to the line of cops.

"We don't want any trouble! We just want to talk to the mayor!"

A voice boomed over a bullhorn. "Disperse your crowd now or you'll all be arrested!"

A rumble swept through the marchers. Danny turned and called out to them. "Everybody move off the street, but keep going. There's no law against walkin' down the sidewalks!"

But Danny was wrong. The police meant to break up the crowd wherever they moved. They advanced on the marchers split between the opposite sides of the street and tried to herd them back where they came from with loud threats and intimidation. The crowd refused to budge, and the police began to use force. Batons flying, they struck at whoever was in their path. A woman screamed as the man next to her was bashed in the head and fell to the ground, blood flowing from a gash in his skull. People panicked when they couldn't move forward or backward. Those at the edge of the crowd broke away and ran. Tear gas cans were tossed into the thick of the marchers and people cried out as the stinging gas burned their eyes and lungs.

A newspaper photographer crossed the street to get closer to the melee, but two policemen snatched his camera and smashed it on the pavement.

Cole stood stunned at the back of the crowd, a feeling of rage growing inside him. He snapped to attention when he saw the police close in from behind him, bearing down with special relish on the black marchers. Cole dug in his pockets and glanced helplessly around to grab anything he could hurl back at their attackers. He moved toward one of the baton swinging bullies ready for a clash, when his ears pricked up at the sound of a boy shouting over a child's crying. It was Ralph.

"Help me, somebody, help!"

Cole drove through the bodies ahead following Ralph's pleading voice. He found him kneeling next to his mother holding Molly shrieking in his arms. Helen was sitting propped against the side of the building clutching her elbow and moaning.

"Are you okay?" he yelled over Molly's voice.

"It's busted," Helen answered and when she took away the hand cradling her arm, Cole saw the huge lump that distorted her limb.

"Come on," he said as he lifted Helen to her feet. He shielded her and the children with his body as he herded them toward an opening. The crowd was quickly becoming an angry mob fighting to defend itself. It was exactly the excuse the police needed to justify further action. Cole steered Helen and her family between two buildings and down an alley as the crack of gunshots echoed in the streets behind them. They kept running until the sound of screaming voices and scuffling bodies slowly faded in the distance.

***

Cole helped Helen back to her shelter. Her arm, now splinted and cast in plaster, hung in a sling completely useless. Ralph followed with his little sister in tow. It was late afternoon and none of them had eaten a bite of food that day.

The other marchers had straggled back into the camp and sat despondently near their makeshift dwellings. They had achieved nothing in their march except exhausting their already malnourished bodies.

"I'm going out to find food," Cole said. "Will you be okay?"

"Sure," Helen said grimly.

The city streets were quiet at dusk with no trace of the turmoil earlier that day. Cole searched the garbage cans of alley after alley only to find they'd already been scavenged through. He walked farther and farther north until he realized that he was no longer in the city, but had entered the neighborhoods of a well-to-do suburb. He guessed that his presence would not be wanted here and he stuck to the shadows of dusk. Through lighted windows of tastefully appointed homes, he could see that the inhabitants were untouched by the hard times. A truck pulled up to a large

English Tudor with every window lit. Cole watched two men in grey uniforms, one short, the other thin, climb out of the truck and walk to the service entrance. Cole noted the name on the side of the truck: Watson Caterers, Let Us Serve Your Party. The two men returned shortly, opened the back of the truck and began to unload platters of food.

"Did you get a look at the maid?" the short man asked his pal.

"Yeah, what a set of gams!" the other man answered.

One of the caterers looked up suddenly as he felt someone behind him. He whirled around and found a figure staring down at them wearing a black hood similar to an Executioner.

"Put the trays back in the truck," the Executioner ordered as he held a gun pointed on them through the pocket of his trousers.

"Please. We don't want any trouble," the short caterer said.

"Good," said the Executioner gruffly. "Now, give me the keys to the truck."

"What?!" the thin man exclaimed.

"I've got a party to serve," the Executioner told them.

The thin caterer dropped a set of keys into the Executioner's free hand.

Five minutes later, the two caterers, their mouths gagged with cloth napkins and their hands tied with festive ribbon, watched from the bushes as their truck drove out of sight.

***

Danny stood at the edge of the camp, restless and frazzled. She worried that the cops hadn't given up, that they might come into the camp for reprisals. Today had been a nightmare and she had led her people into it. She would never forgive herself. Two people had been shot, one killed, many others were wounded. The march had been a disaster.

Two headlamps appeared and she froze like a deer in the light as a wave of fear swept over her. A truck drove past, but didn't stop. It wasn't a police wagon, yet she couldn't make out the sign on the side. It continued into the camp and disappeared behind a line of shacks. She followed it quickly and when she caught up, there was already a crowd forming around it. The back door of the truck was flung wide open and men were pulling out trays of...food!

Danny ran over to the men.

"Where'd it come from?"

"We don't know," they answered, continuing to unload tray after tray of hors d'oeuvres, cold cuts, fruit platters, loaves of bread, and racks of roasted beef. People emerged from their shelters with mouths watering from the aroma. They swarmed around the truck, but the men unloading insisted on order.

"Set up some tables and form a line. We'll do this calm and fair!"

The crowd obediently and quickly retrieved planks of wood and old crates from their shacks to make tables. The platters were set out, then each person quickly and deftly grabbed a plateful and stole away to a quiet eating spot. There was plenty for everyone. Danny sent word to the neighboring camp and the black families got in line. Many in their group were hurt or injured, but they forgot everything at the sight of a meal.

"Thank the Lord," a woman murmured.

"Talk about the bad and the good rolled into one day,

whooee!" whistled a man shaking his head. "Where'd this come from?"

"Nobody knows," the woman answered.

"Nobody cares," another added.

"Where's the driver," Danny asked one of the men who unloaded the truck.

"Didn't get a look at him. He hopped out and took off."

"As soon as all the food is out, we better get this truck out of here," Danny said.

"I'll take care of it," the man said.

Helen, Ralph and his sister had joined the diners and sat huddled over their plates, gulping down their food.

"How is it?" a voice asked behind them.

Ralph turned and smiled at Cole. "Swell!" he answered with strawberry jam smeared above his lip and chicken gravy dripping down his chin. Cole got a plate of food and sat with them.

"Whoever did this is a saint," Helen mumbled with her mouth full. Molly sat next to her, absorbed with licking chocolate icing off her small chubby fingers.

Someone brought in wood scavenged from the park nearby and a big fire was lit. People sat around talking about the events of the day, commiserating over the death of the marcher, and marveling over the miracle of a six course dinner appearing out of nowhere.

Molly sat in Helen's lap, a contented smile on her round face. Ralph was leaning against Cole's shoulder. He, too, had a rare, peaceful look as his eyelids drooped sleepily.

"Sing the animal song, Mama," Molly begged.

"Okay," Helen said with a smile and started singing softly.

"I went to the animal fair,

The birds and the beasts were there,

The big baboon by the light of the moon
was combing his auburn hair."
Ralph giggled and joined in.
"The monkey he got drunk,
and sat on the elephant's trunk."
Cole broke in and sang along.
"The elephant sneezed and fell on his knees
and what became of the monk,
the monk, the monk?"

They all laughed and Cole looked at Helen. Her eyes sparkled from the young woman inside, and he felt glad she was having at least this small moment of happiness. His smile faded, however, when he thought of her future.

The next morning, a drifter brought in a newspaper he bummed from a coffee shop. Danny read the headlines to a small group of early risers.

"Unemployed start riot in downtown!" she growled, infuriated. She skimmed the article then spat on the ground. "Oh hell, we knew the paper wasn't on our side anyway." She went on to another headline and stopped. "Hey, listen to this! Masked bandit makes off with Grosse Point banquet...a truck full of gourmet food prepared by Watson's caterers, that's it!"

"That was gourmet?" a scruffy bearded man asked. "Tasted like roast beef to me."

"I'll be damned," Danny continued. "Says the thief tied up the caterers and made off with the truck before anybody saw him. No witnesses and no clues. How bout that. Pretty slick I'd say."

"What is?" Cole asked, walking by.

"This," she answered and handed him the paper. He read the article, quickly searching for reports of any witnesses to the crime. He handed the paper back and headed toward the street.

"Where you off to?" Danny asked.

"To get a job."

"What do you do anyway?" she asked curiously.

"Didn't I ever tell you?" Cole grinned. "I'm a trapeze artist in the circus."

"Yeah, right," Danny smirked. "And I'm heir to the Rockefellers."

Cole walked onto The Halley Circus lot and breathed a sigh of relief. He never felt quite right on the outside, but here, where he didn't yet know a soul, he felt completely at home. Halley's was a small, one ring truck show under tent. Cole spotted some acrobats working out on a trampoline and walked over to them. They eyed him with suspicion, but with a quick phrase he let them know he was okay.

"You kinkers know where I can find the boss?"

"In the ticket wagon most likely," one of them answered.

"You should tuck your knees higher on that last trick," Cole informed the acrobat on the trampoline."

"Oh, yeah? Think you can do better?"

"Well, if you insist."

"Be my guest," the acrobat replied sarcastically, making way for Cole with a sweeping gesture of his arm.

Cole swung up on the trampoline and started showing off his usual stunts. Halfway through his routine, he noticed a short, wiry man with curly grey hair watching him from the sideline. He ended his act and jumped back on the ground. The man walked up to him.

"Not bad. What's your name, kid?" he asked with a heavy Italian accent.

"Cole Artel. What's yours?"

"Vincent Zambini. Ever do any flying?"

"Some," Cole answered.

"You come with me and we have a talk, okay?"

"Okay," Cole said as Zambini threw an arm around his shoulder and steered him away.

Cole stood at the performers' entrance that afternoon watching Halley's show and smiling. He had definitely lucked out. Zambini's son had been knocked out of the catch trap and had broken his collarbone three days ago. Zambini was in need of a catcher.

Cole had been nervous as hell when Zambini sent him up to the catch bar to try him out. Cole knew what to do. That wasn't the problem. He'd caught for his mother hundreds of times, however, that was six years ago. But like riding a bike, the skill was not lost and when Zambini came flying across on the trapeze, Cole caught him firmly in his grasp. They worked out a deal even before their feet touched ground again, and he planned to leave with Halley's when they pulled up stakes the next night.

Cole still couldn't believe he was really in a flying act. It had been four months since he left the Olympic and he'd traveled nearly two thousand miles looking for work, any work. Now he had not only joined out with a circus, but he was getting to fly! The season was nearly over, but if he did well, maybe Zambini would keep him on.

Cole's brow furrowed, however, when he remembered the people in the Hooverville camp. He wondered if they'd miss him when he didn't return that evening. He pictured Ralph and Molly sitting beside their dugout home. What would happen to them?

The Detroit police were busy that evening. The first call came in about 7:00 p.m. A wealthy businessman had been robbed leaving his office. A masked gunman held him up as he was about to get into his car. The thief made off with fifty bucks. About an hour later, another robbery took place across town. An affluent couple leaving the city's finest restaurant was robbed at gunpoint, again the perpetrator wore a mask. Then, barely a half hour later, five men allegedly playing a clean game of cards in the back of a cigar store were held up and the thief came away with half a grand. The police probably wouldn't have known about the last offense, except that one of the card players got arrested for drunken driving later that night and whined about being robbed as his excuse for breaking the law.

All of the robbery victims gave identical descriptions of the criminal, a man in a black hood resembling an Executioner. It was definitely the same man who had stolen the catering truck the night before. In the space of a few hours, the cops were already labeling this masked crook a sort of Robin Hood who stole from the rich and who was probably a victim of the Depression. The police were comparing him to the likes of John Dillinger and "Pretty Boy" Floyd who were handily cleaning out Midwestern banks.

It was close to midnight and Danny sat cross-legged by the campfire. A wave of loneliness swept over her as she thought about her hometown and the family she'd left there. Her parents ran a small grocery store, which barely provided for their five children. Danny had left home to help out and had landed a factory job in the city. When the factory laid off half its workers, she hadn't wanted to return home and be another mouth to feed. She had ended up in the camp instead, waiting for better times to come.

At moments like this when she got homesick, she could almost smell the aromas in the grocery store, her mother's home baked pies mixed with hickory smoke from the pot belly stove, the hint of vinegar from the covered pickle barrel, and the sweetness of hard rock candy and chocolate bars. It was her mother and father's store that the children ran to after school every day, and that their parents came to for credit. Danny was determined not to be a burden to them.

Someone crouched down beside her and she looked over to find Cole staring into the fire.

"Any luck?" she asked, referring to his job hunt.

"Yes," he answered.

"No kiddin'. Congratulations," she said.

"Thanks. I'll be leaving tonight," he told her. "I just wanted to give you this. He stuck a wad of money in her palm and closed her hand to shield it from other eyes.

"What the...?" she exclaimed.

"Don't ask. Don't spend too much at once, and only divvy it out to people you can trust to buy for everybody. I hope it lasts you awhile," he said.

Danny stared at him open mouthed. He responded by pulling the Executioner's mask out of his pocket and putting it in her other hand. She gazed at it in disbelief.

"It was you?!" she whispered. "Everybody's been talkin' about it. The police were here askin' questions tonight. People are callin' you a hero!"

"I'm not a hero. I just don't like to see kids starving that's all. Tell Ralph, Molly and Helen I said good-bye and that I hope everything goes like they want." He took the mask back from her and tossed it in the fire. The dark cloth caught instantly, but he was not watching. He stared into the distance and it was a fire inside him that Danny saw, but only briefly. Cole stood quickly.

"I've got to be going."

Danny stood up, too, and shook his hand. "Good luck." She held up her fist with the roll of bills. "We'll put it to good use. Thanks."

She watched Cole disappear into the darkness with a mixture of wonder and sadness. She noticed for the first time how he walked slightly forward on the balls of his feet, how he swung his strong arms free and gracefully. She remembered what he had said that morning and began to laugh. Damned if he didn't look like he could be a trapeze artist. He sure had the guts for it.

She shoved her hands in her trouser pockets and tilted her face up to the night sky. She felt the bulge of money in her hand and the rain of hope that fell from the stars.

Cole left with Halley's that night and within a week, was performing twice a day with Zambini. To his dismay, he was billed on the program as Cole Zambini, and as they grew closer, most people who met them thought he and Zambini were truly father and son. Their flying act began to attract attention.

"The son's collar bone healed, but he was never a very good catcher in the first place," Cole said, finishing his story for Lila and Jack. "By that time, I'd convinced Zambini that he couldn't do without me and he asked me back for the full season," he said proudly.

"I see you've developed an ego to match those biceps," Lila laughed. She watched the sheepish grin that had nearly won her heart spread across his face, and added, "What I really mean is that I'm as proud of you as you seem to be of yourself," she added. "I'm glad things worked out for you."

"When can we see you perform?" Jack asked.

"Tomorrow night if you want. Here," Cole said, pulling two tickets out of his pocket. "It's a small show like I said, but they've picked up some good acts. We're only in town for two nights, but I managed to come on ahead so I'd have time to see you."

"Tomorrow night?" Jack asked, conferring with Lila.

"Definitely," Lila answered and she signaled the bartender for another round of drinks.

Chapter Twenty Two: The Ghost

When Lila gave up her post as hostess to join Jack and Cole, she didn't notice the foursome that was ushered in and seated in the back of the restaurant. Now she was aware however, of a growing disturbance from their booth. She turned to see what the commotion was and saw two men arguing. It seemed a friendly argument so far as the men kept smiling during the exchange. They sat facing each other at the outside of the booth leaving the two women tucked inside, barely visible from view. One of the men was clearly inebriated and as Lila watched, the yelling suddenly became one-sided as the drunken man hurled insults instead of arguments.

Everyone in the restaurant turned to stare and the room became silent except for the shouts of the drunken man. The other man had become quiet and still, and it was actually he that worried Lila the most. Darkness narrowed his large eyes as he stared with rage across the table. He was a small man, almost child-like in appearance, but Lila guessed that the hand that quietly reached into his pocket was not fingering a harmless toy.

Jack stood up and headed for the booth with Cole

following close behind.

"Evening, folks," he said with a calm smile. "I'm Jack Riley, the owner. Is there a problem?"

Being interrupted left the drunken man suddenly without words and he sat there with his mouth hanging slack for a moment, then he slowly stood up.

"No, there ain't a problem. We was just leavin'. Come on, Sally. The company stinks around here." He glared at the small man across the booth then he and his female companion weaved toward the front door and left.

Jack watched him go and relaxed his shoulders, then turned back as the small man addressed him.

"The guy's a real jerk. Sorry to disturb everybody, Jack. By the way, my name is Frank, Frank Dinetti.

Cole, who was standing behind Jack, winked back at Lila that everything was okay, although Jack did not leave the booth. Cole heard him question Frank further.

"Is your lady friend all right?" Jack asked.

"She's fine," Frank answered.

"She looks a bit ill," Jack persisted. "I'd be glad to call a doctor for you..."

"I said she's fine," Frank repeated, irritated, then his voice became friendly and fast again. "She's just gettin' over the flu. I told her she shouldn't have come out tonight, but you know how stubborn women are," he said, laughing conspiratorially with Jack.

Jack did not join in the laughter, however. He continued to stare at the young woman slumped against the wall of the booth with her eyes barely open. Her skin was pallid and sickly green, and her hands lay in a loose heap in her lap. Her hair was uncombed and straggly and Jack noticed the lines of dirt in the creases of her neck.

Cole wondered what was keeping Jack standing at the booth. He was feeling awkward waiting behind Jack so he stepped up next to him to see what was drawing his attention. He saw the fast talking little man called Frank then he looked at the woman next to him and understood Jack's concern. Her dark hair fell across her face so it was hard to get a real look at her, but it was easy to see that she was in bad shape.

"Miss, are you all right?" Jack said to the woman, ignoring Frank's annoyance at being usurped.

The young woman slowly rolled her head toward them and the strand of hair that had covered her eyes, fell away. Cole froze next to Jack and his hand reached out unconsciously to steady himself on the frame of the booth. Sepia looked up at him without the slightest hint of recognition, though it was hard to tell if she was really looking at him at all. Her eyes were totally blank and barely able to stay open.

Cole's first thought was that she was dying and he was not far from the truth. Frank had barely kept her alive, doping her up with cocaine and alcohol and using her however he wished. She had been with him for two months, but it might as well have been two years for all she knew. She had not had a clear thought in weeks. If she was dying, she seemed not to care.

Cole's face went deathly pale and he immediately wheeled around and walked away. He knew he was going to be sick and he stumbled past Lila toward the restrooms.

Lila stared after Cole in surprise, but she did not follow him. She went instead to the booth where Jack still stood waiting for an answer from Sepia.

Sepia's eyes were now fixed ahead in response to the unseen pain Eddie's fingers caused digging into her thigh.

She was desperately trying to respond to Jack in the way Frank would want her to.

"I'm okay," Sepia managed to get out in a strained whisper.

At first, Lila was repulsed at Sepia's seeming disregard for her hygiene and her dignity. Then Sepia looked up at her and Lila realized that something was terribly wrong. She saw that Sepia was not conscious of her own appearance nor did she have the capacity to care. The large brown eyes that stared back at Lila wore the saddest expression she had ever seen. A lump rose in Lila's throat and she balled her hands into fists. It was all she could do to stop herself from grabbing up the weasely little man in front of her and tossing him out on the street. Instead, she forced a pleasant smile on Frank and turned to Jack.

"Jack, leave these two alone," she said. "I need some help in the kitchen. The chef is throwing a tantrum and you're the only one that can manage him." She took Jack's arm and gently, but firmly guided him back toward the rest rooms. When they were out of sight of the booth, she said in a low voice. "Go into the john and get Cole."

A minute later, Jack and Cole walked out, Cole's face still as white as the new napkins on the table.

"You know her, don't you?" Lila said.

"It's Sepia," Cole said hoarsely, trying to control his emotions. "But I don't understand...," he started to say, his voice trailing off with guilt and anguish.

"It doesn't matter," Lila said. "We've got to get her away from him."

"I'll get her away from him," Cole said, the color rushing back into his face as he started toward the booth.

Jack stopped him. "No. That guy is trouble. We've got to

get her away so he doesn't know where she is...ever."

A waiter brought two dinner plates to Frank and Sepia's booth, but as he was setting Frank's plate down, he slipped and dumped half the plate into his lap.

"You fuckin' idiot!" Frank yelled.

"I'm really sorry, sir," the waiter said convincingly as he tried to mop the spaghetti off Frank's shirt.

"Get away from me," Frank growled, pushing the waiter off. "Where's the fuckin' men's room?" he demanded as he stood up and slid out of the booth.

"Straight back and to your left, sir," the waiter told him. He watched Frank quickly follow his directions then he glanced down at Sepia, turned toward the bar and nodded.

Within seconds, Cole and Lila were at the booth.

"Come on, honey," Lila said to Sepia as she slid in next to her. She threw Sepia's arm around her shoulder and pulled her out of the booth.

"Frank will be mad," Sepia murmured, but she didn't resist as Cole and Lila helped her stand up. As inconspicuous as possible, they walked her out the front door.

Jack was waiting in his car. As Cole led her to the curb, Sepia's feet gave out and he scooped her up in his arms and carried her the rest of the way. As he set her gently in the back seat, he heard shouting behind him.

"Hey, where you goin' with her?!" Frank yelled as he came out of the restaurant, his shirt stained red with sauce. Lila ran out after him.

Cole glanced over his shoulder then left Sepia in the car and strode over to Frank. He grabbed him by the collar and threw him up against the restaurant wall.

"If you ever come near her again, I'll kill you!"

"Okay! Okay," Frank promised, but he pulled the switchblade from his pocket.

"Cole! Look out!" Lila screamed.

Cole saw the flash of metal as Frank jabbed upward. He dodged sideways, but the blade managed to graze his ribs. He grabbed Frank's wrist and slammed it against the wall, causing the knife to fly out of his hand. He then rammed his fist into Frank's stomach and landed another blow to his face. Frank collapsed unconscious on the pavement.

"Get going!" Lila shouted.

Cole jumped into Jack's car and it sped away.

Cole held Sepia cradled in his lap as Jack headed for the nearest hospital. She began to shiver and he instantly removed his shirt and wrapped it around her. It was stained with blood in one spot but he ignored the wound on his side.

As he sheltered Sepia in his arms, he couldn't believe how thin and frail her body felt. He vividly remembered her strong muscles and tight frame, but the woman he held in his arms was a ghost of the person he had known before. She seemed barely conscious of what was happening to her now.

"Sepia," Cole said quietly as he held her against his bare chest and gently stroked her hair.

Sepia moaned something unintelligible.

"It's okay. You're safe now," Cole whispered. "Nobody is going to hurt you anymore."

Cole thought he felt Sepia sigh against him, but it was merely that her body had given up and she had fainted.

Jack pulled into the emergency entrance to Mercy Hospital, got out and went around to help Cole with Sepia.

"Do you want me to come in with you?" he asked.

"No. You go on back," Cole told him.

"Call us, would you?"

"I will," Cole promised and then he carried Sepia through the door of the hospital.

He entered a wide hallway where several people sat on a long wooden bench, waiting to be cared for. A tough looking man held a handkerchief spotted with blood to his ear. A frowning mother sat with a teenage boy in a baseball uniform gingerly holding his arm. Cole glanced around for help and was met by an orderly in a blue striped coat who came walking toward him.

"What is the problem?"

"I'm not sure," Cole said.

The orderly leaned closer to look at Sepia and screwed up his nose at the odor of whiskey. "Is she drunk?"

"Maybe, but..."

"She's hurt," the orderly said, noticing the bloodstained shirt.

"The blood's mine. I don't know what's the matter with her, but there's something wrong."

"Okay, sit down here and I'll go get a sister."

"I want to see a doctor."

"Yeah, okay, but you'll have to wait. You can see there are people here..."

Cole pushed past him and strode down the hall. He turned into a large room with six beds, all occupied by patients.

Cole scanned the room and spotted a man in his late thirties, wearing a white coat and spectacles. "Are you a doctor?!"

The man in the white coat looked up as the orderly rushed in behind Cole and shouted, "You're not allowed in here!"

Cole hadn't noticed the sister who now stepped over to

him. She wore the large white winged hat of a nun and a white apron covering her dark habit.

"Can I help you?" she asked calmly. "I'm Sister Agnes," she added, already starting to examine Sepia by taking her pulse and placing her ear to Sepia's chest.

"She's drunk," the orderly informed the sister.

Cole ignored the orderly. "No, something's not right."

"You're right," Sister Agnes said. "She's not breathing. Bring her over here," she ordered. "Doctor, I have a woman in collapse!"

Cole laid Sepia down on a wooden gurney covered with a white sheet and pillow. The doctor rushed over, put his stethoscope to her heart then raised her eyelids to check her pupils. "Prepare 5cc. strychnine sulphate .002 gm.," he said to the sister as he pulled off his scope and began artificial respiration.

"Orderly, we need hot water bottles and more blankets!" Sister Agnes yelled at the surprised attendant. He jumped at the nun's command and headed for a nearby cabinet.

Cole stood frozen as the doctor continued breathing air into Sepia's lungs, stopping every few moments to tap below her breastbone with a small hammer. Sister Agnes brought the hypodermic injection and the doctor immediately disinfected Sepia's arm and inserted the needle. He went back to his resuscitation, and within moments, Sepia took a sudden gasp of air and the doctor watched with relief as her chest began to rise and fall on its own. Again he listened to her heart and the furrow at his brow lessened a bit. He took a bottle of ammonium salts and held it under Sepia's nose. Her head jerked away and she moaned slightly.

"What's her name," the doctor asked, startling Cole by

addressing him.

"Sepia," he responded.

The doctor called to her. "Sepia?" then a bit louder, "Sepia! Okay, come on, let's get you up."

Sister Agnes was already holding a metal pan with a long tube curled inside. The doctor lifted Sepia up to a sitting position then inserted the tube into her mouth and down her throat. She instantly began to gag and when the contents of her stomach were removed, the doctor laid Sepia back down and the sister began to strip her clothes off. The doctor stepped aside and took a handkerchief from his pocket to wipe his brow.

"Doctor," Sister Agnes called in a firm voice.

The doctor came back to the table to see what the nun was indicating. Cole saw what his hands had already felt, Sepia's incredibly wasted body plus the added horror of bruises covering much of her skin.

"That bastard," Cole hissed vehemently.

"It could be tissue damage. She appears very malnourished," the doctor said, but as he turned Sepia over he saw fresh red welts on her back. "Do you know who did this to her?" he asked as he began to palpitate Sepia's skull, then work his way down her body, searching for injury.

"Yes," Cole answered furiously. "He won't do it again."

The doctor glanced up at Cole and noticed the knife wound in his side. He went back to examining Sepia.

When the doctor was assured that there were no broken bones or signs of internal injury, he signaled to Sister Agnes who first laid hot bottles around Sepia's body, then covered her with several blankets and began briskly massaging her legs.

The doctor stood by for a moment, surveying Sepia's

condition, then he glanced over at Cole and saw the stricken look on his face. He walked over to him.

"Don't worry. She's doing much better now. By the way, I'm Doctor Nabors."

"Cole Artel."

"Are you okay? Let me take a look at that cut of yours."

"It's nothing."

"Is it something the police should know about?"

"It was just a fight."

"Are you a relative of Sepia?" Nabors asked.

"No," Cole said.

"Do you know where we can get in touch with one?"

"Not exactly. Her father works in the circus. I don't know where he is."

"So, er, what is your relationship to Sepia?"

"A friend," Cole answered simply.

"Maybe you can help me then. Is Sepia an alcoholic?"

"An alcoholic? I...I don't know," Cole said, upset. "I've been away. I haven't seen her in a while."

"How long?"

"Almost a year."

"Was she drinking then?"

"No."

"That's good. When she's conscious, I'll speak to her. I'm much more concerned about her immediate physical condition now." He saw the look on Cole's face. "We'll take good care of her. There's not much you can do for her now. She'll be asleep for quite awhile. Why don't you go on home and come back in the morning if you want to."

"I want to. Thanks, Doctor," Cole said.

Sister Agnes handed Cole his shirt and he put it on. He stepped over to see Sepia before leaving. As sick as she looked, her face was like an angel as she wound her way through her drugged sleep. He smoothed her hair gently back from her forehead, then walked away. All he could do now was hope that she was in good hands.

Outside, in the cool night air, Cole aimlessly walked the streets, wracking his brain to figure out what could have happened to Sepia. He wondered now if she had ever returned to the circus and if so, why she hadn't stayed. He tried to think what or who could have driven her away then it became obvious. Both he and his mother shared the blame.

He realized that Sepia must have been in the city at the same time that he was last summer. She, however, did not have the benefit of knowing someone like Lila. She probably tried to get a job and failing that, any number of paths could have propelled her toward the state in which he found her.

Cole was filled with guilt for not having made sure Sepia was safe. He had been so humiliated by her discovery of his charade as the Executioner that he had left her prematurely. He had abandoned Sepia and unintentionally obeyed his mother's bidding after all.

All of the past months of trying to rid himself of his mother's pull on him vanished in an instant. Anastasia still exerted power over Cole, accompanying every weak and guilty thought that entered his head. He was determined that she not ever be in control of him again, and he wrestled with his mind to keep her away as he continued wandering the streets.

Hours later, Cole found himself back at the restaurant as Jack and Lila were closing up. Lila was anxious to hear about Sepia.

"The doctor thinks she'll be okay," he told Lila, but his face revealed his doubt.

"Come back to the house with us," Lila insisted.

When they got to Lila's, the comfort Cole had known there gave him some sense of relief. Jack said good night and went up to bed, leaving Lila to give her full attention to Cole. She insisted on dressing his wound, then she fixed some tea and they faced each other across the same kitchen table he had first sat down to a year ago.

"Did the doctor say how long she would be in the hospital?"

"No, but if you could have seen her...her body. She'd been beat up pretty bad," Cole said quietly.

"I guessed as much," Lila said.

"The doctor thought she's probably been drinking for a long time, too."

"That wouldn't surprise me either. I'm so sorry," Lila said.

"It's my fault. If I hadn't left her, this never would have happened," he told Lila.

"Why do you say that?"

"I'm sure it was my mother who made her leave the circus. I should have gone back with her, made sure she was safe," he said, then paused as his eyes brimmed with tears. "God, Lila I hardly recognized her. She looked so bad," he said, barely audible.

"She's going to be okay now," Lila reassured him. "What happened in the past is done. You got her away from that weasely little bastard and probably saved her life. That's what's important now."

Cole closed his eyes and ran his fingers through his hair, trying to concentrate on the present. "I should find Sepia's father. I also need to look for work here." Cole said.

"Why?" Lila asked.

"I want to stay with her," Cole told her.

"You would leave your job with the circus?" Lila asked.

"Of course," he answered. The bravado in his voice covered the fear of giving up his hard won independence. "I have to stay with her," he said adamantly.

Lila saw the look of determination on Cole's face and the exhaustion in his eyes. "Why don't you try and get some sleep and we'll talk about it in the morning. Stay here tonight."

Cole nodded, suddenly overcome by fatigue, though he doubted he would really be able to sleep.

Lila made up the couch in the living room and then said good night. As she climbed the stairs and got ready for bed, thoughts churned in her head. She slid quietly into bed and lay on her side thinking in the dark then Jack rolled over and placed his arm across her waist.

"Everything okay?"

"I think so. I want to help the girl," she said as a plan began to form in her mind.

"So, help her," he said, pulling her close. "Once a bartender, always a bartender," he mumbled as he nuzzled her ear.

She dug her nails into his thigh, but smiled as she drew him closer.

"You don't deserve me," she purred.

"Haven't I always told ye so?" he agreed. "The trouble is, you don't deserve me either. How we ever ended up together is a miracle." His hand was inching under her nightgown as he spoke.

"Haven't you had enough excitement for tonight?" she asked.

"I'm feelin' I have to prove myself to ye after you've been with that brawny lad."

She wiggled round to face him. "Number one, he's a kid. Two, he's hopelessly in love with another woman, and three, where else would I find such a clever business partner as you?"

He rolled on top of her and pinned her wrists to the pillow.

"Business partner is it? Then stop talkin' and let me conduct my business." He bent his head and covered her mouth with his. She wrapped her thighs around him in response and let her partner commence with his work.

Downstairs, Cole was exhausted, but lay in the moonlight thinking. So much had happened over the last year and he realized that until now, he had not had the time to sort through the changes. His experiences had moved him through time and space and he had perhaps intentionally avoided pondering what had happened.

Lila woke early. She dressed quickly without waking Jack and tip-toed downstairs. She passed Cole asleep on the couch and carefully slipped out the front door.

When Lila arrived at the hospital, she was not allowed to see Sepia at first. Sister Agnes explained her condition and what would be the sequence of events for her recovery. Apparently, Doctor Nabors had spoken to Sepia and determined that she had indeed been drinking heavily for months. She also told him about the cocaine.

"If a person has been drinking alcohol for a long period of time," the nun explained, unaware she was talking to an ex-speakeasy owner, "and then suddenly doesn't get it anymore, the body starts to rebel. There can be quite a violent reaction; vomiting, tremors, hallucinations, sometimes even seizures, along with extreme mental anguish. Not everybody goes through it, but Sepia is already experiencing some of these symptoms."

"How long does it last?" Lila asked. The violent symptoms the nun described were unknown to her.

"It can go on for several weeks."

"Can't you do anything for her?" Lila asked astonished.

"We can help her get rid of the poison that has built up in her body from the alcohol and we can give her sedatives to calm her down. Her condition seems to be worsened by the fact that she was mixing alcohol with cocaine."

Lila was taken aback by the struggle Sepia faced. She had never known anyone who had become so sick from drinking. She knew plenty of drunks, but she realized that she'd never seen them try to stop drinking.

"I don't believe Sepia is a drunk," Sister Agnes said, as if reading Lila's thoughts. "By that I mean somebody who would find it very hard to stop drinking. I heard her speaking to the doctor and she seemed quite upset about something that happened. She didn't say what it was, but it must have been very painful. Most likely it has something to do with the person she was with, the one that hurt her."

"I suppose so," Lila responded though she was quite sure that from what Cole had told her, Sepia's troubles went back further than that. "When can I see her?"

"You can see her now, but only for a few minutes. She's still in great danger. Her heart is very weak."

Sepia had been put in a large room with at least a dozen other patients. When Lila spotted her, the first thing she noticed were the straps binding Sepia's wrists to the bed. Her eyes were squeezed shut, almost as if she was afraid to open them.

Lila walked over to Sepia's bedside and laid a hand on her forehead. It was ice cold.

"Sepia," she said quietly.

Sepia's eyes opened for a moment and she looked up into Lila's face.

"My name is Lila. I'd like to help you."

Help? Sepia wasn't sure if Lila was an angel come to save her or another of Satan's helpers come to torture her.

"I won't lie to you," Lila told her. "The nurse said it's going to be tough, but you won't be alone. I'll stay with you and help you any way I can," Lila said.

Sepia tried to form a word on her lips as her eyebrows arched on her frigid brow.

"Why?" Lila said, reading Sepia's silent question. "Because nobody deserves to go through this and I'm sure you deserve it less than most." Lila knew Sepia was probably not following, but she went on anyway. "You were sold a bill of goods that didn't belong to you. I want to help you find the right ones."

Sepia prayed that she was really hearing even half of what Lila said. For some reason, this strange woman was reaching out to her. Sepia closed her eyes again, but her mouth relaxed into something resembling a smile.

A tear rolled down Lila's cheek as she gazed at Sepia's sweet, sad face. She couldn't be more than eighteen or nineteen, Lila thought, then her chest tightened with the pain of recognition.

Lila had never imagined her baby growing up. Though a day never passed that she didn't think of her, it was always the memory of an infant being carried away, her hand raised above the blanket, fingers opening to the light. Lila had been seventeen and unfit to be a mother the nuns said.

Now Lila imagined her daughter as a grown up, ready to face the world. What would she look like? Would she have Lila's dark, angular lines or would she resemble the fair-haired young private Lila spent a night with before he left to fight the Great War? Would she have Lila's stubborn streak or the soldier's easy going confidence?

She stared out the hospital window and knew her real motive for helping Sepia. Somewhere out there her daughter might need the aid of a stranger. If she helped Sepia, someone else might...

Sister Agnes appeared and Lila pressed her hand gently over Sepia's, then left.

As Lila headed down the hallway, she saw Cole speaking to a nurse. He caught sight of Lila and started toward her.

"How is she?"

"She's asleep," Lila told him.

"I want to see her."

"Cole, can I talk to you for a minute first?" Lila asked.

"Okay," he said reluctantly, anxious to go to Sepia.

Lila moved to a nearby bench and sat down. Cole followed her, but remained standing.

"What is it?" he asked.

Lila waited a moment, trying to choose her words carefully.

"Do you think Sepia recognized you last night?"

"No," Cole answered. "Why?"

"I know how much she means to you, but are you sure that she wants to see you?"

Cole was hurt by Lila's question, but almost instantly the truth of it sank in. He sat down on the bench and hung his head. The fact was that Sepia most likely would not want to see him. Looking back on the times they'd spent together, Sepia couldn't have many fond memories. Cole remembered when they first met and how he had treated her. He thought of the time in the boxcar and the things he had called her. It was only as the Executioner that he had been kind to her, but of course she hadn't even known it was him, and she may only recall his hoax as another betrayal. He hadn't stopped to explain things to her. He had run off like a coward. The more Cole thought about it, the more he saw that he was incredibly arrogant to think he might help her. Lila was right. He might even do her harm.

Lila read his thoughts. "Cole, I'm not saying you are bad for her. You are a different person than you were before."

"I just want to tell her how sorry I am for all of the things I did to her, and I want to tell her how much...," he paused, shaking his head. "But I don't want to upset her. I don't want her hurt any more than she already has been," he said firmly, the pain and conflict showing clearly in his eyes. "What should I do?" he asked Lila.

"I've been thinking about it and I have an idea," Lila said. She took in Cole's look of surprise and went on. "I want to help Sepia, too. I could talk to her for you, see how she feels, see what she needs...and wants."

Cole's face lit up. "You would do that?"

"I would do more than that," Lila said. "I'd like to help her get back on her feet if she'll let me. What she needs most after she gets out of here is hope and good nursing. I'd like to try and give her both."

Cole was speechless. He knew Lila was generous, but he never quite saw her as a Florence Nightingale type. Either she was showing another side of herself or she was doing this all for him.

"I couldn't let you do that, Lila," he said.

"You don't understand. I want to help her. I also want to help you. I know how much you want to be here with her, but I would hate to see you lose what has taken you so long to find. What I'm saying is, I don't think you should leave the circus."

Cole started to object, but Lila held up her hand. "Just hear me out a second. If you went back to the circus while Sepia is recovering, I could let you know how everything is going. It would also give me time to find out how she feels." She smiled at Cole. "Look, if she cares even a tenth as much about you as you do about her, I would do anything to help you two get together. I may act tough, but I'm still a sucker for fairy tales."

Fairy tales. Cole remembered Sepia saying something about fairy tales, too, that the way he had helped her as the Executioner was like a fairy tale. He still didn't believe in them, but he would do whatever it took to make Sepia well again. "You'd let me know how she's doing?"

"Yes," Lila promised.

"I'd call you from every stop we make."

"Right," she agreed.

Cole was quiet for a minute as he wrestled with his strong desire to see Sepia now only yards away, and his equally strong desire to do what was best for her. "Okay," he said, trying to reassure himself. "Okay," he said again, trying to calm his heart at the thought of leaving Sepia again. He trusted Lila implicitly. If anyone could help Sepia it was she. "Okay," he said one more time.

"I'll take good care of her," Lila answered, seeing his struggle.

"I know," Cole said in a whisper.

Lila hugged him. "She's going to make it. You're her hero,

you know. You saved her life again."

Lila's words were little consolation. Cole did not feel anything like a hero, though he would gladly have given his life for Sepia. He looked down the hallway toward Sepia's ward. Leaving her again would be the hardest thing he'd ever done.

"Come on," he said quietly to Lila and they stood up and walked toward the hospital exit without speaking.

When they got outside, Lila broke the silence. "Will you still perform tonight?"

Cole had forgotten about the show. "I can't do it. Not tonight."

Lila smiled up at him. "I know it's asking a lot, but would you do it for me? Please?"

Chapter Twenty Three: Delirium Tremens

Cole sat on the catch bar waiting for Zambini's signal. He knew that Lila and Jack were sitting below in the darkness and he wanted to perform well for them, but it took all of his effort to stay focused.

Cole had been back to the hospital that afternoon to find out from the nurses how Sepia was doing. They tried to be positive, but he could tell they were shielding him from bad news.

The truth was that Sepia had worsened throughout the day. The withdrawal symptoms were extreme as her body suffered from the shock of no alcohol. Every time the sedatives wore off, she cried out from the agony of craving the two drugs she was no longer allowed to have, a craving that made her skin crawl, her insides rot and her mind alternate between dark quiet depression and hysterical, pleading outrage.

Cole happened to be there when she burst forth with one of her tirades. He started toward her room, but a nun held him back. "Just remember that when she's screaming like that it means she's still got strength in her. She's stronger than any of us thought," the sister told him.

Now, as he sat on the catch bar ready to begin his act, Cole could hear Sepia's blood curdling scream echoing in his ears and he visibly shook his head to clear it.

Flying had been his salvation and the moment Cole was in the air, he was able for a few moments to forget everything else. It freed him from his worst enemy, his own thoughts, for he was obliged to direct his concentration on the act since he wasn't the only one who depended on the absolute precision it required.

Zambini had truly been like a father to Cole, patient yet encouraging. He had given Cole the confidence not only to fly again, but to believe that he could be really good at it. And Cole was good.

Lila watched him from the stands with her mouth hanging open as he swung across the tent above her. The show, as Cole had said, was small with only one ring, but it made the experience more intimate. Cole wore no shirt, only his royal blue tights with a gold belt, and Lila could see what the bulges under his street clothes had suggested. His chest had grown even larger than when she'd known him and his powerful arms pumped the air with a beautiful grace. She watched as Zambini released the trapeze, spun into a back somersault and was caught in Cole's strong grasp. Lila thought her heart had surely leapt into her throat, but she found she was still able to scream her approval when Cole swung back up to a sitting position and saluted the crowd.

Lila turned to Jack who raised his eyebrows at her, but he, too, was clearly impressed by Lila's young friend. It was exciting and fun to know someone that the whole tent found both dashing and daring. Lila was beside herself with pride, but tried to restrain herself for Jack's sake. She knew how she would feel if the roles were reversed and Jack was ogling some beautiful female flyer that she more than suspected had been his lover.

Jack, however, seemed just as tickled to watch Cole perform as Lila was and they yelled and applauded together after every trick.

Cole had managed to accomplish quite a lot in the last six months. He could now catch Zambini's two-and-a-half back somersault. Though others compared him to legendary catchers, Cole only competed with himself. Like Sepia, the thrill was in the flying and increasing the difficulty of the tricks only made it more fun.

He ended his act, dropped into the net and exited. Outside in the dark, he caught his breath and let his thoughts return to Sepia. He paced under the stars and tried to fight off the urge to change his mind and stay in Chicago. He repeated the words Lila had said to him that morning, knowing she was right but needing to reassure himself again and again. By the time the show ended and Cole met Lila and Jack out front, he had calmed down. They tried to cheer him up by telling him repeatedly how wonderful he was. They celebrated at the restaurant, opening a bottle of champagne, knowing that it was a drink that almost never made one melancholy. While Cole wasn't exactly merry, he did manage to smile a few times, and he fell asleep quite rapidly on Lila's sofa that night.

Cole woke late the next morning to a huge Sunday breakfast that Jack prepared. Lila had slipped away again to visit Sepia at the hospital and returned with a good report. Sepia had kept down her first meal, even if it was only chicken broth. She had been asleep when Lila saw her, but the nuns relayed that Sepia had actually had a few moments of peace from the ravages of her body.

What Lila didn't tell Cole was that Sepia had been up most of the night, convulsing and shaking until the nurse had to change her sheet drenched with sweat. Lila withheld the nurse's description of Sepia screaming for someone to kill her and end the unbearable pangs that racked her body. Lila also kept to herself that by dawn, Sepia was reduced to unintelligible mumbling as she described to the nurse the hallucinations that tortured her mind. Finally, Sepia had collapsed under the straps that kept her safely secured to the bed. All of these things Lila kept from Cole knowing that he was already unsure about leaving Sepia and would grab at any excuse to stay.

Cole said an unemotional good-bye to Lila and Jack outside the restaurant, and then he returned to the circus for their final performance in Chicago. Halley's moved in large vans and Cole took the wheel of one of the trucks with a forced detachment that he hoped would last at least for the next few hours.

Zambini sensed the change in Cole, but respected his privacy. He still did not know what caused the pained expression that came over Cole at intervals and made even Zambini, who had seen his share of tragedy, stop and say a prayer for him. He was however, not one to allow someone he cared about to wallow in unhappiness, so he kept a watchful yet sensitive eye on his young friend and partner.

When Zambini perceived that Cole had gone too far inside himself, he found a way to bring Cole back by talking about flying or by playing a practical joke on him. The jokes did not always go over well, but they usually succeeded in snapping Cole out of his self-absorbed moods. Zambini was exactly the sort of friend Cole needed, especially now when he threatened to lose himself in dark thoughts almost constantly.

***

Sepia continued to alternate between bouts of extreme excitability and deep depression. During the few moments when she was lucid, she felt disoriented and confused. She didn't remember how she'd gotten where she was or why. It made her anxious and she tugged at the straps that held her down on the bed. Her skin remained cold and clammy, and her pulse was feeble. After a week she slipped into a coma-like state.

Lila became frightened, thinking Sepia's plight had definitely worsened, but Sister Agnes assured her that while there was cause for concern, the symptoms were typical for someone recovering from delirium tremens or "D.T.'s."

Lila continued to visit, though she doubted that Sepia even knew she was there. Lila sat next to the bed and talked about the restaurant, the weather, things that happened to her on her walk over to the hospital, what she had for breakfast.

One day when Lila arrived, however, Sister Agnes informed her that Sepia had taken a turn for the worse. She had developed a fever of one hundred and four and was showing symptoms of uremia, a potentially fatal infection.

When Lila saw Sepia, her stomach tightened. Sepia's face had turned grey and her sweating body was trembling beneath the sheet. Lila had seen this look before and it terrified her. It was the same look she had seen first on the face of her mother then on her father before she lost them to the great flu epidemic when she was nine. It was as if a shadow had covered Sepia's face, threatening to draw her life's breath away. Lila knew there wasn't much time. She sat down next to the bed and took Sepia's burning hand in hers.

"Sepia, please, you must listen to me. You've got to fight this. There is someone who cares about you very much, someone who loves you deeply. He found you and brought you here. He saved your life. He wants to see you, but only if you want to see him."

Sepia heard Lila's words, but only faintly. She was no longer there in her hospital bed. She was high above it, as high as her trapeze, staring down at her body lying feverish below. She should have been frightened, but she wasn't. Instead she felt incredibly peaceful. There was something Lila was saying, however, that caught her attention. She strained a little to hear.

"Cole has changed, Sepia. I know that he would do anything for you."

Cole. Sepia suddenly felt the hard bed beneath her. She felt her parched throat and her burning, fiery limbs again. Cole. That one word had made her instantly rejoin her wasted body. She heard Lila clearly now.

"Please hold on, Sepia. He loves you. Please don't go."

Lila imagined she felt the slightest movement in Sepia's fingers, but she couldn't be sure. She sat next to the bed praying, until her head drooped to her chest and she dozed off, still holding Sepia's hand.

Sepia tried to squeeze Lila's hand. She felt Lila's love and she wanted to thank her. The feeling of peace had gone away, but the feeling of love had not. It was the unexplainable love for the man she'd tried to forget that now grew inside her, creating a pocket of warmth, a small glow that brought strength to her weakened heart. It grew and slowly traveled through her body like the spotlight moving across the Big Top, replacing dark, empty spaces with bright, healing light. It filled her whole body with a longing so powerful that it became a force equal to life.

When Sister Agnes entered the ward at dawn and touched Sepia's forehead, she was amazed to find it cool and dry. Sepia was sleeping peacefully with the hint of a smile curving her lips.

"Thank God," Sister Agnes murmured.

Lila woke, startled. "What is it?" she asked fearfully.

"It's all right. The fever has passed. Look, she's sleeping quietly now," the sister said.

Lila looked over at Sepia's face and saw that the dark shadow had indeed vanished. Sepia appeared beautifully alive, and Lila stared at her with wonder and relief. She opened her fingers and laid Sepia's now cool hand on her chest where it rose and fell with her even breath. Lila and Sister Agnes exchanged smiles then Lila went home. She quietly climbed into bed at morning's light and Jack sleepily rolled over and scooped her into his arms. "Did I tell you I love you today?" he murmured into her ear.

"It's already tomorrow," she smiled.

"I love you, I love you. Now I'm caught up," he said drowsily.

"I love you, too," Lila said.

"Actually, I don't tink tellin' you is enough. I tink I better show ye," he mumbled as his hands roamed under her nightgown.

"Go ahead," she smiled, overwhelmed by the power of love.

***

When Sepia finally woke the next morning, her mind was clear and her stomach was growling. The morning nurse smiled when she saw her.

"Welcome back, young lady," she said.

Sepia couldn't remember what brought her from the brink of death, but she did feel a grain of hope planted inside her.

After two weeks, she was eating normally and quickly gaining her strength back. She was also able to go for short walks outside. It felt good to get out of the stuffy hospital and into the late spring air, but she was shocked by the number of displaced people on the streets. There seemed to be a shoe shine or an apple seller on every corner, people relying on their own ingenuity to survive.

Sepia, too, was trying to survive. She looked up through the newly leafed out trees at the blue sky above and felt her heart begin to open again. She felt as vast and empty as the cloudless sky, as if she'd risen from the depths and the huge weight of her past had been left behind. She didn't know quite how or why she deserved a second chance, but she knew Lila was counting on her.

When she came to see Sepia after her fever broke, Lila's voice had been more familiar than her appearance. Sepia had then studied the face of the woman who had given her courage. She saw Lila's soft, grey eyes, high cheek bones and dimpled smile. She saw the silver streaked hair that fell in untamed curls around her face. She was determined to get well because she did not want to let Lila down.

Lila, however, knew that Sepia had to get well on her own or there would always be the chance she'd slip back into the hell she'd risen from. She had spoken to Doctor

Nabors several times during Sepia's recovery.

"She'll need a lot of encouragement," Doctor Nabors said. "She also needs someone who can help her figure out why she needed to drink so much in the first place. I'm not of the school that thinks people drink as heavily as Sepia did just to get intoxicated. Do you know what might be behind her behavior?" he asked.

"I have a pretty good idea," Lila said. "But shouldn't she have special help?"

"We can't afford to provide psychological treatment right now except for those who are mentally ill. And frankly, our chief of staff is not sympathetic toward patients suffering from drinking problems. He still believes that a drunk is a drunk and there's not much to be done about it. If Sepia had money, she could be admitted to a private sanitarium for treatment, but as it is, as soon as she's physically well enough, I'll have to release her."

"So, what you're saying is that if she's going to get any help, I'm it?" Lila said.

"From what I've seen, she could do a heck of a lot worse," Doctor Nabors smiled.

"Thanks, Doc," Lila said, though she was far from convinced. The best she could offer was years of experience talking to clientele in her bar. She had learned from them that most people's troubles stemmed from childhood and that most bad feelings came from guilt and fear. From what Cole had told her, Sepia probably had her share of both.

A week later, when Sepia was released from the hospital, Lila took her home. When Sepia walked into the house, Jack saw the incredible change in her. He barely recognized Sepia from the desperate woman they'd whisked away from the restaurant a month before. Her hair was pulled back in a ponytail and the sallow color was gone from her skin, replaced by a faint pink. He also saw a clarity in her brown eyes that made him smile. She was still very thin, and her shoulders were drooped from embarrassment and lack of self-esteem, but when he shook her hand, it was a strong grip, full of emotional energy that couldn't be suppressed.

Sepia had agreed to let Lila give her temporary refuge, but now when she saw Jack and Lila together, she felt like an intruder. She was about to protest being there when Lila looped an arm through hers and led her into the living room.

"I made some tea," Jack said, indicating the teapot and tray of sandwiches on the coffee table.

"Thanks, Jack," Lila said then watched him retreat into another room.

Lila poured Sepia a cup of tea and they sat in silence drinking. Sepia glanced around at the warm tapestry on the wall and the muted reds, golds and browns in the up-holstery and Turkish rug. It wasn't at all like the elegant surroundings she used to fantasize having, but she realized with a smile how much more comfortable and inviting this room was.

"I like your house," she said shyly.

"Thanks," Lila said. "It used to be my aunt's and I had the great fortune of inheriting it from her. If Jack and I stay together, we'll definitely keep it unless we move out of the city."

"Jack is swell," Sepia said.

"The cat's meow," Lila beamed. "It took twenty years to find him though," she laughed.

"Do you have any other family?" Sepia asked.

"No. I was an only child and both my parents died when

I was young," Lila replied. "Sepia, when you were still very sick, I asked you if there was someone I could contact in your family and you said 'no'."

"There's only my father, but I don't want to see him right now," Sepia replied.

"Is he here in Chicago?" Lila asked even though she knew the answer.

"No. I'm not sure where he is," Sepia said truthfully.

"Mind if I ask where you're from?" Lila asked as if she were tending bar to a new customer.

Sepia looked away from Lila, then back at her, then down at her cup. "I'm from the circus," she answered and it came so completely out of nowhere that it needed explaining even if she wasn't quite ready. "I grew up in the circus," she began and then suddenly, without intending to, she started telling her story. She was surprised how easily it flowed out. She didn't stop until she reached the time she arrived at the Olympic.

Lila sat riveted to her cushion, amazed both at what Sepia was saying and at the fact that she was saying it. It was almost a deja vu of when Cole had revealed his history.

Sepia told Lila everything, about her mother's death, her father's drinking, his abusive behavior, how she'd learned to fly, and how her father had totally run her life. Sepia left out little of the facts, but a lot about how she felt about them. Lila guessed how Sepia felt about Bruno, but she couldn't tell how she felt about her mother. She really hadn't said much about her mother except what Bruno had drummed into her head. It was a start though, Lila thought to herself. Sepia had ended her story before she told Lila about joining the Olympic and Lila understood why. That part of her history was tied too closely with her downfall.

"It must be an incredible feeling to fly on the trapeze," Lila said.

"It is," Sepia answered.

The unspoken question was left hanging in the air, but Sepia could not answer it yet. She was afraid to tell Lila why she had left the circus. With her fear came the urge to suppress it with something she knew would do the trick.

Lila saw the panic enter Sepia's eyes and she jumped up. "I forgot to show you my garden!" she fairly shouted, forcing Sepia out of her thoughts and her chair as they headed through the kitchen and outside.

Lila spent the next few days keeping close to Sepia, bringing out other details of her past then distracting her from dwelling on them with a walk in the park or a household chore. The first time they stopped by the restaurant, Sepia shuddered when they walked inside. She knew she'd been there before, but she had never asked Lila exactly what happened the night she was taken to the hospital.

"It was pretty simple really," Lila told her. "We saw how bad off you were, we rigged a way to get that creep you were with out, then we got you to the hospital," Lila explained, leaving out who the "we" included.

"I've never thanked you for everything you've done," Sepia said.

"You just did," Lila said. "Come on, I'll show you the kitchen."

Sepia wanted to find a way to repay Lila's kindness and when she saw the restaurant kitchen, she spoke up. "Lila, I'd like to do something for you. Is there work I could do for you here?"

"You really want to?" Lila asked.

Sepia nodded.

"You may regret this," Lila kidded, then found an apron for her. "We always need help."

Sepia started off washing dishes, but within days, was aiding the cook. Her strength was coming back quickly and after working in the restaurant kitchen a week, her weight began to increase, too.

One Sunday morning, Lila asked Sepia to help her wax the bar during closed hours. As they knelt on the floor polishing the dark oak front, Lila posed the question she'd been holding back.

"Sepia, why did you leave the circus?" she asked.

Sepia was quiet a long time, but Lila could tell that she was forming an answer. "I left the circus to find someone."

Lila held her breath, thinking Sepia was finally going to tell her about Cole then it occurred to her that it wasn't Cole that was lost.

"You didn't find her, did you?" Lila said gently.

"No," Sepia replied. "She kept running away."

"I think you've stopped running now."

"Yes," Sepia nodded with her own shy smile. It was true and if there was ever a time to find out who she was, it was now.

They both continued working for a few minutes and then Lila stopped.

"Sepia, did you hate your mother when she died?"

Sepia looked at Lila suspiciously. "Hate her? What do you mean?"

Lila explained. "It's just that when my parents died, at first the only thing I felt was really sad, but after awhile I realized I was angry at them, especially my mother. I hated her for leaving me. I loved her so much and then she left me all alone. For a long time, I couldn't forgive her."

"I don't remember my mother," Sepia said abruptly. "All I know is that she wasn't a good person."

"That's what your father said," Lila commented.

"Yes," Sepia said. "He didn't want me to be like her. That's why he was so hard on me," she explained.

"He never said anything good about her at all?" Lila asked. "No," Sepia answered.

"She must have been very bad then," Lila agreed.

"He had a reason to hate her," Sepia explained. "She didn't love him. She only married him because she was pregnant with me by somebody else."

Lila was taken aback by this new revelation. "Do you know who your real father is?" Lila asked.

"Yes. I never knew his name. He was hurt in an accident. My mother left him and then married my...Bruno."

"You say your mother left this other man? Do you know why?"

"His face...it was covered with scars. I guess she didn't want him anymore."

"Who told you all this? Bruno?"

"No, he never told me any of it. I found out from someone else."

"Someone told you that your mother left a man she supposedly loved because he was maimed then married a man she didn't love because she was pregnant?" Lila asked.

"Yes."

"How do you think your mother felt about you?" Lila asked.

"She didn't love me."

"Why do you say that?"

"If she loved me, she wouldn't have left me with...him," Sepia responded.

"I see, or at least I see it the way you saw it as a child. But now I could look at it any number of ways," Lila said as she began to polish a worn spot above the foot rail. "If there is one thing I've learned it's that people aren't always as strong as we want them to be. They get sick. They become weak, even broken hearted. Sometimes they do things they don't really want to simply because they don't have the heart to go on, but," she paused and looked at Sepia, "that doesn't make them a bad person, does it?"

"I don't know," Sepia said.

"Can you remember one good thing about your mother?"

"I told you..."

"One good thing?" Lila pressed.

"I can't..."

"What did she look like?" Lila asked more gently.

"She had... dark hair," Sepia said haltingly, "like mine," then she stopped as a memory suddenly flashed through her mind. "Sometimes, she would wash my hair outside of our wagon. I would kneel down over a bucket and while her fingers worked the soap into my hair, she would start singing this loud song in Italian, a love song. She would sing and sing and when my head was full of soap, she would form my hair into horns, or elephant ears or whatever, then I would reach up and feel the slippery shapes and we would laugh together." Sepia was smiling as she looked off in the distance, like she could see the whole scene.

Lila smiled, too. The image Sepia created was not exactly the picture of an evil woman.

"Do you remember anything else?"

"Anything else?" Sepia asked still lost in reverie. "We used to steal cans of peaches from the cookhouse and sneak into the Menagerie, then sit in the hay and eat them. My mother would tell me funny stories about when I was small and I would laugh so hard I'd spit the fruit out and end up so sticky that I let the baby leopards lick my arms clean." Sepia sat with her arms straight out in her lap as if she could feel little sandpaper tongues running across them. Then she went on.

"My mother was the one that started teaching me to fly. We used to practice acrobatics together. She would put her arms under my waist while I tried to do a back flip. At first, I always lost my balance and she would swing me back up and twirl me round and round until we ended up dizzy and laughing on the floor." Sepia paused. "Sometimes, she would look at me and hug me so hard it hurt. There would be tears in her eyes and I wouldn't know why."

"Do you know why now?" Lila asked.

Tears now filled Sepia's eyes. "Because...she loved me."

"You were probably the only good thing in her life."

"Not enough to make her want to live," Sepia said bitterly.

"Maybe you'll find a way to forgive her," Lila answered.

"Bruno never has. He still hates her," Sepia said with a hurt look through her tears.

"Yes, and he took it out on you. He sounds like a very bitter man. He had no right to blame you for his problems. You were a totally innocent child. Sepia, your mother wasn't bad and neither were you."

Sepia looked at Lila. "I loved her so much, but I tried to forget what she looked like, what her voice was like. It hurt too much."

Lila reached out and took Sepia's hand. "I know," she said.

The two women sat on the floor holding hands, remembering their separate losses, but sharing a common grief.

After that day in the bar, Sepia began to recall more stories about her mother and she related them all to Lila. Lila grew to know Angelina quite well, and it only strengthened her belief that Angelina was an incredible woman. But it saddened her to know that there was something so painful in Angelina's life that it made her willing to leave her daughter with such finality.

For Sepia, the memories of her mother literally changed her life. Angelina was no longer the insensitive monster Bruno had created in her mind. She became instead, a person with all the strengths and weaknesses of any other human being. Sepia still felt hurt and sometimes angry over her loss, but she no longer blamed her mother for leaving her. When she stopped blaming her mother, she slowly began to stop blaming herself.

"I used to think I was the reason my mother killed herself, that I had done something wrong and made it happen," she said to Lila.

"I thought the same thing about my parents," Lila replied. "I thought it was my fault they got sick. You know when you're a kid and you get so angry sometimes you wish your parents would die? I thought I had made it happen. I think it's common to feel like it's your fault when somebody close to you dies even when you're an adult."

"There's a dream I've had ever since my mother died, that I'm being smothered because I'm bad."

"You know now that you weren't bad, don't you?" Lila asked hopefully.

"Yes," Sepia answered. "But it's like a habit that's hard to break.

She did try to break it though. She began to see how

feeling bad about herself had made her ripe for Bruno's criticisms, pulling her even deeper into self doubt until she was totally manipulated by his view. Her only escape from his abuse had been to wish him dead. But he was not dead. He was alive and someday she would face him with her anger.

Thoughts of her mother naturally drew Sepia back to wondering about her real father, the Executioner. She wanted more than anything to understand what happened between her parents. Perhaps then she could understand why her father, seeing Sepia's resemblance to Angelina, had wanted to hurt her. Her thoughts grew louder until one day they came out unintentionally as words.

"I wish I had known my father better," Sepia murmured over her morning coffee.

Lila turned from the stove where she was frying eggs. "You met your father?!" she asked incredulous.

Sepia realized that she had wanted to tell Lila the rest of her story ever since that Sunday morning in the restaurant.

"I met my father in a circus called the Olympic. I had only been there a week, one week," she repeated to herself in amazement. So much had happened in that week, a lifetime. "Bruno and I joined the Olympic here in Chicago after the circus we were with closed down. We felt incredibly lucky. I thought it was the best thing that ever happened to me," she said with an ironic smile.

Lila listened while Sepia related everything that had happened during her short time with the Olympic, about Billy, Rosie, Charlene...and Anastasia. She described how she and Bruno got center ring, the night the reporters came and the morning she got the triple. She did not, however, talk about Cole and she hadn't yet described meeting her father.

"And your father?" Lila prompted.

"He was part of the circus, too, a rigger and a clown. His face was covered with horrible scars so he wore the hood of an Executioner in a clown act."

Lila's eyebrows shot up when she heard about the disguise. She remembered the hood she had pulled from Cole's pocket and now wondered how he came to have it.

"From the first time he saw me, I could tell that he hated me," Sepia continued. "I guess I reminded him of my mother or maybe he even thought I was my mother. I think there was something wrong with his mind. I could also see pain in his eyes when he looked at me. He may have hated my mother, but I don't think it was always that way. Anyway, he cut the rope on my trapeze the night I tried the triple in front of an audience. The rope broke and I fell. After the accident, I left the circus."

Lila was already familiar with this last part of the story, but from Cole's perspective. Sepia had yet to mention him.

Cole had told Lila that he had taken Sepia away because he was afraid of what Anastasia might do to her.

"So you left the circus because you were afraid of the Executioner?" Lila asked confused.

"I didn't actually leave on my own. Someone took me away thinking I was still in danger. The odd thing was that at first I didn't understand that he was trying to help me because the person who took me away was the Executioner! Or at least I thought it was the Executioner."

"Who was it?" Lila asked in anticipation.

"Cole Artel, Anastasia's son. He was wearing the Executioner's hood," Sepia explained.

Sepia revealed to Lila what happened while she was with

Cole disguised as the Executioner. She spoke with obvious affection and longing for that person beneath the hood and Lila hid her joy at knowing how much Sepia cared about Cole.

"When I found out that it was Cole, he left. I'm sure he only helped me because he felt sorry for me. He told me it was Anastasia who got the Executioner to cut the net. He said that Anastasia was afraid that I would take her place."

"Was that true?" Lila asked fascinated.

"I still don't know," Sepia said. "I went back to the circus after Cole left me and I talked to Anastasia. She said Cole had lied about her because he was mad at her. She said he couldn't be trusted, and in many ways, she was right. Anastasia also told me the truth about my father. She had heard Rosie telling Billy about him after the fire."

"Fire?" Lila asked. Cole hadn't mentioned a fire.

"The night of my accident there was a storm and the Menagerie was hit by lightning. It burnt to the ground and my father was killed in the fire."

"I'm sorry," Lila said.

"Anastasia told me how upset Billy was about the accident and the fire and my father's death. I felt like it was all my fault. I was sure I'd brought bad luck to the Olympic."

Lila kept quiet even though she knew that Sepia had not brought bad luck to anyone. Lila was convinced now that the circumstances in which Sepia's mother left her disfigured lover were probably not as Anastasia described. Anastasia had done a horrifyingly good job on Sepia. This was the infamous mother that Cole had described. Lila was astounded at the depth of deceit Anastasia had maintained without discovery. Anastasia was impressive to be sure, terrifying, but impressive.

Sepia continued her story haltingly now as she described what happened after she left Anastasia; about Roscoe Tyler, Tony, and finally her months with Frank Dinetti. Toward the end, there were many things she couldn't remember or didn't want to.

There was the night she was in the back of Frank's car while Frank sat in front with the snake man driving. The snake man's name was Charlie, but Sepia never thought of him as anything but a reptile. Frank was edgy and kept flicking his switchblade open and closed. The car suddenly pulled over outside a restaurant and Frank ordered Sepia to stay in the car. She was heavily drugged, but the tension in Frank's voice kept her alert and she watched him enter the restaurant. Charlie kept the car engine running and minutes later, gunshots were heard. Frank came running out of the restaurant followed by two men, one bearing a gunshot wound in the arm and the other in the cheek. Frank jumped in the car totally calm even as the two men fired at him.

"Better get a move on, Charlie," Frank said, but Charlie rolled down his window, aimed his own gun and shot the wounded-arm man in the forehead. Sepia sat frozen, watching the man collapse on the sidewalk in a pool of blood. His buddy staggered back in fear and Charlie finally put his foot to the gas and sped away. Frank turned around to Sepia. "You didn't see nothin'. You rat on me and you're dead." His threat did not scare her though. She wasn't afraid of him, but of what she had seen and that she was with people who could do such things. Somehow she had thought Frank only did bad things to her. After that, she retreated farther and farther into her drug induced world.

When Sepia finished, it was Lila who was overwhelmed

by the telling. Mostly she was in awe of how Sepia had survived everything that had happened, especially at the end. Lila doubted that she could have survived such abuse. She told Sepia as much, but Sepia shook her head.

"It wasn't what other people did to me that really hurt," she said. "It's what I did to myself. I knew I was a coward, but I didn't have the guts to do the things I wanted to do."

"What things did you want to do?" Lila asked.

"I wanted to go back to the Olympic and tell Billy what happened. I wanted to stop Bruno from running my life. I wanted to say to Anastasia that if she thought I was trying to compete with her she was wrong. And I wanted to..." she stopped as the words caught in her throat.

"What, Sepia? What else did you want?" Lila asked.

"I wanted to find Cole and tell him that I loved him whether he cared about me or not," she said, full of emotion.

"Do you still love him?" Lila asked.

Sepia looked at Lila with tears brimming in her eyes. "I will always love him," she answered.

"Sepia, do you still want to do all of the things you just said?"

"I don't know anymore. I don't know what I want to do."

"Do you want to fly?" Lila asked.

"Flying was my whole life and I don't want it to be that way. I don't want it to be an escape anymore. Cole said something to me, that I had to be as strong on the ground as I was in the air, and he was right."

Lila smiled at Cole's words of wisdom, and then looked Sepia in the eye. "You said that you were a coward, but I must tell you that a coward would never have suffered through what you did. You were punishing yourself and you took it like the bravest soldier. Something kept you going. Even the doctor and nurses saw it. They didn't think you would make it. I don't know what kept you alive, but I suspect it was love. Somewhere inside is a part of you that loves that daring young woman on the flying trapeze."

"I've lived my whole life thinking that I'm not worth loving," Sepia said in response.

"But it's pretty obvious that there are people who love you. I'm positive that your mother loved you very much. The people at the circus, Billy and the seamstress Rosie, it sounds like they cared a lot about you. Jack and I love you. I hope you know that. And there is someone else that I think you guessed wrong about. I think Cole does care about you, but he was too scared to show it."

"If I thought that was true, I'd do anything to find him." Sepia replied.

"I'll make you a deal, Sepia. If you do the other things you said you wanted to do, I will help you find Cole. I promise."

Sepia looked at Lila with surprise, but saw that she was serious. "It means I have to go back to the Olympic."

"Yes."

"I'd have to find out where they are," Sepia said to herself, turning the possibility over in her mind.

"The Olympic is coming to Chicago in three weeks," Lila answered.

***

Lila gradually stopped worrying about the possibility of Sepia drinking again. Sister Agnes was right. Sepia was not a drunk and the need for oblivion had disappeared as quickly as it had come. However, when Sepia was mysteriously absent several afternoons in a row, Lila grew concerned. Sepia returned from her outings sweating and flushed, but seemingly clearheaded, saying she'd been out for a walk. Lila didn't want to intrude on her privacy, but the next day when Sepia showed up late for work at the restaurant, she couldn't hold back any longer.

"Sepia, what's going on?" she asked worried.

"I'm sorry I'm late," Sepia apologized then a huge grin spread across her face. "Lila, I can tell you now. It's all coming back! I haven't lost it!" she exclaimed.

"Lost what?" Lila asked, perplexed.

"I didn't want to tell you because I was scared that I wouldn't be able to do it, but the last few days I've been going to a gym where they let me work out on their trampoline. I was really rusty at first, but now it feels great!"

Lila stared at Sepia dumbfounded.

"I'm starting to build up my muscles again. I'm so weak! I want you to tell me when you can see a difference," Sepia said glancing at her biceps hopefully.

Lila was at a loss for words. "Okay," she said simply.

Satisfied, Sepia walked past Lila toward the restaurant kitchen to start work. Lila watched her, astonished, but smiling as she noticed that Sepia walked a little taller through the kitchen door.

Sepia entered the kitchen and attacked a pile of dirty glasses. While she loaded them in a sink of soapy water, she suddenly remembered a tune and started humming it. It was the love song her mother used to sing. Sepia remembered only part of the melody and none of the words, but she plunged her hands into the sudsy water and kept on humming until it was time to quit.

Sepia returned to the gym everyday after that. She had

forgotten how good it felt to physically work her body. At first, she had been clumsy and stiff, but the more she stretched out her muscles and limbered up, it was as if her body had only been waiting to do what was ingrained in every fiber of her being since childhood. The more she bounced and flipped in the air on the trampoline, the more anxious she got to leave the ground completely. She wanted to fly!

Sepia thought about the deal Lila proposed. She had already decided to visit the Olympic when it came to town. Whether she stayed there or not depended on a lot more than her own desires. Billy might still be angry at her for leaving so abruptly. He might still feel, as Anastasia had told her, that Sepia was the cause of the bad things that happened to the Olympic when she was with them. Sepia was not anxious to face Bruno, either. She did not want to lose control in front of him, so she rehearsed what she would say to him until it sounded forceful, but calm.

Chapter Twenty Four: The Olympic

Rosie sat on a low wooden stool repairing a palm-size rip in the menagerie top. The Olympic had arrived in the predawn hours, and even though it was still early morning, the set-up was almost complete. After repairing the tent, Rosie would have a few hours of needed rest. Twenty years in circus had not made sleeping on trains any easier for her. She was glad to be in Chicago where the show ran for a week and she could stay put in her wagon for a while.

Being in Chicago also turned her thoughts to their last run in this city and then, of course, to Sepia. The series of events since she last saw Sepia played often in Rosie's mind. When Billy showed her the note Sepia left him, Rosie had stared at it in disbelief. For a long time she tried to convince herself that Sepia had a good reason for leaving, that she was doing it to help herself, to get away from Bruno, to have her own life, but she was never sure. Something didn't seem right. She had felt it in her gut and still felt it today, that Sepia had left for the wrong reason. Rosie had been worried about her ever since.

Rosie knit her brow as she worked her oversized needle in and out of the stiff canvas, remembering the night of

Sepia's accident. The rumors of what happened had circled and eventually died, even the rumor about Cole. Whether she believed Cole Artel was involved or not, Rosie was certain the Executioner had a hand in causing Sepia's accident. When he was found dead, Rosie was plagued with guilt from not having told Billy about him sooner. She was glad at least that she had spoken to the Executioner, though she guessed that he may not have understood what she told him. She had seen in his eyes a faint glimmer of recognition, but mostly he seemed beyond reach, as if he had entered a world protected from pain. If only she had realized earlier who he was, she could have tried to help him.

When Bruno Stefani's accusations had shifted from Anastasia to Cole, Rosie was not convinced. She still suspected that Anastasia was at the bottom of it all. Rosie guessed Anastasia had taken advantage of the Executioner to help her and would have found a way to manipulate the Executioner's already twisted mind. It made Rosie furious, not just because of what Anastasia had done, but because there was no way to prove it.

Like Billy, Rosie's main concern, however, had always been Sepia. She wished very hard for her safe return. There was so much she wanted to tell her. Sepia deserved to know the truth about her past no matter how tragic it was. The only thing Rosie was unsure about revealing was the truth about the Executioner being her father. She was afraid it would be too painful and perhaps unnecessary for her to know now. Rosie decided not to worry about what she would say to Sepia. She only hoped that she would get the chance to see her.

Rosie looked up from her work to rest her eyes and noticed a figure in the distance. She blinked, rubbed her eyes then slowly stood up.

"Louie!" Rosie shouted. "Go get Billy!"

Louie, who was working close by, followed Rosie's stare and saw a woman walking toward them. It took him a moment, but even Louie, who took pains not to get too familiar, recognized the auburn hair and large brown eyes of the woman approaching. He dropped his work and trotted toward Billy's office.

Rosie stood up and began walking toward Sepia. They met at the edge of the circus grounds and Rosie threw her arms around her.

"God, kid, I hoped you'd come back. Are you okay?"

"Yes," Sepia said through smiling tears. She hadn't realized how glad she would be to see Rosie.

Billy came walking over with Louie, and Sepia's smile faded. She held her breath, unsure how Billy would react to her return.

"Sepia," Billy said in a cracked voice.

"Hello, Billy," Sepia replied, still not able to read his mood. "Hi, Louie," she added, remembering his serious but honest face.

Louie's mouth crooked into what could be interpreted as a smile, then he immediately found an excuse to leave them. "I need to keep an eye on them guys bringing the cats out," he said and shyly darted off.

Sepia looked at Billy. "Billy, I'm sorry for running out on you. I don't blame you if you're sore at me," she said.

"What?" Billy exclaimed. "Why would I be sore? I've never been anything but worried about you!"

"I thought because of everything that happened, you might think I brought you bad luck," she said.

"You didn't bring us bad luck. Whoever tried to hurt you

was the bad luck. As far as I'm concerned, any bad luck we had just changed," Billy said, grinning at her.

Sepia's fears about Billy had been unfounded and she breathed a huge sigh of relief. She remembered all the things Anastasia had said that night a year ago and wondered what other lies Anastasia had told her.

"So, what have you been up to?" Billy asked.

"I've, uh, been staying in the city," Sepia answered hesitantly.

Rosie noticed Sepia's reluctance to explain. "Can you stay awhile and visit? You want a cup of coffee?"

"Sure," Sepia answered.

"Let's go over to the cookhouse. I bet there's plenty of folks around that'll be glad to see you. Join us, boss?" Rosie asked Billy.

"Let me set the men working on their own and I'll be over," he said as he headed back toward the Big Top.

"Is my fa...is Bruno still here?" Sepia asked Rosie as they began walking toward the cookhouse.

"He's still here," Rosie told her. "He wasn't doing so good after you left, but the oldest Terelli brother broke his shoulder and Billy got Bruno to fill in." She paused and looked at Sepia. "He hasn't changed any."

Sepia smiled. She wouldn't have figured Bruno had changed. Neither was she surprised that he had survived okay without her.

Sepia hadn't been sure what it would feel like to step onto the circus grounds again. She had thought it would make her tense, but when she walked past the familiar sights and felt her body suddenly relax, she realized that it was everywhere else that had made her tense.

As people recognized her, they called out their welcomes,

and when they entered the cookhouse tent, Sepia was immediately surrounded by a group of performers led by Charlene.

"Sepia! Wow! I thought we'd never see you again!" Charlene yelled then gave Sepia a hug. Each of the others; Wanda, the Terelli brothers, Zelda, the tattooed lady, even the Sheik welcomed her with open arms.

Sepia sat on top of a dining table and everyone crowded around her. She was overwhelmed by her reception. She didn't expect everyone to remember her much less be happy to see her. She felt guilty for having misplaced these wonderful faces in her memory when they had clearly not forgotten hers. There had been people who cared about her before. She just wasn't able to accept it then. As she let their welcome sink in, she caught sight of Bruno coming toward her. She sat quietly, waiting to see what he would do.

Bruno walked over to Sepia in a casual manner and the other performers parted to let him through.

"So, you're back," Bruno said.

"Hi, Papa," Sepia said, though the words felt foreign to her now.

Billy joined the group then and stood near Sepia. He kept a close eye on Bruno.

"Are you back to stay?" Bruno asked bluntly.

"I...I don't know," Sepia said glancing at Billy, embarrassed that the topic had come up.

"We haven't talked, Stefani," Billy told Bruno.

"In that case, I got nothin' to say either," Bruno replied then turned and walked back out of the tent.

The other performers watched open-mouthed, but Sepia didn't seem upset. She had words to say to Bruno, but now wasn't the time. She was just as happy to have him go.

The other performers gradually left, too, expressing their hopes to see her again. Finally, Rosie and Billy were left alone with Sepia.

"There's a place for you if you want to come back," Billy said.

"Thanks, Billy. You don't know how good that makes me feel. I need to work some things out first," she said. "But I do want to fly again."

Rosie and Billy glanced at each other over the news that she hadn't been flying. Billy had thought she looked different and now he realized that she had lost weight and muscle. He wondered what had happened to her this past year.

Louie interrupted them. "Boss, you want to take a look at these orders coming in?"

Billy looked at Sepia. "Don't leave without saying goodbye, okay?" he asked Sepia.

"I won't," she promised.

After Billy left, Sepia slid off the tabletop and sat on the bench next to Rosie. They each took a sip of coffee in silence.

Rosie wasn't sure it was the right time, but she couldn't keep it inside any longer.

"Sepia, I must tell you something. I wanted to tell you before. I should have told you before, but I didn't get the chance. Sepia, I knew your mother." Rosie waited for a reaction, but got none. "We worked in the same circus together when she was young, before she met your father, not Bruno, but your real father." Again, Rosie paused for a response, but didn't expect the one she got.

"I know," Sepia said.

"You know about your father?" Rosie asked with surprise.

"Anastasia told me. I came to see her the night you pulled up stakes here."

"Anastasia?" Rosie exclaimed. Somehow Anastasia had found out. "You were here that night?" she asked then a slow wave of recognition spread across her face. Anastasia had used the information about Sepia's father to drive her away. Rosie refrained from using the expletives that were on her tongue.

"I came to Anastasia because I was trying to find Cole," Sepia explained.

"We all thought you were with Cole," Rosie said.

"I was, but then he left," she replied and her voice changed in tone. "None of that matters now. Rosie, tell me about my mother and father. Do you know what really happened between them?"

Rosie had been thrown off track by the news of Anastasia's treachery, but she began again to tell Sepia about her past.

"Your mother had been with another man before Bruno, not married, but lovers. His name was Patrick Dannon. He was your father."

"Patrick Dannon," Sepia repeated. She now had a name that could finally replace the only other reference she had had for her father, Executioner.

"Why didn't my mother stay with him?" Sepia asked.

"She couldn't," Rosie explained. "They had planned to go away together, but Patrick was hurt in a terrible accident. Both of their parents had been against their being together. The accident became the way to keep them apart. Your mother was not allowed to see Patrick and his parents must have told him that she didn't want to. She waited for him to come just like he waited for her. When he didn't come, your mother was forced into marriage because of the baby she was carrying. She didn't love Bruno, but she married him so that you would be taken care of. She never saw Patrick again."

"What happened to him?"

"I don't know. I never saw him until he came to the Olympic."

"And then he died in the Menagerie fire," Sepia said.

"Yes. Before he died, I spoke to him. I tried to tell him that your mother had never stopped loving him. I believe he understood me. I hope so. I met him briefly when he and Angelina were together. He had the kindest eyes I have ever seen. Like yours, Sepia."

"She never stopped loving him," Sepia murmured. "That's why she killed herself."

"Yes," Rosie agreed.

"She must have hated me for ruining her life, for forcing her to marry Bruno."

"No, you're wrong. You were the only thing she had left of Patrick. She adored you...but Angelina was not strong. She could not live with a broken heart and a broken spirit."

Sepia nodded. She had learned what having both could do. She understood what her mother had felt, why she had let the ache in her heart consume her. It could have happened to Sepia. It almost had. She looked at Rosie with tears in her eyes. "Do you really think I'm like my father?"

"You have his quiet strength and good heart," Rosie smiled.

Even Rosie, however, did not know the extent of Patrick Dannon's strength. In his deranged, tortured state, he had first saved his daughter from Anastasia then given her up to someone else. When Cole had faced him in the Menagerie,

Patrick was prepared to die to protect Sepia, but Cole had kept talking, using the calm steady voice a trainer uses on a wild animal. At first Patrick hadn't trusted the voice. Cole was the son of the woman who had deceived him, but when he looked up into the young man's eyes, he saw the same determined love that he had felt for Angelina, and he let Cole take Sepia. When they left, Patrick laid down in the straw and fell into a deep, restful sleep only to be wakened by the frantic cries of the animals around him. His throat was assaulted by the burning smoke, but he moved choking through the tent, cutting as many animals free as he could find. Then a flaming tent pole fell against him and he was finally at peace.

It was time for Sepia to leave. She hugged Rosie and thanked her for filling in the pieces of her past. Sepia held tightly to her memories now. There were so many things she wished she could ask her mother. More than anything, however, she wished she could have saved her mother from unhappiness.

Billy was not in his office, so Sepia headed for the Big Top to find him. The feeling that swept through her when she entered the tent was overwhelming. It was as if a thousand sensations hit her at once; smells, voices, music, and warmth. Her eyes were immediately drawn to the peak of the tent and the rigging that already hung in place. She wanted to be up there so badly she could taste it.

Sepia sensed someone behind her and a chill ran down her spine. She turned around and saw Anastasia standing there in her rehearsal outfit looking as vibrant and powerful as ever, like the poster Sepia had seen on the abandoned building, except that Anastasia was not smiling now.

"Hello, Sepia."

"Hello." Sepia felt suddenly light headed and a tingling sensation spread through her body. She clenched her fists to keep from fainting.

"What brings you here?" Anastasia asked.

"I'm just visiting," Sepia answered. There were so many things she wanted to say to Anastasia, but she stood silent. She wanted to ask about Cole, but felt foolish. She didn't know that Cole was exactly who Anastasia was thinking about, too.

"What have you been doing?" Anastasia asked.

"Working in the city," Sepia stammered. Damned if she would let Anastasia know the hell she sent her to a year ago.

"Doing what?"

"Working for a friend in a restaurant," Sepia answered, slightly embarrassed.

"So you haven't been flying."

"No."

"Have you given it up?"

"No, in fact, Billy just offered me a job if I want it. He wanted me back. Funny, all this time I thought he was sore at me. He wasn't sore at all," Sepia said with emphasis. She was gaining courage. "Have you heard from Cole?"

"Cole never came back. For all I know he is working in a restaurant, too," Anastasia said in an insulting tone, "Or dead. You wouldn't happen to know, would you?"

"No."

"I didn't think so," Anastasia said.

Sepia felt the anger rise inside her and took a deep breath.

"If it's true you had something to do with my accident, I'll never be able to prove it, but I do know what you did to me the night the Olympic left Chicago. I let your lies almost kill me."

She took a step toward Anastasia who stared at her wide-eyed.

"I should hate you for what you did, but I can't. I feel sorry for you. You are too scared to care about anyone and someday you will die alone."

"How dare you talk to me like that!" Anastasia hissed. "You know nothing of my life or what I've been through!"

"Yes I do," Sepia said with conviction. "I've been through as much as you ever have. If I decide to come back here, it will be because I love to fly not because I want to compete with you or be anywhere near you. I'm not afraid of you so back off."

Sepia walked past Anastasia and left her standing there speechless. Sepia headed for the exit shaking, not from fear, but from the thrill of standing her ground. As she reached the tent opening, she jumped up and slapped the top border with her hand, a joyful signal of her triumph.

Sepia spotted Billy near the Menagerie and took a moment to calm herself before she walked over to him.

"Goodbye, Billy," she said.

"You'll be back?"

"I'll be back," she said, though both were unsure exactly what that meant.

***

"So, how was it?" Lila asked anxiously when Sepia walked into the restaurant for work.

"Mostly great," Sepia said with a smile. "I saw everybody. I saw Bruno."

"And?"

"He wasn't much interested in talking unless I'm coming back," she laughed, remembering his reaction. "He's such a bastard," she added with growing detachment. "I saw Anastasia, too."

"You did?"

"I'm not so in awe of her anymore. I'm not scared of her either. You were right. Everything she told me was a lie, but when I can stop being angry, I feel sorry for her. I told her that."

"I bet she didn't take that real well," Lila said with a smirk.

"I found out something else from her. She hasn't heard from Cole."

"Doesn't surprise me," Lila commented.

"I wonder where he is?" Sepia asked, mostly to herself.

"Maybe he joined another circus," Lila suggested. "Speaking of which, did Billy ask you to come back?"

"How did you know?" Sepia asked, surprised.

"Wild guess," Lila grinned. "So?"

"I want to go back. I might have to work with my father for awhile, though."

"Could you do that?"

"I think so. If he starts to yell at me again, I'll just yell back," she laughed. Her voice became serious. "What I've been through the last year, especially the last three months, I would never want to go through again, but I've learned to stand on my own two feet and I will always be grateful for that. I could never let Bruno run my life like he did before. Never," she said firmly.

Lila had seen the gradual changes in Sepia over the last two months, but now as she saw Sepia standing before her with her shoulders back and her chin up, speaking with proud determination, she realized how far Sepia had come. Lila remembered Cole's description of Sepia as a scared kid. She was no scared kid now. Sepia was a woman standing tall and ready to make a life for herself.

"I'll miss you, Sepia," Lila said with a smile.

Sepia had avoided thinking about leaving Lila. Lila had been her guardian angel, then her friend, then like a second mother to her. Sepia found herself saying things to Lila that she had wanted to say to her mother. As she had done with Cole, Lila had given Sepia the chance to fly again.

Sepia couldn't help compare Anastasia to Lila, two powerful yet totally different women. One had led her into darkness and the other into light, but both had saved her from her life before and both had helped form the person she was now. Anastasia had forced her to grow. Lila had encouraged her to. It was obvious who Sepia felt indebted to.

"I'll miss you, too, Lila, more than I can say."

"Well, we can always write and I'll get to see you at least once a year, right?" Lila observed through tears.

"Right," Sepia said then they reached out to each other and held on tightly.

The next morning, Sepia returned to the Olympic and knocked on Bruno's wagon. He was sharing it now with two other performers. Bruno came to the door yawning with his dark hair sticking out at the sides.

"Billy asked me to come back," Sepia told him. "I want to fly again. Do you want to be my catcher?"

"I am your catcher," he said.

"Not unless we work as equals, equal in money, equal in decisions," she said firmly.

"Do I have a choice?" he asked, grumbling.

"You could keep working with the Terelli brothers."

"It's wrecking my shoulders," he complained, rotating one of them sorely.

"I'll meet you in the Big Top," Sepia replied.

When Sepia climbed up the rope to the trapeze platform, Charlene stood there waiting.

"Louie told me you were going to workout. Thought you could maybe use a hand," Charlene explained.

"I could. Thanks. Thanks a lot," Sepia replied.

Bruno hadn't arrived yet, so Sepia took some practice swings on her own. She couldn't help feeling nervous being up on the platform again, but when she took the wooden trapeze bar in her hands; it felt as natural as eating or sleeping. She swung out into the air, her body surging with adrenalin. She closed her eyes and felt the wind on her body as she soared across the tent, then as she reached the apex of her swing, she twisted around and flew back to the platform. After Charlene helped her to her feet, Sepia took a deep breath and let the rush of excitement flow through her body. There was nothing quite like it…except, and Sepia could not stop the thought coming…except when she was with Cole.

"Are you okay?" Charlene asked as she watched Sepia's broad smile fade.

"Yes," Sepia answered, bringing her thoughts back to the present.

"You looked great out there!" Charlene told her.

"Thanks," Sepia said as she grabbed the bar and flew out again.

Charlene had been dying to ask Sepia her whereabouts for the last year, but there hadn't been the right moment. Gossip was rampant, but the only thing anybody could say for certain was that she had been working in Chicago in a restaurant and she was not with Cole. That news had been disappointing. All this time, Charlene had hoped that Sepia and Cole had run away together and were working in another circus somewhere. Now she was not only curious about Sepia, but also worried about where Cole had ended up. Charlene's thoughts were interrupted when she spotted Bruno climbing the ladder to his trapeze. She wondered how Sepia and Bruno would get along now, though she guessed Sepia wasn't going to take the same abuse Bruno used to dish out.

Sepia swung back up to the platform and watched Bruno climb onto the catcher's bar. She had a slight knot in her stomach at the familiarity of the scene, but she remembered the deal she had made with him and she swore to herself that if he didn't go along, she wouldn't either.

Bruno sat on the catch bar, getting the feel of being sixty feet off the ground again. He took a deep breath, thankful to be back in the air. He had almost lost hope that Sepia would come back, but there she was just like old times and they could start where they left off... sort of. She was different now, making demands and acting like she knew as much as he did. He had no choice but to go along, but he would see how long she kept up her act of being high and mighty. Besides, he was rusty and couldn't make any demands on her anyway.

"We try very simple tricks, eh?" he shouted to Sepia and watched her nod. When Sepia took hold of the bar and swung out, he slipped down into position and wrapped his legs tightly in the ropes. As she swung toward him, he was surprised how smooth and comfortable she looked. He, on the other hand, was shaking from nerves, but he managed to grab her calves and catch her, if awkwardly. He was relieved when she returned to her trapeze and he swung back up to a sitting position, sweat breaking out on his forehead. He needed practice that's all, lots of practice.

Sepia and Bruno worked through the morning, and by the time they both decided it was time to quit, it was clear that Sepia had returned to form much quicker than Bruno. There was a marked difference in her flying, however. Charlene noticed it right away.

Sepia's body had not regained its former weight in muscle, but the flesh that had replaced it gave her a more rounded, womanly appearance. Where before she had performed with athletic precision, now there was a sanguine quality of whimsy and grace.

When Billy walked inconspicuously up to the arena entrance, he stood stock still, watching Sepia sail across the tent as if it was second nature, as if the past year was fiction and she had never really left. He, too, saw the change in her. She was a woman now, even more beautiful with maturity, no longer the frightened bird that needed protection. Billy guessed the price of learning to protect herself was the dark shadows that remained under her eyes. She lacked the bitter edge, however, that often accompanies hard learned lessons, and she still projected an openness and desire for life that only hope can bring. A lump rose in his throat as he murmured yet another quiet thank you that she had returned safely to the Olympic then he walked back out of the Big Top.

Sepia dropped into the safety net, swung down to the ground and waited for Bruno. He had kept his comments to a minimum during their practice, and overall, she had felt okay about working with him. Maybe they really could reach a common ground that would satisfy them both, she thought.

"Are you stayin' then?" Bruno asked.

"I told Billy I would practice everyday and if it went okay,

I would go with him when he left Chicago."

Bruno clearly did not like this new way she talked to him, but he was forced to nod his head. "See you tomorrow mornin'," he said then left the tent.

Sepia laughed inside as she watched Bruno hunch his shoulders and stifle his frustration with her. It was an obvious effort on his part and she enjoyed watching him make it. It amazed her, this feeling of smugness, knowing that Bruno needed her more than she needed him.

Sepia tried to avoid thinking of the person she needed more than he needed her. Needed or wanted, she wasn't quite sure of the difference. She reminded herself that Cole had only helped her to stop Anastasia. She recalled the anger and bitterness in his voice as he spoke of Anastasia beneath the Executioner's mask. Yet, he had not cared enough to tell Sepia himself that he had betrayed his mother to help her. He did not care enough to confront Anastasia. If he wanted Sepia, he would have fought to come back. He wouldn't have run away.

Sepia knew all of this and yet when she thought of Cole, her heart forgot everything. She remembered only the sandy brown mane of hair, the deep blue eyes, the ir-resistible smile, the muscular arms and broad chest. She breathed in his scent, heard the beating of his heart, and felt the power of his arms as if it had only been a moment ago that he held her pressed against him.

Sepia thought she heard someone call her name and she turned to look, but no one was there. It had happened before when she thought of Cole. Some spark of memory she couldn't place, a time she couldn't remember when he had held her safe against a hurricane of darkness. Perhaps it was a dream so real that it will stay with me forever, she thought, though there was little of it she remembered except Cole holding her and saying her name, and that she was about to die. She decided it must have been when he carried her unconscious from the circus the night of her flying accident, yet she wondered why the dream hadn't started until so much later, after she was in the hospital. Even if it were possible to fade Cole from her mind, this dream, this memory would never fade. Perhaps because he saved her life, it was inevitable that she would remain somehow linked to him forever, like the lifeline knotted to the mechanic.

Chapter Twenty Five: The Bank Game

Anastasia sat in her wagon nursing a shot of leftover Prohibition whiskey. Sepia was in the Big Top practicing for the third morning in a row and for the third morning, Anastasia had kept away. She knew she should be in the tent, establishing her dominance and rehearsing her act, but she was losing her energy to fight.

Things had not gone well this last year as the crowds dwindled and the Olympic struggled to stay afloat. Anastasia was still Queen of the Circus, but she felt the magic slipping away. The cheers were not as loud, the adulation not as strong. Even her body was beginning to resist the constant strain of her act. She found herself holding back, doing simpler stunts and dropping the number of one arm swingovers. None of the performers ever said anything, but she felt their stares of curiosity, wondering if the goddess was mortal after all.

No one really wanted to see Anastasia retire. She was the glue that kept the show together, by far the biggest attraction, but as they watched her performance slip, they were forced to wonder who could possibly take her place. It was no small wonder that when Sepia showed up again, the other performers began to speculate on her potential. Where before they had believed the idea of Sepia taking Anastasia's place had been fantasy, now it became real. Anastasia had, of course, always believed it was real. Anastasia had believed more in the girl's potential than Sepia ever did. Having been right all along gave her no satisfaction however. It only made her feel drained.

Sepia's return was a problem, but not one Anastasia could share with anyone. Before, when something upset or angered her, she could vent her emotions on Billy or Cole and get sympathy, but this matter with Sepia was different and she would get no sympathy there.

There were two possible solutions to her problem. She could continue to fight Sepia's rise by whatever means she could devise or she could accept what was inevitable, that someday she must step down from her place at the top. The former no longer appealed to her and the latter was unthinkable.

She recalled her confrontation with Sepia in the Big Top. Sepia's words had struck harder than Anastasia wanted to admit, the part about being scared, not about being alone. Anastasia had always been alone even when she was married and with her son. She had always had to support herself because she always had more ambition than those around her. No one had ever taken care of her or coddled her, but just once, it would have been nice to have someone to lean on, someone who could take away her fear of the future, for what was to become of an ex Queen of the Circus? Sepia was right. Anastasia was scared, and whether she admitted it or not, she had already given up.

***

Billy sat at his desk shuffling bills from one pile to another when Louie delivered the telegram. He read it quickly then crumpled it up in his hands.

You don't own me yet, Hunter!" he shouted to the ball of paper. "Dammit!" he added in frustration as he tossed the wadded telegram across the wagon. He stared at the wall. "All I asked was that they give us 'til the middle of the season. We could have made up our losses by then."

Louie shook his head, knowing what the bank's answer was. He didn't want to think what that meant for Billy...or himself. He turned his thought to the immediate, reminding himself that the show must go on. "We're all squared away for tonight, boss."

Billy looked across his desk at Louie. "Get everybody together in the Big Top."

Sepia and Bruno joined the other Olympic performers and workers already gathered in the stands of the Big Top. When everyone was assembled in front of Billy, he began. "I asked you all here because I believe in giving it to you straight. There's an outfit that wants to buy me out."

Billy was interrupted by cries of protest. Sepia was stunned. She didn't want to hear what Billy was going to say.

"It's a big outfit and I hear they won't be under a tent much longer. Think of it, boys," Billy said to the group of roustabouts sitting together, "no more bustin' your butt to bring this old gal to her feet, and no more fires or windstorms to bring her down."

There were smiles and understanding nods in the stands

even if they didn't like what Billy was getting at. Billy stood very quiet and scanned the group before him. "But, if enough of you still like the smell of sawdust, canvas and sweat, and knowin' you can count on each other, then I sure as hell wanna' stick around. You people built this circus. We're makin' a name for ourselves, and I don't want to give up now. The only way we can stay alive is to show the bank folks we're somethin' special, that we can still draw the crowds wherever we go. One of their big shots is comin' to see the show tonight. I'm askin' you to be extra good. I know you're the best. Just go out there and show 'em what you got."

As soon as Billy finished, he walked briskly out of the tent. There was a stunned silence in the stands then everyone broke out in nervous talk.

Bruno leaned over to Sepia. "If Thompson sells out, it'll be good for us."

Sepia stared at Bruno. "What?"

"We'll be a bigger act in a bigger show," Bruno explained.

"You don't care if Billy goes under?" Sepia asked.

"We gotta think of ourselves," Bruno said.

Sepia stood up and looked down at Bruno. "No, I've got to think of myself," she said as she started climbing down from the stands.

Bruno called after her. "What's that supposed to mean?"

When Sepia didn't answer, Bruno stood up. "Come back here!" he ordered, but Sepia did not. Bruno shouted once more, risking the stares of those around him. "Sepia!"

When still Sepia kept going, Bruno stood humiliated in front of the other performers. They, however, were staring after Sepia in awe.

Sepia was deep in thought as she walked out of the Big

Top ignoring Bruno's cries. She wasn't thinking of Bruno or of herself. She was thinking of Billy and she wanted to help him. There was really only one thing she could do and that was to perform tonight, but not just any act. She had to perform an act that would astound the audience and show the bank that the Olympic was big box office.

She and Bruno had worked hard the last few mornings and they were gaining back their timing and skill. She had moved past the simpler stunts and was throwing somersaults again. Just this morning she had thrown a two-and-a-half backward somersault and Bruno had caught her, raggedly, but he had caught her. They had not tried a triple however, and it was the triple Billy needed tonight.

She unconsciously looked down at her body as if checking to see if there was enough power within it. She was stronger now, but was she strong enough? She knew, too, that it wasn't only physical strength she needed. She needed to recapture that feeling she had a year ago, that she really could do it.

"You can do it," Lila said after hearing what had happened that day and Sepia's plan to help Billy.

Lila had stopped by the circus one morning to visit Sepia. She was fascinated to see what it was like behind the scenes, the everyday life of the circus. As she walked across the grounds, she saw people washing clothes, feeding babies, grooming animals, and repairing equipment just like ordinary people. They weren't unfriendly, but Lila sensed that she was an outsider and under suspicion even if she was with Sepia.

Sepia ushered her toward the Big Top and it was a surprise to step into the large empty tent, a totally different space without the crowds, lights and music. It seemed more like a gym where performers, looking distinctly unglamorous, worked out in shorts and undershirts.

Lila climbed up into the open stands and sat waiting while Sepia ascended to the trapeze. Sepia didn't bother introducing Lila to Bruno, preferring not to spoil the moment by his probable rudeness. Sepia had told Lila about Charlene who now waved down at her from the platform. Lila instantly liked Charlene's open, expressive face and toothy smile. She could also see Charlene's loyalty to Sepia as she pointed to Sepia behind her back and signaled to Lila with a conspiratorial thumbs-up signal.

Lila was enjoying the whole experience, but it was when Sepia took hold of the trapeze and flew out into the air, that Lila was truly agog. She had imagined what it would be like to see Sepia fly, particularly after watching Cole, but it was nothing compared to seeing her in real life sailing across the tent like a beautiful bird, graceful and effortless. Sepia was truly at home in the air, like a fish in water or a gazelle on land. When she tucked her body into a back somersault, she spun so fast Lila couldn't keep track of how many turns she made. It seemed like at least three. If it wasn't, Lila had no doubt that Sepia could do three if she wanted to.

"You can do it," she repeated, seeing the worried look on Sepia's face.

"I have to try anyway. It's the only way I can help Billy," she said.

***

"Would you let us come and watch?" Jack asked.

Lila and Sepia had been talking in the restaurant kitchen, but Jack was chopping onions nearby and had heard their conversation. He was usually slightly on the outside of their conversations, though never excluded. He liked listening to them talk to each other. Where he tended to try and find immediate solutions to problems, he found it mysterious yet refreshing to hear the more circuitous yet supportive way that Lila and Sepia discussed things.

Sepia looked over at Jack, considering his question, wondering if she would be too nervous if Lila and Jack were in the audience. She decided that she'd probably be so nervous it wouldn't matter who was watching.

"Sure, why not?" she answered.

"Good. I for one would like to see history in the making," Jack stated.

Chapter Twenty Six: Now Or Never

The stands were empty and waiting. The circus band tuned up as the candy butchers filled their trays with popcorn and bottles of soda. Roustabouts finished raking the sawdust smooth.

Billy stood at the arena opening with Louie.

"All set, boss?" Louie asked.

"Let the folks in," Billy replied.

Outside, a shiny black Packard pulled into the circus grounds. George Hunter from Midwest Bank and Trust stepped out of the car wearing a dark pin-stripe suit and a Stetson. He walked down the Midway, following the crowd toward the Big Top. He stopped to buy his twenty-five cent ticket like any other customer and was whisked through the line by the lightning fast sellers. There was a heightened feeling in the air that even Hunter noticed. No one could ignore the power of five hundred performers and workers all hoping at the same time.

When Hunter entered the Big Top, Billy signaled one of the ushers who showed him to a choice spot. Billy watched Hunter take his seat and immediately assume a critical pose, his arms and legs crossed.

Billy was nervous, no doubt about it, but he was also a showman used to high stakes. He refused to think that losing his circus would be the end. Besides, he had no intention of losing the Olympic. His luck had changed, Sepia was back, and he knew his people were behind him a hundred percent. That gave a person a strong feeling, the best there is.

The crowd quickly filled the stands, every seat, full house. Billy had made sure of that, handing free tickets out on the street at the last minute.

Lila and Jack took their seats in the middle of the stands with a clear view of center ring. Lila decided she was more nervous than Sepia. She held her breath as the lights went down and the Announcer strode into the spotlight.

"Ladies and gentlemen, children of all ages, we welcome you to the most spectacular show of exotic animals and death defying feats in the world! And now, the one and only great Olympic Circus!"

The Grand Entry parade began as the floats streamed into the tent and circled the arena. Charlene smiled and gave Billy a reassuring wink from atop her float as she passed by.

From that point on, the night became a blur for Billy as he watched each act, then glanced at Hunter's face for a re-action. The Terelli brothers balanced three men high as the drums rolled and they pumped their fourth brother square-ly atop their human tower. A tightrope walker flipped over backwards and nailed a perfect landing on the slender rope. Princess pranced across the ring with the Sheik perched on her back, praising her, praising the crowd, and praising Allah in a complete renewal of faith. Nothing had caused Hunter to change his position, however. He remained arms crossed and stone faced until Billy began to think he was lucky that Hunter hadn't gotten up and left.

Louie tapped Billy on the shoulder. "I think you better come outside, boss."

Billy was relieved to have an excuse to leave the Big Top. He walked out into the cool darkness of the backyard. The light was shining above Anastasia's wagon door and he saw a group of performers surrounding someone there. When Billy caught sight of who it was, he immediately walked over. The crowd parted for him and he faced Cole Artel.

"Hello, Cole.

"Hello, Billy."

"Been a long time."

"Yeah, it has."

"Where you been, kid?"

"Working out west with an outfit called Halley's."

"You left us in quite a hurry. Lots of rumors were flyin'."

"They were probably true."

"Meaning what?"

"Meaning I took Sepia away from here the night of her accident."

The other performers glanced at each other, their long held suspicions finally confirmed.

"Why'd you do it?" Billy asked.

At that moment, the door to Anastasia's wagon opened and Anastasia slowly emerged. She was in costume with her cape pulled around her shoulders. She stood on the step and stared down at her son. Cole met her gaze.

"Hello, Mother."

"Cole."

"Billy was just asking me why I took Sepia away the night of the accident."

"I can't imagine," Anastasia said coolly.

"It was to keep her from being hurt," Cole said turning from his mother back to Billy.

"By whom?" Billy asked.

"He means that clown rigger who got killed in the fire," Anastasia answered for Cole. "I told you it wasn't Cole that cut the trapeze," she added, trying to redeem herself in front of her son and keep him from talking.

"He was killed in the fire?" Cole asked, hearing only the first part of his mother's response. He was visibly shaken. He hadn't known that the Executioner died after handing both Sepia and his identity over to Cole. He was more determined than ever that the truth be told.

"It wasn't the Executioner I was worried about. He wouldn't have hurt Sepia again," Cole told Billy.

"So it was him that cut the trapeze," Billy said, remembering Rosie's suspicions.

"Yes. I knew about it because I was asked to do it first, right, mother?" Cole said, looking up at Anastasia.

"I don't know what you're talking about," Anastasia answered, keeping her nerve.

"You were so worried Sepia would take your place that you had to get rid of her," Cole explained.

Anastasia glared at him. "You kidnap Sepia then disappear without a trace for a year and come back thinking people are going to believe your wild stories?" she challenged.

"I believe him," a voice called and Charlene stepped out from the half circle of people surrounding Anastasia's wagon.

"He's telling the truth."

"Hah, what do you know about the truth?! You had an affair with my husband behind my back!" Anastasia shot back.

"I loved Harry. You didn't care nothin' about him," Charlene responded.

"She's right," Cole said.

"You shut up," Anastasia growled at Cole.

"No," Cole responded. "That's the problem. I've been quiet too long."

"Quiet about what?" Billy asked.

Cole looked down at his feet then slowly up at Billy, "The night my father was killed, he and my mother had been fighting. I was afraid he was going to hurt her. He had her on the ground, threatening her. I picked up the trapeze bar and swung it at him. I didn't mean to hit him so hard. I just wanted him to stop, but the bar caught him in the head... and killed him. My mother thought the police wouldn't believe it was self-defense, so she made up the story of the robbery. She also made sure I understood she had saved me from prison." He paused for a moment as he left the past and returned to the present. "The idea was to get rid of Sepia, and when I refused to do it, she got the Executioner to do it for her."

"If you're telling the truth, why didn't you try to stop him?" Billy asked accusingly.

"I did or at least I thought I did...but I should have come to you, Billy. I should have told you. I could have saved Sepia from getting hurt."

"You did save me."

The performers and Billy turned and saw Sepia standing alone. She was dressed only in her costume, but the goose-flesh on her arms and legs was not just from the cool night air. A chill of recognition ran through her body.

"Everything Cole said is true," Sepia told Billy. She could

not bring herself to look directly at Cole yet. Her heart was racing and her eyes were stinging with tears, but she held them back.

Billy turned to Anastasia. "Is it true?"

"Of course not. That man, the one you ironically call the 'Executioner' might have had some fixation with Sepia and tried to hurt her. I don't know. We'll never know, will we? Anyway, I had nothing to do with it. Obviously my son has been persuaded to think otherwise," she said, glaring down at Sepia from her wagon step.

Sepia stared up at Anastasia, directing her words calmly and carefully. "Before I fell asleep last night, just as I closed my eyes, I suddenly remembered something, a sensation. It was terrifying because it felt like someone was trying to smother me. I tried to tell myself it was a dream, except that I was still awake. It wasn't until just now that I remembered when it happened. It was after the accident when I was alone with you in your wagon. You covered my face with a pillow and tried to suffocate me."

All eyes turned to Anastasia. She was backed into a corner, but not about to give in. She met the crowd's gaze with a burst of fury.

"I don't have to stand here and listen to these lies!" She shouted angrily.

Louie called out from the back of the group. "Miss Artel, you're on!"

"Excuse me, I have an act to perform," Anastasia said haughtily as she breathed a hidden sigh of relief, then stepped down from her wagon and pushed through the crowd.

No one stopped her, but Billy took her firmly by the arm and escorted her to the Big Top.

The rest of the group remained around Cole and Sepia.

Charlene was the first to speak. "I believe you, both of you."

Sepia finally looked up into the face that had remained blazoned in her mind for a year. "It doesn't matter anymore, does it?"

Cole stared down into her copper brown eyes and saw the strength there. "No," he answered.

Just before they reached the Big Top, Billy stopped and grimly faced Anastasia. She seemed like a stranger to him now. He was shocked and angry about what she had done, but in a way, he blamed himself. He had been blind to how far she would go to stay at the top. He had only seen her passion and love for the circus, not her ruthlessness.

"It's all true what Sepia said. I know that," he said.

Anastasia stared at Billy with a dazed look.

"Why did you do it?" Billy asked.

"She was going to take it all away," Anastasia said, her eyes becoming distant.

"You're wrong. Sepia was no threat to you," Billy said.

Anastasia focused her eyes on Billy again. "No, you're wrong."

Anastasia left Billy and walked on through the dressing room and up to the performer's entrance. She straightened her cape, lifted her head, and stepped into the Big Top.

When Anastasia appeared, Hunter shifted in his seat for the first time that evening. He sat up, uncrossed his arms and stared intently at the dazzling figure in the golden cape. He recognized the value of a legend and he saw from the moment Anastasia entered the arena that she was the genuine article.

Lila sat up and took notice as well. She was finally getting to see the woman she had heard so much about, the woman who had nearly destroyed two people Lila held dear. There was nothing in Anastasia's charming and magnetic presence, however, that betrayed any ill intent. Lila realized that if there was good in Anastasia, she was seeing it now. Anastasia obviously loved performing. It was the only thing she did that was truly selfless. She gave everything she had to the crowd. Lila understood now why Anastasia fought so hard to keep the limelight. It was her redemption.

Anastasia dropped her cape, grabbed the web and began rolling herself up the long rope. She reached the roman rings and gracefully took hold of them. There was something about the reckless gleam in her eye however, that made the crowd move to the edge of their seats. As she began looping her body over and under between the rings, her movements became unusually swift and powerful, too powerful. Several times she almost missed catching herself.

She paused for a moment, then decided to position herself to do a trick she had long since excluded from her act. She dropped down, swung her legs over her head and released one hand from the rings; however, the other hand lost hold of the ring and slipped off. She caught the web with one arm and hung on. The audience gasped as Anastasia slowly reached over and pulled herself back onto the rings. She waved at the crowd who burst into relieved applause.

Cole had heard the scared reaction of the crowd from outside and dashed into the Big Top. Sepia followed behind and joined him at the performer's entrance staring up at Anastasia. They watched rigid as Anastasia's motions became jerky and a sickly smile appeared on her face.

Anastasia looked down at Cole with Sepia by his side, then she stopped her act, seemingly lost. The band conductor hesitated, but kept the music going.

An alarm went off inside Billy and he called to Louie, "Get her out of there!" then he signaled the announcer and walked out into the ring. The music changed as the announcer shouted in the background.

"One more round of applause, ladies and gentlemen, for the great Anastasia Artel, the Queen of Circus!"

Anastasia was confused. She looked below at Billy who was waving her down then she looked out at the cheering crowd. As if in slow motion, Anastasia moved into position to do the trick again. Her legs dropped and she arched her back as she swung in the air. She spun freely, beautifully, but never touched the rings again.

The crowd screamed as Anastasia hit the ground. Billy was immediately at her side and Cole ran out to join him.

Sepia remained at the performer's entrance in shock. Her hands were still covering her ears where they'd instinctively shot when she heard the crowd scream.

The elephant trainer, totally stunned by Anastasia's accident, nevertheless dashed out into the arena track and led his herd into their act to cover.

Anastasia lay still, but her eyes were open as she looked up at Billy and Cole kneeling over her.

"It was easy. I just closed my eyes and let go..."

Doc had broken through the roustabouts surrounding Anastasia and was feeling the light erratic, pulse from her wrist.

"Don't talk," he said softly, but Anastasia didn't listen.

"I showed 'em, didn't I?" She whispered defiantly. "At least I went out...on...top," she said, fierce until her last breath.

Doc searched for a pulse then Billy and Cole watched in

disbelief as Doc slowly touched his fingers to Anastasia's eyelids and gently closed them forever.

Lila saw through the circle of elephants as Cole picked Anastasia up in his arms and carried her inconspicuously out of the ring. As he passed by Sepia at the performers entrance, Lila watched their eyes meet for a moment then Cole moved on. Lila couldn't help them anymore. Whatever happened was between them now.

Bruno walked over.

"We're on next," he told her.

Sepia ignored him. She walked up to Billy standing at the arena opening, staring vacantly out at the arena. The three rings were already full of acts performing their hearts out to bring the crowd back, but Billy was looking beyond them, off in the distance. He was in total shock. He noted Sepia's presence, but kept his gaze outward.

"I'm sorry, Sepia. I never knew she would go that far," he said.

"This may not make any sense, Billy," Sepia answered, searching for words to explain. "But no matter what she did or wanted to do to me, Anastasia gave me a way to escape. I was dying before I met her."

Whether Billy understood Sepia or not, his face only showed anguish and defeat. "Anyway, it's all over. Despite what she did, I will miss her. I will truly miss her." He stared at the crowd. "And without her, we're sunk."

"What if you had the first woman in the world to do a triple?" Sepia asked.

There was a long pause before Billy finally turned and looked at her. "Don't try it. Not now," he told her.

"Tomorrow will be too late," Sepia replied.

***

Cole carried his mother out of the Big Top, past the other performers who had rushed in to see what happened, and back to her wagon. He brought her inside and laid her on the bed.

She looked so small. He covered her with a blanket, but could not cover her face, not because it was difficult for him, but because he had never seen her so tranquil. Her mouth, which remained a tight line except when she was performing, was now parted in a serene pose. For the first time, Cole saw her as a human being, not the larger than life figure that had so dominated him. He could not forgive her for what she had done, and yet, he could not prevent the pain in his heart.

Rosie appeared at the door. "I'm sorry, kid," she said quietly.

Cole nodded in response, still looking at Anastasia.

"You gotta remember that she loved you," Rosie said.

"She loved herself more," Cole said.

"She looked out for herself more. There's a difference."

"Not to a kid," he answered.

"People let things get in the way, the wrong things. She got mixed up and forgot what was important. Maybe she never knew," Rosie said.

"If she didn't know, how was I supposed to?" Cole asked.

"You weren't. That's why you can't be too hard on yourself, kid. Give yourself a chance." She wasn't looking for a response and she got none. She stepped out of the wagon, leaving Cole still standing over his mother.

Cole didn't react to Rosie's words, but they sank in. He

had carried the guilt of his father's death so long that he wasn't sure he could ever let go. That was how he and his mother were different. He would never lose the capacity to care when he had done wrong. Something, however, had caused Anastasia to lose her conscience. She had hardened herself, thinking it was the only way to survive. Cole had suspected for a long time that Anastasia was operating out of fear rather than strength, but he had not known how to help her. Everyone else had thought she was fearless. Cole took one last look at his mother then he drew the cover over her face.

Despite his grief, Cole felt a huge weight lift from his shoulders. He needed something, however, to hold him to the ground. He had lost his sense of direction and he wanted desperately to find it again.

***

The elephants finished their act in center ring and circled the arena. Bringing on the huge, lumbering animals had helped the audience forget the frailty of humans and the accident they had witnessed. No one knew, of course, that Anastasia was dead. It was an unwritten rule of circus that the show must go on.

The elephants had not distracted George Hunter from the accident, however. It had shaken him badly. He was, after all, not an unfeeling man. He hoped she was okay, but knew that such a fall would require a long recovery. Anastasia was an amazing creature that captivated the audience like no one he had ever seen before. He had been enormously attracted to her and had already decided that he would somehow arrange to meet her. He admired her gutsiness and aura of power, traits he hadn't found in many women he'd met. In his world of finance, women were always subordinate and usually demure, working as secretaries or at best, assistants. Here was a woman who was second to no one and hardly shy. She was also smart. She couldn't have gotten where she was without being clever. Actually, she reminded him of his mother. His mother had not achieved the same level of power, but she'd pushed her son to do so.

Hunter thought it tragic there had been no net to catch Anastasia. He would change that policy in the future, that's for sure. He gathered up his Stetson and prepared to go and find out how Anastasia was, though he knew it was likely that the Olympic's greatest asset was likely out of commission for a good while. As he started to rise from his seat, the announcer introduced the next act.

"And now, high above center ring, a daring duo perform spectacular feats on the flying trapeze. I present to you the magnificent Flying Stefanis!"

Hunter decided to stay for one more act.

Sepia and Bruno prepared to enter the arena as the last of the elephants was exiting. Timba, forever the showoff, trailed behind the others and stopped in front of the performer's entrance. Sepia patted her trunk and stepped around her. Bruno started to follow, but Timba moved in front of him and blocked the opening.

"What's the matter with her? Get her out of the way!" he shouted.

Timba curled her trunk, let out a trumpeting call and nodded upwards. Sepia looked up and saw Cole sitting on the catcher's trapeze. He waved her up with complete assurance. She glanced back toward her father, then up at Cole again in total disbelief. Her gaze shifted to the audience and her body turned in a full circle, taking in the whole Big Top. In that moment, she realized that her life had truly become her own. She began walking toward center ring. She picked up her pace, grabbed the edge of the safety net, swung herself up and headed for her ladder.

Timba moved away from the performers entrance, but when Bruno strode out into the arena, he stopped dead when he noticed Cole and yelled back at Billy.

"Thompson, stop the act! Get him outta there!"

Billy stood at the arena opening, ignoring Bruno's shouts and staring open-mouthed up at Cole.

Louie stood at his side. "What should I do, boss?"

"I don't know," Billy murmured.

Sepia had climbed the ladder and now reached the platform where Charlene stood waiting.

Charlene had watched the events of that night happen like a surreal dream, though nothing had really surprised her until Anastasia's accident. She could never feel happy about Anastasia's death, but like Cole, she had felt her body lighten from baggage she had carried for a long time, and she couldn't help feeling relieved. At the moment, however, Charlene was mostly feeling astonished. She crossed her fingers that Cole knew what the hell he was doing then she handed the fly bar to Sepia.

"Whatever you intend to do, you better do it fast," Charlene told her, indicating below.

Sepia looked down at Bruno's livid face, then out at Cole whose determined expression had not changed. She took the trapeze from Charlene and flew out. Cole caught her badly, causing her body to jerk and the trapeze to get knocked out of rhythm. Charlene waited until she could match their swing and sent the bar back.

"What are you doing?!" Sepia yelled to Cole as she hung briefly in his grasp.

"What does it look like?" he answered. "Throw me a single," he called as he sent her back to her trapeze.

She swung back up to her platform with her heart pounding.

"That wasn't so great, was it?" Charlene said nervously.

"He just needs practice," Sepia answered then took a breath and swung out again.

Billy watched as Sepia sailed through the air, threw her body into a somersault and was caught in Cole's hands. His catch was ten times better, and though Billy's heart was in his throat, he did not make a move to stop the act despite Bruno's continued screams.

"Thompson, dammit, he'll kill her! Get them down!" Bruno yelled, then he finally strode toward the safety net to stop Sepia himself. Louie, however, ran over and dragged him back to the performers' entrance.

"I'll sue you for this!" Bruno sputtered at Billy.

Louie tightened his hold on Bruno's arms. "If Sepia wanted to stop, she would stop," he growled, not taking his eye off the air.

Sepia flew out once more and threw a double somersault to Cole. This time he caught her almost perfectly and the crowd broke out in cheers.

"You're a lot lighter than Zambini," Cole grinned. "Next time, throw me a triple," he called as he sent her back to her trapeze.

Sepia returned to her platform, spun around and faced Cole.

He swung up to a sitting position and stared back at her.

"What'd he say?" Charlene asked.

"He wants me to do a triple," Sepia answered, keeping her eyes on her catcher.

"Sepia," Charlene responded with alarm. It was all she could say. She couldn't say "no", but Sepia had heard it anyway.

The band had softened its tune and the crowd was growing restless, but Sepia kept her gaze fixed on Cole. He smiled and cocked one eyebrow, a question. She laughed softly to herself and slowly nodded her head. Her heart was near bursting from the feeling inside. She didn't know if she was crazy or not, but she would risk her life for this feeling without hesitation. She slowly reached down and raised the starting bar.

Bruno yelled up to her. "Sepia, come down!"

Sepia stepped up onto the starting bar instead. Billy signaled for the band to stop playing and the arena became still. Cole suddenly lifted himself to a standing position on the catch bar to draw the crowd's attention. He stretched out his arm and pointed to Sepia then opened two more fingers giving a number three sign to the crowd. They got the idea. It was like "The Babe" pointing to the center field bleachers before his famous home run in last year's World Series. The gesture was bold and daring and the crowd went wild.

Billy was sweating bullets, but he gave a signal to the Announcer who filled his lungs with air.

"And now, Miss Stefani will attempt a feat never before achieved by a woman, the triple back somersault to a hand catch! We ask for your total silence, please!"

Lila had watched the latest turn of events with her stomach in knots. She knew how good Sepia and Cole were, still she squeezed Jack's arm in a vise grip.

Cole lowered himself into position and began swinging. Sepia took a deep breath, grabbed the trapeze and flew out.

She pumped herself back and forth then forced the trapeze as high as it could go. She soared to the top of the tent and every heart stopped as her body made three complete revolutions in the air. Cole swung up, and like two magnets of opposite fields, they met and locked wrists. The Big Top thundered with applause.

Hunter jumped from his seat, clapping and cheering. Billy let out a triumphant whoop and threw his hat in the air. Louie released a stunned Bruno and slapped his thighs. Charlene stomped her feet on the platform, crying and laughing. Rosie grabbed the nearest body and squashed the surprised Sheik in a bear hug. Lila turned to Jack, smiled then screamed with joy.

Sepia did not return to her platform. She could not let go of Cole's grip. The audience watched as they stopped swinging and hung quietly in the air. Then Cole slowly pulled Sepia up until their lips met and a new act was born.

Acknowledgements

The Triple started as an idea for a screenplay so I thank screenwriter Diane Simon for conversations about the Greek Myth of Psyche and Eros, which stirred in me the idea of retelling it then writing it as a novel. Much gratitude goes to many people. To the readers of my various drafts who shared suggestions, spurred me on, and inspired me with their own great work: Karen Hammer, William Meis, Sr., Shelley Morhaim, Dennis Hardcastle, Richard Montgomery, Monica Wellman and Karen Berger. To the road trip from Baltimore to Chicago with one of my sisters during which I practiced an "audio version" of the book by recounting the whole novel out loud. She was a captive but receptive listener and I treasure that journey of love and support. To John M. Kelley, a former attorney for Ringling Brothers, for establishing the Circus Museum in Baraboo, Wisconsin, which holds one of the largest collections of circus materials in the world. Ringling Bros. and Barnum & Bailey Circus is still the greatest show on earth even in a technology-based, virtual world. To filmmaker Exsul Van Helden and circus manager Holly Harris who introduced me to the amazing Circus Flora that still performs under a Big Top. I got to walk through the "backyard" to meet performers including the children of circus families. I'm indebted to these extraordinary people who let me see into a world that most "townies" aren't privy to. To my editor, Bill Meis, who believed in my work and got this book off my computer and out to the public in a superb and un-compromised fashion. To Fallen Bros. Press for publishing delightful books and including me in their selections! And my amazing family, Terry, Brynn and Wil, who gave me space to create, kept me strong, and remind me daily of the power of love.

About the Author

Having hailed from the Midwest then lived on both coasts, Mary is happily settled in Baltimore. Like many "boomers" her career path has followed some twists and turns. She studied plant physiology, enjoyed success as a teacher and indie filmmaker, and has recently returned to her environmental roots to promote city parks. She is currently finishing her second novel, Kidnapped, a time travel epic that sends a disillusioned Next Gen law clerk back to the early 1830's where she meets a young Abe Lincoln just beginning his career.

www.ingramcontent.com/pod-product-compliance
Lightning Source LLC
Chambersburg PA
CBHW061927170626
46813CD00006B/2326